D0431031

Praise for New Y

"Kat Martin is a fast gun when it comes to storytelling, and I love her books."
—#1 *New York Times* bestselling author
Linda Lael Miller

"It doesn't matter what Martin's characters are up against—she dishes up romantic suspense, sizzling sex and international intrigue…. Readers better set aside a block of time to finish this unputdownable tale of adventure and romance."
—*RT Book Reviews* on *Against the Sun*
(4½ stars, Top Pick!)

"[Kat] Martin is a terrific storyteller."
—*Booklist*

**Praise for *USA TODAY* bestselling author
Delores Fossen**

"Clear off space on your keeper shelf, Fossen has arrived."
—*New York Times* bestselling author Lori Wilde

"Delores Fossen delivers a sharp-witted narrative and kick-ass main characters."
—*RT Book Reviews* on *Veiled Intentions*

Kat Martin is the *New York Times* bestselling author of more than sixty historical and contemporary romance novels. To date she has over sixteen million copies of her books in print in twenty countries, including Sweden, France, Russia, Spain, Japan, Argentina, Poland and Greece. Kat and her husband, author L. J. Martin, live on their ranch outside Missoula, Montana, and spend winters at their beach house in California. Kat invites you to visit her website at www.katmartin.com.

Delores Fossen, a *USA TODAY* bestselling author, has sold over fifty novels, with millions of copies of her books in print worldwide. She's received a Booksellers' Best Award and an RT Reviewers' Choice Best Book Award. She was also a finalist for a prestigious RITA® Award. You can contact the author through her website at www.deloresfossen.com.

New York Times Bestselling Author

KAT MARTIN

AGAINST THE SUN

⊕ **HARLEQUIN**® BESTSELLING AUTHOR COLLECTION

If you purchased this book without a cover you should be aware that this book is stolen property. It was reported as "unsold and destroyed" to the publisher, and neither the author nor the publisher has received any payment for this "stripped book."

ISBN-13: 978-1-335-14493-5

Against the Sun

Copyright © 2018 by Harlequin Books S.A.

The publisher acknowledges the copyright holders of the individual works as follows:

Against the Sun
Copyright © 2012 by Kat Martin

Veiled Intentions
Copyright © 2004 by Delores Fossen

All rights reserved. Except for use in any review, the reproduction or utilization of this work in whole or in part in any form by any electronic, mechanical or other means, now known or hereafter invented, including xerography, photocopying and recording, or in any information storage or retrieval system, is forbidden without the written permission of the publisher, Harlequin Enterprises Limited, 22 Adelaide St. West, 40th Floor, Toronto, Ontario M5H 4E3, Canada.

This is a work of fiction. Names, characters, places and incidents are either the product of the author's imagination or are used fictitiously, and any resemblance to actual persons, living or dead, business establishments, events or locales is entirely coincidental.

This edition published by arrangement with Harlequin Books S.A.

For questions and comments about the quality of this book, please contact us at CustomerService@Harlequin.com.

® and TM are trademarks of Harlequin Enterprises Limited or its corporate affiliates. Trademarks indicated with ® are registered in the United States Patent and Trademark Office, the Canadian Intellectual Property Office and in other countries.

Recycling programs for this product may not exist in your area.

HARLEQUIN®
www.Harlequin.com

Printed in U.S.A.

CONTENTS

Don't miss Until Midnight,
*Kat Martin's newest book from HQN,
in stores February 2019.*

AGAINST THE SUN

Kat Martin

To the FBI, DEA, ICE and other agencies of Homeland Security, and the men and women who work so hard to keep us safe.

Chapter 1

Middle East Unrest Travels to Houston
One Dead in Protests.

Jake Cantrell turned off the engine of his Jeep and glanced over at the front page of the *Houston Chronicle* lying on the passenger seat. The headline in the morning paper was a reminder of why he was there, parked in front of the mirrored-glass, fourteen-story Marine Drilling International building.

It was still hot as Hades today, the first of September, the sun and humidity baking him in his navy blue suit and white shirt as he strode toward the wide concrete steps leading up to the front doors. The clothes were the worst part of a protection detail—wearing a jacket and tie instead of the jeans and T-shirts he lived in most of the time. But the pay was top-notch and he'd been getting more and more restless sitting behind a desk at Atlas Security, handling the day-to-day management of the company while the owner, his best friend, Trace Rawlins, and Trace's wife, Maggie, were off on an extended honeymoon in Australia.

Jake was damn glad they were finally home.

Pushing through the heavy glass doors, he entered the lobby, icy-cold in comparison to the wet heat outside. He headed for the bank of elevators and stepped inside one, pushed the button for the twelfth floor, then waited through the ride to the executive level.

The time hands on his heavy steel wristwatch said he was a few minutes early for his ten o'clock appointment with Ian Dumont, the founder of Marine Drilling, CEO and chairman of the board. The family-owned business, originally Dumont Drilling, had been in oil production since the fifties, when Ian had made his first big strike along the Gulf Coast.

Today, they were mostly in offshore oil and gas production, thus the name change to Marine Drilling International. The Dumont family was well-known in Houston society, with big money and everything that went with it.

Walking out of the elevator, he made his way across shiny black granite floor to the reception desk, where his shoes sank into thick gray carpet. The waiting area was all black leather sofas and chairs, the desk itself smooth dark walnut and chrome. Nothing but the best for the Dumonts.

A good-looking woman in her late twenties with wavy, shoulder-length, mink-brown hair was busily searching the drawers and cabinets behind the desk.

The way she bent over in her tailored pencil skirt provided him with a perfect view of a very shapely ass.

He almost smiled.

Even the help was first-class.

She jerked upright at his approach, noticing him for the first time, and her face colored. It was a pretty face with amazing golden-brown eyes that looked him up and down, which took a while, Jake being six-five, two hundred thirty-five pounds.

"May I help you?" she asked.

He gave her a smile. "I'm Jake Cantrell. I've got an appointment at ten with Ian Dumont."

She frowned, looked down at the computer screen on the desk, but apparently didn't see his name. "He didn't mention it. He's getting ready for another meeting. You might have to wait awhile."

"Not a problem. In the meantime, I could sure use a cup of coffee."

Amusement tipped her mouth up, making a tiny dimple appear next to those plump, rose-colored lips. He could see the curves beneath her tailored suit, suggesting her breasts were just the right size, and her waist was small.

Jake's groin tightened. Which surprised him, since he needed the coffee to recover from the night he'd spent with Deanna Leblanc, an old flame who was in Houston to film a TV commercial.

The receptionist cast him a look. "I'll see what I can do." But she didn't make a move, just turned to the woman hurrying toward her across the waiting room.

"Oh, I'm so sorry I'm late, Ms. Dumont," the newcomer said.

Son of a bitch. A Dumont, Jake thought. Asking her

to fetch him a cup of coffee was probably not the best idea he'd ever had.

"Is Paulo all right?" the Dumont woman asked.

"My son wasn't driving, thank God." The real receptionist, attractive and in her mid-forties, had straight black hair pulled back in a bun and smooth, olive skin. "Paulo has a concussion and a couple of fractured ribs, but it looks like he's going to be okay. Thank you for covering while I was gone."

"Your boy was in a car accident, Marie. It wasn't a problem. I'm just glad he's going to be all right." The Dumont woman tipped her head toward Jake, her soft mahogany curls sliding around her shoulders, making the muscles across his abdomen clench.

"Mr. Cantrell is here to see Ian," she said. "I have to get to the meeting. Could you fetch him a cup of coffee while he waits?"

Jake felt the slight rebuke in the glance she cast his way. Clearly, she wasn't used to fetching a man much of anything.

"Of course," Marie said. Ms. Dumont walked away, heading for the tall walnut door leading into Ian Dumont's imperial domain. Her strides were long and purposeful, Jake noticed, as if she had someplace important to go. He liked a woman who didn't dawdle. And his earlier assessment was right—she had a great ass and a pair of legs that wouldn't quit. She was only about five-six, but her expensive spike heels pushed her somewhere close to six feet.

He watched her disappear behind the door, wondering what role she played in the Dumont empire, then turned his attention to the receptionist.

Marie was smiling. "Mr. Cantrell?"

"That's right."

"Mr. Dumont mentioned yesterday that you would be coming in this morning. I believe he wants to see you as soon as you arrive." She indicated the office door. "I'll bring coffee for everyone into the meeting."

"Thank you, Marie."

The woman blushed as Jake turned and walked away. It was his size mostly, he figured, that made women take a second look. He was used to it by now.

He swung open the walnut door and stepped inside, finding only two people in the room—the woman he had subtly insulted and a silver-haired gentleman in his late seventies, slightly stooped but still impressive, undoubtedly Ian Dumont.

"Mr. Cantrell, I assume," the man said. "Our mutual friend, Trace Rawlins, had nothing but good things to say when he recommended you for this job." Trace knew Ian well. He'd recently helped design the state-of-the-art alarm system for Marine Drilling when the building was renovated. "Please join us."

The Dumont woman was staring, one of her dark eyebrows slightly elevated in question. He noticed she was wearing a flashy diamond engagement ring. Since he felt a jolt of heat whenever he looked at her, it was probably good she was out of his reach.

Ian Dumont walked the length of the long conference table to greet him, reaching out to shake his hand—a strong, solid handshake that set the tone for the discussion ahead. He'd once had calluses on those hands, Jake figured.

"Why don't we all sit down?" the CEO suggested.

They grouped themselves at one end of the table, which was done in the same walnut and chrome as the waiting area. Wide plate-glass windows looked down on the city streets, and modern artwork in bold bright colors lined the inner walls.

The door swung open and Marie walked in with a silver coffee service. She set the tray down on the table and poured each of them a cup.

"Thank you, Marie," Ian said as she quietly headed back out the door. He fixed his attention on Jake. "I asked you here today to discuss providing security for one of our people during an upcoming business negotiation."

"Right. An S. E. Dumont, you said, when we spoke on the phone."

"That is correct."

"Wait a minute," the woman interrupted, her gaze sliding toward Jake. "Ian, you aren't thinking—"

"Mr. Cantrell, I'd like you to meet my granddaughter, Sage Elizabeth Dumont."

The room fell silent. Son of a bitch. *She* was his assignment?

"I don't need a bodyguard, Ian."

The older man turned toward her, a determined glint in eyes that looked strikingly similar to the flashing, gold-ringed brown ones belonging to his granddaughter.

"This man has experience in Middle Eastern protocol as well as a background in personal security. Isn't that correct, Mr. Cantrell?"

"This is a business transaction," Sage argued. "I'm not in any sort of danger."

Both men ignored her. "Over the years, I've done a lot of corporate protection work, both in South America and the Middle East," Jake said. "I worked in Saudi

Arabia for three years after I got out of the marines. So yes, I'm familiar with the protocols."

"I understand you were in Special Forces. You served in Iraq, I believe?"

"That's right." Ian Dumont had done his homework.

"Sage is vice president of acquisitions and distribution for Marine Drilling. Currently she is involved in a transaction that may reach the three-hundred-million-dollar mark, a deal being negotiated with Sheik Khalid Al Kahzaz of Saudi Arabia. The sheik and his family are due to arrive in just a few days."

"I see," Jake said noncommittally. Protecting a corporate executive was one thing. Protecting a young socialite who got her job because she was a member of the Dumont family was something altogether different.

"With your experience," Ian continued, as Jake took a sip of his coffee, "I'm hoping you will be able to guide my granddaughter through this visit with our Saudi friends, and should any trouble arise, also keep her safe."

"That's what I get paid for."

Sage shifted in her chair, irritation clear in her face. "We need to discuss this in private, Ian."

The old man smiled indulgently. "We can do that, of course, but the result will be the same. You're representing Marine Drilling International. You will be prominently engaged in entertaining the sheik, his daughter and son, and the remainder of his party. The unrest in their part of the world has reached all the way to our city. A man was killed in a Middle Eastern prodemocracy demonstration last night."

"That was an accident," Sage protested. "He was hit by a car."

"The police are still investigating. They're not completely certain what actually happened. And even if it was an accident, tempers are running hot on all fronts. Your safety is vitally important to me. Mr. Cantrell will make certain you are safe."

"But—"

"It will only be during the day, for as long as the sheik is here, or when you are somewhere entertaining him and his family. Along with that, there are things you need to know that Mr. Cantrell can teach you."

Her shoulders tightened. "I understand there are business protocols, things I need to be aware of. I planned to research the subject. I've just been so busy...."

"You work too hard, my dear. You need someone to help you. Mr. Cantrell can handle that." Her grandfather rose from his chair and turned to Jake when he stood up, too. "When can you start?"

Part of him wanted to refuse the assignment. Jake didn't want to deal with a bossy, cantankerous female. The other part was looking for something interesting to do after weeks of mostly sitting behind a desk. And keeping a pampered young woman like Sage Dumont out of trouble probably wouldn't be dull.

"If we have only a short time before they arrive," he found himself saying, "we had better get started today."

"Splendid!" Ian said.

Sage's spine went a little straighter. She fixed her gaze on Jake. Even in her high heels she had to look up at him, which he could tell she didn't like.

"Fine," she said. "I'll see you in my office in half an hour. Does that work for you?"

"I'll be there."

And then she was gone.

As soon as the door swooshed shut behind her, Jake heard Ian chuckle. "I knew she was going to pitch a fit about this—actually, I expected far worse. But I want her safe. She means everything to me, Mr. Cantrell."

"It's just Jake. And you can count on me to take care of her—whether she likes it or not."

Sage marched into her office and slammed the door. *A bodyguard.* It was ridiculous. She couldn't believe her grandfather would go to such extremes. The sheik and his family would be bringing their own security people. And the police had been officially notified of the visit. There was nothing for her grandfather to worry about.

Still, she knew how much he loved her. And Sage loved him.

She sighed as she walked to her desk. Ian Dumont had raised her since she was twelve years old. She respected him more than any other man she'd ever known.

She thought of the towering hulk who had asked her to bring him some coffee. Typical chauvinist. Marine Special Forces. Served in Iraq. The guy was all male, no doubt of that. She hadn't missed the hot gleam in his eyes when she'd caught him watching her bent over at the reception desk.

She refused to acknowledge the jolt of awareness that had slipped through her when she first saw him standing there. For heaven sake, who wouldn't notice a man who looked like that? The Terminator—only bigger and better looking. Dark brown, neatly trimmed hair, and those eyes. Light blue and beautiful.

Still, muscle jocks and ex-soldiers were hardly her type and even if she found this one attractive, she was engaged to be married. Her fiancé, Phillip Stanton, was vice president of their North Sea drilling operation. He was a few years older than Sage, handsome and sophisticated, from one of the best families in Houston. Exactly the sort of man she had always hoped to marry.

Sage looked up at the clock on the wall. Cantrell would be here soon. When a soft knock sounded, she was sure he'd arrived a few minutes early, but when the door swung open, it wasn't him. Her best friend, Sabrina Eckhart, swept into the office. Red-haired and feisty, and currently dating a brilliant computer geek, Rina was a successful stockbroker who earned a very good living though the market was shooting up and down like an out-of-control fire hose.

"Sorry to barge in," her friend said, though clearly she wasn't sorry at all. Being best friends gave her plenty of latitude, and Sage was always glad to see her. "Marie said you were alone, and it's almost noon. I thought I'd drop by, see if I could talk you into getting some lunch."

Sage sighed. "I wish I could. I'm up to my ears in alligators, and on top of that, my grandfather's hired me a bodyguard."

Rina's blue eyes widened. "Oh, my God—not that good-looking hunk out in the waiting room."

"That's him. Ex-soldier and all that."

"I can imagine. Even in a suit, the guy looks tough enough to eat nails."

He looked exactly like the kind of man her grandfather would choose, confident and capable, and underneath that veneer of civility, a very dangerous man. "It'll just be for the Saudis' visit. Granddad insisted. You know how protective he can be."

"Maybe he's right. Did you see what happened at the university last night? The students were protesting some damn thing and a guy got killed."

"It was an accident."

"Doesn't make him any less dead."

Sage's lips twitched. "There is that."

Another knock sounded, this one firm and faintly demanding. "No doubt who that is," she grumbled.

Rina's face lit up. "The Incredible Hunk? For God's sake, let him in."

Sage rolled her eyes. "What would Ryan say if he saw you drooling like that?"

Rina laughed. "Not much, since I'm usually drooling over him."

Sage started for the door, but before she had time to reached it the knob turned and it swung open.

"You did say thirty minutes?" Cantrell's deep voice boomed into the office.

Sage's mouth tightened.

"I was just leaving," Rina said, wiggling her fingers over her shoulder as she walked past the tall, brawny man standing in the doorway.

"Why don't you come right in?" Sage said with a hint of sarcasm.

"Bad idea." Cantrell closed the door behind him.

Sage's gaze ran over him. She couldn't remember seeing a more impressive male specimen. One she was going to have to put in his place right from the start.

She crossed her arms over her chest. "We need to get something straight right now."

Cantrell cocked a dark eyebrow. "And that would be...?"

"I'm the boss here, not you. You work for me. That means you do as I say."

"Sorry, no. I work for your grandfather, not you. You're in charge as long as it involves your job. Until this is over and you're no longer under my protection, I'm the boss and you do exactly what *I* say. That's what we need to get straight."

Sage just stared. "You can't be serious."

"I'm deadly serious. It's my job to keep you alive. That's what I intend to do."

Sage started shaking her head. "I'm not in any real danger and I can see right now this isn't going to work."

"Until your grandfather says differently, it's going to work just fine."

And that was the moment she realized she had lost the war. Ian would never back down—not on this. If she wanted to stay in charge of the negotiations with the Saudis—make the biggest purchase of used off-shore drilling equipment in the history of the company, and save them millions of dollars—she had to deal with Jake Cantrell.

She let her arms fall back to her sides. "Fine, you win. When it comes to my protection, you're in charge. The rest of the time I'm the boss. Does that satisfy you?"

The look he gave her said that wasn't even close to the kind of satisfaction he wanted from her. Then he blinked and the expression was gone. She might have believed she'd imagined it if her stomach hadn't floated up the way it did.

"That'll work just fine." He pulled an envelope out of the breast pocket of his navy blue coat, opened it and withdrew several sheets of paper. "These are notes I made on some of the protocols you and your people will need to learn. If you're ready, we might as well get started."

His blue eyes ran over her, but the heat was no longer there. Still, just looking at all that masculinity packaged so nicely made her skin feel warm. She told herself whatever minor attraction she felt to Jake Cantrell was unimportant. And that all of this would be over in just a few days.

Walking away from him, she sat down behind her desk. "I'm ready whenever you are."

Chapter 2

The lady was hot, no doubt about it. Jake knew a lot of pretty women, but Sage Dumont had something besides a beautiful face and what appeared to be a spectacular body. No, she wasn't just pretty. She had a certain presence, a kind of aura about her. In the marines, the guys used to say a woman had *It*. That inexplicable quality that drew a man when his brain told him to run like hell the opposite way.

Fortunately, Sage was a Dumont, and to Jake that screamed high society, rich and spoiled. The lady might be great for a night or two in bed, but beyond that, he hadn't the slightest interest.

One thing he knew. She might be engaged, but she wasn't in love. A woman didn't look at a man the way she looked at him when she was in love with someone else.

He couldn't help pitying the unlucky bastard she

was going to marry. Jake was just damned glad it wasn't him.

Settling in one of the two cream leather chairs across from where she sat behind a sleek, black-granite topped desk, he unfolded several printed sheets of instruction.

"Let's start with some general background," he said. "I'll make it short and to the point. If you know this already, stop me." He glanced at her, saw he had her full attention. "Saudi Arabia is a monarchy bordered by Jordan, Iraq, Kuwait, the Persian Gulf and Qatar."

"I know where it is."

"But you've never been there."

"No."

"Then maybe you don't know that if you aren't Muslim, you can't go to Saudi Arabia without an invitation, nor can you leave without permission." He checked to see if she was getting bored. "To give you some idea of the kind of people you'll be dealing with, visitors to Saudi Arabia have to abide by sharia law. You can be imprisoned for possessing alcohol, pornography, drugs or even pork. Thieves still have their hands cut off, and capital crimes are punished by public beheadings."

Her face went a little pale.

"It's a different culture," he went on. "They don't think the way we do. That's the first thing you need to know."

She took a slow breath and started nodding. "All right. What else?"

"Knowing their names isn't enough. You'll need to find out how they want you to address them. If they're members of the royal family—and there are six thousand of those you'll address a malc as Your Highness. Unless he's in line for the throne, in which case you would say Your Royal Highness."

"I'll get whatever information we need."

"Saudi men don't usually shake hands with women. Let them make the first move."

"All right."

"Do you own a skirt that comes below your knees?"

Her lips faintly curved. "Not this season."

"Then buy some. And be sure your arms and shoulders are covered. What you have on is fine, but the skirt needs to be longer."

"These people are coming to my country—I'm not going to theirs. I don't see why I should change to please them."

"How bad do you want to make this deal?"

It meant everything. If she closed this purchase, she could prove to her grandfather that she was the person to take over as president of the company when Michael Curtis resigned next year.

"I'll take care of it," she said.

"I need the details of their visit. How long they'll be staying. Which hotel they'll be in, what security measures are being taken."

"We've booked them into the presidential suite at the Four Seasons. They'll have the entire twentieth floor. It's a five-star hotel and it's close to the office. I was planning to leave security up to their own people."

"Bad idea. They don't know the city or the hotel. I can take a look if you want, see what might need to be done."

"All right, yes. That sounds like a good idea."

"And you'll need to inform the local authorities of the visit."

"Already done. Everything's covered."

They spent the better part of another hour going over the protocols, things like not waving someone forward with your fingers, which an Arab might do to summon a dog. Or making the okay sign, forming a circle with your thumb and forefinger, which meant you were giving the person the evil eye.

Sage was exhausted by the time Cantrell unfolded his tall frame from the chair. Damn, the man was big. He had feet the size of snowshoes and big hands, as well.

She didn't let her mind wander in the direction that led her.

Instead, she thought that for a bodyguard he seemed fairly polished and intelligent. His clothes were perfectly tailored to fit his tall, broad-shouldered frame. His suit wasn't a two-thousand-dollar Armani, but it hadn't come off the rack at J. C. Penney's, either.

He glanced down at the heavy watch on his wrist. "Why don't we take a break?" he suggested. "You haven't had lunch. We can meet back here in an hour, get started again."

Her shoulders sagged. "I thought we were finished."

Cantrell's mouth edged up, a hard mouth, but sexy. "I hate to disappoint you, but we're just getting started."

Sage looked at the stack of notes on her desk, thought of the endless preparations she still needed to complete to get ready for the Saudis. "I've got appointments all afternoon. I won't be finished until at least seven o'clock tonight."

"All right, I'll pick you up here at seven. We'll catch some dinner and continue where we left off."

She gazed up at him and inwardly groaned. She was

exhausted from working the long hours necessary to prepare for the negotiation. Now she had to deal with Jake Cantrell.

To say nothing of the tug of attraction she felt whenever she looked at him. Or worse yet, when she felt him looking at her.

She wouldn't act on any of it, of course. She was committed to Phillip. Which reminded her to call and tell him she wouldn't be able to see him tonight. They would have only tomorrow evening to say goodbye before he returned to Edinburgh, where his North Sea drilling operations office was located.

Reluctantly, she returned her attention to Cantrell. "I'll be ready when you get here," she said. And wished she'd be going home to get some sleep instead.

Jake left the office and climbed into his Jeep. He'd bought it two months ago, a replacement for Sassy, the old, beat-up one that had served him so well over the years. The new Jeep was also black, but shiny, and had a canvas top without holes. He'd had it up all summer so he could run the air conditioner, which actually worked.

He cranked the engine, thinking of the evening ahead. What the hell had he been thinking? Yes, he needed to work with Sage as much as he could before the Saudis arrived. He sure as hell didn't need to take the woman to dinner.

Yet there was something about Sage Dumont that interested him. He tried to think of her as the spoiled rich socialite she undoubtedly was, but somehow it didn't seem to fit.

He reminded himself that she was engaged, and that cooled his ardor a little. Not enough.

He wondered what kind of man she had chosen to marry, and how she really felt about him, then reminded himself it was none of his damned business. Disgruntled that he had taken the assignment at all, he left downtown Houston and drove to his office in the University District, where he did freelance work for Atlas Security.

Jake shoved open the office door and walked in, passing Annie Mayberry, Trace's receptionist and office manager, who was seated at the front desk. A small woman in her sixties with frizzy blond hair, Annie ran the place like a dictator. She also mothered the single men who worked there, and though they grumbled about her overprotective nature and salty disposition, everybody loved her.

"So how did it go?" she asked. "You take the job?"

"I'll probably regret it, but yes, I did."

One of her penciled eyebrows went up. "She's a real beauty, that Sage."

Jake's steps slowed. He stopped and turned. "You knew Sage was the assignment? Why the hell didn't you say something?"

Annie just smiled. "'Cause I was afraid you'd say no. You know how you can be when it comes to women."

Jake frowned. "What's that supposed to mean?"

"It means you think a woman has only one job, and that's to keep you entertained in bed. You aren't interested in a female who might stand up to you. Sage Dumont is just as used to being in charge as you are. That has to chap your behind but good."

Amusement warred with irritation. "She's used to being in charge, all right. She works for her grandfather. Of course she's in charge."

"You might want to do a little checking on that. Sage started at the bottom. She's good at what she does, and that's why she's been promoted so many times over the years."

"How the hell could you possibly know that?"

"Because, smarty-pants, I read the newspapers. They've done a lot of stories about her and her family. Plus I did a little checking on the internet when Trace mentioned he was recommending you for the job."

"All right, so let's say she worked her fingers to the bone to get where she is today. Doesn't change the fact that as long as I'm protecting her, she has to do what I say."

"You told her that? How'd that work out?"

"We talked things over and she agreed to follow my rules."

Annie snorted as if he was deluding himself. "She's engaged, you know."

He scoffed. "That's pretty hard to miss, with the size of the diamond she's wearing."

"Phillip's not the right man for her."

Jake couldn't believe this conversation. And yet this was Annie. She had an uncanny ability to know everything that was going on, and she was usually right. "Really. And why is that?"

"Too soft. The guy was raised with a silver spoon in his mouth. He's never done a hard day's work in his life. You ask me, Phillip Stanton's a social climber. He wants to be part of the Dumont royalty. Sage is his ticket in."

Jake mulled that over, wondering if it might be true. "So why is she marrying him?"

Annie's mouth puckered. "I haven't quite figured that out. If I do, I'll let you know."

"You do that." With a shake of his head, Jake headed for his desk. Trace wasn't in today, but Sol Greenway, Trace's computer whiz kid, was pounding away on his keyboard at the desk in his glass-enclosed office.

Trace employed two other freelancers in the office. Ben Slocum, an ex-Navy SEAL, was off investigating a case, but Alex Justice, also a P.I., was working at the desk next to Jake's.

"Hey, buddy, how's it going?" Alex asked. He was a former navy pilot, a jet jockey who was a lot tougher than his blond-haired, blue-eyed appearance made him seem. "Heard you were taking a protection job for Sage Dumont. She is one hot lady."

Jake grunted. "Why the hell is it everybody in the place knew S. E. Dumont was a woman but me?"

Alex grinned, a dimple appearing in his cheek. "Try watching TV sometime." The guy was a real lady killer. Jake wondered if Sage would rather be working with Justice than with him.

"Yeah, I'll do that," he said. But he wasn't the TV type. He'd far rather be outdoors.

He sat down in front of a stack of messages, calls that needed to be returned, and went to work. All the while, Sage Dumont hovered at the edge of his mind. Maybe it was time he found out some of the things about her everyone else already seemed to know.

Chapter 3

Sage had her personal assistant, Will Bailey, reschedule her afternoon appointments. She was buried in work, but the most important thing she had facing her right now was the upcoming deal with the Saudis. Today, Jake Cantrell had caught her unprepared, and that wasn't going to happen again. She skipped lunch and had Will bring her a ham sandwich off the meal cart that circled the floors every day.

For most of the afternoon, she sat in front of her computer, poring over Middle East business protocols and reading every article she could find on the customs of Saudi Arabia. The more she read, the more she discovered she didn't know. And the more disturbing she found the information.

She had always been independent. It was hard to

imagine living under the oppressive restrictions a Saudi woman was forced to bear.

Sage reminded herself that these people were from another country, another part of the world, and she had to respect their values and lifestyle. They were here as Dumont family guests and she would treat them accordingly.

She finished reading one last article on the screen, feeling even more exhausted than she had before. She had half an hour before Cantrell was due to pick her up. Allowing herself a brief respite to recover a little of her energy, she closed her eyes and leaned back in her chair.

"Napping, Ms. Dumont?"

She shot upright in her chair, nearly launching herself across the desk. She blinked, her gritty eyes focusing on the imposing man standing in front of her.

"I was working. I—I must have nodded off." Why was it he always caught her off guard? Damn the man for his timing, among other things.

"Maybe eating something will help."

"I had a sandwich earlier off the cart," she said a little defensively.

Cantrell looked at her as if sizing her up. "That's not much. You ready to go?" He wasn't wearing the suit he'd had on earlier, but a pair of faded jeans that hugged his long, powerful legs, and a dark blue T-shirt. The T-shirt stretched over a chest that was ridiculously wide and banded with muscle. She had to tear her gaze away.

"I need to make a quick trip to the washroom," she said, "then we can leave." There was a private bathroom in the office, one of the privileges of being a VP.

Grabbing her purse, she darted inside, made a toilet stop, brushed her teeth, applied a little fresh lipstick. She straightened her ivory suit jacket as she walked back out the door.

Cantrell was waiting, taking up far more of her spacious office than most men did. She felt those blue eyes on her, assessing her in some way, and a little curl of heat settled low in her belly. She wondered what those perceptive eyes saw when he looked at her.

He followed her to the door, but it opened before she reached it, and her fiancé walked in. Immaculately dressed in an Italian designer suit, six feet tall and lean, with blond hair, hazel eyes and darkly tanned skin, Phillip looked as if he had just stepped off a Ralph Lauren billboard.

His gaze went to Cantrell, then returned to Sage. "I thought we were going to dinner."

"I'm sorry, Phillip. Didn't you get my message?" She sighed. "Ian hired Mr. Cantrell to help me learn the protocols before the Saudis arrive. We have to work on that tonight."

"I see."

"Phillip Stanton, this is Jake Cantrell."

Phillip extended his hand. Jake shook it and stepped away, clasped his hands in front of him and splayed his legs, going into bodyguard mode. Phillip eyed him sharply. Sage caught a hint of disdain. Clearly, Phillip wasn't happy that she would be working with Jake.

"Ian mentioned you," he finally said to Cantrell. "He told me you would be providing protection for Sage while the sheik and his family are here."

"That's right."

"Ian can be ridiculously protective."

"Maybe. Or maybe he's just being smart."

A muscle tightened in Phillip's lean cheek. He was better-looking than Cantrell, Sage decided, but the bigger man was far more imposing. She tried not to draw a comparison, which Cantrell would surely lose. Phillip held an MBA from Princeton. He knew classical music, appreciated art and ballet. Things they enjoyed together. Cantrell was a marine who knew how to fire a gun.

Which, she noticed as he turned to the side, probably explained the lump in the waistband of his jeans beneath his T-shirt. Surely he didn't think it was necessary to carry a weapon. She made a mental note to broach the subject as soon as they were alone.

"Are you sure you can't put this off until tomorrow?" Phillip asked her, positioning himself between her and Jake.

"I wish I could. You know how important it is to me, Phillip."

"Of course, darling." He leaned over and kissed her cheek, flashed a look at Jake. "Take care of her, Cantrell."

Jake's mouth edged up. "I plan to."

There was something in the way he said it that made her feel like blushing. Phillip cast him a last hard glance and walked out of the office.

Sage waited long enough for Phillip to reach the elevator, hoping to avoid any more of the subtle tension swirling between the men. Then, slinging her leather bag over her shoulder, she started once more for the door.

"There's a Chinese Express just down the block," she said. "We can go there."

"I've got a table for us at Bella's Cusina. It's only a few blocks farther."

She glanced back at him. It was a power play, pure and simple, a move to let her know she might be a Dumont, but he was the one in charge.

"You won't be on the job," he reminded her.

"So you're the boss tonight, is that it?"

"Exactly."

She blew out a breath. What did it matter? It was only dinner. Besides, she had to admit there was a tiny part of her that liked when a man took charge.

It didn't happen often. And it wouldn't last long.

"Italian sounds great. If you want to know the truth, I'm starving."

Cantrell smiled. It was the first real smile she had seen and it made her breath catch. This wasn't good.

Walking together across the reception area, they stepped into an elevator and headed downstairs. There was a security guard at the desk in the lobby. He came in after closing and stayed until midnight, then someone else took over till the company opened in the morning.

"We'll be back a little later, Marvin," she said to the guard, a big, pudgy black man with a kindly face. "By the way, this is Jake Cantrell. He's providing security for the next few days. It's all right for him to go in and out whenever he needs to."

"That's what Mr. Dumont said."

She should have known her grandfather would make it easy for Cantrell to do his job. Ian wanted her safe. He was determined.

"Your grandfather gave me a parking pass," Jake

said. "My Jeep's in the executive lot. With those shoes, maybe you'd better ride."

She looked down at her Jimmy Choos. Riding would be good. "Might be hard to find a parking space at the restaurant."

"I don't think so. Not this time of night."

He led her to a fancy black Jeep that seemed the perfect fit for him, having big wide tires with chrome rims and a roll bar that would show when the top was down. Which, thankfully, it wasn't. As hot as it was, she was glad to get in out of the heat.

He helped her climb inside, which wasn't that easy in a snug skirt and high heels. As she snapped her seat belt into place, Cantrell rounded the car, then slid in behind the wheel and cranked the engine.

It didn't take long to reach the restaurant, and since most people in the downtown area went home after work, there were parking places in the lot. The maître d', a little man with slicked-back black hair, greeted them effusively. Clearly, he knew Cantrell.

Or maybe he was just afraid of him. Sage hid a grin.

"Mr. Cantrell, it's good to see you. I have your table ready, if you'll come this way?"

"Thanks, Mario." A big hand settled at her waist as Jake guided her to a table with a red-checked cloth and a little red candle in the middle. Typical Italian, but the place seemed downright homey. Sage liked it right away.

She sat down and picked up a menu. When the waiter arrived, she ordered the pasta primavera with extra vegetables.

"I'll have the lasagna, and bring us a couple glasses

of Chianti." Jake glanced over at her. "Unless you'd like something else?"

"I'd love a glass, but I wasn't planning to drink. I need to have my wits about me."

"You don't have to finish it." He nodded at the waiter and the man disappeared, returning a few minutes later with the wine.

Sage took a sip, glad Jake had ordered it, after all. She felt suddenly nervous as she looked across the table at the handsome man.

"So you're going to marry Phillip Stanton," he said, taking a drink of his wine.

"That's right. We thought maybe sometime next year."

"But you don't live together. Your grandfather mentioned that when we discussed some of the security issues."

"No. Phillip spends a great deal of time out of the country. In fact, the day after tomorrow he's returning to his office in Edinburgh."

"Makes things a lot easier."

She wasn't exactly sure what he meant by that, especially when she noticed the way those blue eyes slid over her.

Cantrell turned his attention to business, pulling folded sheets of paper out of his back pocket. "First, I've got a couple of questions."

"Fire away."

"How long will the Saudis be here?"

"The trip is open-ended. I'm hoping not more than a week. They arrive on Tuesday. I figure we should give them Wednesday to relax, then bring them into the office on Thursday and begin the negotiations."

With a faint smile, Cantrell started shaking his head.
Sage knew right then it was going to be a very
long night.

Jake leaned back in his chair. He had a nice view
of a very pretty woman, all smooth skin, golden eyes
and softly curling dark brown hair. For several long
moments he allowed himself to enjoy it, didn't even
fight the hardening of his body beneath the table. Unfortunately, his relationship with Sage Dumont was
strictly business. He intended to remind himself of
that on a daily basis.

"To start with, Thursday and Friday are going to pose
a problem," he said. "That's more or less a Saudi's weekend. They'll expect you to entertain them on Thursday,
then Friday is a day of relaxation and meditation. Like
our Saturdays and Sundays."

Jake caught Sage's exasperated sigh as she set her
wineglass on the table. "The office is closed on the
weekend. That means we'll have to wait until Monday
before we even start."

"You might as well resign yourself. The Saudis take
everything slowly. They'll need to get to know you
before they even begin to think about negotiations."

"I read that, but I didn't think it would mean losing almost a week."

The waiter arrived just then with their food. Jake let
the conversation drift while they dug into their meals.
The lasagna was damn good, as always. Bella's was
a personal favorite of his in the area. From the look
of pure pleasure on Sage's pretty face, he figured she
was enjoying it, too.

"This is wonderful," she said with a roll of her eyes.

"I can't remember when I've had a chance to do more than grab a snack here and there."

Jake was beginning to think maybe Annie was right, and Sage had climbed the corporate ladder with a lot of hard work. Not that being a Dumont hadn't opened the door.

"Okay, what else?" she asked.

"You'll need someone you work with to attend the meetings with you. He'll be the one who asks most of the questions."

"But I can handle that."

"If you do, they'll think you're a lackey. They'll figure they should be speaking to someone else, someone who has the actual authority."

Sage shook her head. "I spent half the day reading up on all this, and I still don't have a clue. I hate to say it, but I'm glad you're here to help."

Jake's eyebrows went up. He hadn't expected to hear those words, at least not so soon.

"There is one thing," she said.

He swallowed the bite of lasagna he had taken. "Which is…?"

"I don't like the idea of you carrying a gun. I assume that's what you've got clipped to your belt. Do you think it's really necessary? I mean, as big as you are, and with the training you've had, surely you can handle any problem that might come up without shooting someone."

"Probably." He took a drink of his wine. "The problem is, if the other guy is carrying and I'm unarmed, then you and I are both in deep shit."

Sage sat up a little straighter. "I think we should wait and see if a gun is really something you'll need."

"No."

Her lips tightened. "I don't like handguns."

"Noted." He returned his attention to his food. Sage fumed in silence, but the smell of the delicious pasta was nearly irresistible and pretty soon she was eating with the same gusto as before. She nearly cleaned her plate, and ate at least two pieces of toasted garlic bread. Jake enjoyed food, lots of it. He liked that she wasn't a priss about eating.

They carried on with their work, and he was impressed that she seemed to know more than he'd thought. When the meal came to an end, he paid the bill, which would go on his expense account, and they rose from the table.

"We'll need to brief your people," he said. "And you have to get those Saudi names. I'll be in at nine in the morning. That'll give you a little time."

She nodded, but he could tell she wasn't looking forward to seeing him.

"We got a lot done tonight," he said as they drove back to the office. "More than I thought we would. Your research really helped. Now you need to go home and get some sleep."

She shook her head. "I've still got a few things to do here at work."

Jake reached over and caught her hand, saw the surprise on her face. "I'm beginning to understand how important this deal is to you, Sage. You'll need to be at your best when the Saudis arrive. Get some sleep. We'll start again tomorrow."

She nodded, and he let go of her hand. He didn't say any more as he dropped her off in the executive parking lot, but couldn't help wondering if Phillip Stanton would show up at her apartment and spend the night in her bed.

The thought didn't sit well.

Jake had taken an instant dislike to the man, who was a little too much the way Annie had described him. Soft and self-indulgent, more worried about himself than what might happen to the woman who was going to be his wife.

The Jeep engine purred as Jake waited for Sage to slide behind the wheel of her silver Mercedes S550, start the engine and drive out of the lot. He'd been right about her being rich. Everything about her spoke of money and class. She was a little cantankerous at times, but not as bad as he had expected. He wasn't sure yet about the spoiled part. He'd get around to deciding on that.

In the meantime, he needed to take his own advice and get some sleep. He'd already canceled the plans he had made for the evening. Funny thing was, even the thought of a night of hot, raunchy sex wasn't enough to stir his interest in Deanna Leblanc.

Chapter 4

Jake awakened at his usual early hour, five-thirty, and rolled out of bed. His apartment off Buffalo Speedway was a small oasis in the middle of the huge metropolitan area, a two-story rectangular complex with fountains and lakes in the center, and trees and grass all around.

He'd been born in Iowa, raised on a farm. After his father died, during Jake's senior year in high school, he'd felt compelled to stay and help his mom, but as soon as he'd finished junior college he had joined the marines. He had worked outdoors ever since. The lush foliage and grassy landscape outside the windows made his apartment a respite from the hustle and bustle, the closed-in spaces of the city he worked in, at least for the time being.

Over the years, Jake had never stayed in one place too long. Instead, he'd enjoyed the challenge and excitement, the financial rewards, of taking jobs all over the globe. Though lately he'd been thinking that might change.

He was beginning to feel as if Houston was home, beginning to build a network of people he cared about. Thanks to a friend named Abraham Lincoln Jones, a man Jake had worked with off and on, he had even gotten involved in the Big Brothers Big Sisters program. It felt good to be part of a community for the first time in his life.

Still, he wasn't sure it was possible for a man like him to settle in one place for long.

Jake yawned as he walked into the kitchen and went about making a pot of coffee. He felt refreshed today, almost glad he hadn't been up half the night getting laid.

Almost.

The problem was, he didn't want Deanna. His dumb-ass libido had begun to fixate on Sage Dumont. Last night he'd dreamed about her, a lusty dream that had left him covered in sweat with a raging hard-on. The bad news was he couldn't even remember what they had done together.

Not enough, that was for sure. As he climbed into the shower, he turned down the temperature until the water was just above chilly. He would be spending another day with Sage—hell, he'd be with her at least another week. He almost laughed. If he took a cold shower every day, it wouldn't be enough.

He turned off the water, towel-dried his hair, shaved, then dressed in a yellow oxford cloth shirt and another of the tailored suits he kept for protection details, this one dark brown. In the kitchen, he poured a cup of the freshly brewed coffee and took a sip.

Heading for the front door, he collected the copy of the *Chronicle* that waited for him every morning. As he started back to the kitchen, he read the headlines and jerked to a halt.

Saudi Sheik to Arrive in Houston
   Potential Oil Rig Deal with Marine Drilling International

Jake's jaw tightened. Ian Dumont had assured him the story was being kept out of the papers. He continued reading only long enough to see Sage's name mentioned as the vice president in charge of the transaction.

Son of a bitch. Downing his coffee in a couple of gulps, Jake grabbed his Heckler-Koch .45 and shoved it into its leather holster. Then he clipped the holster on his belt, grip forward on his left side, where it was easy to reach with his right hand. Plucking his suit coat off the back of a kitchen chair, he headed for the door.

He knew where Sage lived, a high-rise in the Galleria District. Her grandfather had already arranged clearance for Jake to access the building whenever he needed.

He fired up his Jeep.

His job had just kicked into high gear.

It was still early, just after six, but Sage was dressed and ready for work. She had her bag slung over her shoulder and car keys in hand when a hard knock sounded at the door. She frowned. Why hadn't the guard in the lobby phoned before sending someone up?

She peered through the peephole and recognized the massive chest blocking her view. When she opened the door, Jake Cantrell strode past her into her condo.

"I thought we were meeting at the office," she said, a little annoyed.

"Have you seen the paper?"

"I saw it. Someone leaked the story. So what? The press would have gotten wind of it sooner or later."

"Helluva lot better if it had been later." Those beautiful blue eyes ran over her, making her stomach flutter. "I see you're ready to go."

"I was just leaving. I've got a lot to do."

"Fine, then, let's head out."

Irritation filtered through her. "Look, you didn't need to come here. I've been driving myself to the office every day for the last six years."

"Maybe so, but from now on you'll be going with me. I'll arrange for a car, so you won't have to ride in the Jeep."

"It isn't the Jeep I mind, it's you."

He grinned, that sexy mouth curving upward. "I'm sorry to hear that." Oh, dear God, that grin... It was devastating.

"How did you get past security downstairs?" But suddenly she knew. "Ian, right?"

"Your grandfather's a very efficient man."

She cast Jake a look, then followed him out the door. They rode in the Jeep to the office, stopping at a bakery along the way so he could buy something to eat.

"Didn't have time for breakfast," he said, and she

thought that a man his size definitely needed plenty of fuel to get started.

Jake insisted she come with him into the bake shop. She nearly swooned at the delicious smells inside.

"Two ham-and-cheese croissants," he ordered, "two chocolate doughnuts, coffee, and whatever the lady wants."

At least he wasn't one of those guys who always had to order for a woman. Well, except for the wine last night, and she had to thank him for that. After the delicious meal, she had slept like a baby for the first time in weeks.

"I'll have a glazed doughnut, please, and coffee."

He flicked her a glance. "You sure that's enough?"

"I'm not hungry in the mornings. I usually skip breakfast altogether."

He cast her a long, sensual glance. "Maybe you need to work up an appetite."

Her breath caught. He was giving her that look again, the one that said he could make her ravenous, and not just for food. Then it was gone, as if she'd imagined it.

"I've got to get to the office," she said.

"Ten minutes and we're out of here."

They sat at a small round table, Jake barely fitting in the little, wrought-iron chair. They finished eating quickly and were on the road again.

It was a little past seven when he pulled into the executive lot and turned off the engine. It wasn't until they rounded the building, heading toward the front door, that Sage understood why he had come to pick her up.

* * *

"I had a hunch this might happen when I read this morning's paper." Jake surveyed the crowd that had begun to gather in front of the mirrored-glass building. "I didn't figure they'd get here so early. Is there a back way in?"

"No. Just the emergency fire exits. They let you out but not in."

He moved a little in front of Sage, putting himself between her and what appeared to be students from the MSA—the Muslim Student Association who had been demonstrating at the university a few days before. Some young men wore traditional Muslim garb: white, flowing robes called *thobes* and headdresses secured by an *agal,* the black rope that held them in place. Caftan-style dresses in various colors and patterns were worn by a number of the women, who had their heads and necks hidden by colorful scarves.

There were other young people there, kids in Western dress who sympathized with the cause, some of them carrying signs. One read Students for Middle East Democracy. Another, Free Libya. A third said Stop the Bloodshed. The group was relatively small, not more than thirty people, and fairly well behaved.

So far.

Another group milled around to one side. Jake couldn't tell exactly who they were. But there were always radicals drawn to protests like these, people just itching to cause trouble, he knew. As the crowd spotted them climbing the wide concrete steps toward the front door, a soft rumble of recognition turned into a muffled roar, and he went into high alert.

Someone shouted, "Friends of the Saudi royal oppressors!"

Someone else shouted, "Freedom from tyranny!" and hurled something in their direction. A tomato splattered against the wall next to Sage's head. She made a little sound in her throat as Jake pushed open the door and shoved her into the lobby.

"Oh, my God," she said, pressing her back against the wall there. "Oh, my God."

The security guard came out from behind his desk and started hurrying toward them. Jake waved him away.

He caught hold of Sage's shoulders, felt her trembling. "It's all right, Sage. The people out there are mostly just kids, trying to be supportive of a cause they believe in, or at least think they do. They're harmless, for the most part."

Her trembling eased a little. She steadied herself, straightened, and Jake released her. "It's...it's not like the sheik is in line for the throne or anything. He's just a businessman."

"As I said, they're mostly trying to make a point. Unfortunately, there are radicals in every group. They're the ones we need to watch out for."

"Oh, God."

"Look, we'll work out a better way to come and go. Put a man on the back door, and develop a strategy to keep things running smoothly. We need more security people in here to make sure none of the protestors try to come inside. And we'll need men outside, too, to ensure your employees' safety."

"Can you handle that?"

"Trace can. I'll call him, have Atlas provide the extra men we need."

Sage looked up at Jake, her eyes bigger and more golden than usual. "I had no idea something like this would happen. Now I see why Ian hired you. I'm glad you're here."

Jake thought of how protests like this had a way of swelling, how there was a good chance things could get worse in the next few day. He thought of the danger Sage might actually be facing. "So am I," he said, and realized he meant it.

Sage led Jake into the conference room. "I hope this will do. There's a phone in here and a computer. Is there anything else you'll need?"

"I just have to make a few calls, get things rolling. I was hoping we'd have another day or two before things got stirred up. Looks like that's not going to happen."

She tried to smile. She still felt shaky inside, a little off-kilter. "Marie just got here. I'll have her bring you some coffee. Let me know if there's anything you need." Sage closed the conference room door and for a moment leaned against it.

She had scoffed at her grandfather, thinking it ridiculous to hire a professional bodyguard. It was beginning to look as if he was right.

Which was usually the way it worked. She'd been twelve years old when her grandfather's detective had found them—Ian's son's runaway wife and daughter hiding in a Chicago tenement. When Louis, Sage's father, had died, Ian had come for them. He had convinced her mother to return with him to Houston.

From that day forward, Ian Dumont had raised her.

Sage had just turned fifteen when her mother died of breast cancer, and after that her grandfather became her whole world. Over the years, she had learned to trust him as she never did another man.

Sage wasn't convinced she was in any serious danger now, but she didn't want to be assaulted or harassed just for coming to work. Jake would make sure that didn't happen.

Jake. Besides being dangerously attractive, he was an interesting man. Smarter than she'd given him credit for. And from the moment he had spotted the threat in front of the building and taken charge, she had known with complete certainty that he was capable of protecting her from whatever might come.

A thought that eased some of the tension inside her.

Sitting down in the cream leather Eames chair behind her desk, she went to work. She started making calls, digging up the information Jake had asked for, and some she needed, as well. She had the name and contact information of the aide who was handling the Saudi end of preparations for the visit, Caseem Al Dossari. She made a list of questions, then phoned the man in Saudi Arabia.

Did the sheik or his family have any special needs? Did anyone require or prefer any special foods? Was there anything in particular the family wanted to see or do while in Houston? Most importantly, how did the sheik and his family wish to be addressed?

The man patiently answered each of her questions and added a few more details he thought might be useful.

Sage finished the cell and spent the next few hours going over her notes and making other calls.

It was almost noon when she finished the call and her assistant buzzed her on the intercom.

"Yes, Will?"

"Mr. Cantrell has a few things he needs to go over."

"Of course. Send him in." She sat up a little straighter, tossed her hair back over her shoulder as Jake walked through the door.

"I just wanted to let you know we've got security coming in this afternoon. They'll be round-the-clock in the building until the negotiations are finished."

"That's a relief." Not wanting to be at even more of a height disadvantage, she stood up and walked toward him.

"You come up with those names?" he asked.

Sage couldn't stop a smile. "The sheik's full name is His Highness Sheik Khalid bin Abd al-Kahtani bin Abd Al Kahzaz."

"There's a mouthful."

"Formally, we're to call him His Highness Sheik Khalid Al Kahzaz. Being a little less formal, we can leave off the His Highness and go with Sheik Khalid."

"That's better."

"I have the son and daughter's names, as well. Roshan's twenty-six and A'lia's twenty-two. I've got a list of all their personal likes and dislikes, which I'll be discussing with the hotel, and some things they'd like to do while they're here."

"Such as?"

"The daughter loves to ride. I thought we'd take them out to Ian's ranch for a couple of days. Give them a real taste of Texas."

"Where is it?"

"Out along the Brazos less than two hours away.

We've got twenty-five hundred acres out there. There's a main house and a separate guesthouse. It should be perfect."

"I'll need to see the place ahead of time, check the security."

A soft knock sounded. Phillip's knock. He didn't feel he should have to go through her assistant to speak to her. It irritated her a little.

Her fiancé smiled as he stepped through the door and kept the smile in place when he spotted Cantrell. "Just wanted to check in, make sure our evening was going forward as planned."

It was Friday, Phillip's last night in Houston. He wouldn't be back in the country for at least two months. Fridays were one of the nights he stayed at her apartment when he was in town. Tuesdays and Fridays they went out to dinner, came home and made love. It fit into both of their schedules.

Sage had never given that fact much thought until she glanced at Jake. She couldn't imagine Jake Cantrell planning his calendar around the two days a week he intended to have sex.

The thought made her feel uneasy, and somehow restless. She didn't know why.

She shoved the thought away, looked up at Phillip and smiled. "It's Friday, and your last day in the city. Of course we're going out as planned."

Cantrell's blue eyes fixed on Phillip. They seemed darker, somehow more intense. "If you don't want company, I'd advise you to change your plans."

Sage's mouth thinned. "What are you talking about? What Phillip and I are planning has nothing to do with you."

"Have you looked outside lately?"

"No, why?"

"Because that little scene you caught this morning has grown, the crowd already more than doubled. My job is to protect you. You're stuck with me until the Saudis are gone."

Her shoulders stiffened. She wanted to tell him to take his protection and shove it. That he was overbearing and domineering, and she didn't like it.

She looked at Phillip, who was waiting for her to do exactly that—tell Cantrell to stay out of her personal affairs. She thought of the night ahead, of Phillip in her bed, of another round of unimaginative lovemaking and very little passion. Suddenly, it was the last thing she wanted.

"I think Mr. Cantrell is right. Ian wouldn't have hired him if he didn't trust his judgment."

"Nonsense. Most of those people are students from the university. They're hardly a threat."

"Until this is over, what I say goes," Jake said. "And if she goes out with you, I'm coming along."

Phillip bristled. But he wasn't a fool and he was certainly no match for Cantrell. Not that he would consider behaving as anything less than a gentleman.

"Why don't we go get some lunch?" Sage suggested, ignoring the guilt slipping through her, the feeling that she was somehow betraying Phillip. "We can say our goodbyes in the dining room."

"I planned to have dinner at the club." River Oaks, the most exclusive country club in Houston. "That's hardly the same as lunch in the executive dining room."

Jake didn't say a word, just stood there with his legs

splayed and his hands crossed, staring straight ahead, looking like an employee—for once.

Sage almost rolled her eyes. He could be as irritating as Phillip.

"Fine, let's go." Phillip waited while she grabbed her bag, then took her arm and walked her out the door. She wondered why he hadn't suggested staying home tonight, having dinner in her apartment. But their relationship had never been one of grand passion. It was comfortable, the kind both of them felt could stand the test of time.

"I'll be in the conference room when you're done," Jake said, following them out of her office.

Phillip's jaw looked tight as he watched Cantrell's tall frame disappear inside the room. Turning, he led Sage toward the elevator and the small but first-class restaurant on the fourteenth floor.

She tried to convince herself she was furious at Jake. That what she was feeling wasn't relief.

Chapter 5

The weekend arrived. Both days, Jake escorted Sage to the office, where only a few people were working in the building. There were just a few protestors out in front, and none of the chaos that had greeted them coming and going on Friday. These were kids. Most of them wanted their weekends off.

While Sage caught up on things at the office, Jake began the work he needed to do before the Saudis arrived. As the protests had grown, his job had expanded. Fortunately, Ian had given him the authority to arrange whatever additional security was needed during the visit.

Jake made a trip to the Four Seasons, walked the twentieth floor, checked the exits, checked the lobby, dining rooms and kitchen. The hotel was well run, and nothing unusual caught his eye. He spoke to hotel security, alerting them to the Saudis' visit, advising them to treat the matter as a celebrity stay and keep the information quiet.

The staff assured him that wouldn't be a problem. Oil-rich Texas was used to visitors from the Middle East. It was only the recent unrest that complicated the situation.

On Sunday afternoon, after Sage finished work, she and Jake drove out in the Jeep to the Dumont family ranch, south and a little west of Houston. The weather had turned slightly cooler. Jake hoped it stayed that way. The Saudis were certainly used to heat, but the humidity was something else.

He glanced over at Sage. She was dressed in jeans, sneakers and a white cotton blouse. The shirt was tied up in front, giving him a glimpse of bare skin. Though perfectly modest, it was driving him crazy. Her dark hair fell around her shoulders, the way she usually wore it, making him want to run his fingers through it.

His heart rate went up and yet again his groin tightened.

He thought of the brief exchange he'd had with Phillip Stanton in her office on Friday, recalled the evil little demon that had driven him to ruin Sage's last night with her fiancé.

The protests in front of the building weren't enough to keep her from dining out with the man she was going to marry. Jake could have escorted her home and checked things out, made sure everything was okay. They had planned to have dinner at River Oaks, and getting inside the exclusive country club was next to impossible.

Jake just couldn't stand the thought of the guy in her bed.

Sage was staring out the window now, her mind somewhere else. Probably on business. "Why'd you do it?" he asked.

She glanced up at him. "Why'd I do what?"

"Let me push you into canceling your date with Phillip. You knew the protest wasn't enough of a threat that I needed to be with you all evening. You also knew if you gave me any kind of resistance, I would have backed down."

She didn't deny it.

"So why didn't you fight me?" he pressed.

A slow breath whispered out. "I don't know."

"I think you do."

Sage shifted in her seat, to see him better. "What are you saying, Jake?"

"I don't think you wanted to be with Phillip that night. I think you were glad I gave you an excuse. What I don't get is why you're marrying him."

He figured she would launch into him, tell him it was none of his business—which it wasn't.

Instead, she leaned back in the seat. "I met Phillip right after I started working for the company. He was already a vice president, not as important a job as he has now, but someone my grandfather had high hopes for. A few years later, we started dating."

"So you've known him quite a while."

"That's right. We got along well from the start. Same interests, same goals. Phillip and I... We're extremely well-suited."

"How's that?"

"We both love classical music and ballet. We're interested in art and the theater."

"That's enough for you? That Phillip likes ballet?"

"Which I'm sure you don't."

He grinned. "Watching a bunch of men prancing around in tights? Not a chance." In the mirror, he saw her lips curve in a smile.

"We share the same interests, as I said, and my grandfather and I talked about it. He thought it was time for me to think about my future. Marrying the right person is important to my career."

Jake clicked on his turn signal and passed a few cars, then pulled back into the right lane. "Your grandfather raised you after your mother died. I saw that in an article on the internet."

"He raised me from the time I was twelve. He's the best man I've ever known."

Jake frowned. "What about your father?"

She gazed down at her hands, then looked back through the windshield at the road. "My father died when I was twelve. It's a long story. It's enough to say that when he died, I hadn't seen him in eight years."

It was obviously a subject she didn't want to discuss, and Jake didn't press her. But his curiosity was piqued. There was something about Sage that didn't add up. She just didn't seem to be the self-centered heiress he'd expected. And he thought he had just uncovered the first clue to solving the puzzle.

They reached the impressive wrought-iron gate that marked the entrance to the property. A sign overhead read Double D Ranch. "Double D" for Sage and Ian Dumont? Or for Ian and his dead son, Louis?

Sage gave Jake the security code. He punched in

the numbers and the automatic gate swung open. They drove till the highway was well out of sight and the Spanish-style ranch house appeared, huge and white, with a red-tile roof, several turrets and patios. Even the matching guesthouse was big.

Sage was right. The place could easily handle the Saudis and the entourage that was sure to be traveling with them.

There was also a large, tile-roofed stable, and an indoor arena surrounded by lush green pastures. Horses grazed and galloped across the countryside.

"Pretty place."

"It's a great getaway," Sage said. "There was a time when Ian raised the finest cutting horses in Texas. Riding is kind of a passion of mine. My only real hobby, I guess you could say. Lately, I just haven't had time." She turned to Jake as he pulled up in front of the house. "Do you ride?"

"Not if I can help it."

She looked disappointed. He tried to imagine Phillip Stanton on horseback, but the image wouldn't come.

They parked the Jeep and headed into the main house. It was fully staffed, and decorated, too, in a Spanish style, with lots of old wood, bright serapes and heavy old-world antiques.

By the time Jake had surveyed the two houses, walked the stables and the grounds, he only had one comment.

"Your security here sucks. You want the Saudis to stay in this place, you're going to have to do something about it."

Her shoulders slumped. "I was afraid you'd say that.

Nothing's been done in years. I guess we just felt safe out here."

There were vast open stretches of grassland. Lots of native trees and abundant wildlife. Horses roamed the pastures, deer grazed in the fields and the bird-life was spectacular. A hawk soared overhead as if to make the point.

"So what do you want to do?" he asked.

She glanced back at the house. "How fast can something be done?"

Jake pulled out his iPhone and punched in Trace's home number. "Hey, buddy, I've got a problem."

A low grumble preceded his friend's soft Texas drawl. "It's Sunday, you know. This is supposed to be my day off. I'm spendin' time with my wife."

Jake could hear the pride in his friend's voice. Trace was married and in love. Jake had never seen him so happy.

"I'm out at the Dumont ranch. The place is huge, with lots of land, main house, guesthouse and stables. Some of the security cameras aren't working and the alarms are years out-of-date. The whole system needs to be replaced. How long will it take you to upgrade?"

Trace muttered a word Jake couldn't quite hear. "I'll get on it. I can have someone out there today. We can do a perimeter installation, mount new cameras, put some temporary equipment in the house, guesthouse and stables, till we have time to do a permanent replacement."

"There's a housekeeper, foreman, some ranch hands. We'll let them know your men are coming."

"We…?"

"Sage is with me. Can you be finished by next weekend?"

"Enough for you to feel safe."

"Good enough."

Jake clicked off and shoved the phone back into the pocket of his jeans. "Trace is going to take care of it. He'll have enough of the system up and running to keep people safe. Let's talk to your foreman, let him know what's going on."

Sage nodded. "I can't believe how complicated this is getting."

"Three hundred million is a lot of money."

"If I make this deal and we get hold of a platform and some used offshore equipment, it'll be a huge savings to the company."

"And that means a lot to you."

"Yes, it does."

"Then let's get to it." Setting a hand at her waist, he guided her toward the foreman's house. Without her high heels, she seemed almost tiny to him. Jake felt a surge of protectiveness, and told himself it was all right to feel that way, since it was his job. He thought about how much softer she seemed out here, miles away from work.

He told himself not to think of how sexy she looked in the snug jeans, with that little bit of skin showing at her waist. Told his mind not to stray where it had no right to go.

He told himself to remember Sage was off-limits. But he couldn't quite convince himself.

Riding the elevator up to her apartment on the tenth floor, Sage felt Jake's hand at her back.

"You don't have to come in," she said, as the elevator doors slid open and he guided her out into the hall.

"That's what I get paid for. I'll just take a quick look around, make sure everything's okay." He walked past her as she opened the door and turned off the alarm, then watched him disappear down the hall. It had been a long day and she was exhausted. The security situation at the ranch was worse than she had expected. The system needed upgrading anyway, so doing it now wasn't really a problem, except that the matter had become urgent.

She thought of the surprisingly comfortable day she had spent with Jake. He was easy to talk to and actually listened to what she had to say. She tried not to compare him to Phillip, whose mind always seemed to be somewhere else.

Things had gone well at first, but as the day progressed, the easy conversation had slipped away, replaced by a slowly building sexual tension.

The ride home had been silent, marked by a shared look now and then that seemed to scorch the air between them. She had never felt anything like it.

Thank God they were home and he was leaving.

She watched him return to the entry, thinking how much space he took up, even in her large, airy apartment. "Did you really expect to find someone lurking in here?"

"No. But don't be surprised if trouble starts again tomorrow. Seems like once these things get rolling, they take on a life of their own."

"I hope you're wrong."

"So do I. It would make my job a whole lot easier."

She looked up at him, standing there in front of her. God, he was handsome, and so damned male.

"Is that all I am to you, Jake? A job?"

His blue eyes ran over her. Something shifted between them, and the air seemed to simmer and heat.

"That's the way it started," he said, his gaze on her face.

"And now?"

His nostrils flared. He was standing closer than she'd realized. So close she could see his chest rising and falling, each breath coming faster than the last. He was wearing a dark green T-shirt and jeans, and when she glanced down she saw there was a heavy bulge beneath his zipper. He took a step toward her, and instead of moving back, she rested her hand on his chest. She could feel the thick muscle, the bands of sinew that tightened beneath the soft cotton fabric.

Her heartbeat quickened. She stared at his mouth and wanted him to kiss her. It was insane. She was engaged to be married. She wasn't the type of woman who betrayed her fiancé by kissing another man.

She tipped her head to look up at Jake's face, saw the hunger in those blue, blue eyes, and her whole body went hot. One of his hands slid beneath her hair, tilting her mouth toward his. She felt the roughness of his palm against her scalp, the raw power he commanded. He bent his head, lightly brushed her lips, and heat and need poured through her.

She exhaled a breath and her eyes closed. She wanted this kiss…wanted it so badly.

His mouth hovered over hers, just a breath away. "What about Phillip?" he whispered.

"Phillip?" Her eyes fluttered, slowly opened. Then

the name hit her like a splash of cold water and her stomach knotted. Sage jerked away. "Phillip. Oh, my God."

Those fierce blue eyes bored into her. "I don't share my women, Sage."

Humiliation burned through her, and fury boiled in her blood. "Get out." She pointed toward the door with a hand that trembled. "Get out of here right now."

The edge of his mouth harshly curved. "I'm leaving. But I'll be back in the morning. Seven o'clock."

"Six!" she demanded, just to save a little pride. "I have work to do." She wanted to throw something at him, wanted to tell him never to come near her again. He had humiliated her, shown her how susceptible she was to him.

Her eyes stung.

"Lock the door behind me," he said a little more gently, and then he was gone.

Sage's throat closed up. He had made a fool of her, preyed on the attraction she felt for him. Clearly, he believed he could have her anytime he wanted.

It wasn't true. She wouldn't do that to Phillip.

She leaned back against the wall and released a shaky breath. It was nothing, she told herself. A moment of weakness, nothing more.

It wouldn't happen again. Sage ignored the little tremor of regret that whispered through her.

Chapter 6

On Monday morning, Jake pulled up in front of Sage's apartment in one of the big black SUVs that belonged to Freedom Limousines, the fleet owned by Abraham Lincoln Jones.

Linc was a longtime friend and a man Jake trusted. As a kid, Linc had boosted cars for a living, until he got busted and tossed into juvenile hall. Unlike other kids his age, he had realized the error of his ways, straightened up his life and become a successful Houston businessman.

He still knew cars, knew how to handle a vehicle better than any Hollywood stuntman. Linc had agreed to be Jake's personal driver during the Saudis' visit.

The Cadillac Escalade rolled to a stop beneath the overhanging portal of the high-rise apartment building where Sage lived.

Jake opened the door and climbed out. "I won't be long."

It was six in the morning. Damn the woman. Ian was right—Sage worked too hard. But the early departure was partly Jake's fault. If he hadn't goaded her last night—if he hadn't given in to that single moment of weakness—she would have agreed to the later hour and gotten at least a little more sleep.

He should have left her alone. But he hadn't expected the hunger to be so intense, hadn't known for sure until last night that she wanted him, too.

It didn't matter. The attraction between them wasn't going anywhere, and he had a job to do.

With a nod to the security guard, he took the elevator up to Sage's apartment and knocked on the door. An instant later, she pulled the door open.

"I see you're on time," she said sharply. "Let's go."

He'd meant to ignore what had happened last night, go on as if it didn't matter. Maybe he would have, if it weren't for the faint purple smudges beneath her eyes, the stiffness in her posture that told him he had hurt her.

She tried to brush past him, but he caught her arm, stopping her. She was wearing her high heels, putting her back in her confidence zone, and he was glad.

"About what happened last night…"

Her chin went up. "Nothing happened. Don't pretend it did." She tried to walk past him, but he wouldn't let her go.

"Nothing happened. But don't think I didn't want it to. I wanted it too much, Sage."

Her eyes found his. They were golden and full of fire. Disbelieving.

"I'm sorry," he said. "I was out of line. Nothing like that will happen again."

For a moment she just stared, her eyes fixed on his. Then she relaxed. "We're both under a lot of pressure. Things happen. It's better if we just forget it."

But he wouldn't forget. Every time he looked at her he would curse himself for not tasting her, not seeing where that single kiss might lead. His gaze remained on hers. "Are you sure that's the way you want it?"

She didn't even blink. "That's the way it has to be."

Jake stepped back and let her pass. "There's a car waiting downstairs. Let's get you to the office."

Sage just nodded.

Walking out of the lobby moments later, she stopped when she spotted the big black SUV with the dark tinted windows. "And here I was expecting a stretch. Should have known that wouldn't be manly enough for a marine."

He grinned. "Just a little too conspicuous." He opened the rear passenger door, waited till Sage slid across the butter-soft, black leather seat, then followed her inside.

"Sage Dumont, meet Lincoln Jones. Linc owns the limo company. He's a friend of mine and the best wheelman around."

Linc, a tall, slim African-American man with short kinky hair and a very white smile, was a good-looking guy. Never married but hopeful, he always said.

"It's a pleasure to meet you, Mr. Jones," Sage said with a smile.

"It's just Linc, and same here, Ms. Dumont."

"Since you're a friend of Jake's, let's just make it Sage."

He grinned and turned back to the wheel, started moving the heavy vehicle forward. Jake glanced at Sage, a little surprised at how accessible she seemed to be. She might be a Dumont, but she treated people as her equal. Another point in her favor.

They reached the office in record time. As they had planned, Linc pulled the Escalade into the executive lot. Jake made a call to the security guard at the back door, and they entered the building that way.

It wasn't until Sage's friend, the little redhead he had seen in her office before, arrived at noon that the problems began.

Sage was sitting behind her desk, the phone pressed against her ear, when the door swung open and Rina walked in. They were planning to go to lunch. Since there hadn't been any problems over the weekend, and no trouble when she'd come to work that morning, Sage figured she'd be able to get away for a couple hours—without her overbearing bodyguard.

He'd surprised her with an apology for his behavior last night—which had been her fault as much as his.

She wished she could have stayed mad at him, convinced herself he was just another arrogant male. But he had spoiled that by actually behaving like a human being.

She blocked him from her mind as Rina rushed toward her across the office, her face flushed, her blue eyes wide.

"Oh, my God, Sage, have you seen what's going on outside?"

Sage stood up behind her desk. "No. What is?" Her

door swung open just then, at the same instant her intercom buzzed.

"We've got a problem," Jake said, striding in as if he owned the place.

Will raced in behind him. "Sage, the police are downstairs."

Sage shot Jake a glance. "What's going on, Jake?"

He tipped his head toward the big floor-to-ceiling windows on one wall of her spacious office. "Take a look."

Will backed out of the room and closed the door.

"Jake, this is my friend Rina Eckhart," she said. "Rina, meet Jake Cantrell."

Rina gave Jake a head-to-toe once-over, which took a while, since she was so petite and he was so big. "Nice to meet you, Jake."

He smiled. "You, too, Rina."

Sage went over to the window and looked out past the wide steps at the front. A familiar sight greeted her—only now the protest was three times bigger.

"I guess the students are back."

"They're back, all right," Jake said, walking up beside her. "Along with two other factions. Besides the students, there's a pro-American bunch thanking God for keeping our troops safe in the Middle East, protesting sharia law, advocating for women's rights and anything else that comes to mind. Another group is demonstrating against Israel and pushing for a Palestinian state."

Sage turned to look at him, felt that same little kick she always experienced when he was near. "I can't believe this. All we're doing is trying to buy a used drilling platform and a shipment of pipe."

"Believe it. There's plenty of friction out there. The cops have arrived to try to keep things under control. It remains to be seen how much good it will do."

"Don't these people have to get permits for this kind of thing?"

"I talked to the police. The main group has done the necessary paperwork. Aside from that, there's a thing called freedom of speech."

Worry knotted her stomach. "The Saudis are due at the airport tomorrow afternoon. What are we going to do?"

"We're going to handle it," Jake said firmly. "Linc's got a fleet lined up to meet the plane and take them to the hotel. They'll have their own security while they're there, and we'll put a couple of people on it, too. The sheik and his family will be at the hotel the rest of that day and Wednesday. The ranch won't be ready till the weekend. That leaves only Thursday and Friday to worry about."

"On Friday they'd like to attend prayers at the local mosque. That's the Da'wah Center. It's right downtown."

"Good. We'll have them taken them there and picked up, return them to the hotel. That leaves only Thursday."

Sage worried her bottom lip. She looked up at him. "I wonder if they've ever been to an IMAX."

Jake flashed her one of his devastating grins. "Probably ten of them in Saudi Arabia, but it's still a good idea. Anything that'll keep them away from the office."

"The daughter wants to go shopping," she said, her mind beginning to work.

"I imagine you can handle that."

"Are you kidding?" Sage smiled, Jake's confidence easing her nerves. "The Galleria is my home away from home."

"She'll have to be accompanied by a male family member. There may be more than one, and they're sure to have bodyguards. I'll get one of the other guys at my office to go along. Alex Justice is an ex-navy pilot. He's capable and he knows the drill."

Sage turned to Rina. "Maybe you could come with us. With two other women in the group, A'lia won't stand out so much."

Jake's gaze flicked to the redhead. "Good idea. Can you make it?"

Rina grinned. She was always up for an adventure. "I'd love to come along. I'm a shop-till-you-drop kinda' gal, and I've never met a Saudi princess."

"All right, then. We keep them busy and away from the office. With nothing going on here, there's a good chance things will start cooling down. By Monday of the following week, you'll have done enough small talk to satisfy their customs and earn their trust. If the protests are over, you can bring them into the office and start negotiations."

Sage shoved back her hair, lifting it away from her face. "You make it sound easy."

"It could be. With any luck, it'll all work out the way we plan." But his smile couldn't hide the unease in those sexy blue eyes. She knew it was the same worry she was feeling.

She looked over at her friend, determined to carry on as normally as possible. "You ready, Rina?"

"Sounds like Jake has everything under control, so yeah, let's go."

Sage turned to him. "We're going to Gravitas for lunch. Rina's car is in the lot. We'll go out the back way so no one will see us. You and I can talk some more when I get back."

Jake just smiled. "I'll tell Linc we'll be needing the limo."

She didn't argue. She didn't care who drove them; she just wanted out of there. "All right." Sage started for the door, but Jake's long strides got him there before she did. He pulled it open, stepped back for them to walk out, then followed on their heels.

Sage stopped and turned. "Please don't tell me you're going with us."

"All right, I won't."

But deep down, she had known he would demand to accompany them. With the protests going on out front, it was his job.

He pushed the button on the elevator, and when it arrived, followed them inside.

She gave it one last try. "Jake, please…"

"I won't sit at your table. In fact, you'll hardly know I'm there. That's the way it works, Sage. This won't be for long. In the meantime, you might as well get used to it."

"I could sure get used to it," Rina teased with a grin.

Sage bit back a smile and shook her head. They headed for the back entrance out of the lobby, which led to the executive parking lot. When the guard pushed open the door, Sage jerked to a halt.

"Son of a bitch," Jake muttered beneath his breath. The group out front had morphed into a mass of people at the back door, slightly smaller, but no less disturbing. He let the door swing closed, but not before Sage got a look at the media trucks parked at the curb, the cameras aimed at the crowd, as well as the back door of the building. It was turning into a circus.

Jake was on his iPhone, in contact with Lincoln Jones. He ended the call and slipped the phone back into his pocket.

"Linc's pulling up as close as he can get. He'll have the passenger door open. When I say go, walk as quickly as you can to the car and get in."

Sage glanced at Rina, who didn't look nearly as perky as she had before. "Are you ready for this?" she asked.

Her friend's slim shoulders straightened. "I guess if I want to eat, I don't have any choice."

"Go!" Jake said, and they hurried toward the car. He was blocking the way like a pro football tackle, herding them into the car, then jumping inside himself. Linc gunned the engine and they shot out of the parking lot, the tires squealing, the crowd surging toward them, waving their signs.

If she closed her eyes, Sage could still see the one that read Keep American Money in America. And right beside it, Dumont Millions Earned at the Price of Betrayal.

"We got company," Linc said, his black eyes fixed on the mirror above the windshield.

Jake turned in his seat, saw the white media van cutting in and out of traffic behind them. "Get rid of them." He checked to make sure the women had their seat belts fastened as Linc gunned the powerful engine.

A couple of screeching turns, roaring through a few yellow lights, blazing down a straightaway, careening around another corner, and the van was no longer in sight.

"Everybody okay?" Jake asked.

Sage smiled. "When you said Linc could drive, you really meant it."

Rina grinned and leaned back in her seat with a theatrical sigh. "Reminds me of my high school days."

Jake's eyebrows went up. "You drove like that in high school?"

"I had a boyfriend whose dad was into drag racing. Jimmy had a hot Camaro. We did a little drag racing at night."

"That's illegal, you know," Linc said from the driver's seat.

Rina laughed. "Fun, though."

Jake almost smiled. He was beginning to like the saucy little redhead. And she seemed like a good friend to Sage. There was no heat in the flirty looks she cast his way. It was just to tease her friend.

They reached the restaurant and Linc drove the Escalade up in front. Jake helped the women out, then escorted them both inside the brick building.

Gravitas was hip and modern, the food upscale and interesting. The maître d' approached Sage smiling, a short guy in his thirties with brown hair thinning on top.

"We have your table ready, Ms. Dumont."

"Thank you, Ned."

He flicked a glance at Jake. "Will there be three in your party?"

"No," Jake answered.

The man seated the ladies, then returned. "One for lunch, sir?"

"I'm Ms. Dumont's personal security. I need to make a sweep of the restaurant, make sure it's safe. Then seat me someplace where I can watch her table, and bring me a sandwich—it doesn't matter what kind."

"Of course, sir. Over the weekend, I read something in the newspaper about the protests at Marine Drilling. I hope there isn't any trouble."

"Just a lot of noise so far. Let's hope it stays that way."

But Jake didn't like the different factions milling around together. It was like putting them in a pressure cooker and turning up the heat.

The maître d' seated him at a discrete table not too close to Sage. She deserved some privacy. And since she wasn't having lunch with Phillip...

The evil demon was back, making him inwardly smile. For whatever reason, his dislike for Stanton hadn't lessened. Jake was damned glad the guy had left the country.

Which returned his thoughts to Sage and how much he wanted her. What would it take, he wondered, to get her into his bed?

He took a long swallow of the iced tea the waiter delivered. What happened Sunday night had been accidental. He knew women. Sage wasn't the kind who slept with men other than the one she was pledged to.

Still, the attraction between them hadn't diminished. He felt it every time he looked at her. Every time she looked at him. Just sitting next to her in the car had left him hard and wanting. He wondered how it had affected Sage.

He had a feeling the desire that sparked between them was new to her, not something she felt with Phillip.

It didn't matter. Jake didn't date married women because he didn't want to think of them in another man's bed. He felt the same way about Sage. She was available or she wasn't.

And clearly, she wasn't.

He made another slow, sweeping perusal of the restaurant, saw that everything was as it should be, picked up his sandwich and dug in.

The delicious pastrami on rye tasted like sawdust in his mouth.

"Your neck isn't getting stiff, is it?"

Sage kept her eyes straight ahead. "What are you talking about?"

"It's okay if you look at him once in a while," Rina said. "He's very easy on the eyes."

"I don't want to look at him. I don't want to think about him. I just want this whole thing to be over."

Rina ate a few bites of her salad. Sage mostly pushed the lettuce around on her plate.

"You know, I've known you for years," her friend said. "I've never seen you this way."

"What way is that?"

"Fascinated by a man."

The bite of tomato stuck in Sage's throat. "I'm not fascinated with Jake. He's smarter than I thought and maybe not so much of a jerk. He's good at what he does and I admire that. But he's just a man. More virile that most, I'll admit, but still only a man."

"He's not just virile, the guy is the ultimate stud. Your female anatomy recognizes that, responds to it. You want him, Sage. I've never seen you in lust before, until now. It's as simple as that."

Her insides tightened. "You think that's simple? I'm engaged, Rina. I'm getting married to Phillip. Surely you don't think I should cheat on him."

"I think maybe you should consider talking to Phillip, telling him you need some time to think things over. Tell him you want to postpone your engagement for a while."

"For God's sake, Rina, just because I'm attracted to my bodyguard doesn't mean I want to give up the future Phillip and I have planned."

"It isn't just that. From the start, you've been hesitant—and don't tell me I'm wrong. I know you. I know Phillip embodies all the things you think you want out of life, the things you think you need to accomplish your goals. But maybe that isn't so. Maybe you deserve more than an arranged marriage—because that's exactly what it is."

Sage set her fork down on the table. "My grandfather has nothing to do with this."

"Pleasing him does."

Her mouth felt dry. Rina was her best friend. If anyone else dared to talk to her this way, she would walk away and never look back. "If you really believe that, why did you wait so long to say it?"

"I said all this before, Sage. You just weren't listening. That you're listening to me now ought to tell you something. Even if you don't give in to your attraction to Jake, give what I said some thought. Give yourself a chance to find out what you really want out of life. Maybe you'll find out it isn't Phillip Stanton."

Sage took a long drink of her tea and realized her hand was trembling. She respected Sabrina Eckhart, and she trusted her. Rina would never do anything to hurt her.

And yet hearing those things did hurt. And they made her wonder....

"I'll think about it—when all this Saudi business is over. Right now, I just don't have the time."

"Fair enough." Rina reached out and caught her hand. "I didn't intend to bring any of this up. It's just that when you look at Jake, there's something in your eyes I've never seen there before."

Sage pulled her hand away. "It's exactly what you said it was. It's lust, Rina. I may not have felt anything quite like it before, but I'm smart enough to recognize it now. And I'm not going to let it ruin my life."

Chapter 7

The Saudis arrived right on schedule. Tuesday afternoon, Sheik Khalid's Boeing 727 landed at Bush International Airport and taxied to the executive terminal.

Jake was there with Sage to greet them, along with her assistant, Will Bailey, and a man named Red Williams. Her assistant was a string bean of a kid in his mid-twenties, with dark hair and big horn-rimmed glasses. Will looked efficient, which Jake was sure he was, or he wouldn't be working for Sage.

Red Williams was the man Sage had chosen to bring with her into the negotiations, the one she considered her best purchasing agent, and apparently someone she respected.

Red had reached the top of his profession by working his way up from the bottom. According to Sage, he was a hard-driving, hardworking man, and he had the calluses to prove it. It was Red's job to fend off the minions willing to do just about anything, no matter how shady or underhanded, to sell goods to Marine Drilling. He had to ignore the tempting offers of all-expense-paid trips to the Caribbean, the bribes, booze and women, and actually buy the products that would serve the company best. Apparently, he did.

Yesterday, after they returned from lunch, Sage had brought him into the office. Jake had worked with him the rest of the afternoon and into the evening, teaching him the basic protocols he would need to know to negotiate with the Saudis.

Aside from asking questions and giving advice when it was needed, Red would remain in the background as much as possible. He seemed to have no problem with that.

Jake liked him right away.

The plane taxied up to the executive terminal and the jet engines shut down. A ladder rolled across the tarmac toward the door, and a few minutes later, the heavy portal swung open. The Saudi entourage descended the steps, crossed the asphalt and entered the building through a private entrance.

Jake stood just behind Sage, Alex Justice beside him.

Jake had brought his friend in mostly for appearances. Though everyone involved in the negotiations knew Sage Dumont was in charge, she was a woman and would therefore be seen as less important. Having two personal bodyguards left no doubt of her status.

The greeting was perfectly executed, all the protocols followed. Sage had done her homework, and so had everyone else.

"As-salam-alaikum," she said, using the standard Saudi greeting. *Peace be upon you.* "Welcome to America."

The sheik seemed pleased. *"Wa alaikum as-salam,"* he replied. *And upon you be peace.* "We appreciate your hospitality," he added in perfect English.

His Highness Sheik Khalid Al Kahzaz was a tall, lean man with high cheekbones, olive skin and black eyes, dignified with his gray-speckled black beard and flowing white *thobe.* He wore the traditional Saudi headdress, as did his son, Roshan, the cousins, Quadim and Yasar, and their four male bodyguards. Dressed in black suits, the guards were all tall, silent and forbidding, giving the exact impression the sheik wanted.

His daughter, A'lia, walked behind him in a loose-fitting caftan that fell around her ankles. Instead of white cotton, the robe was made of delicate embroidered rose silk. A matching scarf covered her neck, head and shoulders and most of her face, but it couldn't hide the girl's stunning beauty—her fine, perfect features, delicate nose and small white teeth. Just before she was introduced, she pulled a thin black veil over the lower portion of her face. Her cousin Zahra, taller and blunt-featured, was even more fully covered, and though her garment was also embroidered, it was completely black. Zahra was a few years older, maybe twenty-four or twenty-five, brought along, Jake was certain, to make sure A'lia stayed in line.

As a former Saudi minister there to negotiate the sale, Sheik Khalid and his family had diplomatic immunity. They whisked through customs and outside into the bright Texas heat, pouring into the line of black SUVs Linc had waiting. The cars sped away while their vast array of Louis Vuitton luggage was loaded into more SUVs.

Riding in the lead car, Alex sat next to the driver, Jake behind them next to Sage, and Will and Red in the rear seat as Linc maneuvered the vehicle through traffic. The sheik rode in the second car with his son and daughter and two bodyguards. Zahra rode with the cousins and two more bodyguards in the third vehicle.

The cars reached the Four Seasons, the timing fairly close together and without incident. The Saudi group was welcomed by hotel staff and escorted up to the twentieth floor.

Sage accompanied them, walking into the entry of the elegant, richly appointed presidential suite, Jake taking a position behind her and to the right, Alex behind and to her left.

She smoothed a nonexistent wrinkle from the front of her pale yellow business suit. Jake's gaze ran over her. Though the skirt reached well below her knees and the cream silk blouse was buttoned to the throat, she still made him think of sex. His pulse quickened and his loins began to fill. The fertility gods were definitely working overtime.

"I hope you find the hotel accommodations satisfactory, Your Highness," Sage said.

He smiled. "The suite is quite lovely."

"I've planned an itinerary I hope will meet with your approval and you will find interesting. While you're here, if there is anything at all you need, please feel free to call my assistant or me and let us know." She handed him their business cards, carefully prepared with the information on the front also printed in Arabic on the back.

The sheik looked down at the cards. "I am certain everything will be fine."

Sage smiled. She was doing everything just right, Jake thought, oddly proud of her.

"Then rest and recover from your journey," she said. "Take a look at the schedule, and if it is suitable, I'll see you again on Thursday."

The sheik gazed at the paper she handed him. "My daughter wishes very much to go shopping here in America, and my son would enjoy the IMAX. There is one at the science dome in Al-Khobar, but I have not been there. I understand the screen is several stories high."

Sage's smile widened. "That's right. It's amazing. There's a movie showing at the IMAX here in Houston, a climb up Mount Everest. It's quite an exciting film."

"Yes, I would like to see that."

Sage made her farewells and stepped out into the hall. As soon as the door closed behind her, she sagged against the wall. "Thank God that's over."

Jake smiled, relieved it had gone so well.

Alex grinned, flashing those damned dimples women seemed to love. "I hate to point this out," he said, "but this is only the beginning."

She gave him the first real smile Jake had seen on her face all day. "True, but I made it this far without doing anything stupid. That's a start in the right direction."

"You did great, Sage," Alex said.

When her smile widened and Alex's damn dimples

showed up again, Jake sliced him a hard look, but Alex just laughed.

"Let's get out of here," Jake said grimly, suddenly wishing he'd brought in someone besides his good-looking friend.

The three of them headed back down to the lobby. Red and Will had already left for their respective jobs. Linc waited in the SUV, which was parked in front, and the three climbed inside.

They were quiet on the drive back to the office, silently preparing themselves for the scene they would be facing when they got there.

"What's the time frame for the shopping trip on Thursday?" Alex asked.

"The mall opens at ten," Jake said. "We'll pick up A'lia and her escorts a little before then. That evening, we'll take the sheik and his party to the IMAX. I've got a private showing arranged."

Alex nodded. The Escalade reached Louisiana Street and pulled into the executive lot. Unfortunately, the group in back of the building had swelled to the size of the group out front.

"Fuck," Jake whispered, too low for Sage to hear, and thought that pretty well summed things up.

Sage hurried along behind Jake as he forged a path through the media toward the back door. Alex followed close behind her, fending off the hordes that tried to get too close.

"Ms. Dumont!" a reporter shouted, shoving a microphone in her face. "What do you have to say about what's going on here?"

"No comment," she muttered, as Jake shouldered the man aside.

"The students are here to show their support for democracy in the Middle East," shouted a female reporter wearing a KTRK TV badge. "Are you sympathetic to their cause?"

"No comment." Sage kept moving, Jake clearing the way, Alex backing him up.

"Ms. Dumont!" The first reporter caught up with her again and shoved the mic back into her face. "Some of these people are protesting the business you're doing with a country they feel is oppressive. How do you feel about Marine Drilling spending American money in the Middle East?"

Jake grabbed the device out of the newsman's hands, nearly knocking him off his feet. "The lady told you she has no comment." Then he shoved the mic at him, so hard the man jerked backward. Tentatively, the reporter reached out and took hold of it, and they continued toward the door.

Jake stepped inside and hauled Sage in after him. Alex followed, and the security guard closed the door.

"You okay?" Jake asked her.

She nodded, but she was trembling, her mouth dry as cotton. "I hate this."

"Maybe you should call off the deal and let the Saudis go back home."

She shook her head, wishing she could do just that. It wasn't going to happen. "I couldn't even if I wanted to. I invited the sheik and his family to Texas. I'm not going to abandon them."

Approval shone in his face. "I didn't really figure you would." Catching hold of her arm, he urged her toward the bank of elevators in the lobby. Through the thick, mirrored-glass walls of the building, she could hear the demonstrators outside, arguing and shouting back and forth.

"Unless you need me," Alex said, "I'll see you Thursday."

"Thanks, buddy," Jake said, and Alex headed out to his car.

Sage stepped into the elevator and Jake followed. "It's getting worse instead of better," she said.

Jake pushed the button to the twelfth floor. "It still may cool down."

"Or they may start killing each other."

His mouth quirked. "There's always that chance."

Sage stood beside him in the elevator. Even in her high heels, he towered above her. She felt feminine and safe in a way she never had before.

She thought of the sheik's daughter, A'lia, beautiful and sheltered. Living in a gilded prison. As lovely as she was, there was a sadness in her dark, exotic eyes, something that seemed to reach out to Sage in some way. In the cousin, Zahra, Sage had sensed no underlying disquiet. It made her wonder if she could be wrong, and A'lia was happy.

Whatever the truth, it was none of her business. She was determined to make a multimillion-dollar deal, save a boatload of money for Marine Drilling and prove to her grandfather she was capable of running the company when Michael Curtis retired next year.

She entered her office, accidentally brushing against Jake's thick chest as he held open the door, and his eyes locked with hers. A jolt of electricity shot through her, making her legs feel weak. It was ridiculous. He probably had the same effect on every woman in the building.

Except she had never seen him look at another woman the way he was looking at her.

Another little curl of heat slipped through her. There was no question Jake wanted her. Every time he glanced at her, it was boldly there in his eyes. And yet she couldn't accuse him of overstepping the boundary between them.

What she couldn't understand was this burning desire she felt for *him*. It had never happened before, not even in her more carefree days in college. She'd had boyfriends. She had even slept with a couple of them. But there was none of the gnawing hunger she felt when she looked at Jake.

It wasn't like her. She was serious and dedicated. She didn't lust for a man.

Sage amended that. She had never lusted for a man before. It appalled her to realize how much she desired Jake.

"If you keep looking at me that way, I might break my rule."

Her face went warm. She knew exactly what he meant. He wanted her, but he wouldn't touch her unless she was free.

She turned away from him, forced her feet to carry her over to her desk.

"It went well today, I thought," she said, forcing her mind toward business.

"You did great," he said, and there was none of the heat she had heard in his voice before. "The sheik is well-educated. Speaks English like a native. The son, as well. Makes everything easier."

"Khalid and Roshan were both schooled at Oxford." He nodded. "I'll be coaching Red a little more this afternoon. I noticed he has a habit of crossing his ankle over his knee when he sits too long. I've warned him it's a major insult to show a Saudi the bottom of his shoe."

"Red may not have a university degree, but he's smart. He'll remember what you tell him."

"He seems like a good man to have on your team."

"He's a very good man. I considered asking one of the VPs, either Charles Denton or Jonathan Hunter, but they're both very busy with their own jobs, and extremely competitive. I wasn't sure how much I could trust them. Red worked for Ian for years before he started working for me. He's loyal to a fault."

"That was my take on the guy."

"So what about Thursday? Looks like the sheik is going to let his daughter go shopping with us. Probably her cousin Zahra will come with her."

"She's got to have a male relative along," Jake said again. "I have a hunch we'll have a small army going with us to the mall. I called yesterday and made arrangements with Saks and Neiman Marcus. They're going to provide a private salon."

Sage grinned up at him. "That's a good start—considering you're a man—but not nearly enough. I'll have Will phone Cartier, Gucci and Tiffany's. The sheik and his crew already own enough Vuitton to open their own shop, so we can probably leave them out."

"Or that might be exactly the place they want to go."

She sighed. "You're right. They sell a lot more than just luggage. I'll have Will let Vuitton know we'll be in."

"For that caliber of buyer, the boutiques may close the doors to the public while we're in there."

"I'm sure they will. Just think of all the money we'll be bringing into the community."

Jake grinned. "Maybe we ought to march around with a sign that says Marine Drilling—Spending Saudi Money in America."

Sage laughed. "Maybe." Her laughter slowly faded. "They'll be safe, won't they?"

His gaze shifted, darkened. "They'll be fine. More importantly, you'll be safe. I promise you that, Sage."

And when she looked into those blue, blue eyes, she knew he would keep his word.

Knew that if he had to, Jake Cantrell would protect her with his life.

Chapter 8

They left the office shortly after six that night. The heat outside was intense, but the sun was a little less vicious as the days marched through September. The crowd had thinned some and the media cameras were gone, which was a hopeful sign. Jake sat next to Sage in the backseat of the SUV, slightly more relaxed now that they were away from the building.

So far no one seemed to know the Saudis had arrived in Houston, or if they did, they were more interested in Marine Drilling's involvement than they were in the Saudis themselves. Jake wasn't sure if that was bad news or good.

The Escalade had traveled only a couple blocks through the office high-rise district when his cell phone rang. Pulling it out of the pocket of his suit coat, he checked the caller ID and saw it was Tanya

Porter. Tanya was the mother of the boy he sponsored in the Big Brother program Linc had gotten him involved in when he'd first returned to Texas.

"Jake, I'm sorry to bother you," she said, "but I've got a problem. I was wondering if you might be able to give Felix a ride home."

"What happened?"

"He went to the show with his friend Desi, and Desi's older brother, Bo. I guess they got to arguing and the boys ended up leaving him there. I know you've been working downtown. He's in front of the AMC. Is there any way you could pick him and bring him home?"

"I'm on the job, Tanya. I can't get to him for at least another hour."

Sage reached over and caught his arm. "What is it?"

"Hold on." He covered the phone. "A friend of mine's got a problem, young kid named Felix Porter. I'm his Big Brother. He's stuck at the AMC theatre and needs a ride home."

"The theater isn't that far. For heaven's sake, pick him up."

"You sure?"

"I'm done for the day. It isn't a problem."

Jake smiled. "Thanks. Felix is a good kid. Not the kind to make trouble. Some of his friends, however, are another story." Jake spoke across the front seat to Linc. "You hear that?"

"On my way."

Jake let Tanya know he would pick up Felix and bring him home. The theater was only a few blocks out of the way. When they got there, Felix was waiting on the corner, the cell phone Jake paid for in his hand. Jake rolled down the window and motioned him over. Linc opened the front door and the kid climbed in beside him.

Felix turned in the seat. "Thanks, Jake." He was a lanky kid, with feet and hands still a little too big for his growing frame. Beneath his shiny black skin, his face looked tightly drawn.

"Felix, say hello to Ms. Dumont. She's the one who's giving you a ride."

"Thank you, ma'am."

"It's nice to meet you, Felix."

"What happened?" Jake asked as Linc began to move the big SUV through traffic.

Felix shrugged, stared down at his hands. "Desi and me... We had a fight. It was no big deal."

Jake knew it was probably Desi's older brother, Bo, who was the troublemaker, but Felix wouldn't snitch on the dumb-ass kid. As soon as Jake got the time, he'd have a little talk with Felix's friends. "No big deal, huh? Seems like with those two, something's always 'no big deal.'"

Felix glanced away.

They left the downtown area, slugged their way through traffic and headed for the house south of Holcombe where the twelve-year-old lived. His mother was waiting on the sidewalk as he slipped out of the front seat.

"Thanks, Jake. Ms. Dumont." The kid closed the door and ran to where his mother stood. Tanya waved, and the two of them headed into the house.

Jake turned to Sage. "Thanks for letting me pick him up. Like I said, Felix is a really good kid."

She smiled as Linc pulled away from the curb. "The

Big Brother program is extremely worthwhile. Our company's a big supporter. I'm really glad you're helping him."

He nodded, realizing the kid was another tie he would have to cut when he took off on another job. This was the second time he'd lived in Houston. The first was after he'd left the service and returned from the Middle East. He'd gotten his P.I.'s license and taken a job freelancing for Trace.

Though he'd enjoyed the work, eventually he'd grown restless and taken a corporate protection job in South America. He'd traveled and worked there for a while, and had just finished a job in Mexico when he got a call from Dev Raines and met up with him, Trace and Johnnie Riggs, old military buddies.

When the job was over, he'd returned to Texas, which had begun to feel more like home than any other place he'd been.

He flicked a glance at Sage, his current, far more intriguing assignment, and looked back out the window. Nothing but traffic, no one on their tail, and aside from the occasional bad driver, nothing that posed any sort of danger.

He was doing his best to keep his eyes off her, trying not to think how pretty she looked even after the long, grueling day. Trying to keep his thoughts in check and his blood from flowing south.

Once the SUV reached the high-rise where she lived, Jake escorted her upstairs, went in and checked her apartment. Finding everything in order, he made himself head for the door—though every ounce of testosterone in his body wanted him to stay.

He reminded himself the lady belonged to another

man, that he had a job to do and there was no place in it for his attraction to Sage.

He reached for the doorknob. "I'll pick you up in the morning." He stopped and turned. "Unless you have plans to go out tonight." So far the threat posed by the demonstrators had stayed confined to the downtown area around the office, but until this was over, he didn't want her going out by herself.

Sage hesitated, then smiled. "I've been sticking pretty close to home. I figured it would be safer that way."

"Good girl."

She walked him to the door. Knowing he shouldn't, he lingered. "You did really well today. You said all the right things, made the right moves. I think the Saudis were impressed."

Her smile reappeared. "Thanks. Coming from you, that means a lot." She didn't move away, and he wanted to reach for her, haul her into his arms. He wanted to kiss her until he had her begging him to take her to bed.

He couldn't. *Wouldn't.*

Jake turned and walked out the door.

It wasn't until later that night that he found himself thinking about her brief moment of hesitation. It didn't mean anything, he told himself. Sage wouldn't risk going out alone.

But it bothered him.

After he finished the rest of the leftover spaghetti he'd picked up at Mama's Take-Out a couple nights ago, he found himself dialing Sage's home number. The answering machine picked up and his nerves kicked in. When he phoned her cell and his call went directly to her messaging center, he tamped down the worry beginning to knot his stomach, damned her for the little witch she was, and headed for the door.

"Are you sure we should be doing this?" Dressed in a sapphire-blue mini that set off her eyes, Rina sat across from Sage at the Post Oak Grill, one of Sage's favorite restaurants.

Dressed more conservatively in a short, black silk dress and platform heels, Sage took a sip of wine. "I'm sure, all right. Absolutely sure we *shouldn't* be doing it. But I'm really glad we are."

Rina laughed, making her long silver earrings jangle.

Sage released a slow breath. "I've had one heckuva day. I had to get out of the house, just for a while." *I had to stop thinking of Jake.*

The episode this afternoon with Felix had shown her a completely different side of him, one that was far too appealing. The hero worship she'd seen in the boy's dark eyes told her how good Jake was with the kid. She wished she hadn't noticed. She didn't want to like Jake as well as lust for him.

"Well, we aren't that far from your apartment," Rina said, taking a sip of the rich Stag's Leap cabernet they had ordered, "and this place should certainly be safe enough."

Sage took a bite of perfectly cooked, medium rare filet mignon, savoring the delicious port reduction sauce. "God, I love the food here. Since all this started, I've barely had time to eat. Believe it or not, I've actually lost a couple of pounds."

Rina rolled her eyes. "That should happen to me."

Sage scoffed. "You don't need to lose weight. You're perfect."

"I don't need to lose weight because I constantly watch what I eat. If I didn't, I'd be as big as a house."

Sage just smiled. Rina ate healthy food, and both of them went to the gym at least three times a week. That is, until she had gotten involved with the Saudi deal. Fortunately, there was a fitness center in the apartment building where she lived.

"So tell me about today," Rina said. "How did it go with his high-and-mightiness, the sheik?"

"Actually, I think it went pretty well. But, Lord, it wasn't easy. And this is just getting started." She sipped her wine, set the glass back down on the table. "You're still on for the shopping trip, right?"

Rina grinned. "You couldn't keep me away."

"A'lia will probably be bringing her cousin Zahra, so there'll be four of us women altogether. I think that'll make things a little easier. Or at least with you there, it'll be easier for me."

"What's she like?"

"Beautiful. Absolutely gorgeous. But kind of sad, I think. It has to be hard to have your entire life completely laid out for you and be totally dominated by men."

"And some of them will be coming with us to the mall, I gather."

"That's right. A male relative and probably at least one bodyguard. Along with Jake and Alex."

"Alex?"

"Alex Justice. He's the guy who's helping Jake with security. Apparently, they work out of the same office." She took a bite of scalloped potatoes and decided she had never tasted anything so delicious. Then again, everything tasted good when you forgot to eat.

"I think you'll like this guy," Sage said.

"I'm involved, remember?"

"So am I, remember? He seems interesting. That's all I'm saying."

"Interesting how?"

"Six-two, a hundred eighty pounds. Dark blond hair and blue eyes. He's got the cutest pair of dimples."

Rina eyed her across the top of her wineglass. "But he's not Jake, right? So you're passing him on to me."

"I'm not passing him on to anyone. I just mentioned him."

"That's good, because I'm not interested."

"I thought you and Ryan were having trouble."

"Everyone has trouble. We'll work things out eventually."

She thought of Phillip. Since he left, they'd spoken several times on the phone, but their conversations were brief and unfulfilling. There were never any arguments, not even any serious disagreements. Maybe that was the problem. Both of them always kept their emotions carefully controlled. No outbursts, no fighting. Never saying what was really on her mind. Maybe that bothered her more than she'd realized.

Sage glanced up. There was something going on in the restaurant. People were beginning to whisper and shift in their chairs. She gazed around the room, caught something pressed against one of the plate-glass windows, a big white square with words written on it. When she saw what it said, the delicious filet mignon nearly came back up.

Dumont Drilling Traitors. Keep U.S. Money in the U.S.

"Oh, my God." Rina stared out the window, and the noise in the restaurant grew louder. Sage turned to see a man storming toward her, his face beet-red, his brown hair standing on end, his lips thinned in anger.

"It's people like you!" he shouted. "People like you who are ruining our country!"

Her mind went blank. Opening another drilling platform would mean dozens of new jobs for the area. It would be helping the country end its dependence on foreign oil. The environment had to be protected—she adamantly agreed with that—but Marine Drilling did everything in its power to keep people and the ocean safe.

All those arguments and half a dozen others rushed into her head. She wanted to explain, but as she stared into the man's furious face, not a single syllable came out of her mouth.

His fist slammed down on the table, making the silverware jump and water slop over the rim of their glasses. "You hear what I said? It's people like you!"

"You don't...don't understand." It was all she could manage to say as she spotted the valets pushing through the door and starting toward her, caught a slice of the commotion outside, more signs, more people who wanted her to fail.

"Send them back where they belong! You hear me?"

She heard the words, but they were muffled by the ringing in her ears. Then Jake was there, striding toward the table, his face set in hard, determined lines. He grabbed the red-faced man by the back of the neck and hauled him away from her, putting himself be-

tween her and the danger. The man looked at Jake
and his lips curled back, ready for another damning
tirade. Jake's hand settled on his shoulder, and an instant later the man went limp.

Sage watched in awe as Jake propped him against
his side and hauled him out of there as if he weighed
nothing, as if maybe he was just a friend who had
drunk a little too much. The maître d' stepped out of
the way, letting them pass, and the pair disappeared
through the door.

"Oh, my God," Rina said again, staring at the place
where Jake had been.

Sage just sat there trembling. She could still see
the fury etched on the man's ruddy features. And the
matching fury in Jake's. She had never seen him angry
before, at least not like that. And part of it was clearly
directed at her.

On top of that, she had never seen him in action.
The scene was over before it had truly begun. Jake had
taken the man down with unbelievable ease, put an
end to the threat in seconds. Sage felt certain the guy
wasn't really hurt, just immobilized and then neatly
dispensed with.

Though she could be wrong.

She fought to compose herself as she looked at
Rina, whose blue eyes looked as big as saucers. Then
Sage spotted Jake striding back toward her, and wished
she could slide under the table.

"Time to leave," he said, hauling her to her feet,
her napkin falling to the floor. "You, too, sweetheart."

Rina shot up from her chair. Numbly, Sage let Jake
pull her toward the door, herding Rina along in front
of them.

"What...what about the bill?" Sage asked, her voice high-pitched and shaky.

"They're sending it to your office."

She swallowed, realizing for the first time that he was guiding them through a side door that led into the alley.

"I'll drop you off on the way," Jake said to Rina, apparently planning to drive Sage home.

"I drove us here tonight. I can get home by myself."

"You sure?"

"It wasn't me they were after."

Jake's scowl deepened. Sage stood there trembling as he surveyed the outside of the restaurant, searching for any remaining sign of danger. But the people who had been at the window were gone. So was the man who had barged up to her table. Jake took her arm as he walked Rina over to her little red Mercedes SLK, waited until she buckled herself inside, then watched as she drove out of the parking lot.

Sage didn't resist as he pulled her toward his Jeep, lifted her up and dropped her into the seat.

"Buckle up," he said darkly, then slammed her door and strode around to the driver's side. With her hands shaking, she couldn't get the clasp fastened. Fumbled, tried again. Jake reached across her lap and shoved the buckle into the catch. Without a word, he started the engine and roared out of the parking lot.

Sage just sat there, her mind going over and over the scene in the restaurant. All the way back to the apartment, Jake didn't speak. When they reached the tenth floor and walked out of the elevator, he took the key from her hand and started to unlock the door.

Sage swallowed. "I shouldn't have done it. I—I

know that now. I just…" She shook her head. "After everything that's happened, I just… I wanted a couple of hours to myself. I just wanted to pretend for a little while that everything was normal." She looked up at him and her eyes filled. "Please, Jake, don't be angry."

The stiffness in those wide shoulders melted. Jake reached out and simply folded her into his arms. She knew she should resist, but all she wanted was to burrow into him more deeply, let him make her feel safe.

"It's all right, baby, this is new to you. You scared me, that's all."

She didn't let men call her *baby* or *honey* or any of those ridiculous terms. She should have told him that, put him in his place. Instead, she just hung on.

"I'm sorry," she said. "It was a stupid thing to do. I won't do it again."

He nodded. She felt the tension begin to seep back into his big body, knew his concern was shifting to sexual awareness. The moment was over, and she pulled away.

"I'd better go in."

Jake nodded again and focused on opening the door. He used her key in the lock and turned the knob. As she disabled the alarm, he drew his pistol, a big, black semiautomatic, and began checking the rooms.

"Everything's all right," he said when he returned to the entry, shoving the gun back into its holster.

She looked up at him, trying not to think how good it had felt when he'd held her. "What happened to that man in the restaurant?"

Jake's lips curled. "Guess he wasn't feeling very well. Seems he fainted dead away."

She cast him a glance. "But not really dead, right?"

He grinned. "Not really dead. He was fine by the time he got outside. By then the police were there and the demonstrators were dispersed."

"How many were there?"

"Five, including him."

Her mind strayed back to the scene in the restaurant and she shivered. What would have happened if Jake hadn't come when he did? Things could have gotten ugly. Very ugly.

Sage frowned. "How did you know where to find me?"

Jake pulled out his iPhone, brought up the screen. "GPS. Handy little app that lets me know where everyone is. At least everyone whose cell number I've loaded."

"Wait a minute. The way I understand it, you have to have my permission to do something like that."

He smiled. "You must have given it to me. Maybe you just forgot."

Sure, that must be it. The man was impossible. And she was incredibly glad he had shown up when he did.

"How did they find me at the restaurant?"

"They must have had someone watching the building. Not hard to find out where you live. Whoever it was must have followed you. I'll talk to the security guard, bring him up to speed, tell him to watch out for anyone who doesn't belong around here."

She nodded. "The people who work here are very conscientious."

"The police had a chat with the guy who bothered you. They warned him what would happen if he continued to harass you. They'll also be keeping an eye on the building. Still, after what happened, I don't like leaving you here alone." His eyes found hers and lingered. She felt a sweep of heat, then suddenly short of breath. "Maybe I should stay."

Sage forced some air into her lungs, breathed out slowly. Finally, she shook her head. She wanted him to stay. Which was the reason he had to leave. "I'll be fine."

He nodded, seeming almost relieved. He wanted her, but not as long as she was engaged to another man. Still, she tempted him. Just as he tempted her. But neither of them wanted to do something they would regret.

"I'm only a phone call away, Sage. Call if you need me."

"I will." She needed him, all right. But not for protection.

She walked him to the door.

"I'll see you in the morning," he said. "Lock up behind me."

She nodded and watched him walk away. With a sigh, she closed the door, slid the dead bolts into place and turned the alarm system back on.

Tonight had shown her one thing—that until this was over, she needed Jake Cantrell.

Chapter 9

Jake kicked himself all the way home. What the hell was he thinking? Sage wasn't his *baby*. She wasn't his sweetheart or even his date. She was his assignment. He had no right to hold her, no right to whisper soothing words in her ear.

In all his years of working protection details, he'd never done anything like that before.

Maybe if he hadn't been so angry... But she had lied to him, or at least let him believe she would be staying safely at home. When he'd driven up to the restaurant and seen the angry people outside, when he'd walked inside and found the guy leaning over her table, threatening her, he had damn near come undone.

Then she'd told him she was sorry and looked up at him with those big, tear-filled golden eyes, and he'd melted like a bowl of ice cream on a hot Texas day. Damn, what the hell was wrong with him?

The thing she didn't understand was that the whole situation with the Saudis was explosive. Jake knew from experience how quickly things could shift from volatile to deadly. It was his job to keep Sage safe, and tonight he had almost failed.

As he walked into his apartment and tossed his keys onto the kitchen table, he blew out a breath. *What a day.*

Earlier this evening, before he'd called Sage's apartment, he'd phoned Tanya Porter, concerned about Felix. Tanya had managed to get her son to admit it was Desi's older brother who had been hassling him, trying to get him to try some kind of drugs. The argument had started when Felix refused.

Jake was proud of the kid. Which, since he saw the boy only one weekend a month, he'd told Felix on the phone.

He really thought a lot of the kid. Until he'd come back to Houston, Jake had never allowed himself to get involved in other people's problems. Maybe at thirty-five he was changing, becoming less of a loner.

As a boy, he had been close his dad. Then a heart attack struck as he worked in the fields, and Sam Cantrell was gone. Two years after he died, Jake's mother had married one of her high school sweethearts, Sam's bitter rival for Letty Cantrell's hand. Since Jake looked just like his dad and by that time was just as big, he was a constant thorn in his stepfather's side.

Figuring it was better for everyone, Jake had joined

the marines and left Iowa. And aside from an occasion phone call to his mother, he'd never looked back.

He stretched out on the sofa in his living room now, his long legs hanging over the arm, and shoved his hands behind his head. He was too keyed up to sleep. And he knew if he went to bed, he'd think of Sage. She was getting under his skin and he couldn't let that happen.

After the little scene in her apartment tonight, he vowed nothing like that was going to happen again.

The demonstrations mushroomed again on Wednesday. There were at least three groups of people in front and behind the tall glass building, most of them at odds with each other. Some were the college students advocating for democracy in the Middle East, while others demonstrated against Israel in support of a Palestinian state. Some were Americans against Sharia Law, and there were those like the men last night who believed spending American money on Saudi Arabian equipment made Marine Drilling a threat to the country.

Any minute, Jake expected the scene to erupt into violence. So far that hadn't happened.

On Thursday morning, Linc picked him up and they went to collect Sage for her shopping trip. Next, they picked up Rina at her apartment not far away. It was time to go shopping and all of them were ready for their day at the mall. Alex, who was meeting them at the Four Seasons, was waiting when the big black SUV pulled into the portico in front of the glass lobby doors. A second Escalade was already there and waiting.

Before they went inside, Sage made introductions.

"Alex, this is my friend, Sabrina Eckhart." Sage smiled. "Rina's here to give me moral support."

Rina smiled slightly. "Hello, Alex."

"Rina."

Jake watched his friend with interest, saw his baby blues slip over the petite redhead. He must have liked what he saw, because his smile came easy.

"Pleasure to meet you." Alex was from Connecticut, born to a wealthy family, attended all the right schools. He was intelligent, had the polish that came with money and social position, and yet to his family he was a big disappointment. Seems his father wanted Alex to study law and go into politics. Instead, he joined the navy and became a fighter pilot. All he'd ever wanted to do was fly, and he was damned good at it.

And a helluva lot tougher than his polished good looks made him seem. Jake found it interesting that the smile Rina gave Alex was a whole lot more reserved than the teasing smiles she had given to Jake.

"All right, now that we're all acquainted," Jake said, "let's get this show on the road."

So they went as a group of four up to the presidential suite, where Sage introduced Rina to the sheik, his son, Roshan, and the others, some of who returned with them downstairs.

Alex rode in the rear car with Rina, a male cousin named Quadim, Zahra and a bodyguard. Jake rode in the lead car with Sage, A'lia, A'lia's brother, Roshan, and another of the bodyguards.

At twenty-six, Roshan was a real pretty boy and, based on the comments he made, a spoiled self-centered jerk. A'lia was beautiful and quiet, yet there was a shrewd intelligence in her heavily fringed black eyes.

They arrived at the mall and poured out of the vehicles.

"I'll call you when we're ready to leave," Jake told Linc as the group headed for one of the entrances.

Linc smiled. "We won't be far away."

The group climbed the steps and walked into the mall, the flowing robes worn by the men and the colorful head scarves and caftans worn by the women garnering interested glances from the people they passed. As they headed for their first stop, Saks Fifth Avenue, Roshan started speaking in Arabic to his cousin Quadim, and both of them laughed.

Jake inwardly smiled.

They were talking about the American women strolling past them, commenting on their too-short skirts and low-cut blouses, admiring the women's plump breasts. They were saying what they would make the women do to them in bed.

Almost the same conversation two American men might be having. Except in the eyes of a Saudi male, a woman had very little choice. He wondered how the conversation would change if the men knew he spoke enough Arabic to know what they were saying. He'd served in Iraq, worked security in Saudi Arabia. He was hardly fluent, but he'd learned enough to do his job, more than enough to get by.

Roshan said something lewd about a couple of high school girls who ambled past, giggling as they peered into store windows, and Jake's dislike of him grew. There was something about his smug glances, his subtly derisive view of Americans, that rubbed Jake the wrong way.

He'd sensed none of that in Roshan's father, or Cousin Yasar or either of the women. Time would tell.

Jake wondered what else he would discover that might come in handy.

No matter where you came from, the Galleria was impressive. It was the fourth largest mall in the country with more than three hundred and fifty shops and restaurants. The place was a city in itself.

Along with its size, the architecture was stunning, with spectacular glass atriums, skylights and suspended glass balconies. There was even an ice rink, which was a big attraction in Texas.

Walking with Alex and Jake, Sage herded the women toward the entrance to Saks, and as they walked into the exclusive department store, some of A'lia's solemnity began to fade. She looked even prettier when she smiled.

"It is very nice here," she said, taking in her surroundings.

"But not as nice as the Kingdom Mall in Riyadh," Sage said, thinking, *Thank God for the internet*. She had intended to impress the girl with the Galleria until she'd stumbled on photos of the fabulous Saudi mall that included most of the exclusive shops in the Galleria and more the mall didn't have. "I bet you've shopped there, right?"

A'lia smiled. "I went to university in Riyadh, but I lived with my aunt, who is very strict, so I did not get to go there often. Sometimes my father would take me when his travels brought him to the capital."

Sage waited as Alex opened the door, then walked

past him inside. "I saw photos of it on the internet. It's beautiful."

"We have shopping in Dhahran, where I live, but it is not so fine as the Kingdom Mall. And the best part is the entire third floor is accessible only to women. It is a place we can go where we are allowed to dress in the American-style clothes we cannot wear out in public." The sadness had crept back into her voice. Sage wanted to ask about it, but it was none of her business.

"Here men and women shop together," Sage said, "but we've arranged a private room for you and Zahra so that you may try on whatever you please."

A'lia beamed. "That sounds wonderful." She flashed a look at her brother. Half brother, Sage mentally corrected, having read somewhere that the two had different mothers.

"Roshan will not like it," she said softly, so he couldn't hear. "He believes a woman can easily be seduced by sinful American ways." She surveyed the beautiful displays filled with expensive perfumes and cosmetics, and smiled again. "Perhaps he is right."

"This way, ladies," Jake said, urging them toward the elevators. Roshan led them inside, looking grim. Apparently, A'lia was right. Her brother did not seem to approve of the freedom American women claimed as their right.

He stood in the elevator with his back against the wall and his head held high, looking down his nose at the rest of them. With his high cheekbones, smooth dark skin and small, neatly trimmed beard, he was unbelievably handsome. He had the longest, thickest eyelashes Sage had ever seen.

Behind them, Rina chatted with Zahra, who also

spoke English, though not as well as A'lia. Sage could hear them discussing Zahra's family. Apparently she was another Al Kahzaz cousin, married, but her husband had remained in Saudi Arabia with the rest of his family.

"Does your husband have more than one wife?" Rina asked Zahra as they walked toward the salon where the private showing was scheduled to take place.

Sage held her breath. She had gone over the basic protocols with Rina, but they hadn't discussed which topics might be taboo. Sage had no idea how such a question would be received.

She released a sigh of relief when Zahra answered easily, "My husband, Mahmood, has three other wives. I am his latest. We have not been married long and as yet have no children. But I am from a very fertile family and I am certain that in time we will have many offspring."

"I'd like to have children someday," Rina said. "But not right away."

"You are married?"

"No. I'm not ready for that, either."

"Your father must be very displeased."

Rina just laughed. "My father could never choose a husband for me. He gave up trying years ago."

Sage was hoping Rina would change the subject before it came to light that she was living with a man, and he wasn't her husband.

That's when Alex stepped in. "I'm sure Miss Eckhart's father will help her choose exactly the right man when the time comes."

She opened her mouth, but Alex's hard look silenced whatever she was about to say.

Rina pasted on a sugary smile. "I'm certain he will," she said demurely, and cut Alex a glance that warned him not to push his luck. The corner of Alex's mouth tipped up, but he made no further comment.

They crossed the floor of the designer clothing department and two high-level managers hurried toward them, introduced themselves to Sage and led the group toward the private salon. Jake went in to check security. When he returned, the women were ushered inside. Sage cast a last quick glance at Jake as he closed the door behind them.

With the women safely inside, Jake joined Alex, Roshan and the rest of the entourage in the quiet, poshly furnished alcove set up for them to wait. They were offered tea or coffee, but all of them declined.

"I will be back in an hour," Roshan said. "Make certain A'lia is ready to go when I arrive."

"All right," Jake said.

The young man, his cousin and one of the bodyguards wandered away to entertain themselves, Roshan clearly not interested in playing the role of A'lia's protective older brother.

The other bodyguard positioned himself just outside the salon door.

"So far so good," Alex said as he sat down on the deep leather sofa next to Jake. "Looks like none of the problems downtown followed us to the mall."

"We've done our best to keep things under wraps, and it seems to be working."

Alex glanced at the tall, silent man in the black suit standing beside the door. "Interesting group," he said.

"That's for sure. The kid's a real piece of work."

Alex nodded. "Way too full of himself."

"The daughter seems nice enough," Jake said. "When I lived over there, I saw how hard it was on some of the women, trying to cope in a male-dominated society."

"Gotta be tough."

"I'm surprised she's not married. She's a real beauty."

"Yes, she is," Alex said absently, his eyes moving toward the door of the salon. "The little redhead's not bad, either." He smiled. "Take some taming, though, to bring that one in line."

One of Jake's eyebrows went up. "You interested in the job?"

Alex scoffed. "I don't have that much time."

"Good, because she's living with a guy."

Alex glanced back at the door. "Better for both of us."

Considering the looks Alex had been casting Rina's way, Jake wondered if he meant it.

Time slipped past. Jake walked the floor several times, looking for anything out of place, but everything seemed in order. He was checking his watch, waiting for Roshan to return, when the salon door opened and the women reappeared. They were carrying armloads of boxes, giggling and smiling. Only Zahra looked a little dower, but she usually did.

Jake's gaze swept the group. As beautiful as A'lia was, it was Sage who took center stage. Those golden eyes and that thick, wavy dark hair... There was just something about her. He couldn't remember a woman who attracted him the way she did. Or who left him hard and aching, alone in his bed every damned night.

Alex moved forward to help the ladies with their load. Jake didn't offer. His job was to protect them, and he couldn't do that with his hands full. The bell chimed above the elevator doors. They slid open and Roshan strolled out, exactly on time. Jake noticed the lighthearted laughter faded from A'lia's voice.

"It is time for you to leave," Roshan said to her sharply.

Though Jake didn't like the kid's tone, he was happy to be leaving. He wasn't much of a shopper, just bought what he needed and was done with it.

They left the store and began their trek through the mall. Seeing the smiles of anticipation on the women's faces, Jake groaned. It was going to be a very long day.

Sage liked A'lia. She was a sweet girl, and smart. Inside the private salon, as soon as the door had closed, she'd turned into a different person. More outgoing and at ease with herself and the people around her. It was clear her cousin Zahra didn't like the change, but she made only an occasional comment.

"You shouldn't dress like that," Zahra said when A'lia took off her embroidered, turquoise silk robe and did a little pirouette to show off the Vera Wang designer sheath she wore underneath. She had long slender legs and a fabulous figure, which the above-the-knee dress showed off perfectly. It seemed a shame to keep such beauty hidden.

Saks did their usual spectacular job of presenting the merchandise—gowns, sportswear, bags and jewelry—displaying them in a private fashion show. As much money as A'lia wound up spending, along with the clothes Sage and Rina couldn't resist buying, their extra effort certainly should have paid off.

From Saks they went to Cartier, Gucci, Louis Vuitton—where Roshan added to his personalized luggage collection—and ended the day at Neiman Marcus.

Jake insisted they leave in time to avoid the traffic heading back downtown, and Sage was secretly grateful. She was exhausted. But also pleased that another day had passed without incident and, in her estimation, had proved a great success.

They took the Saudis back to their hotel. Alex drove off in his shiny, dark blue BMW coupe, Linc dropped Rina and her armload of bags at the apartment she shared with Ryan not far from Sage's, then took Sage back to her apartment.

"I might as well stay," he said as he helped her out of the Escalade. "We've only got a couple of hours before we have to head for the IMAX."

The thought of tonight made her inwardly sigh. "All right."

"You'll need to be back here in time to get us down to the hotel," Jake said to Linc through the rolled-down car window.

He grinned. "Will do." Their driver seemed to have far more stamina than Sage. Then again, he hadn't been shopping in high heels all day the way she had.

Jake escorted her upstairs and she waited while he checked her apartment as usual.

"You can nap for a while if you want," he said. "I'll wake you up in time to change." His mouth curved in a sexy smile. "With all the stuff you and Rina bought today, there's no way you're going out tonight without wearing something new."

Sage laughed. "Trust me, nothing I bought today has a skirt that comes down past my knees."

Jake laughed. "I suppose that would be a problem." His expression slowly shifted and his gaze ran over her, settling on her lips. She knew that look and her stomach contracted.

"You went to Victoria's Secret," he said, his voice softer now, a little husky. "You must have bought something there you can wear." Challenge sparked in those sky-blue eyes.

Sage never could pass up a challenge. "Oh, I definitely bought something at Victoria's Secret. Among other things, a pair of pretty blue satin thong panties. And since you suggested it, I'll make sure I wear them tonight."

Jake's whole body tightened. He looked as if he couldn't breathe. With a triumphant smile, Sage turned and walked off down the hall, leaving him staring after her.

Sometimes being a woman was just too much fun.

She closed the bedroom door and leaned against it for a moment. She was tired, but satisfied with the way the day had turned out. Still, she needed to recoup for the night ahead. Trying not to think of Jake on the opposite side of the door, she pulled a cap over her hair, turned on the water and took a long, hot shower.

By the time she got out, she felt better, some of the tension in her muscles having drained away. She thought of the night ahead with less dread. Will Bailey would be going with them to act as her escort for the evening—a way for the sheik to get used to his presence in the meetings as one of her assistants.

Sage pulled on a robe and lay down on the bed, determined to take Jake's advice and catch a quick nap. Instead, she stared up at the ceiling and tried not to wish he would come striding through the door and demand to join her in bed.

Guilt washed over her. She was engaged, for God's sake. She had to stop thinking of Jake. She remembered the old adage about trying not to think of an elephant, after which the image of an elephant completely filled your mind.

It seemed to be that way with him.

Whatever the reason, she never relaxed enough to get the nap she so badly needed. She felt just as tired when she left the apartment as she had when she arrived.

Chapter 10

Accompanied by Jake and Alex, Sage went up to the presidential suite at seven o'clock that night to collect the sheik, his son and the usual entourage of cousins and bodyguards. The women weren't allowed to join them.

Sheik Khalid was waiting when the group walked into the foyer. Greetings were made, all the protocols followed. Sage glanced down at her watch, worried they'd be late for the show. She started to suggest it was time to leave when the sheik walked over and picked up that morning's *Chronicle*.

"It seems that in coming to Houston we have created somewhat of a disturbance," he said, holding the newspaper out for her to see. At the bottom of the page was an article on the protests outside the Marine Drilling office building.

Sage had known their guests would find out sooner or later, since the news was all over the local TV. She felt lucky it had taken this long. She took the paper from his hand and glanced at it, grateful the story was on the bottom of the front page instead of in the headlines.

"Whatever endeavor one undertakes," she said carefully, "there are always people who disagree. It's the way a democracy works."

Shrewd black eyes assessed her. "Things are much simpler in my country."

Sage met his gaze. "I'm sure they are. Though I imagine your country has its own set of problems." Living under the rule of the Saudi monarchy had its downside, particularly for women. His daughter was a prime example.

The sheik tipped his head as if to acknowledge the statement. "As you say, there are always disturbances. But business must be done."

"Exactly," Sage said, feeling a surge of relief that the protests hadn't upset the sheik enough for him to go home.

The party headed downstairs and climbed into the waiting limos for the short drive to the IMAX theatre at the Houston Museum. Two hours later they were on their way back out, with Sage and Will walking together, Jake and Alex behind, heading into the warm, moist night air.

Fortunately, when Will started talking, they were out of earshot of the sheik and his son.

"I guess A'lia and Zahra weren't allowed to come," Sage's assistant said. "It's kind of hard to get used to that whole thing about women being treated so differently."

"I keep telling myself it's just the way it is in their world. But you're right. It's difficult to imagine living that way."

"Worse, I suppose, for you, being a woman."

Sage didn't answer. From the dark look Jake was giving Will, she knew the conversation was over.

She smiled as she approached the sheik. "I hope you enjoyed the movie." *Everest, Roof of the World* seemed to have kept the group enthralled.

"Yes, we enjoyed it very much." He was a tall man, dignified and imposing, obviously a product of his culture. Yet in some ways he seemed far more modern than his son.

"The Himalayas are vastly different from the warm places we both live," Sage said.

He nodded. "I would like to see the mountains someday. I have never seen snow."

"I'm afraid I can't help you with that while you're here. The ice rink at the Galleria is as close as we get."

A smile appeared above his gray-speckled beard. "My daughter enjoyed her day," he said. "She likes you very much."

"She's a sweet girl and incredibly bright. She told me she graduated from your university. I'm sure she had very high marks."

"My daughter is very intelligent. It is her dream to continue her studies in America. I wish I could grant her that dream, but it is better she remain in her own country and assume her wifely duties."

"I didn't think she was married."

"A'lia is not yet wed, but it is past time I chose a husband for her."

Sage opened her mouth, then felt the subtle pressure of Jake's hand at her waist. "The car is waiting," he said firmly.

Sage just nodded. It was none of her business, and women's rights was a very touchy subject among the Saudis. One of the protocols, she remembered, was never to ask a man about his wife.

"I guess we had better get going," she said. Beside her, Will shoved his glasses up and offered her his arm. Sage walked with him toward the line of limos waiting to drive the party back to the hotel.

Once they arrived, the Saudi men exited the cars and walked inside, quite a sight in their flowing white robes and headdresses. As soon as they were gone, Will departed in his own car. The evening was finally over.

Sage breathed a sigh of relief. "Thank God."

Jake chuckled. "You were great. It was a tough day from start to finish, and you handled it like a pro."

She smiled up at him. "I am a pro."

He smiled back. "I know." Their eyes met, held for several long seconds. Then Sage glanced away, and they climbed into the Escalade, sliding into the seat behind Linc.

"You know, you were pretty great yourself," she said, once they were settled and the limo pulled into the street. "Thanks for keeping me on the straight and narrow. It's hard for an independent woman like me to keep from speaking her mind."

"Damn good thing you weren't born in the Middle East."

Sage laughed. "Damn good thing," she repeated, swearing, which was also not done.

Jake grinned and just shook his head. "We're off

the hook tomorrow. Linc will be driving the Saudis to the mosque and back. We don't have to return to the hotel until Saturday morning, when we take them out to the ranch. Trace will be there on Friday to make sure the security is all in place."

"Your friend seems very capable."

"He's the best."

"Then at least we won't have that to worry about." The visit to the ranch would be safe. And once they were there, she had plenty of activities to keep her foreign guests entertained. Hopefully, no worries in that regard, either.

"I read in the paper this morning that the police have declared the man killed during the protest at the university an accident," Sage stated.

Jake nodded. "Apparently, the accelerator stuck and the driver of the vehicle lost control of his car. The victim just happened to step in the way."

"Another possibility we don't have to worry about."

He nodded again, but she could tell he was thinking of problems that might lie ahead. Sage thought of the protests that continued at the office, the volatile situation facing her in the morning when she went to work, and knew she had plenty of other things to worry about.

She flicked a glance at Jake, felt his eyes on her, as hot as the tip of a flame.

One of those worries was sitting beside her.

Sage sighed.

Jake was still awake at midnight, even tired as he was. Cicadas hummed in the trees outside his bedroom window, and a slice of moonlight filtered in between the curtains. His eyelids were finally beginning to droop when the phone rang. It was nearly one, he saw on the clock, as he rolled to the side of the bed and grabbed his cell off the nightstand. His stomach tightened when he read the name on the caller ID.

"Sage, what is it?"

"I've got a problem, Jake. I know you don't want me going out by myself, so I'm calling to tell you I'm leaving my apartment. Roshan and his cousin are down at Galaxy, causing trouble. The owner, Joey Romero, is a friend of mine. I guess he read about the Saudi visit in the newspapers, and called to tell me what was happening. He says if I don't get Roshan out of there, he's going to phone the police."

"Just stay there and I'll come get you. We'll go down together."

"There isn't time, Jake. Just meet me there."

"No way. I don't want you going—"

The phone went dead and Jake cursed. He grabbed a pair of jeans and pulled them on, clipped his holster to his belt, grabbed his Heckler-Koch and shoved it in place, then dragged a clean, dark green T-shirt over his head to cover the weapon. Tying the laces on a pair of low-topped leather boots, he headed for the door.

Galaxy was a posh nightclub near the Galleria. It wouldn't take Sage long to get there. Damn woman. Jake had thought she'd learned her lesson at the restaurant. His jaw hardened. Sage Dumont was a handful, just as he'd figured from the start.

And it was his job to make sure she didn't get hurt.

This late at night, it didn't take him long to reach his destination. As he pulled his Jeep up to the valet in front, Jake spotted Sage's silver Mercedes parked in the lot.

He handed the kid a twenty. "Keep her close by and leave the keys in the ignition."

The valet eyed the wide tires and chrome wheels and grinned. "No problem."

Jake strode toward the heavyset black bouncer working the door.

"Your boss called about a problem," Jake said. "I'm protection for Sage Dumont. She just went inside."

"I talked to her. She told me you were coming. Go on in."

At least she had eased the way for him to get into the club, and so far it didn't look as if she'd caused any trouble.

Music throbbed as Jake stepped onto the stainless-steel floor in the entry. The place was slick and modern, with lots of brushed chrome and dark wood. Mauve and blue lights gleamed beneath the black granite bar and along the walls, and the ceiling twinkled with tiny white lights.

The dance floor was also stainless, and crowded with people gyrating to a hip-hop beat. There was a bank of padded booths along one wall, and Jake headed in that direction. As he drew near, he spotted Sage speaking to a group of men, none of whom were wearing Saudi robes.

Roshan sat in the middle, a blonde on one side, a redhead on the other. His cousin Quadim sat in the booth, along with Roshan's two bodyguards. Empty champagne bottles and broken martini glasses littered the table, though clearly, the bodyguards weren't drinking.

Sage stood next to a good-looking, dark-haired man—the owner, Joey Romero, Jake figured. They were trying to talk to Roshan, but the anger in the kid's pretty-boy face, the tight lips and dark scowl, said he wasn't listening.

"You need to go back to the hotel, Roshan," Sage was saying.

"Go away and leave me alone. You have no business here." He scoffed. "You American women. You are badly in need of discipline."

The blonde on his left giggled. "You can discipline me, Roshan. I'd love a good hard spanking."

He looked down at her, his eyes dark and hungry. "You will please me greatly, I think."

"Look, we don't want any trouble," Romero said. "You've broken a half-dozen glasses and nearly hit someone with an empty champagne bottle. Either you do as Ms. Dumont asks or I'm calling the police."

"I will pay you well for damages. As for the police, I have diplomatic immunity. There is nothing you can do."

"That isn't exactly true," Sage said. "This is America and property rights here are protected. At best, the police will escort you out. At worst, your family attorney will have to appear at the police station to prove your diplomatic status."

Jake's voice came out low and soft. "You need to do as Mr. Romero asks," he said, leaving Sage out of it since she was a woman and, although she was right, the last person Roshan would listen to. "Your father has a big day tomorrow and he'll expect you to be at your best."

What he didn't say was, *There's something I can*

*do, you little bastard. I can haul your ass outside and
knock the crap out of you.*

But he wouldn't. He was on the job. Sage was trying to negotiate an extremely important deal, and she
didn't need the son being openly hostile toward her.

Roshan tipped up the bottle of Dom Perignon he
gripped by the neck, and took a swig of the expensive
champagne. "Go away."

"Your father know you're here?" The second mention of the sheik had the effect Jake intended.

"My father does not run my life." But Roshan
stood up in the booth, swaying a little on his feet, and
dragged the blonde up with him. "You are fortunate.
I grow bored with this place, and I am in need of a
woman." He turned to his companion. "Come, we will
see how well you can please me."

The blonde giggled.

Sage opened her mouth to say something, but Jake
caught her arm and she fell silent.

"I've got a limo waiting out front," Romano said.
"I've instructed the driver to take you wherever you
want to go."

Roshan ignored him and started for the door. His
cousin fell in behind, the redhead latching on to his
arm. They were followed by Mutt and Jeff, the names
Jake had given the bodyguards.

"I didn't think they drank," Sage said, staring after
them as they made their way toward the door.

"Roshan is clearly not his father."

"And he's married. In fact, from what I read about
the family, he has three wives."

"Doesn't matter. He's a man, and the rules for them
are different." And since the men all had separate

rooms on the twentieth floor, getting the blonde and redhead in and out wouldn't be much of a problem.

"I realize that, but still..."

Jake cast her a glance. "Since you're hoping to make a deal with the sheik, we need to make sure they all get back downtown safely. I'm not letting you out of my sight again tonight, so you'll have to come along."

Sage sighed. She was dressed in a pair of faded jeans and a T-shirt, and looked tired. And just plain beautiful. "I'm disliking Roshan more and more," she muttered.

Jake chuckled. "How would you like to be married to him?"

Sage just rolled her eyes.

Chapter 11

The sun blazed down on the pastures of the Double D Ranch, with only a few stray clouds floating in the clear blue sky. The air, heavy with humidity, hung over the lush green fields, but the heat was bearable this morning, and the Saudis didn't seem to mind.

As they had planned, Ian was there to greet the guests when they walked into the big, Spanish-style house. He was the head of Marine Drilling, but today he was merely Sage's grandfather, the head of the Dumont family, nothing more.

Ian's thick silver hair glinted as he extended a hand to the sheik. *"As-salam-alaikum,"* he said in greeting, an old pro at this game.

"Wa alaikum as-salam," the sheik replied. And so the day began. Introductions were made all around, then the Saudis were taken to the guesthouse to refresh

themselves and change into clothes more appropriate for a casual Western setting.

Sage stood next to Rina beneath the wide covered patio as she waited for her guests to reappear. She had called her friend first thing that morning and asked her if she could possibly get away and come with them to the ranch.

After the scene at Galaxy with Roshan, Sage figured she needed a friend to help her get through the next two days. Having another woman along would make things easier, especially since, a little to Sage's surprise, Rina seemed to have made a nice connection with both Zahra and A'lia.

"Thank God you came," Sage said to Rina softly. "I swear this is getting harder instead of easier."

He friend grinned. "Ryan's out of town. I didn't have anything better to do, and I figured the weekend would definitely be entertaining."

Sage laughed. "That it certainly should be."

During their earlier phone conversation, Rina had asked only one question. "Is Justice going to be there?"

"He's one of the bodyguards. He'll be there. You really don't like him, do you?"

"The guy's a total male chauvinist. Men like him are exactly the reason I'm living with a sweet guy like Ryan."

And walking all over him, Sage thought, but didn't say so. "Can you put up with him for a couple of days as a favor to me?"

"Of course. He's just a man. It's not a problem."

But Sage thought maybe it was more of a problem than Rina wanted to admit. She wasn't so sure her friend wasn't attracted to the hot-looking guy with the amazing dimples.

She glanced across the patio to where Jake stood with Alex, both men with their legs splayed and their hands crossed in front of them. They were making their presence clear, to impress the sheik, and so far it seemed to be working.

Most of the time Jake remained in the background, yet Sage was always aware of exactly where he was. It was as if she had some special radar where he was concerned and could somehow sense him even when she couldn't see him.

It was another reason she was glad Rina had agreed to come. Secretly, she hoped having a friend along would help insulate her from Jake. She cast him a sideways glance, felt those sky-blue eyes on her, felt the current instantly swirl between them, and tore her gaze away.

She should be thinking of her fiancé, not her bodyguard, but Phillip had scarcely entered her mind since the day Jake had walked into her office. And the fact she so rarely thought of the man she was engaged to marry worried her in a way it never had before.

It was cool out here beneath the heavy wooden beams and red tile roof. Situated at the back of the house, the patio looked out over the lush green pastures and paddocks of the ranch. Horses galloped through the fields, and frolicking colts raced after their mothers.

While Jake and Alex stood with their backs to the wall a few feet away, Sage, Ian and Rina sat on comfortable wicker sofas and chairs upholstered in cheerful striped fabric, bright orange, red and dark green.

They talked for a while, then stood up as the first

of their guests reappeared—Roshan and his cousin Quadim. As handsome as Roshan was, Quadim was unattractive, with a broad nose and low brow over eyes set a little too close together. Both were dressed in American fashion, Roshan in a pair of designer jeans and a red-plaid Western shirt. Quadim wore a brand-new pair of jeans and a light blue Western shirt with pearl snaps up the front.

The rest of the group arrived in more traditional apparel, the sheik and Cousin Yasar in lightweight white trousers beneath a long, loose-fitting robe that fell to just above the knees. Mutt and Jeff, as Jake jokingly called Roshan's personal bodyguards, wore their usual black suits. They had to be sweating in the moist Texas heat.

A'lia appeared in a loose-fitting, soft peach caftan, an embroidered scarf around her head and neck. Since she planned to ride, Sage figured there were matching pants underneath. Zahra wore a lightweight, dark gray robe, and a head scarf that covered most of her face.

Refreshments were served, iced tea and lemonade, and trays of tiny quiche and finger sandwiches, nothing that contained pork. No mention was made of the scene at Galaxy last night. It was as if the incident had never occurred, which was perfectly fine with Sage.

As soon as they finished the snacks, Sage and Ian led the group out to the stables, followed by Jake and Alex.

"I hope you all enjoy your ride," Ian said, declining to join the excursion and instead remaining with the group who wouldn't be going along—Zahra, Yasar, Rina, Alex and both the sheik's personal bodyguards.

The horses were led out of the barn and over to the riders, a pretty little pinto mare for A'lia, a prancing black gelding for Roshan and a dappled gray for the sheik. Sage had chosen each of their horses personally, having discovered their level of skill from the liaison in Saudi Arabia, hoping each animal would please its rider.

The rest of the horses were a mix of sorrels and bays, all of them easily handled by even a novice rider. Sage rode Sunrise, the palomino mare she had received from her grandfather as a colt for her eighteenth birthday. Sunny was perfectly trained for trail riding, and in her earlier days had won medals as one of the finest cutting horses in Texas.

Sage looked around for Jake, who, of course, had insisted on coming along. She frowned when she saw him leading Thor, a big red gelding and one of the stable's best quarter horses, out of the barn.

Sage led Sunny toward him, the mare's hooves clopping against the hard-packed earth. "I asked Jimmy to saddle Buster for you. He's easy to handle."

Jake shrugged. "He was a little on the small side for me. Jimmy thought Thor might work better."

"Thor's a great horse, but he can be a little cantankerous at first. I thought maybe—"

"He'll settle down." Jake had on scuffed cowboy boots today and a slightly dusty straw hat her grandfather had loaned him and insisted he wear, and he looked way too good in them.

Sage frowned as he shoved a boot into the stirrup and swung up into the saddle with an ease she didn't expect. "I thought you didn't ride."

"I said I didn't ride unless I had to, not that I didn't know how." He settled himself in the saddle, stretched his long legs out in front of him, stood up to test the length of the stirrups, seemed satisfied they were the right fit. "Some of the places I've worked, horseback is the only way you can get around."

"Where was that?"

"South America, mostly. That area's kind of my specialty." He tugged the hat a little lower on his forehead. "You coming?"

Sage released a breath. Damn, the man was maddening. She wondered if he was really as comfortable in the saddle as he looked. Some mischievous little part of her imagined Thor tossing him on his tight derriere, but the horse was behaving as if Jake had ridden him for years.

The group was finally mounted, with their stirrups adjusted to the proper length. The sheik rode next to his daughter and they made a handsome pair. Roshan hung back, riding next to his cousin, the two of them speaking quietly in Arabic.

Sage settled in next to the sheik and A'lia, who sat her mount easily, as did her father.

"It is wonderful to ride out here," the girl said with a wide, bright smile. "Thank you for giving us a taste of your American West."

Sage felt a trickle of satisfaction that her plans seemed to meet with approval. "My pleasure."

A few of the wranglers fell in behind them, their saddlebags filled with the snacks and drinks that would be served at the halfway mark down by the river. Sage planned for them to be out only a couple of hours, including the stop for refreshments and to rest and water the horses.

As much as she liked to ride, with the tension she was feeling, she was already looking forward to getting back to the house.

* * *

The lady was magnificent, Jake thought. There was no other word for it. Sitting astride her pretty palomino mare, Sage rode with the ease of a true Texas woman, someone who'd spent years in the saddle. Dressed in crisp blue jeans, an embroidered, pink flowered Western shirt, expensive custom-fitted boots and a white straw hat with a turquoise-and-silver band, she should have looked like a socialite playing cowgirl.

Instead, she actually was one. There was no way to fake it. You either had the confidence, the know-how to handle a high-spirited animal, or you didn't. The mare had plenty of spunk, but Sage controlled her easily, using a mixture of voice commands, knee pressure and light tugs on the reins.

She was in her element on horseback, out here on the ranch, something Jake never would have expected. When they were here before, she'd been worried about security, thinking about the visitors she planned to host. None of the passion she felt for riding or the land itself had shown that day, but it was showing now.

It made her even more appealing. And it raised questions about her.

He'd done a cursory search of Sage Dumont on the internet. He'd read about the charity benefits she attended, the donations she and the company often made. He'd seen the photos of her engagement party at the River Oaks Country Club, an event the newspapers had called one of the social highlights of the year. He knew she had graduated from Vassar and gone on to the Harvard Business School.

Now he saw that he hadn't dug deep enough. Some piece of the puzzle was missing, some element that had made her the woman she was today, and he wanted to know what it was.

Jake rode behind Sage. Trace had done a good job of upgrading the alarm system and adding perimeter sensing devices, but twenty-five hundred acres was a lot of ground. Jake kept his eyes open, scanning the area they rode through for any sign of trouble, and hoped for the next two days he wouldn't find any.

Alex had purposely stayed behind at the ranch house. As head of the Dumont clan, Ian could also be a target, or any of the guests, since it was clear now that there were people who didn't want this deal with the Saudis to go through.

As the hour slipped past, the sun beat down hotter and brighter, and the horses began to sweat. Jake hadn't ridden in a few years and the inside of his thighs were beginning to ache. He was glad it would soon be time for a rest stop.

He spotted the lunch site just as Roshan and Quadim broke into an impromptu race. Their horses' hooves thundered against the ground, flinging up dirt, both men obviously excellent riders. The race ended on the banks of the Brazos with Roshan in the lead. Jake figured Quadim was smart enough to let him win.

They rested in the shade down by the water, seated on granite boulders under the spreading branches of an ancient oak tree. An array of snacks were laid out on an old picnic table that looked like it had been there for years, though it was covered today with a white linen cloth. They drank ice water and lemonade with the food, explored the banks of the river, then prepared for the ride back to the ranch.

Jake made a brief reconnaissance of the area as

the group remounted. Roshan and Quadim ended up riding just ahead of him, off to one side. Jake caught snippets of laughter as the men talked about their evening at Galaxy and the women who had spent the night in their beds.

Roshan said he had given the woman what she wanted. He said he had tried to pay her afterward, but she'd refused the money. "Stupid American woman," was the rough translation of what he said.

As Thor moved steadily beneath him, cutting through the high green grasses, Jake focused on scanning the landscape, looking for anything out of place. All he saw were lush fields scattered with low, leafy trees and the occasional live oak. A deer darted out of the bushes next to a meandering creek, and the women pointed and laughed.

Roshan and Quadim were still talking. Jake's memory of Arabic was slowly returning, the words getting clearer in his head. The conversation drifted. He was mostly ignoring the pair until he caught a couple of words that put him on alert. *Money. Shipment.* And then a reference to narcotics.

Jake told himself he was mistaken. He had just misunderstood. He hadn't used the language in a while and he had never been completely fluent, though he'd been able to communicate fairly well. He started listening closer, paying more attention. The words *shipment* and *arrival* came up, this time with the added information that the delivery would be soon and that there would be plenty of money.

Money and plenty. *Floose* and *quarn al katra,* a reference to the horn of plenty. That was what Quadim had said. There was no mistake. He and the sheik's son were involved in something and it didn't sound good. Jake had caught the word for drugs only one time, so he couldn't be sure, but he had a feeling he'd heard right. And whatever Roshan was doing, he was doing it right under their noses.

Jake's jaw tightened. As if Sage didn't have enough trouble already.

He softly cursed.

"So I guess you're not much of a cowboy," Rina said to Alex, who stood on the patio with his back to the wall, looking out at the riders approaching across a broad green pasture.

Alex's blue eyes turned in her direction, ran over her head to toe, and his mouth curved up. "Guess it depends on what kind of riding we're talking about."

Rina's face heated. She couldn't believe it. A man hadn't made her blush in years. She ignored a ripple of irritation. "Sage says you're a pilot. What kind of planes do you fly?"

"Pretty much anything with wings. Since I've come to Houston, mostly I've been flying choppers. Kind of double duty. Getting the client where he wants to go, then protecting him once he gets there."

"You don't look much like a bodyguard."

"Mostly, I'm a P.I."

She glanced at him in question. "Private investigator?"

"That's right."

"I see."

"Yeah?" Those blue eyes assessed her. "What exactly is it you think you see?"

She stiffened. There was something in his tone....

Just the way his mouth lifted at the corners when he looked at her made her mad. "I see a smart-ass flyboy who thinks he's brighter than everyone else and especially me. But he would be wrong about that."

Alex's dark blond eyebrows went up. "That so?"

"Yes."

"Actually, I think you're a damned intelligent woman. A little too sassy. Maybe a little too smart for your own good. That's the reason I make you mad. I'm a man—the kind a woman like you needs, but won't let through the door. You're afraid of a guy who takes charge, afraid of giving up control."

She'd started to open her mouth, tell him where he could stick his ridiculous notions, when the door opened and Ian walked out on the patio.

"Ah, there you two are. I thought I'd better let you know our visitors have returned."

For Ian's sake, Rina pulled in her claws and pasted on a smile. "Then we had better go and greet them." She walked over and took Ian's arm, flashed Alex a final haughty glance and floated past him into the house.

Men. What did Alex Justice know about the kind of man she needed? Not a single damned thing.

When the party arrived back at the ranch, lunch was waiting in the main house. While the guests retired to their quarters to shower and change before the meal, Jake followed Sage into a sunny salon off the living room, a room filled with green plants, Spanish antiques and shelves full of leather-bound books.

"I think your guests enjoyed themselves," he said, easing into the subject he needed to broach.

"So far so good." Sage tossed her straw cowboy hat onto one of the tables and ran her fingers through her hair, lifting it away from the nape of her neck, exposing the smooth pale skin there. Jake felt a surge of heat.

"What's next on the schedule?" he asked.

"Lunch, then a nap for those who want one. A barbecue this evening."

"With entertainment, as I recall."

"That's right, the Brazos Boys."

They were a local country band. Jake had vetted them to make sure they wouldn't be a problem. They were well respected in the area, not known for making trouble.

"Tomorrow morning before it gets hot, we'll be trap shooting," Sage said. "The sheik and Roshan enjoy a similar sport in their country and my grandfather loves it."

Jake had checked out the range. The setup looked secure. "Ian's a good man."

Sage smiled. "He kept everyone entertained while we were gone."

"And Alex and Rina from sniping at each other."

"As much as possible," she said. "You noticed, I guess."

"He likes her. He wouldn't give her such a bad time if he didn't."

Sage laughed. "Well, she doesn't like him. She thinks he's a male chauvinist."

"He is. But she likes him just fine."

Sage cocked an eyebrow. "Even if you're right—and I'm not convinced—it couldn't go anywhere. Rina's not into macho men."

Jake looked down at the stack of magazines on the

round oak coffee table. A *Forbes* rested on top. "What about you? Considering the type of guy you're going to marry, it doesn't look like you're much into macho men, either."

Her eyes met his. "Big strong guys like you are for flings, Jake. They aren't the kind of men women marry."

Jake made no reply. Sage was right. He wasn't the kind of man a woman married. Not if she had a lick of sense.

His eyes slid over the snug jeans covering that perfect little ass, the pretty pink shirt with the flowers across her breasts. Didn't mean he didn't want her in his bed.

Which, from the way Sage was looking at him, was exactly what she was thinking.

"I, um, need to shower and change," she said, grabbing her hat off the table and starting for the door.

Jake stepped in her way. "So do I, but before you head upstairs, there's something I need to talk to you about."

She lifted her head. "What is it?"

"Something's going on with Roshan and Quadim. I overheard them talking while we were riding. Quadim said something about money and a shipment coming in. He used a word that means narcotics."

"You can't be serious."

"I know you've already got problems enough, but—"

"From what I've read, using drugs in Saudi Arabia gets you thrown into prison. I can't imagine Roshan would be that stupid."

"We aren't talking about Saudi Arabia. We're talking about here in the States."

"What possible motive could he have? His family is filthy rich. He can buy anything he wants."

"With his father's money, not his own."

"I don't want to hear this, Jake. In the first place, you told me yourself you aren't fluent in Arabic, so you could have misunderstood."

"I thought I had at first. I hoped I had. I didn't, Sage."

"I don't care," she said stubbornly. "I don't give a damn what Roshan and Quadim do while they're in Houston, as long as it doesn't affect our deal. We start negotiations Monday morning. As soon as we reach an agreement, the sheik and his family will be heading back home. Until that time, I don't want to hear anything about drugs or money or anything else—and don't even think about saying anything to Ian."

Jake clamped down on his temper. "I'm not talking to Ian, I'm talking to you. This could be important, Sage. We need to know what the hell is going on."

She firmly shook her head. "No, Jake. We're going forward exactly the way we planned. We aren't stirring up trouble. We already have more than we can handle."

"Sage—"

"Don't bring this up again." She looked at him and her voice softened. "Please, Jake. I'm asking you as a personal favor to let the matter drop."

He wished to hell he could. What Sage didn't understand was that they had to find out what Roshan and Quadim were doing in order to protect themselves. The Marine Drilling deal with the Saudis was already making headlines in the papers. If Roshan was into something illegal, the whole thing could come down on Sage's head.

"I won't say anything to Ian or anyone else," Jake said. He didn't have enough information, anyway. "But you need to keep your eyes and ears open. That just makes good sense."

She released a long sigh. "All right, I'll do that much, but that's as far as it goes." She looked up at him with those golden-brown eyes. "This deal means everything to me. And I really appreciate your help," she added softly.

Jake just nodded. Something was going down and it involved people who had come to matter to him. Sooner or later, he'd find out what it was.

And he'd damn well put a stop to it.

Chapter 12

The aroma of hickory smoke lingered over the patio long after the barbecue was over. In their jeans, boots and dusty straw hats, the Brazos Boys strummed guitars, fiddled, and sang till midnight. No one seemed ready for bed as they packed up to leave, so Rina brought out her guitar and started strumming old cowboy tunes. For an amateur, she was darned good.

Seated nearby, Sage flicked a glance at Alex Justice, who watched her with an interest he didn't bother to hide. Every once in a while, Rina cast a hostile glare his way. Alex either returned the glare or gave her an indulgent grin, which only seemed to annoy her more.

Sage figured Jake was way off base when it came to that particular pair. They weren't able to get along for an hour, let alone time enough to develop any kind of relationship—though the heat they generated as they eyed each other might make for a wild night in bed.

As Rina finished a soft country ballad, Sage glanced up to see Sheik Kalid rise from his chair. He was once again dressed in a long white robe and head-dress. As he drew near, his lips curved faintly behind his beard.

Sage rose to greet him. "Sheik Khalid."

"My family and I wish to thank you for a very interesting evening," he said. "My son Roshan and his cousin Quadim have been to America a number of times, so they are familiar with your Western music. But it is new for the rest of us. My daughter A'lia particularly enjoyed it."

"A barbecue with country music is kind of a Texas tradition. I'm glad you found it entertaining."

He nodded. "Your grandfather and I talked about the shooting match to be held in the morning. We both look forward to testing our skills. I am certain my son will, as well."

"Good. I also look forward to it."

"Then it is time for us to leave. *Massa al-khair.* I bid you good evening."

"Massa al-nur," she said in reply, silently thanking Jake for teaching her the words. She watched the sheik lean down to speak to his daughter. In a pale blue caftan with sparkling silver beads on the front, A'lia rose gracefully, along with Zahra, who as usual was gowned in black. As they left the patio, Yasar, who was perhaps a few years younger than his cousin the sheik, a man in his late forties, fell in behind them. Sage had spoken to Yasar a couple times today. He was shorter than the other Saudi men, a little heavier, but he had a ready smile, laughed more frequently and

seemed much more easygoing. It was clear he had a close friendship with the sheik.

The group headed off toward the guesthouse, followed by the sheik's bodyguards. Roshan and Quadim had already left with the other two bodyguards, so for Sage the evening was over. Even Rina had packed away her guitar and slipped quietly off to her room upstairs.

Finally able to let down her guard, Sage dropped onto the brightly striped wicker sofa, giving in to a wave of exhaustion. When she turned her head, she saw Jake watching her with those amazing blue eyes. As tired as she was, her heartbeat kicked up. He strode over and sat beside her.

"Your guests were extremely impressed," he said. He was wearing jeans and a loose-fitting, pale blue knit shirt. She was used to seeing the gun hidden at his waist. She wished he didn't look so damned attractive.

"You did everything just right," he added.

Sage smiled. "It was a good day."

His return smile made her pulse beat even faster. "You didn't think you would enjoy yourself," he said, "but you did."

"That's true. I haven't ridden in a while. Too long, really. When I was younger, Ian and I spent every weekend out here. He raised cutting horses back then, some of the best in the country. I used to compete."

"You're a damned fine rider. Now I know why. You have to be good just to stay in the saddle of a well-trained cutting horse."

"I love to ride. I'm hoping, once my career gets further along, I'll be able to raise some horses of my own."

"You mean out here. You're part owner of the ranch." It wasn't a question.

"How did you know?"

"The name on the gate, Double D. Had to be Ian and your father or Ian and you. Since neither of you ever mention your dad, I figured it had to be you."

Sage looked at Jake. She rarely talked about the past and yet the words came spilling out. "My mother ran away from my father when I was four years old. When I got older, she told me he was abusive. She never said he beat her or anything like that, but living with him must have been really bad. She wasn't his equal socially and he never let her forget it. I think he destroyed her self-esteem. I know she was wildly unhappy."

"Do you remember any of it?"

"I remember being scared of him as a child."

"What happened?"

"My mother told me she left him one night after they'd had a big fight. She just bundled me up and took off for Chicago. She went underground, completely disappeared. If Louis had found her, he would have taken me away from her—there was no question of that. He never found us. I'm not sure he tried very hard."

"Your mother was married to a very wealthy man. She must have been used to the finer things in life. How did she take care of you without your father's financial support?"

"She wasn't rich before she married him. My mother was beautiful. I guess that's why he married her. At any rate, after she left, she went to work as a waitress. We lived in a ratty old tenement building in a low-rent district, but she had a job and she made enough to pay the bills. As I look back on it, I realize in her own way she was happy. It meant a lot to her, I think, being able to take care of me."

"What about you? Were you happy?"

"I went to school in the neighborhood, made friends there. I knew we didn't have any money, but neither did anybody else. Mom loved me, and yes, I was happy."

"I'm guessing it was your grandfather who finally found you."

She nodded. "I was twelve when my father died in a car accident. My grandfather started looking for us the day he was buried. He hired detectives. One of them tracked us down, and Ian flew out to Chicago to convince my mother to come back to Texas and live with him."

"Why'd he wait so long?"

"I think maybe he knew what was going on with my mom and dad. I think he was afraid of what would happen if he brought us back to Houston."

Thinking of those days, Sage felt a tightening in her throat. She had dealt with all this a long time ago, moved on with her life. Still, the pain was there.

"Three years later my mother got breast cancer. If it hadn't been for Ian, I don't know what would have happened to me." Sage felt her eyes burn when she glanced up. "I owe him everything, Jake. More than anything in the world, I want to make him proud of me."

"He is, Sage. I can see the pride in his eyes every time he looks at you."

She didn't expect to feel Jake's hand cupping her cheek, the gentle brush of his thumb over her lips.

"I read about you on the internet," he murmured. "I tried to figure you out, but I knew something was missing, some part of you that makes you the woman you are today. Now I know."

A tear rolled down her cheek. He wiped it away with his finger. "I've never wanted a woman the way I want you. I don't expect that to change things. I just wanted you to know."

Her throat tightened even more. She had never wanted anyone the way she wanted Jake, either. She wanted him to kiss her, so badly she ached with it, deep down inside.

She watched him rise from the sofa, hold out a hand. "Time to go in," he said a little gruffly. Sage took the hand he offered and they walked into the house.

Jake said nothing had changed.

But something *had* changed. In the matter of a heartbeat, everything she wanted, everything she had worked for, seemed unimportant. Only one thing mattered and that was being with Jake.

It was mostly physical attraction, she was sure. A little caring tossed into the mix, a little respect. But whatever she felt, it wasn't going away. That her need for Jake affected her so profoundly meant she had to deal with it before she could get on with her life.

She had waited, wanting to be certain. Now she knew for sure what she had to do.

It was a hot Texas morning, not a cloud in a sky so blue it hurt your eyes. Jake loved it, loved the smell of damp grass in the air and the wind in his face, loved the green open spaces and watching the horses gallop across the fields.

He was standing behind the group that had gathered at the range for the trap shooting match. The day was quickly warming, so most of them had dressed comfortably. Since he'd been at the ranch, Jake had been wearing jeans and loose-fitting, short-sleeved shirts. He pitied the four Saudi guards, who braved the heat in their tailored black suits.

Roshan and Quadim wore jeans; the others wore lightweight robes. The women sat in the shade of a lean-to built in a safe place behind the shooting range, a spot for visitors to watch and stay out of the sun.

Four of the five participants took their places—Ian and Sheik Khalid, Roshan and Quadim. Jake blinked when Yasar turned and made his way toward the lean-to to join the observers. Instead, Sage put on her ear protection, shoved on a pair of shooting glasses, picked up a shotgun from the rack and walked over to the fifth position.

Jake shook his head. The lady continued to amaze him.

He fixed his attention on the match. In trap, the participants stood in an arc behind the trap house, firing at twenty-five targets, five from each of five stations in rotation.

The match officially began. Jake watched Ian position his shotgun against his shoulder, getting ready for a clay pigeon to be released. "Pull!" he shouted as he sighted down the barrel. The red disk flew into the sky and Ian squeezed the trigger, the blast echoing, buckshot shattering the disk, sending broken shards careening into the air.

Roshan had a turn, then Quadim. Roshan hit the target. His cousin missed. Jake watched as Sage rested her shotgun against her shoulder, pressed the stock against her cheek.

"Pull!" she shouted, then neatly blasted the red disk into a thousand pieces.

The match continued. By the time they had finished the round, Sheik Khalid and Ian were tied for the lead, Sage and Roshan tied for second.

Jake almost smiled. No way was Sage going to beat the arrogant little bastard. Jake would have bet his last nickel on that. She wanted her deal too badly.

He wondered what Ian would do, and wasn't surprised when the older man won the match one point ahead of the sheik. Respect was involved. They were both clan leaders. Losing on purpose would not have served either of them well.

Jake wasn't surprised when Sage missed her final target and Roshan hit the clay bird dead center. Sage grinned so widely the tiny dimple he'd noticed before popped into her cheek. Setting her twelve-gauge back in the rack, she walked toward him.

He cast her a glance. "I thought you didn't like guns," he said, slightly irritated that she had given him such a bad time over the pistol clipped to his belt.

"I said I didn't like handguns. I didn't say I couldn't shoot."

His mouth edged up. "Good to know."

"Granddad taught me how to handle a pistol, a rifle and a shotgun when I was a teenager. I keep a .38 Colt revolver locked in my apartment, but I won't use it."

"Not unless you have to," he said, just to see what she'd say.

"That's right. Not unless I have to."

Jake grinned.

The observers had moved out from under the lean-to and joined the others in an area a little ways from the trap machine.

"Come over here a minute, will you, Jake?"

He followed the sound of Ian's voice. "Yes, sir." When he reached the silver-haired man, Ian handed him a rifle. Jake looked it over, a beautiful Remington 700 .308 with a hand-carved, inlaid hardwood stock and a powerful Leupold Mark 4 scope.

"You shoot long distance, right?"

"I guess you could say that." When he'd been in Marine Special Forces, he'd been a sniper. With the right weapon, he could hit a target a mile away.

Ian turned as his ranch foreman approached them, a guy named Chico Muñoz whom Jake had met when he'd been out to the ranch before. Hispanic, his skin burned a dark chestnut from his years in the sun, his face weathered and lined beneath his battered straw cowboy hat.

"You got that target in place?" Ian asked.

"Sí, señor."

Ian turned to Jake. "Over there, through those trees, you'll see a hill beyond. Chico set up a target. We figure it's about seven hundred yards out. Think you can hit it?"

"Long way for this caliber rifle."

"Damn long way," the older man agreed.

Jake hefted the rifle, jerked it up to his shoulder a few times, sighted down the barrel. The gun was a showpiece. It felt good in his hands. "I'm only as good as my weapon."

"Rifle's dead-on at two hundred yards," Ian said.

Jake aimed the gun toward the space between the trees. Through the powerful scope, he spotted the tiny speck of a target against the hillside. At seven hundred yards, a .308 bullet would drop about twenty-eight inches. He bent and picked up a pinch of dry grass, held it up and let it fall, testing the wind. "About two knots," he said.

He walked over to a fence post, lifted the gun and settled it against his shoulder, steadying the rifle on top of the post. He felt the weight of the gun in his hands, the warmth of the hardwood against his cheek, felt himself settle into the quiet zone.

He found his mark and gently squeezed the trigger. The gunshot echoed and the weapon recoiled. It was done.

Ian turned. "All right, Chico. Let's see if Jake hit his mark."

The foreman grinned and took off toward a red four-wheeler parked not far away. Jumping on, he fired up the engine and roared off toward the trees.

Jake ejected the casing, leaving the breech open, which was range etiquette. From the corner of his eye, he saw Sage watching him, her look assessing.

She turned to her grandfather. "I've got a ten-dollar bill says Jake hit the target."

Ian smiled, cast Jake a sideways glance. "Twenty dollars says he didn't."

"You're on."

"If your man made the shot, he is a quite a marksman," the sheik said. "I will match your twenty…if your daughter is willing to take the bet."

"I will also bet he did not hit the target," Roshan said smugly.

Sage's smile suddenly looked less enthusiastic. "Of course I'll cover all bets." But the glance she cast Jake said she was starting to hope he'd missed. The moment passed and Chico roared up in the four-wheeler, waving a black-and-white paper target. They all circled around it.

All but Jake. If the gun had done its job, he'd hit the target. He was pretty sure he had.

"Dead center!" Ian shouted, coming over to slap Jake on the back. "Damn fine shooting, son."

"Very well done," the sheik said. "That was quite an impressive exhibition of marksmanship."

"The kind of lessons I had stay with you."

Ian eyed him shrewdly. The older man knew Jake's background. There was no need to ask what a sniper did with his expertise. "I imagine they do," he said.

The match was over and they walked back toward the house, the women following behind the men. As soon as the Saudis disappeared inside the guesthouse, Sage turned to Jake.

"You were amazing."

"Hitting a target was once my job. When things go wrong, it still is."

He thought he saw a shudder pass through her. He was a bodyguard, after all, and currently he was guarding her luscious little body. That she needed him at all must have had her thinking of the demonstrations downtown and the man who had accosted her in the restaurant.

"What about tomorrow?" she asked, confirming that he had been spot-on. "You think it's safe to start the negotiations at the office?"

"You watch this morning's news?"

"No. What happened?"

"The protests are still going on. Police made a couple of arrests last night. You'd be better off going to plan B."

"Our attorney's office." Sage had already spoken to Weis, Weis, Silverman and Schultz, the law firm that represented Marine Drilling. Should the demonstrations continue, Robert Schultz had arranged for the meetings to be held at his midtown office.

"All right," Sage said. "We go to plan B."

"I'll let Linc know tomorrow's destination has been changed."

"Quadim won't be going to the meeting. According to the sheik, he's staying at the hotel with Zahra and A'lia. Oh, and Roshan has asked for a car and driver for the evening. He wants a stretch. He and Quadim are going out."

"I'll have Linc arrange it. Let's hope the arrogant little prick stays out of trouble this time."

Sage smiled. "Maybe we'll get lucky." Her eyes stayed on Jake's face for several long seconds. He thought she was going to say something, but instead she shook her head and looked toward the house. "It's almost time to head back to town. I need to go upstairs and pack my things."

Jake checked his watch. "The limos will be ready to leave in half an hour."

"Perfect." She walked back toward the red-roofed structure and Jake fell in behind her. His gaze moved over her trim figure and narrow waist. He tried not to stare at that sexy little ass in those snug-fitting jeans, but it was impossible.

His groin tightened. He wanted this woman. And since he couldn't have her, he'd be damned glad when the job was over.

Before they reached the door, Sage stopped and turned. "You haven't... Roshan and Quadim... You haven't heard them say anything more, have you? Anything else that sounds suspicious?"

Jake shook his head. "Not so far."

"Good. That's good."

But it wasn't good. It just meant he didn't know more than he had before, and he was sure there was plenty more to learn.

Jake held the door and Sage walked past him into the cool interior of the sprawling house.

They needed to know what was going on, and he had just been given a chance to find out.

Chapter 13

It was late Sunday night and Sage was back in her apartment. She had taken a long hot shower and shampooed her hair. Now she paced the floor in her white terry cloth robe.

Before Jake had brought her upstairs and checked the apartment, he had spoken with Security, found there'd been no unwelcome visitors outside, no one prowling the area who shouldn't be there. She was home at last, wishing she could relax.

It wasn't going to happen.

Out at the ranch, she had made an important decision. One that could determine the course of her life. It was time to implement that decision.

She stared at the phone on the desk in her study, turned, paced a few steps, checked the clock for the ten-thousandth time. *Midnight.* She picked up the receiver and dialed Phillip's number. It was 6:00 a.m. in Edinburgh. She had purposely waited to make sure he would be awake, and since he was an early riser and usually one of the first to get to the office, it should be a good time to call.

The phone in his apartment rang a few times. He sounded a little groggy when he answered. "Stanton here."

"Phillip, it's Sage. I hope I didn't wake you. You're usually up by now. If this is a bad time—"

"I'm up. Just getting the coffee on. How are you?"

"I'm fine, Phillip… It's just… Something's come up."

"I hope nothing's gone wrong with your platform deal."

"No, it's not that. The negotiations are just starting. Today is our first official meeting. This…this is something to do with us."

She heard the sound of a chair scrapping the floor, imagined him sitting down at the table in his kitchen. "What is it, Sage?"

She moistened her lips, took a deep breath. "I've been doing a lot of thinking lately…about us."

"Us…?"

"That's right. I've decided I need a little more time."

"Time for what, exactly? If you're talking about our wedding, we haven't even set the date."

"I'm talking about our engagement, Phillip. I need…need a little more time to work through this whole idea of getting married."

He didn't say a word, and yet she could feel his annoyance streaming over the line. "I'm afraid I don't understand what it is you're getting at."

"What I'm saying is I want to postpone our engagement. I need to decide if getting married is the right thing for me to do." Her pulse was pounding, thrumming so hard it was difficult to concentrate.

"That's insane. We went through all this before. Have you discussed it with your grandfather?"

Her stomach tightened. She hadn't mentioned it to Ian, couldn't imagine what he would say when she did.

"It isn't Ian's decision, it's mine. I need more time, Phillip. I—I'm breaking our engagement."

"You can't be serious."

"I'm afraid I am."

"It's this deal you're working on, darling. It's got you tied in knots. You need to pass it to someone else, let Charles or Jonathan take the reins."

She bristled at the mention of the other two VPs. "I'm not letting Charles or Jonathan take over my project. This is a personal matter involving you and me. I need some time, Phillip. A marriage between us won't work as long as I have doubts."

"You didn't have doubts when I left." A long pause ensued. "Does this have something to do with that brute your father hired? If that's it, Sage, you need to think this through very carefully."

She swallowed, tried not to see Jake's image. "That's exactly what I'm trying to do, Phillip," she replied, dodging the question. "I'm sorry I've upset you, but I've made my decision. I'm ending our engagement. Perhaps in time I'll be ready to think about the future, about marriage. When you come back to Houston, if you're still interested in a relationship, maybe we can talk things out, see how both of us feel."

"That's nearly two months away, Sage."

"I know. I'm hoping by then I'll be able to see things more clearly."

Phillip's voice thinned. "You're making a very bad decision, Sage. Sooner or later, you're going to regret it."

"Perhaps I will, but this is something I have to do."

His voice hardened. "All right, fine. From now on, I shall consider that both of us are free to do as we wish."

The implied threat should have bothered her. What Phillip might do. What she might do. Instead, she felt as if a weight had been lifted off her shoulders.

"That's only fair."

"Nothing about this is fair, Sage. I'm hoping you'll see that before it's too late." The line went dead.

If Phillip were a different man, she might have felt sorry for him. But their decision to marry had been based on friendship and practicality. Phillip would be upset, even angry, but he wouldn't be hurting.

Sage hung up the receiver. It was over. She wasn't exactly sure what she was feeling. Lighter, in a way. Less burdened. Part of her worried about how to tell Ian, and what he would say when she did. Part of her was terrified she had made the wrong decision.

She told herself she had time to reconsider. Phillip wouldn't tell Ian. Or at least she didn't think he would. He'd be certain she would rethink her decision, eventually come to her senses.

Maybe she would. In the meantime, she would take things slowly. Just do what felt right.

As she crossed to the kitchen sink and filled a glass with water, the exhaustion she had put on the back burner hit her again. She would worry about all this later. She had a big day tomorrow.

Sage drank the water and trudged off to bed, hoping she'd be able to sleep. And trying to convince herself everything would work out.

"I need you to make a stop this morning," Jake said to Linc as he climbed into the SUV the following morning. "Atlas Security. I need to check on a couple of things and talk to Alex."

Jake figured he'd be there. Alex was usually in early, and Jake didn't want to talk to him on the phone or with other people around. And the office wasn't far away.

Annie was already there when he arrived, sitting behind the front desk, working on something at the computer.

"So you're still around," she said. "I was beginning to wonder, since I hadn't seen you in a while. Thought maybe you'd made a run for it. Couldn't handle a strong woman like Sage Dumont, and hightailed it back to Mexico."

Irritation slipped through him. "I'm handling Sage just fine." *He wished.* He'd like nothing better than to get his hands on that sweet little body. But after the conversation they'd had out at the ranch, and knowing now what she and her mother had suffered, he figured she didn't need the guilt she was bound to feel if she cheated on the man she was going to marry.

And if she did, Jake knew he wouldn't like it one damned bit when she was back in Phillip's bed.

"Alex in?"

"In the back, getting coffee." Annie's sour expression softened. "You look like you could use a cup yourself." She came out from behind the desk. "I made some brownies. You know how you like my brownies. Why don't I get you one? Might as well bring you some coffee, too."

"Thanks, Annie." She might have a caustic tongue, but deep down she was a cream puff.

He headed into the main part of the office. Alex was just walking out of the kitchen, carrying two cups of coffee. "I heard you come in." He handed one to Jake, who blew across the top and took a grateful sip. "Thanks."

Annie appeared and handed him a brownie. "A growing boy needs to keep up his strength."

Jake and Alex both grinned, then walked over to Alex's desk and sat down.

"What's up?" Alex asked.

Briefly, Jake filled him in on the conversation between Roshan and Quadim he'd overheard at the ranch, about the money, the shipment, the possibility the men were involved with drugs.

"You sure you got it right?" Alex asked. "Been a while since you were over there."

"Ninety percent certain. Need to be a hundred percent before we go any further."

Alex shook his head. "Man, when you took this job, you sure got than you bargained for."

"True enough. But I'm in it now. Nothing I can do but charge forward. Which is the reason I came by to see you. Tonight Roshan and Quadim are planning to go out on the town. I talked to Linc. Went over last night and put a bug in the limo he arranged for them to use. Got a parabolic mic hooked into a hidden USB recorder. We'll get everything they say."

Alex grinned, flashing his dimples. "That oughta be interesting."

"If we pick up any hint they're involved in something illegal, I'd like you to talk to that professor friend of yours who teaches Arabic out at the university."

"Adam Haddad? Good idea. You get something, we'll have him translate. He can confirm you heard right the first time."

"Bugging a car is a serious breach of privacy. Haddad might not want to get involved."

"Then we'll keep his name out of it. And we won't tell him who's speaking on the recording or where we got it. That ought to keep him out of trouble if something goes wrong."

Jake nodded. "That'd be great. Thanks."

The two men left the office and headed out for the day, Jake in the SUV with Linc, Alex in his own car.

Three hours after he'd arrived with Sage at Weis, Weis, Silverman and Schultz, Jake walked the floor outside the conference room where the meeting was being held.

Legs splayed, Alex stood next to the closed door. With his blond hair, blue eyes and perfectly tailored Italian suit, he looked like a model in *GQ* magazine. Of course, the average male model didn't carry a Smith and Wesson .45 in a shoulder harness under his jacket.

Inside the room, Sage and her assistant, Will Bailey, along with her purchasing agent, Red Williams, sat across the gleaming mahogany table from Sheik Khalid, Yasar and Roshan. The lawyers were also in there, Robert Schultz and his assistant acting for Marine Drilling, Eric Nadar and a junior attorney representing Saudi interests.

One of the sheik's bodyguards stood across from Alex, another roamed the floor of the elegant offices styled in an old-world design with dark green carpets, plush sofas and gold-framed paintings of English hunting scenes on the walls. The negotiations were now officially in progress.

"How do you think she's doing?" Alex asked, leaving his post to join Jake, out of earshot down the hall from the elevators.

"Sage is a smart lady, and the sheik, aside from whatever prejudices he carries, is a well-educated man. My bet is she'll do just fine."

"I wouldn't bet against her. I like her." Alex glanced at Jake. "From what I can tell, you more than like her."

He shrugged. "I won't lie about it. She's beautiful and intelligent and sexy as hell. But she belongs to another man. Long as that's so, I'm not interested."

"Right."

Jake's mouth twitched. "Well, I'm plenty interested, but I'm not dumb enough to make that kind of mistake."

Alex didn't say more. He didn't date married women or those who were spoken for, either. He didn't have to. With his looks, Alex pretty much had his pick of women. Jake's mind flashed to Sabrina Eckhart, with her fiery hair and sassy smile. Well, at least most women.

The door opened just then and the sheik walked out, his white robes flowing around him. He was followed by Roshan, Yasar and their attorney.

Sage came out with Robert Schultz, followed by Will and Red.

"Nadar is taking Sheik Khalid and the others in their party to lunch in a private room at the Bristol Café. It's right next door."

Alex came to attention. "I'll check it out, make sure there's no problem with security." He strode off toward the elevator, pushed the button and disappeared inside.

"What about you?" Jake asked Sage.

"Robert's having some sandwiches and soft drinks brought in. We'll have a working lunch right here."

Jake nodded. "Sounds good." Safer, anyway. "How's it going so far?"

She flicked a glance toward the conference room. "You know basically what's going on in there. We're trying to buy a deepwater drilling platform and as much class one, five-inch pipe as they've got available. We've bought pipe from them before, but we need more. The deal also involves some miscellaneous drilling equipment, diesel engines, drill collars, those kinds of items, but the main thing is the platform. Used, it's valued at over two hundred million."

"Not small change," Jake said.

"No. These days used platforms are hard to find, and new ones take forever to build, plus the cost is out of sight. We've offered two hundred fifty for the package. Sheik Khalid wants three-fifty, plus a few hundred thousand extra for the pipe and miscellaneous."

She flashed Jake a look. "Let's see…we're only a hundred million apart, so we're doing just great."

He felt the tug of a smile. "Nothing's ever easy."

Red Williams walked up just then, his graying red hair neatly combed and his suit smartly pressed.

"Don't let her kid you. She's got 'em on the run. It's the way the game is played, and Sage is making all the right moves."

Jake smiled again. "I figured."

Sage smiled for an instant, then her eyes met his and slid away. "We need to get going." She tapped the notepad she held in one hand. "Lots of things to talk about."

She was all business today. Keeping her distance, concentrating on her work. He told himself it was exactly the way it should be. Sage was damn good at her job and she was determined to put this deal together.

It should have been a turnoff, a woman that preoccupied with her career. Instead, he liked her efficiency, her drive to succeed.

Jake told himself she wasn't really avoiding him. The uneasy looks she gave him when she thought he didn't see meant nothing. But his sixth sense was telling him that something was going on, that something had subtly changed.

The afternoon passed the same as the morning, with a couple of breaks that didn't last long, and everyone getting more and more uptight. By six o'clock, the group was exhausted, and Schultz called for an end to the session.

When the conference room door opened and the tired-looking crew walked out, Jake's gaze went to Sage.

"You look beat," he said as he reached her. Tired but beautiful, though he didn't say that. "Let's get you home."

She sighed. "I need to stop at the office." She raked a hand through her heavy dark hair, shoving it back from her face. "Pick up some notes and files I need to go over."

"Not a problem." The demonstrations were still going on, but had begun to weaken. According to the morning news, less than half as many people were marching around outside the building now.

The Saudis dispersed to the SUVs waiting for them, and Sage walked out between Alex and Jake.

"I'll see you in the morning," Alex said, and waved as he headed for his flashy BMW. Will and Red had also driven their own cars. Jake led Sage toward the shiny black Escalade that Linc was driving, and helped her in.

"Everybody buckled up?" Linc asked when they'd settled in.

"All set," Jake said.

Sage sat rigidly beside him. She was still keeping her distance, making a point of staying away from him as much as she could. Jake was beginning to believe that instead of her being stressed over business, her reaction had something to do with him.

He might be wrong. Maybe it was just some personal matter that didn't involve him. Still, he couldn't shake the feeling that something had shifted between them. Something important.

You're losing it, buddy, he told himself, but he couldn't shake the feeling.

Chapter 14

Sage let Jake guide her through the diminishing crowd at the rear of the building, then hurried in through the back door the security guard held open for them.

She said nothing as they walked into the elevator and the doors slid closed, sealing them inside. She didn't look at Jake as they were whisked up to the executive floor, but her senses were keenly aware of him, as they had been all day. She knew exactly how far away he stood, recognized the faint scent of his cologne. The brush of his coat sleeve as the doors opened and they walked out had goose bumps feathering her skin.

Jake was tall and powerfully built, and that alone attracted her. That he was handsome and strikingly male made him even more appealing. She tried not to wonder how he would look with his shirt off, how it would feel to run her fingers over all those hard muscles.

Add the chemistry between them that made her heart pound every time he walked into a room, and it was the perfect recipe for wild, erotic sex.

At least the kind of fantasy sex she had only imagined and never actually experienced.

From the start, she had fought to keep her desire for Jake under control. Now, as he followed her into the office and closed the door, that control was slipping badly. As Jake tossed his jacket over the back of a chair, she forced herself to focus on what she was doing. Her hand shook as she went to the mahogany credenza behind her desk, pulled open one of the drawers and found the files she had come for. She looked inside the folder, saw the notes she needed, turned and spotted Jake.

His intense blue eyes were watching her—perceptive eyes that saw more than she wanted them to.

"Something's happened," he said flatly. "What is it?"

She moistened her lips. She didn't have to tell him. She told herself to wait, think things through, take it slowly. Told herself she couldn't afford to make a mistake.

"Tell me," he demanded, and it wasn't her bodyguard talking, it was Jake Cantrell, the man.

"I phoned Phillip last night in Edinburgh. I…" She swallowed. "I broke our engagement."

Jake's nostrils flared. "You talked to Phillip?"

"That's right."

"You told him you aren't going to marry him."

"I don't know… I mean, I told him I wasn't ready. I needed more time. I said maybe later…after we'd both had a chance to think things through...we could talk about it again."

"But right now you're a free woman. You've got no obligation to Phillip."

She squared her shoulders. "No."

"Then why are you still wearing his ring?"

She looked down at her hand as if it belonged to someone else, saw the flash of a clear white diamond. "I don't want the questions...not yet, not while I'm in the middle of this deal."

Jake's eyes bored into her. He took a couple of deep breaths. When he turned and locked the door, Sage's senses went on alert. Those long, powerful legs carried him toward her. Jake hauled her into his arms and his mouth crushed down over hers. There was nothing gentle in the kiss, nothing tender. It was a man's kiss, hot and fierce, a man letting her know what he intended.

Desire washed through her, thick and heavy, so potent it made her dizzy. "Jake..." she whispered as her arms went around his neck. She swayed against him, kissed him back as wildly as he was kissing her.

She wasn't sure what she had expected—not the wet, deep, openmouthed kisses, not the slick tangling of tongues or the spiraling heat. Or being pulled into the V between his thighs, feeling his hardness, his hunger for her.

She didn't expect his lips to turn gentle, coaxing. To find they would be softer than she had imagined, that they would meld perfectly with hers and turn her legs to jelly, that Jake would have to hold her up.

"Easy," he whispered.

"Don't stop."

"I'm not stopping," he said, and kissed her deeply, kissed her like she'd never been kissed before. "I'm taking you right here, right now. It's way past time and we both know it."

She made a little sound in her throat as he covered her lips again, ravished them. Need speared through her, tugged low in her belly. Her skin felt hot and damp, stretched too tight. All she could think of was getting closer, touching him, having him touch her.

He tugged her silk blouse free of the waistband of her skirt, began to work the small pearl buttons up the front. Her hands trembled as she tried to help him, and several buttons tore loose, one popping off and rolling across the floor.

"Don't stop," she said again, though there wasn't the slightest chance he would. The blouse disappeared. Jake unsnapped the front of her blue satin pushup bra, drew it off her shoulders, tossed it away.

"Beautiful," he said, reaching out to cup a breast, running his thumb over the crest, making it tighten and throb.

Sage trembled. She reached for him. His jacket was gone. She began to work the buttons on his short-sleeved white shirt, getting most of them open before Jake grabbed the fabric at the back of his neck and pulled the shirt off over his head.

Her gaze ran over his perfect V-shaped body, all solid muscle, thick slabs that rippled wherever he moved. His waist was narrow, his stomach flat and ridged with muscle. His biceps bulged as he bent his head and fastened his mouth on her breast, and Sage whimpered.

The rough glide of his tongue across her nipple

made her quiver with need. She slid her fingers into his short dark hair and arched her back to give him better access. Desire burned through her, more intense than she could have imagined, so hot she thought she might faint.

She hardly noticed when he lifted her and set her on the edge of the desk. The calendar, desk pad and expensive black onyx pen set Phillip had given her went flying. Jake kissed her deeply, slid her skirt up over her hips, reached down and caught hold of her panties, dragging them down her legs. Her high heels clattered onto the floor and her mouth went dry.

She looked down, saw the blue satin thong panties she had teased him about the night they had gone to the IMAX. They draped over his hand, looking even tinier. She told herself she hadn't worn them on purpose, hadn't expected this. Hadn't hoped it would happen.

Knew it was a lie.

"Next time, I want to see these on you before I take them off." And then he was leaning over her, kissing her breasts, stroking her, finding her slick and wet and hot. She was trembling, couldn't quite catch her breath. She had no idea when he had removed the pistol and holster from his belt, but they were gone. She heard the buzz of his zipper as he freed himself.

Her eyes widened. "Oh, my God."

"I'm a big man, Sage."

"Yes, I—I see that."

He kissed her deeply. "We'll take it easy. I won't hurt you. Trust me to take care of you." He kissed her again, kissed her until she was breathing hard, squirming against the desktop, silently begging him to take her. He didn't disappoint, just eased himself deeply inside.

"You okay?"

She swallowed, nodded, gripped his powerful shoulders. She was more than okay. By the time he was fully seated, she was on fire. Unconsciously, her hips bucked beneath him, and Jake groaned. Then he began to move.

Faster. Deeper. Harder.

"Don't stop," she pleaded, wanting what his hard body promised, wanting that elusive something that was building inside her.

"Just hang on," he said gruffly. "We're a long ways from stopping."

And when he drove deeply, when he took her with all that power and strength, when Sage started coming and didn't think the pleasure was ever going to end, she knew that whatever happened, Jake had just made her secret fantasy come true. And she would never forget it.

Jake waited outside the bathroom in Sage's office. He'd known it would be good between them. It was way better than that. He might have smiled, if thinking about it wasn't making him hard all over again.

His weapon was clipped back on his belt. The condom he'd used was gone. He was dressed once more, and when Sage walked out of the bathroom, so was she. When she looked at him, her cheeks colored and she glanced away.

"We'd better go," she said, straightening the items on her desk a second time. She didn't mention it, but the pen set looked a little worse for wear. "I've got a long day tomorrow."

Long night, too, he figured. Or at least that was his plan. "I called Linc, told him we got tied up. He's waiting out back."

Sage just nodded and walked out of the office in front of him.

The crowd outside the building had diminished even further. It looked as if things were starting to settle down. There was no media around and only a couple of people carried signs. One said Free Palestine, another said Dumont Traitors. That one bothered Jake. He thought of the guy in the restaurant. Big balls, no brains. He didn't like to think where that might lead.

Sage didn't say anything on the way to the Escalade. She managed a smile for Linc as they settled themselves inside and fastened their seat belts.

"Drop us off at my place," Jake said. "We're going to go out and grab a bite, then I'll drive Sage home. No use you having to wait for us."

"You sure?" Linc asked, meeting his gaze in the mirror. He was always conscientious, but there was hope in his voice. It had been a long day for him, too, and it was going to be another long day tomorrow.

Jake flicked Sage a glance. "I'm sure," he said, when he caught that deer-in-the-headlights look in her eyes. She wasn't sure what she should do, but he was. He wanted a helluva lot bigger taste of her than he'd just had, and he figured, whether she knew it or not, the feeling was mutual.

Linc dropped them off at Jake's apartment. "See you both in the morning," he said with a tired smile.

Jake grabbed his suit coat out of the car and closed

the door. He guided Sage up the front steps, and she waited while he unlocked the door, then walked inside and turned off the alarm. When he looked up, she was prowling the living room, wandering over to the big window looking out at the fountains, trees and flowers in the open rectangular area surrounded by apartments.

"I didn't know there was any place like this in Houston."

He tossed his coat over the arm of an overstuffed chair. "It's a real find. A little slice of green right in the city."

She turned, looked up at him. "We've just had the most incredible sex, but the truth is I don't even know you."

His mouth hitched up. "Oh, I think you do. After what just happened, I think we know each other pretty damned well." But not as well as they would by morning.

"That's not what I mean."

He crossed his arms over his chest. "All right, what would you like to know?"

Sage moved restlessly, stopping in front of him. "I checked you out on the internet. I know you were born in Iowa. I know you were in Marine Special Forces— Ian told me you were a sniper."

"That's right."

"And you worked in South America."

"I did a lot of corporate protection down there."

"Like you're doing with me."

He grinned. "Honey, it was nothing like what I'm doing with you."

Her cheeks flushed. She was always so in control. He liked that he could fluster her a little.

"What about your family?" she asked. "Are your parents still living?"

"I was a senior in high school when my dad died. Heart attack. As soon as I got out of junior college I enlisted."

"Because of your dad?"

"Maybe. Dad was a marine and I admired him. Serving my country was important to me, something I'd always planned to do."

"What about your mother?"

"She married a guy she'd dated in high school. Big rivalry between him and my dad over which one she would choose. My dad won. Thing is, I look a lot like him. Same size, same build. I'm a constant reminder of Sam Cantrell, which made a problem for my mother. It was one of the reasons I left when I did. One of the reasons I don't see her very often."

Jake reached out and wrapped a hand around Sage's waist, drawing her closer. He caught a hint of her perfume—jasmine, maybe, or lilac. It made him hard. "Anything else you want to know?"

"Why did you leave the military?"

"I never planned to make it a career. I had things I wanted to do, places I wanted to see."

She looked up at him, moistened those tempting lips. "Are we really going out to dinner?"

Jake slid his fingers into her hair, tilted her head back and kissed her until she was molded against him, gripping the front of his shirt. "What do you think?" he whispered against her ear.

Sage let go of his shirt, reached up and slid her

arms around his neck. Hot, deep kisses followed and his arousal strengthened. Man, the lady could kiss.

"I've never felt this kind of hunger," she said, "but it isn't for food."

"I'll second that." Nipping the side of her neck, he lifted her up and carried her into the bedroom, took his time stripping off her clothes.

She had a slender, beautiful body, with long legs and ripe, full breasts tipped with small pink nipples. He liked kissing her, liked the way she tasted, the way she smelled. Once they were in bed, he took his time with her breasts, enjoying the way they felt in his hands. He loved the little noises she made when he took them in his mouth.

He rose above her, entered her in a single deep thrust that had her arching up from the bed. He tried to go slow, be gentle, but ended up taking her hard. He'd wanted her so damn long, so damn much. Sage took all he could give and wanted more.

After another heated round they got out of bed and wandered into his kitchen, actually feeling hungry for food this time.

"All I've got is bacon and eggs, and some leftover pizza."

Sage smiled. "Pizza sounds great."

"Nuke it or heat it in the oven?"

She grabbed the box out of his hand, set it on the granite countertop and opened the lid. "Pepperoni— my favorite." Picking up a slice, she started nibbling her way from the point toward the crust.

"You're kidding. You actually like cold pizza?"

The big bite she took said yes, and watching those pretty lips wrap around all that sausage and cheese made him think raunchy thoughts, so the blood rushed back into his groin.

Sage finished off the slice while Jake zapped a couple pieces in the microwave.

"I love pizza," she said. "Any way, shape or form. I don't have it often because I try to eat healthy, and pizza is too fattening." She grabbed another slice out of the box. "I'm making an exception tonight."

"Second exception of the day."

"What was the first?"

"I'm betting it was having sex on the desk in your office."

She blushed, turned away. "You'd win the bet."

The microwave dinged and he went to retrieve the bubbling slices of pizza. He carried them on a paper plate to the table and sat down across from where Sage was now sitting in front of the empty box.

"How about the kitchen counter?" he asked, thinking of those blue satin panties, and no longer interested in food. "Ever done that before?"

She glanced up, looking interested, which made him even harder. "There are lots of things I haven't done before."

His erection throbbed. "I can take care of that."

Sage yelped as he left his pizza on the table, lifted her up and carried her back to his bedroom. The counter could wait. He had a couple of things to show her right there in his bed.

Chapter 15

Jake slept like a dead man until Sage shook him awake at four o'clock in the morning.

"I need you to take me home. I've got to shower and put on fresh clothes."

He just nodded, yawned and rolled out of bed. He couldn't help a smile when he glanced over at the woman standing across from him, her mink-brown hair a tangle around her shoulders, little red love bites on her neck, her lips swollen from his kisses. He went hard just looking at her.

She turned away, still a little shy around him, and gasped when she caught sight of herself in the mirror. "Oh, my God, I look awful."

"You look well-loved, honey. Nothing wrong with that."

"There's plenty wrong with it when you're a business-woman trying to negotiate a multimillion-dollar deal."

He grinned. "That's why makeup was invented."

She almost smiled. But already her mind had returned to business. Jake forced his thoughts in the same direction. He had a job to do. He'd been hired to protect her. That he'd taken the lady to bed didn't change that.

He pulled on a pair of jeans and drove her home. Walked her up to her apartment, checked each room. Found nothing out of order.

Sage walked him to the door. When she looked up at him, he saw in those golden-brown eyes what was coming.

"About last night…"

Here it was. He was only a little surprised. "Go on."

"What happened between us…it was amazing, Jake, really, but…"

"But what?"

"But it…it really shouldn't happen again."

He lifted an eyebrow. "Probably shouldn't," he agreed, and caught a flash of something in her face. "But it's going to. Count on it, honey." Then he reached for her, hauled her into his arms and very thoroughly kissed her.

Sage made no protest. Instead, she kissed him back. Her warm gaze followed him out the door.

Cocky SOB, Sage thought as she marched toward the shower. Cocksure of himself and of her. Maybe he had it right, she thought, because sure as hell, she wasn't through with Jake Cantrell, and apparently he wasn't through with her.

She'd said it shouldn't happen again. Said it because it was true. She should have kept her life in order, gone forward with her plans to marry Phillip. It would have been the smart thing to do.

But mostly she had said it to see what Jake would say. See if he was one of those guys only interested in a one-night stand, in making a conquest. She hadn't expected the sharp ache that struck her when he had momentarily agreed.

Or the relief when he'd made it clear it wasn't over between them.

She told herself it was only sexual attraction. How could any woman resist a man with the body of a god, beautiful blue eyes that had a way of seeing inside her, and a brain to go with such a virile package?

She told herself the fire would burn out, that it was just an itch that had become so strong she'd had no choice but to scratch it.

But when he'd been kissing her, touching her, moving deep inside her, it felt like so much more.

Just take it slowly, she told herself. *Let things unfold in their own time, their own way. See where it leads.*

She really had no other choice.

Jake didn't go back to sleep, just went home, showered and dressed for the day in a conservative dark blue suit. His first stop was Freedom Limousine. He phoned Linc ahead and his friend met him there. The shiny black, nine-passenger stretch that Roshan and Quadim had used for their adventures last night was parked in its usual place.

Linc clicked open the locks and Jake climbed in to collect his gear. The partition between the driver and passengers was still rolled up. With any luck, the body-guards had ridden at the opposite end of the car, far enough away to allow Roshan and Quadim to speak privately.

The mic was good enough to pick up even the faintest whisper.

A pair of empty highball glasses lay on the floor. The Scotch decanter sat empty in the otherwise fully stocked, wood-grained bar. Jake reached underneath to retrieve his recording equipment, anxious to learn what secrets might be revealed.

Maybe nothing. Maybe he'd heard wrong. He'd had time to think about it. The wind could have distorted the words or his memory could have been playing tricks. He prayed the tape would end this nagging feeling that Roshan was into something that could completely derail Sage's carefully laid plans.

Jake thought of his departure that morning from her apartment and smiled to himself. She might not *want* to want him, but she did. The fire burning between them wasn't out, not by a long shot.

"You get it?" Linc asked, his thick black brows pulling together as Jake emerged from the car.

"I got it. Now we need to find out what's on it."

"You want to use my computer?"

He checked his watch. "Gonna take some time to play it all back. If the men made the rounds and traveled to and from the hotel, they could have been in the car off and on for a couple of hours."

"We got some time. I'll make us a pot of coffee."

"Thanks." Jake followed Linc into the office, a sparsely furnished main room that held a few desks with computers. A brown vinyl sofa and chair around a walnut coffee table served as a waiting area.

While his friend headed for the employee lounge to

make the coffee, Jake went into Linc's private office, sat at the metal desk and turned on the computer. Reaching down, he plugged in the USB flash recorder he had retrieved from the limo, and the tiny light that said it was working came on. Clearing his mind, he leaned back to listen, trying to absorb the Arabic words and recall what they meant as the two cousins laughed and conversed. The bodyguards, seated at the opposite end of the limo as Jake had guessed, rarely spoke.

Half an hour later, downing his second cup of black coffee, he turned to see Linc walking back into the office.

"Time to pick up your lady," his friend said, making Jake wonder if he'd guessed that Sage had spent most of last night at Jake's apartment. But his friend's dark face was carefully blank.

"She won't be happy if we're late," Linc finished.

"Knowing Sage, if we aren't there on time, she'll take off by herself, and I don't want that to happen. Let's go." Ejecting the drive, he shoved it into his pocket, and they headed out to the big black SUV.

They were talking as they headed outside. They had almost reached the Escalade when Jake heard the faint sound of a click. An instant later, the black car exploded in a fiery flash of heat and blinding light, a shattering roar that split the air and rocked the ground.

"Get down!" Jake yelled, hurling himself against the more slender man, taking him down behind a low brick wall, dodging the eruption of fire and killing debris.

A second blast went off, sending one of the car doors whizzing through the air, while flames erupted out the windows and pieces of glass and metal sliced into the wall in front of them like shrapnel. The crackle of fire and the smells of burning fuel and melting rubber filled the yard.

Jake climbed slowly to his feet, his gaze shooting to the pile of burning metal that used to be an expensive SUV.

Linc rubbed his side. "Dammit, man, I think you broke a couple of ribs." But he brushed off his clothes and got gingerly to his feet.

"Better that than being dead," Jake said, feeling a sting where a piece of hot metal had scorched a path across his thigh. He fingered the hole in his trousers and silently mourned the loss of one of his good suits.

Beside him, Linc's eyes remained riveted on the burning car. A little of the color had drained from his dark face.

"Man, oh, man, couple more minutes, you and me would have been toast."

"Twenty minutes and Sage would have been in there with us."

"Jesus."

"Any chance this was aimed at someone else? Another one of your customers?"

"You mean some lowlife drug dealer who rents my cars to smuggle dope? Or maybe one of my pimp customers?"

"Very funny."

"The answer is no." Linc grinned. "I haven't pissed anyone off lately and I don't cater to clients with those kinds of enemies. At least I didn't until you came along."

Jake flashed him a dark look and pulled out his cell. He dialed 911, told the dispatcher what had happened, then called Sage.

"We've got a problem."

"What is it?"

"Somebody planted a bomb in our ride."

"What?" Her breathing quickened. "Someone blew up the car? Oh, my God."

"Take it easy. The good news is no one was inside when it went off."

"Are you…are you all right? You weren't hurt?" A slight tremor rang in her voice. "You and Linc… you're both okay?"

"We're both just fine. The police are on the way. This may take a while."

"I—I can't believe this. I've got…got to get to work. The sheik will be waiting. We've got meetings scheduled all day."

Jake's fingers tightened around the phone. "Dammit, are you hearing me, Sage? Someone tried to blow one or all of us to kingdom come. Your damn meetings are the least of your problems."

A long silence streched. "You're right… I'm sorry. I—I'm not thinking clearly. What should we do?"

His mind went back to the explosion. Aside from the fact the car was a melted, burned-up heap of metal, there was a lot they didn't know. He knew how important this deal was to Sage, how hard she had worked to put it all together.

"I'll tell you what. I'll call Alex, tell him what's going on. He can pick you up and take you to midtown. You can talk to the sheik, tell him about the bomb, see what he wants to do. He may want to go home, Sage. He's got his family to think of. It's probably what I'd do."

"Yes…yes, of course. But…"

"But what?"

"We've been using the same car every day, right? So the bomb must have been meant for me."

Jake's stomach knotted. Not much question of that. Whoever had rigged the explosion wouldn't have been interested in him or Linc. Sage Dumont was the target. The knot twisted tighter. "Most likely. So...?"

"So that's what I'll tell Sheik Khalid. The bomb was meant for me, not him. Maybe he'll decide to stay."

"The sheik might also be in danger, Sage. It's only fair that he knows it."

"I'll tell him the truth."

Jake released a slow breath. "All right, I'll see you in midtown. Till then, do exactly what Alex tells you. *Exactly.* You got that?"

"I will, I promise."

Jake hung up the phone. All he could think of was getting to Sage, making sure she was safe. But he trusted Alex Justice, and he needed to talk to the police. He needed to find out who the hell had planted that bomb and why it had gone off before Sage was in the car.

He needed to find out why nobody was dead.

Sage sat tensely in the seat next to Alex Justice as he pulled his dark blue BMW coupe up to the curb in the yellow loading zone in front of Weis, Weis, Silverman and Schultz.

"Stay here." With a warning glance in her direction to ensure she did what he told her, he climbed out of the car. After a brief surveillance of the area from where he stood, he started toward the glass front doors.

As he made his way there, Sage watched how his head moved from side to side, up and down. How he looked backward and forward, checking for someone who might be sitting in a parked car, on a nearby roof-top, or walking down the block, anyone who might pose a danger.

Apparently satisfied it was safe to go inside, he re-turned to the car, opened Sage's door and helped her out of the vehicle. He must have felt her trembling. The minute they stepped into the foyer, he turned and caught her arm to steady her.

"You okay?"

She nodded. On the way to Midtown, it had finally hit her that this morning she could have been killed. All of them could have been.

She clamped her teeth together to stop the chatter-ing and steeled herself. "I'm okay."

"Let's go." Alex stayed close beside her, putting himself between her and whatever might be waiting. They went into the elevator, rode up to the third floor and stepped outside.

Alex led her to the conference room, opened the door for her then closed it behind her, and took up a position outside.

She was a few minutes late, so everyone was al-ready there—Will and Red, Robert Shultz and his as-sistant, the sheik, Roshan and the rest of the Saudi entourage in their immaculate white robes. Eric Nadar and his assistant were there, all seated around the long mahogany table sipping mugs of coffee or tea.

Shoving aside her battered emotions, Sage drew herself up. "I'm sorry to keep you waiting. Some-thing's happened I need to tell you about."

For the next twenty minutes, she relayed what had occurred at Freedom Limousine, telling them about the bomb and what little she knew about the circumstances of the explosion. She told them that the attempt was probably directed at her, and since no one was in the car at the time the bomb went off, perhaps it was just meant to be a warning.

At least that was her hope.

"As you know, there have been continuing protests outside the Marine Drilling offices, different groups demonstrating differing points of view." She fixed her attention on the sheik, whose expression was closed and hard. "A small group among the others seems to be violently opposed to our company doing business with you. Most of the protests have been peaceful and harmless, but it's possible some are willing to go further than just carrying signs."

The sheik eyed her darkly. "You say this happened early this morning?"

"That's right. I wasn't in the car yet. That's why I believe it was supposed to be some sort of warning. Whoever did this wants to stop us. Their goal is to keep us from making a deal that would benefit both our families. Both our countries."

The sheik leaned back in his chair. Yasar appeared clearly upset. Roshan and Quadim whispered together in tones too low to hear.

"This is quite an unexpected turn of events," the sheik said.

"Yes, it is," agreed Sage.

They discussed the situation awhile longer, talking about what should be done. Sage knew the police would want to speak to her as soon as possible, and would probably wish to speak to the sheik. She tried not to glance toward the door, hoping Jake would appear.

Finally, Khalid rose to his feet, followed by the rest of his entourage. "We will need more information before we decide what is to be done," he said. "I need to be certain of my family's safety."

The door opened just then and Jake walked in. Sage felt a powerful sweep of relief.

She flashed him a look that said she was glad he was there, then returned her attention to the sheik. "Marine Drilling will be bringing in extra security until this is resolved." Her gaze went to Jake, looking for reassurance. She prayed he and Trace Rawlins would be up to the job.

"We've already begun making arrangements," Jake said, picking up where she'd left off. "We'll have security people waiting at the hotel when you and your party arrive. The police are already working on a suspect list. With any luck, they'll have the man responsible in custody very soon."

The sheik turned to Sage. "I need to check on my family, tell them what has happened and make certain they are safe."

"Of course."

"The cars have all been thoroughly searched," Jake said. "You don't have to worry about that, Your Highness."

Khalid arched a silver-flecked eyebrow. "My people will make their own assessment." He returned his attention to Sage. "We will speak again at the end of the day."

She just nodded. There was nothing more she could do. The Saudis swept out of the conference room, Yasar, Roshan and Quadim, following the sheik. The bodyguards appeared as if they'd been conjured up, and the group and their attorneys headed for the elevators.

Sage walked over to Jake. She felt drained and filled with uncertainty. And when she looked at him and thought that he might have died in that car, something tightened in her chest. "Are you sure you're all right?"

He smiled. "Ruined my suit. Tore a hole in the pants, but aside from that, I'm fine. Linc wound up with a couple of bruised ribs. He still hasn't decided if he's going to forgive me."

She didn't see the humor. Clearly, he had shielded his friend with his body. It was just what Jake would do. "You could have been killed. Both of you. As much as I don't want to, I think I should cancel the rest of the meetings."

His gaze didn't waver. "You can do that, but it might not make any difference."

"Why not?"

"Whatever his reason for planting that bomb, if this guy is focused on you, he might not stop just because the Saudis go home."

Her stomach contracted. She sank down in one of the high-backed conference chairs, her legs suddenly weak. "I never thought of that."

Jake walked over and poured a mug of coffee from the service on the sideboard, came back and handed it to her. Sage's hands shook as she blew on it, then took a bracing sip.

He reached down and touched her cheek. "I won't let anyone hurt you, Sage. We'll beef everything up, make doubly sure you aren't at risk."

She thought of her grandfather and her eyes suddenly widened. "Oh, my God. Ian. We need to put a man with Ian. Someone good. Someone you trust, Jake."

He didn't hesitate. "Ben Slocum. Ex-SEAL. Works with me at Atlas. He's one of the best."

Sage moistened her lips, which felt like cotton. "Do it now."

"Already done."

"You talked to Ian?"

"Soon as I got off the phone with you. He's worried about you. He wants the meetings ended."

Exhaustion washed over her. "You're right in what you said. It might not make any difference. I'm not ending the negotiations unless the Saudis decide to go home."

"Which they very well may."

"I know. But the sheik is a proud man and I have a hard time seeing him back away from a fight."

"Or you," Jake said.

Her shoulders went a little straighter as she shoved herself to her feet. "Or me. I have a hard time letting some sick creep dictate my life. I want him caught, Jake."

"The police have the name of the guy who accosted you in the restaurant. They're bringing him in for questioning. We'll know more about the bomb after their explosive experts take a look at it."

"Why did it go off so early? Why not later, when we were all inside the car?"

"Had to be either a malfunction of the device, or whoever put it there only wanted to scare us."

Sage sighed, raked back her hair. "Well, if he wanted to scare us, he succeeded."

A protective gleam entered Jake's eyes and his jaw hardened. "Yes, he did."

Chapter 16

Not needing Alex until the following morning, Jake drove Sage from midtown to her Marine Drilling office downtown. Ian was there when they arrived, pulling Sage into a hug, telling her how worried he was, hugging her hard again. He introduced her to Ben Slocum, who was acting as his bodyguard, then led her into his office and firmly closed the door.

Ben stood guard outside. Six-two, lean, sculpted and hard as a brick wall, he was swarthy skinned, with the palest blue eyes Jake had ever seen.

The Iceman, they'd called him in the SEALS. Cool as ice, Jake figured, and it was true.

Jake looked at Ben and tipped his head toward the tall mahogany door in the CEO's impressive office. "Ian handling this okay?"

"He doesn't like having a babysitter—that's what he

said. But the man's no fool. He'll handle it fine. Mostly he's worried about his granddaughter."

"I don't blame him." And along with the danger Sage was facing from an unknown assailant, there was the emotional danger she faced from Jake. Already he had derailed her perfectly laid out future. She had ended her engagement because of him, because she'd wanted him and didn't know what to do about that. She hadn't been able to ignore it, had to find a way to deal with it.

And it wasn't over yet.

How Jake felt about the situation, he wasn't quite sure. Not sorry. After last night, he would never be sorry. He'd ached with wanting her. Still did.

At the moment, his main concern was keeping her safe.

"How's Sage doing?" Ben asked.

"She's a lot like her grandfather. She's tough when she needs to be."

His colleague watched him closely. "Seems like a good lady."

Jake glanced away. "Seems to be."

"She's definitely hot. Maybe I should ask her out."

Jake's gaze swung to his friend. "You do and you're a dead man."

Ben actually laughed, which he didn't do that often. "I figured. Just thought I'd check."

Jake stared at Ian's closed office door. "Who else is in there?"

"One of the VPs, her assistant, a couple of other employees."

Jake looked down the hall to find the black-haired

receptionist, Marie Castelo, walking toward them with cups of coffee in her hands.

"I thought you might need this," she said, handing each of them a cup.

"Thanks, Marie," Ben said, having already made a conquest. Marie was older and probably married. She had a son, Jake recalled, but she was female and she wasn't dead. Ben was the epitome of tall, dark and handsome, and women seemed drawn to his forbidding nature. When it came to the opposite sex, Ben was far more ruthless than Alex, but the ladies didn't seem to mind.

"I heard what happened this morning," Marie said. "We all did. Mr. Dumont is terribly worried."

"The police are on the job," Jake said. "They're hoping to make an arrest very soon."

"I pray they do." She glanced at the closed office door, looked back at him. "I'm glad you're here to take care of her."

He smiled. "So am I."

"Well, let me know if there's anything either of you need." Turning, she headed back to her desk.

Sage walked out a moment later and made her way over to Jake.

"What's the verdict?" he asked.

"Ian's agreed to wait until we hear from the sheik." Her smile looked weary. "Convincing him took some doing, I can tell you."

"He wants you safe."

"I know."

She turned to Ben. "My grandfather's ready to leave. You can go on in."

He gave a slight nod. "It was nice meeting you, Sage."

"You, too."

Ben cocked his head toward Jake, but spoke to Sage. "You can trust him to take care of you."

Sage looked at Jake. He could read the trust in her eyes, and his chest tightened.

"I know," she said simply.

Slocum turned and walked through the office door, heading toward the silver-haired man sitting behind his massive mahogany desk.

"I've got a couple of things to do in my office," Sage said. "It shouldn't take long."

"I'll be here whenever you're ready."

As she crossed the reception area toward her office, Jake's gaze ran over her. The tailored light blue business suit with its calf-length skirt and trim-fitting jacket did nothing to show off the luscious figure beneath. But after last night, he knew every curve, every sensuous hollow and valley, the exact shape of her upturned breasts. His hands fisted with the need to touch them, to peel off her clothes and take her again, learn even more of her secrets.

He reminded himself he needed to stay focused, keep his distance, do his job. He would, he knew. He would do whatever it took to keep her safe.

A man he didn't recognized walked up to the reception desk, wearing an immaculate dark gray suit and aviator glasses on his long, thin face.

"I'll tell her you wish to see her, Mr. Hunter," Marie said, reaching for the intercom.

Jake made his way over. "Jake Cantrell," he said. "I'm Ms. Dumont's protection. Do you work for Marine Drilling?"

"Jonathan Hunter. And yes, I work here."

"Mr. Hunter's one of the vice presidents," Marie interjected with a hint of uncertainty, since it was clear the man didn't appreciate Jake's interference.

Jake stepped out of the way. "Go ahead."

Hunter turned and headed for Sage's office, knocked lightly, walked in and closed the door.

Figuring he had a few minutes, Jake made a round of the floor, looking for anything suspicious, anything out of the ordinary. Finding nothing, he came back and stood next to Sage's office door.

She'd had a long, stressful day. He was hoping when she finished with Hunter, she'd be ready to go home.

Which was a whole new can of worms. Because no way was he letting her stay in her apartment alone, not without protection, not until they caught the joker who had tried to kill her. Jake was staying with her whether she wanted him to or not.

He figured she'd balk. It was one thing to sleep with a man, another to let him move in. *Should be an interesting argument,* he thought. One he meant to win.

"I'm sorry I missed the meeting," Jonathan said. "I had an appointment on the other side of town. Charlie just told me what happened. I wanted you to know how glad I am you weren't injured. Or for that matter, how glad I am no one was hurt."

The executive sat down in one of the cream leather chairs across from Sage. In his late forties, of medium height and build, he had black hair with the merest trace of gray at the temples. Jonathan's nose was too narrow, his lips a little too thin for him to be truly good-looking, but he was attractive, smart and capable, and aggressive in building his career.

If Sage didn't prove herself, he or Charlie Denton would be appointed president next year.

"I appreciate your concern, Jonathan. The police are interviewing suspects. We're hoping they'll be able to make an arrest very soon."

"They think it was one of the demonstrators?"

"It seems most likely. You should have seen the man who came barging into the Grill the other night. He was so mad he was spitting."

"I heard about that."

"Yes, well, it wouldn't be a stretch for me to imagine him planting a bomb."

"It could be him or any number of people. And from the signs I saw outside, it's hard to tell who the explosion might have been meant for."

She frowned. "You don't think I was the target?"

"I'm just saying...there's a lot of ill will in this country toward people from the Middle East. They could have been targeting the sheik or his family."

"The car that blew up was the one I've been riding in."

"Maybe whoever rigged the bomb didn't know that."

Her stomach twisted. It was a distinct possibility. All the black SUVs did look alike.

"I suppose that's true."

"I imagine the sheik will have to go home. It's the only sensible thing for him to do."

She glanced down at the notes she'd been making in the unlikely possibility he would stay, deal points she hoped might get him to consider a lower bid. "He's supposed to call me tonight and give me his decision."

"It could be dangerous for him to stay. Surely he knows that."

"Then you think he'll leave."

"I think he should, don't you?"

She closed her eyes and tipped her head back. She felt so weary. "I guess maybe he should."

"If he does, it isn't the end of the world. You can continue the negotiations long-distance. Or you could make a trip over there."

She shook her head. "The sheik already has other offers. If this doesn't gel, odds are he'll accept one of those."

Jonathan rose from his chair, smoothed the creases on his slacks. "Whatever happens, Sage, everyone knows you've done the best you could."

But sometimes doing your best wasn't enough. She rose from her chair, rounded the desk and walked him to the door.

"Thank you, Jonathan, for coming by. I really appreciate it."

He leaned over and kissed her cheek. "Be careful, Sage."

"I will." As he walked out, Sage saw Jake striding toward her. For an instant, she thought of the way they'd made love last night, and a wave of heat washed through her. She bit her lip. This wasn't the time to be thinking of sex. Not when some lunatic was out there trying to blow them up.

She sighed as Jake walked in and closed the door. He was standing so close she could touch him. She had to curl her fingers into her palms to keep from reaching for him. One look at her obviously weary expression, he caught her face between his big hands, bent and very softly kissed her.

"Everything's going to be all right."

Her throat tightened. She should have reminded him that she was still working, that at the office their relationship had to remain impersonal. Instead, she leaned into him, felt his hard arms wrap around her. She didn't pull away, just let him hold her, let some of his strength flow into her.

With a fortifying breath, she finally pulled away. "I hope you're right."

"The police picked up the guy from the restaurant. His name's Bert Hobson. They're questioning him as a person of interest."

She nodded. "That's good."

"Have you heard from the sheik?"

"Not yet. He's due to call anytime now."

"Or he might not phone for a couple more hours. He's got your cell number. I think you should go home and wait for him to contact you there."

She thought of the day she'd be facing tomorrow. If the sheik decided to leave, it was over. All the weeks of preparation, all the plans for assembling the offshore rig, to say nothing of the money all this had cost.

The whole project would end in failure. Along with the chance to do something that would make her grandfather proud. Something that would prove to him she could handle running the company.

"I'll take you home, Sage," Jake said softly.

She nodded and let him guide her toward the door.

"I need to stop by my apartment," Jake said mildly as they took the elevator down to the lobby. "I've got to pick up a couple of things."

His Jeep was parked in the executive lot some distance from where the last of the demonstrators were milling around the building. "I'll get the car. Stay in-side until I come back and get you."

He caught the flash of fear in her eyes.

"Don't worry, I'll check it before I get inside."

A tired, relieved smile curved those pretty lips. "Great."

A few minutes later he had her loaded safely aboard, and the Jeep was rolling down Montrose, turning onto Westheimer, weaving its way back to his place. Sage said little. He knew she just wanted to get home. But a quick stop first. He hadn't mentioned that the things he needed from his place were his shaving kit and change of clothes.

As they drove toward his apartment, Sage pulled out her cell phone. "I need to call Rina. I don't want her reading about this in the paper."

He overheard some of the conversation, the part where Sage downplayed the danger and Rina tried to get her to come over to her place and stay.

"I can't do that. I need to be home." She flicked a glance in his direction. "Jake's with me. I'll be fine."

He almost smiled. Jake was with her. What she hadn't figured out was that he didn't intend to leave.

He pulled up in front of his garage just as Trace's Jeep Grand Cherokee pulled into the visitor parking space right beside him. Jake turned off the engine, went around and opened Sage's door.

"Come on," he said. "There's someone I want you to meet."

She had trouble climbing down with her snug skirt longer than she was used to wearing. Jake lifted her, then set her on her feet in front of him. Her high heels pushed her up six inches. He could feel the tickle of her hair against his cheek, her soft breasts against his chest. Heat pooled heavily in his groin and he had to remind himself that at least for the moment, he was her bodyguard, not the guy in her bed.

She stood so close he could bend his head and settle his mouth over hers. Sage didn't move, but her breathing quickened and his arousal strengthened.

"Thank you," she said softly.

He clamped down on his hunger as Trace walked up. Like Ben and Alex, Jake's friend was tall, lean and solidly built. His hair was dark brown and so were his eyes. A former Army Ranger, he was the owner of Atlas Security and technically Jake's boss.

"Sage, this is Trace Rawlins. The two of you have been doing business together for a while. It's about time you met face-to-face."

"Ma'am," Trace drawled, tugging on the brim of the white straw cowboy hat he wore. "It's a pleasure."

"Same here. And you can skip the ma'am. I'd like it if you just called me Sage."

"Yes, ma'am," he said and grinned. "I mean Sage."

She laughed. It was a sound Jake hadn't heard in a while.

"Let's get in out of the heat," he said, though the warm Texas days were beginning to cool.

Trace followed them into the apartment and Jake closed the door. He kept the AC cranked up, the place almost chilly. It felt damned good right now.

"You want something to drink? I got Coke and beer."

"I'll have a beer," Trace said.

"So will I," said Sage.

Jake took a bottle opener to a couple of Lone Stars

and handed them around, then popped the top on a Coke for himself. He was still working. He wouldn't be drinking anything alcoholic until Sage was out of danger.

"What's up?" he asked as Trace and Sage walked to the breakfast bar and climbed up on a pair of brown leather stools, Sage struggling only a little.

Jake almost smiled. She hated the dowdy skirts she'd been wearing since the Saudis arrived. He didn't mind them. Long as he got to strip her out of 'em.

"I talked to a friend in the department," Trace said, "asked him to do a little diggin', see what the cops have found out about the bomb."

"Sayers?" Jake asked.

"Yeah." Trace and Mark Sayers, a lieutenant in the homicide division of HPD, were longtime friends. A while back, Trace and Sayers had worked together on a murder investigation that had, in a roundabout way, led Trace to the woman he had married.

He took off his white straw hat and set it on the bar, ran a hand through his dark hair, then took a long swig of ice-cold beer. "According to Sayers, Bert Hobson has lawyered up. Says he doesn't know anything about a bomb. But he doesn't have much of an alibi for last night. He went home after work, then went out and had a couple of drinks with some friends, stayed till around eleven. They've verified he was at the bar, but according to Hobson, he was home before midnight and went there by himself. He's got no way to prove it."

"What kind of work does he do?" Sage asked.

"Hobson owns some acreage west of town. Got a bunch of wind machines on it. He earns a living off the power he sells."

"Makes sense he hates people in the oil business," Jake said. "Sees them as competition. I wonder if he hates 'em enough to want one of them dead."

Sage's face went a little pale.

"Police don't have enough to charge him yet," Trace said, "but they can hold him for forty-eight hours. They're hopin' their explosives experts will turn up something before then."

They talked a few minutes more, then Trace downed the last of his beer. "Listen, Maggie's waitin'. I gotta run. Sayers is keepin' an eye on things. If anything new turns up, I'll let you know."

"Thanks, buddy."

Trace grabbed his hat off the counter and settled it low on his forehead. He turned to Sage, tugged on the brim. "Pleasure, Sage."

"Thank you, Trace, for everything you've done."

He headed out the door, and Jake came around and sat on the bar stool his friend had vacated. Lifting his can of Coke, he took a long swallow. As he set it back down on the counter, his cell phone started to ring.

A reprieve, he thought, since he was just getting ready to broach the subject of Sage's protection. He looked down at the number on the screen, saw it belonged to Felix's mom, Tanya Porter.

Or maybe just more trouble. With a sigh, Jake pressed the phone against his ear.

Chapter 17

"Jake, I'm so sorry to bother you, but Felix is in trouble. I didn't know who else to call."

"What's happened, Tanya?"

"He was caught fighting. I'm not sure who it was with. I guess the other boys ran away, but the police took Felix down to juvenile detention. I don't want to go down there by myself. I hoped maybe you could come with me."

He looked over at Sage, sitting at the breakfast bar beside him, her golden eyes were filled with concern. "Let me make a couple of calls, then I'll come and get you. Don't worry. We'll handle this one way or another." He hung up the phone, then turned back to Sage.

"What is it?" she asked.

"Felix Porter's in trouble. They picked him up for

fighting, took him down to juvenile hall. I'm going to call Alex, have him take you home and stay with you till I can get back."

"Isn't the detention center downtown?"

He nodded. "Congress Street. I've passed the building a couple of times on my way to your office."

"Maybe there's a faster way to handle this. Why don't we just go down and get him? I like Felix. He seems like a really nice boy, and he must be scared to death."

The kid did his best to stay out of trouble, and Sage was right. He'd be scared to death.

"You've had a helluva day and tomorrow may not be much better. Let me call Alex."

"Honestly, I don't mind. I'm too wired to do much of anything but worry, anyway. I've got my cell in case the sheik calls. Let's just go get him."

Jake leaned over and kissed her. "All right. I trust Alex, but not as much as I trust myself. I'd rather you were with me. I'll just grab a couple of things and we'll go."

Jake went into his bedroom and changed into jeans and a T-shirt, tossed clean underwear into a black canvas bag, folded a suit and a fresh white shirt and laid them inside, then grabbed his shaving kit. When he had everything together he carried the bag into the living room.

"What's that?" Sage asked.

"Long story." Jake kept walking, urging her toward the door. On the way to the Jeep, he phoned Tanya and told her he was going directly to the detention center. "Let me talk to them, see if I can take care of this. If I need you, I'll call."

Twenty minutes later, he was pulling into a parking space just down the block from the eight-story building, and turning off the engine. He helped Sage down, led her inside and up to the front desk.

"I'm here for Felix Porter," Jake said. "I'm a friend of his mother's."

"I'll see what I can do." The receptionist, an older blonde woman, disappeared for several minutes, then returned with the news that they had already decided to drop any charges against Felix and release him into his mother's custody. A call was made. Tanya okayed the release of her son into Jake's care so that he could bring him home.

A few minutes later, Felix appeared from the back, looking scared and shaken.

"What happened?" Jake asked.

The boy looked down at his oversize feet and just shook his head. One of his eyes was swollen and there was a cut on his chin. Probably hadn't done too well in the fight.

Jake realized the kid wasn't going to talk in front of Sage.

"It's all right now," she said gently, sensing his distress. "Jake's going to take you home and make sure everything's okay."

Felix relaxed a little and looked up at her with grateful brown eyes. "Thank you."

They walked outside and down the block. Jake waited till the boy climbed into the back of the Jeep, then helped Sage in, went around and slid in behind the wheel.

"You doing all right?" Jake asked over his shoulder.

Felix just nodded.

"This have something to do with Desi and Bo?"

Felix nodded. "Desi and Bo wanted me to try some stuff. I told them I didn't do drugs, then me and Desi started fighting, and then the cops showed up and Desi and Bo ran away."

Jake gritted his teeth. "I'll talk to them."

"You said that before."

He blew out a breath. "I'm sorry, son. I'm just really busy right now."

Sage turned in her seat, laid a hand on Felix's arm. "Jake'll take care of this. You don't have to worry."

He looked up at her, seemed to believe her, gave her a faint, tentative smile.

"In the meantime," Jake said in the voice he'd used to command his men, "I want you to stay away from Desi and Bo. You got that?"

Felix's eyes went wide. "Yes, sir."

They left the downtown area, slugged their way through the last of the evening traffic and headed for the house south of Holcombe where Felix lived. Just as before, his mother was waiting on the sidewalk. Jake got out and helped Felix out, leaving the car door open so he could introduce the women.

"Tanya, I want you to meet Sage Dumont," Jake said. "She's the client I'm working for. She let me take care of this."

"Oh, I surely do thank you, Ms. Dumont. I don't know what could have happened. Felix is always such a good boy."

Jake flicked Felix a warning glance. "I'm sure it won't happen again. Right, Felix?"

"Yes, sir."

Jake turned to Tanya and gave her a brief white-washed version of what had happened, keeping her in the loop as much as he could without losing Felix's trust.

Tanya settled an arm around her son's narrow shoulders. "Thanks, again." Waving, she turned and directed the boy toward the house.

"I feel sorry for him," Sage said as they drove toward her apartment. "It has to be hard to be Felix's age and stand up to his peers that way."

"Damned hard. I'm proud of him. Tomorrow, while you're at the office, I'll have a little chat with Desi and Bo, make sure they know what will happen to them if they don't leave him alone."

Sage sighed. "I hate drugs. I hate what it does to the kids."

"It sucks them dry. It takes away their will to accomplish anything, and ultimately, it kills them."

The Jeep hit a bump. Sage glanced into the mirror above the dash and caught something in Jake's expression. "What is it? What are you thinking?"

He just shook his head. "Be better if you didn't know."

"Drugs," she repeated, recalling the look on his face the last time they'd been talking about them. "Oh, my God, were you thinking about Roshan? Did he say something else about smuggling narcotics?"

Jake sighed. "To be honest, I don't know yet. I've only played part of the recording. And if I tell you how I got it, it makes you an accomplice."

Her mind was spinning. She chewed her bottom lip. "Okay, let's see if I get this right. Last night Roshan and Quadim went out clubbing. You knew they were going so you…you hid some kind of recording device in their limo." She caught his glance in the mirror again. "That's it, isn't it? That's why you went down to Linc's this morning instead of waiting for him to pick you up. You were retrieving your equipment."

His mouth quirked. "No one ever said you were dumb."

She slid her hands into her hair, lifting it off the back of her neck, letting the air conditioner cool her skin. "So you've got the recording." She leaned back in her seat. "I don't even know if I want to know what's on it."

She glanced over at Jake. "Maybe it won't matter. Maybe Khalid will take his son and go home. At this point, I almost wish he would."

"When we get to your apartment, I'll play the rest of what I got. Maybe there won't be anything important. If there isn't, that's the end of it."

Sage silently prayed that was exactly what would happen. She didn't need any more trouble. But now that Jake had the recording, she had to know if he was right and Roshan was involved in something illegal.

She didn't say anything more. Jake drove into her apartment's underground garage, parked in one of the visitor spaces, came around and helped her climb out. Reaching into the back, he pulled out the black canvas bag, slung the strap over his shoulder and started for the elevator.

Sage came to a halt in front of the stainless-steel door. "You haven't said what's in the bag. Are you planning to stay the night?"

"That's right. I'd prefer to spend the night in your

bed, but if you'd rather, I can sleep on the sofa. Either way, you've got company till all of this is over."

"You've got to be kidding."

The elevator opened and Jake walked in, held the door and waited patiently for her to join him.

"I'm tired and I'm not in the mood for sex," she said sharply, though for the last half hour she'd been thinking of little else. "I may need protection during the day, but I'm safe inside my own apartment."

"I hope that's true. Unfortunately, after what's happened, there's no way to know for sure."

The elevator made a speedy assent to the tenth floor. The doors dinged opened and they walked out into the corridor. Sage dug the key out of her purse and unlocked the door, went in and turned off the alarm.

When she looked up, Jake was standing in the living room, the canvas bag on a chair.

Sage walked toward him. "I don't like this, Jake."

"You didn't mind last night."

Before she could form some kind of reply, he reached for her and pulled her into his arms. For an instant, when his mouth came down over hers, she resisted. He had no right to make assumptions. Just because they'd made love last night didn't make it a permanent thing.

He didn't let go, just kept kissing her until she softened against him. The hot lips moving over hers turned gentle, coaxing now instead of taking, making her insides quiver and her heart pound in her ears. His hands cupped her bottom and he pulled her into the V of his powerful thighs, letting her feel how big and hard he was, how much he wanted her.

She had never been with a man who dominated her

sexually and it was an incredible turn-on. Her fingers dug into his massive shoulders. She could feel the moisture building between her legs. She was on fire for him, barely able to breathe.

"I'm staying," he said against her mouth, deepening the kiss. "I'm taking you to bed and I'm spending the night there."

A little whimper came from her throat. She wanted him to stay, had wanted it from the start. She wanted to feel him inside her so badly she ached with it. He helped her off with her suit jacket, unfastened the buttons on her pink silk blouse and tossed it away, unfastened the catch on the front of her bra. Bending his head, he took her breast into his mouth. Sage moaned as he suckled and tasted, laved and teased a nipple.

"I think I'll have you here," he said, "then maybe again in the shower. You've got a nice big one, room for both of us."

Somehow her skirt was gone; she didn't recall quite how it happened. Desperate to touch him, she reached for his T-shirt, pulled it off over his head, pressed her mouth against the thick slab of muscle across his chest. Her tongue found a flat copper nipple, circled it, and Jake groaned.

He still wore his jeans, but she was naked except for her tiny thong panties, pink this time, and lacy.

"I like those even better than the blue ones," he said roughly as he buzzed his zipper down, then he turned her around, bent her over the arm of the sofa, pulled the panties aside and entered her.

Sage gasped at the feel of him inside her, the fierce, erotic sensations. Moving deeply, he took her and took her, giving her a series of orgasms so hot and delicious they left her weak and shaky.

Jake reached his own release and little by little they began to spiral down. Big hands circled her waist as he turned her around and kissed her softly one last time.

"You could have stopped me anytime, you know."

"I know."

Lifting her into his arms, he started for the bedroom. "I'm staying. You got a problem with that?"

Sage slid her arms around his thick neck and shook her head.

Jake smiled. "I didn't think so," was all he said.

The spray coming from two different nozzles was finally getting cold. Jake reached over and turned off the water, grabbed a fluffy white towel off the rack and began to dry both of them off. He almost smiled. The moment they'd stepped into the shower, Sage had surprised him by taking control.

"Two can play this game," she'd said, and dragged his mouth down to hers for a kiss as steamy as the water. He went instantly hard. He liked sex and he liked a woman who enjoyed it as much as he did. They'd climaxed together, Sage's head against his shoulder, her legs wrapped around his waist.

When he finished drying her off, she slipped into a fluffy white robe and sat down in front of the mirror to dry her hair. It was too early for bed, though he'd be happy to make an exception, since Sage looked so damned beat. She'd had a stressful day—they both had—though it hadn't dimmed the desire that continued to burn between them. Her sexual needs matched his own. In fact, in all the ways that counted, the woman was his equal.

And wouldn't Annie get a kick out of hearing him say that.

The fact was, Jake liked this woman. More than liked her. She was intelligent and interesting, competent, determined and sexy as hell. Once he took a woman to bed, his interest usually waned. With Sage, he only wanted to know more about her. She intrigued him in a way a woman never had.

The question was, what should he do about it?

"You hungry?" he asked as Sage pulled on a lightweight blue jogging suit and he dragged his jeans and T-shirt back on.

"I wasn't before, but I am now." She grinned as she fluffed out her hair, letting it dry into those soft curls he liked so much. "You have a way of doing that to me."

The lady had a way of doing a lot of things to him, which at the moment he was trying not to think about.

"Maybe we should order some pizza," he said.

"We had pizza last time. How about Chinese?"

"Sounds good." They walked into the living room just as the intercom buzzed, signaling a visitor downstairs.

Sage walked over and pushed the button. "Yes, Henry?"

"The police are here," the security guard said. "Detectives Brady and Vasquez."

Sage flicked Jake a glance and he nodded. "Send them up," she said.

"I'm surprised it took them this long." Jake had spoken to the detectives at Linc's after the car bomb explosion. But Sage had been moving around all day. Maybe they'd just finally tracked her down.

A few minutes later the doorbell rang. Jake stepped up to the peephole, recognized the men he'd talked to earlier. They were dressed in rumpled dark suits that looked as if they came off the discount racks, their shoes slightly scuffed—the uniform of plainclothes detectives. Brady was gray-haired and a little overweight. Vasquez was Hispanic, younger and good-looking.

Satisfied they were who they said they were, Jake opened the door.

"Hello, Detectives," Sage said. "I've been expecting to hear from you."

Brady spoke first. "Sorry to bother you this late, Ms. Dumont," the Texan drawled, "but we need ta ask you some questions 'bout the explosion this mornin'. I'm Detective Brady and this is Detective Vasquez. We're with Houston PD."

"As I said, I've been expecting you. I believe you've met my bodyguard, Jake Cantrell."

Brady nodded. "We talked to him earlier."

"Can I get you something to drink? Iced tea or a glass of water?"

"Nothing for me," Vasquez said.

"We're fine," said Brady.

"Why don't we go into the living room?"

Sage, Brady and Vasquez sat down on the overstuffed, pale peach sofa and chairs facing the big windows looking out over the city.

The entire apartment was done in soft peach, cream and black. A black lacquer table sat in front of the sofa, and Asian accents added an interesting touch. The apartment was modern but comfortable, and Jake thought it fit Sage perfectly. Feminine but without a lot of frills.

He walked past the group and stood at the wall behind Sage.

Brady pulled a notebook out of his pocket and began to flip through the pages. "From the statements made by the owner of Freedom Limousines, a Mr. Lincoln Jones, and those given by Mr. Cantrell this morning, I gather the Escalade was the vehicle you generally rode in to work."

"Just since the arrival of our visitors from the Middle East. My company is involved in business negotiations with Sheik Khalid Al Kahzaz. There've been some protests, things happening around the office. Mr. Cantrell thought hiring a limousine service would be wise. Before that, I drove myself to work."

"Was there anything different about your schedule this morning?" Vasquez asked. "Anything out of the ordinary?"

"No, we were scheduled for a meeting in Midtown. The car was on its way to pick me up. We did the same thing yesterday morning."

"Was anyone besides you, Mr. Jones and Mr. Cantrell supposed to be ridin' in the car?" Brady asked.

"No."

The detectives continued asking questions, all of them routine. Jake had given them the same information that morning. The detectives were just confirming, doing their job.

It took a better part of an hour before the men stood up to leave.

"Anythin' you want to add, Cantrell?" Brady asked.

"I wish I had something. You get anything out of Hobson?"

"Nothin' I can disclose at this time."

Which was bullshit. They didn't have a damned thing.

Vasquez handed Sage a business card. "If you think of anything, even if it doesn't seem important, call the number on the card."

"I will."

The men left the apartment and Sage gave a sigh of relief. "I feel like I'm moving in circles. Everything's turned upside down. Nothing seems to be going in a straight line anymore."

"Maybe Hobson will talk. Or the explosives team will come up with something."

She shook her head. "I keep thinking of what might have happened."

He'd had a few thoughts about that himself. He walked over to where she stood, eased her into his arms. "What might have happened didn't. And now that we know what we're up against, we'll be on guard."

Like he hadn't been already? He didn't tell Sage how hard it was to stop a killer whose mind was made up.

Jake just held on to her, more determined than ever to keep her safe.

Chapter 18

It was late, nearly midnight, and still no word from Sheik Khalid. Sage had been asleep next to Jake, but now was awake and couldn't seem to go back to sleep. They had made love again, slowly this time, Jake treating her as if she were made of glass.

He was extremely intuitive. He seemed to know when to be rough and when to be gentle. He liked to take control, but he also enjoyed it when she took the lead. The man was the perfect lover. And he was becoming a friend.

A dangerous combination. Sage couldn't allow her feelings for Jake to grow too deep. He wasn't a marrying kind of man, and even if he were, he wasn't the sort who fit into her plans for the future. He was hard-edged, dangerous and sexy. Certainly not the kind of man who enjoyed an evening at the country club.

She stared up at the ceiling. So much was going on in her life. She tried to stay focused, objective, tried not to be afraid that if she walked out of her apartment, someone might try to kill her—or someone she loved.

Her grandfather's beloved face popped into her head and she felt a rush of fear for him. She wished she had called him before it got too late. What if something had happened? Was he safe or was he in danger?

Next to her, Jake came up on an elbow and looked over her shoulder. "Everything's going to be all right, Sage. You have to believe that."

"I should have called Ian."

"I talked to Ben while you were in the bathroom brushing your teeth. I would have told you, but I got... sidetracked."

She smiled at the reference to their lovemaking. It was nothing like what she'd experienced with Phillip. Whatever happened, she would always have the memory of her days of fantasy sex with the most virile man she had ever known. "Then Ian's okay?"

"Both of them are home and settled in. Ben says Ian's house has a first-class security system."

She nodded. "That's good."

Jake turned around, swung his long legs to the side of the mattress, stood up and reached for his jeans. As he zipped them up, he walked around the bed, bent and picked up her white terry robe. "Come on." He held it up for her to slide into. "Speaking of Ben, I saw some Ben and Jerry's in the freezer. Maybe it'll help you fall asleep."

Those hot blue eyes were reminding her that he had the perfect sleeping pill, but he didn't say it.

Sage sighed as she slipped into the robe. "The sheik

hasn't called. The police haven't come up with any-thing. I don't know what to do."

"We'll know more tomorrow. Best to take things as they come."

It seemed like good advice. While Jake got the ice cream out of her stainless Subzero freezer, Sage opened a cupboard and took down a couple of bowls.

He had just finished scooping ice cream when Sage heard the distant chiming of her phone.

"That's my cell!" Racing back to the bedroom, she grabbed the phone off the side table. The caller number wasn't one she recognized. Her heart was pounding as she pressed the phone against her ear. "Sage Dumont."

"Ms. Dumont, this is Sheik Khalid. I am sorry to call you at such a late hour, but a problem has come up."

Her fingers tightened around the phone. "What is it?"

"I am afraid my daughter is missing."

Sage could feel the blood draining out of her face. "A'lia... A'lia's been kidnapped?" She looked up to see Jake striding toward her. From his dark expres-sion, she knew he had overheard her words. He bent to her level and she held the phone so he could hear.

"That is what I thought at first," Khalid said, "but she left a note for me with her cousin Zahra. It is with a great deal of sorrow that I tell you my daughter has run away."

Sage's stomach churned. She flicked a glance at Jake, who was scowling. "Have you called the police?"

"My daughter is twenty-two years old. She is of legal age. I am hoping she will contact me. I intend to stay in your country until I can speak to her."

Sage's heart was racing. She wasn't sure who she felt sorrier for, A'lia, alone in a strange city, or her father, frightened for his youngest child. "Is there anything I can do?"

"I am not certain. If she contacts you, I ask that you let me know. Tomorrow, we will talk again. I will meet with you as we planned at your attorney's office at nine in the morning."

"All right. I'll arrange for our security people to pick you up at the hotel."

"Good night, then."

"Good night." Sage ended the call and looked at Jake. "You heard what he said. A'lia is missing."

"I heard."

"I can't believe this is happening on top of everything else."

Jake's gaze strayed down the hallway. "We need to find out what else is on that recording."

Sage took a shaky breath, and they went to study. She thought longingly of the ice cream melting in the kitchen, and of curling up in bed with Jake.

Apparently, sleep would have to wait.

Sage's wood-paneled study was inviting, a little less formal than the rest of the house. It was filled with books, and had a walnut desk with a computer on top, an ergonomic chair behind it. A butter-soft, fawn leather sofa sat against one wall with a matching chair beside it. A shaggy sheepskin throw rug cushioned the brass feet of a wood-and-brass coffee table.

Jake sat down at the computer, plugged in the flash drive and started playing the recording from where he'd left off the morning of the explosion. He yawned as he listened to the flow of Arabic, and tried to keep his attention focused. It was a half hour before he heard words similar to those he had overheard at the ranch.

First there was laughter, and Roshan saying something to Quadim about a girl they had been talking to in a bar, and that maybe the next place would provide better entertainment.

There was silence for a while as the limousine rolled toward its next destination.

Then Roshan said, "You are certain…" Words Jake didn't get. "The delivery is on schedule?" Jake's senses went on alert.

He paused the recorder, wrote Roshan's name on a yellow pad and what he'd just said, including the blank spots, then clicked to continue.

"The last delivery will be…" Something Jake didn't understand. "…on Friday," Quadim answered.

"Unless my father…" Something about a new deal. "…there will…one more…pipe…after this one."

Wishing he knew more Arabic, Jake paused the playback and wrote down the rough translation of what he had heard. Standing behind him, Sage looked over his shoulder and read what he'd written.

"I think Roshan is saying something about the negotiation his father is currently involved in with us," she stated. "Unless his father makes a new deal, there'll only be one more shipment of used five-inch pipe coming into Houston—that's what we contracted for some months back. There're only two shipments left. One's coming in this Friday."

Jake clicked Resume and the conversation continued.

"It does not matter." More words Jake missed. "For now…finished."

"When will…the money?" Roshan asked, and Jake scribbled that down on the pad.

"Tariq will be there with…" Jake couldn't get the rest of what Quadim said. "He will…the money and bring it back to us." Something else was said but Jake missed it.

He paused the replay and wrote down roughly what he'd heard. "I'm getting some of it but not enough."

Yet it was sounding as if he had been at least partially right before. The gaps in the translation would have to be filled, of course. He hoped Alex could arrange for that tomorrow.

"Roshan mentioned money," Sage said. "What money is he talking about? We pay the balance due on the pipe the day it's delivered. The money goes directly into the Saudi bank account the sheik set up for the transfer. None of it goes to Roshan."

"I'm not sure, but I think maybe there's something coming in with the shipment. Something worth money."

Sage seemed to be weighing the information. "Tariq is one of the bodyguards, right? The one you call Mutt."

"That's right. Mutt and Jeff. Jeff's name is Yousef. The sheik's men are Kiron and Kamal."

"They haven't said what's coming in with the shipment. Maybe it's a message or something."

"Could be." But Jake didn't think so. He clicked the play button again.

"I will…when this is over," Roshan stated. Very clearly, he said, "I do not like taking risks."

The men started talking faster, arguing over something, and Jake lost track of the conversation.

Sage read the last of what Jake had written down. "You mentioned drugs before. You thought they said the word. I don't see it in your notes."

"I missed a lot. I can try it again, but I'd rather wait until tomorrow. Bring someone in who speaks the language."

Sage tapped a finger on the yellow pad. "Are you sure about this, Jake? Is your Arabic really good enough to know this is what they're saying?"

"I caught a lot of it. Alex has a professor friend who works at the university. Tomorrow I'll have the whole thing translated."

They played the rest of the tape, but the conversation veered off in another direction. Then the limo stopped, presumably at a nightclub, and when the men returned, they had women with them.

Jake pulled the USB flash drive out of the computer.

"We don't know what's coming in with the shipment," Sage said, as he turned off the machine and rose from the chair behind the desk. "Or if this has anything to do with A'lia's disappearance."

"Let's hope it doesn't," Jake replied. "If it does, the girl could be in serious trouble."

"Oh, God."

He reached for her, eased her into his arms. "We just have to keep going, honey. Sooner or later, we'll get all of this sorted out."

Sage just nodded.

Jake took her hand. "You like melted ice cream?"

She smiled up at him. "I like the other kind of sleeping pill better, the one you were thinking of earlier."

He grinned. "So now you're a mind reader."

"It was more a matter of body language."

Jake laughed. Sweeping her up, he carried her back to the bedroom.

It wasn't too long before both of them fell asleep.

Rina turned the key in the lock on her front door. Though technically she was living with Ryan, she hadn't given up her own apartment, a nice two-bedroom in Uptown. No relationship was ever a sure thing, and she wasn't about to give up this small piece of personal security, a place she came to whenever she needed a little space, a place to hole up and think, or just get away from the stress of her job. Being a stockbroker definitely had its ups and downs, lately mostly downs.

She hadn't been there for a while and the place smelled faintly musty. She walked over and cracked open a window, letting in the moist night breeze, then headed for the air conditioner, turned the temperature down and cranked the fan up to high.

She glanced around, admiring the job she had done on the decor, combining a comfortable eggshell sofa and chair with an array of French antiques: a Louis XV armoire, a pair of fauteuil chairs, a marble-topped burlwood sideboard.

She'd always had a passion for France. Had even gone against her mother's advice and taken French in high school instead of Spanish, which would definitely have been more useful in Houston.

Since her parents were poor, she had studied hard, won a scholarship, then been chosen as an exchange student and gone to France to study for two years before finishing school in Houston. She spoke the language fluently, not that she had much use for it now, just as her mother had said.

Still, her apartment, with its many French touches, always felt like home.

Even at one in the morning.

Rina exhaled a sleepy sigh and yawned. First the call had come from Sage this morning, sending her reeling. A car explosion that could have killed her best friend. But Sage was with Jake tonight, and after seeing them together, Rina felt sure the big man would do whatever was necessary to keep her friend safe.

Then, an hour ago, she'd gotten another unexpected phone call, one that had led her here. Since Ryan was traveling there wasn't a problem getting away from the place they shared.

She thought of what she was about to do and chewed her thumbnail, an old habit she thought she'd conquered. She didn't have to worry about a bomb, but Sage was definitely going to kill her when she found out what was going on—not that any of it was actually her fault.

Well, maybe a little.

During the weekend out at the ranch, Rina and A'lia had become friends of a sort. When the girl found out Rina was a stockbroker, a completely independent woman, she'd been filled with a thousand questions. A'lia was amazingly smart and so eager to learn. Little by little, she had confided her deepest desire—to stay here in America.

"I wish to continue my education," she'd said wistfully, a topic that had also come up the day they'd gone shopping in the mall. "I want to go to a real school where men and women students are treated as equals. I want to see things, do things." She smiled. "I want to drive a car."

They'd been sitting outside on the patio that Sunday morning, while the rest of the group got ready for the shooting match Sage had planned.

"So why don't you stay?" Rina had asked. "You're legally old enough, right?"

"I am twenty-two. But in my country, I am still under my father's protection and guidance. I have cousins who live in this country, one whose family now lives in New York. I have begged my father, but he refuses to give me his permission to stay. He says it is time for me to marry. He plans to choose, for me, a husband. I wish to choose my own husband."

"What you're asking doesn't sound unreasonable. Maybe your father will change his mind."

"I do not think so." A'lia smoothed the front of her beaded silk robe. "He will not agree, and my brother Roshan is even worse. He believes all women are beneath him."

Rina reached over and squeezed the girl's slender hand. "Maybe you'll find a way." She had given A'lia her business card and written her cell number on the back. "If you ever need my help, don't be afraid to call."

Which was the reason Sage was going to kill her.

Because tonight, A'lia had taken Rina up on her impetuous offer of help, and had phoned. The girl had grabbed the bull by the horns, as a Texan would say. She'd devised an elaborate plan and escaped from her cousins, Zahra and Yasar, and one of the bodyguards, during a visit to the University of Houston campus.

According to A'lia, there was some sort of festival going on she had read about in the paper. According to plan, she had slipped away in the crowd, pulled off her robe and head scarf, and run away in the jeans and T-shirt she'd been wearing underneath.

For several hours, she'd stayed hidden, until she could get safely away, then had used some of the allowance money she'd been stashing away for months to hail a cab. Apparently, she had wandered the streets till well after dark, trying to work up the courage to make a call to Rina.

Hearing the near-hysterical tone of A'lia's voice over the phone, Rina had given her the address of her Uptown apartment and told the girl she would meet her there in an hour.

A knock at the apartment door sounded, dragging Rina's thoughts back to the moment. With a resigned sigh, she opened it.

A'lia stood on the threshold looking pale and teary-eyed, dressed in the jeans and T-shirt she had been wearing when she'd run away, though her head scarf was now back in place.

Rina managed a smile. "Come on in, sweetie. Don't worry, everything's going to be fine." How that was going to happen, she had no idea. But the girl looked so forlorn that Rina's heart went out to her. When she opened her arms, A'lia stepped into them, then burst into tears.

Rina swallowed past the lump in her throat and hugged the girl tightly.

Sage was going to kill her.

Chapter 19

The following morning, after a thorough inspection of his Jeep, Jake drove Sage to Midtown for her meeting with the sheik. Alex wouldn't be coming, not today.

The car bomb had changed the equation. Odds were the sheik would be heading back to Saudi Arabia. Today's meeting was just a formality, Jake figured. Sage would be wildly disappointed, but the way things were at the moment, none of them were safe.

It was early when they arrived at Weis, Weis, Silverman and Schultz. Outside the conference room, Jake waited while Sage went in to prepare herself for whatever the sheik might have to say. On the surface, she appeared cool and in control, but Jake was coming to know her. He recognized the faint hint of nerves, the edginess, the worry in her voice.

He didn't blame her. She had a helluva lot at stake.

He took up a stance beside the door, thinking of the call from Ian he had received earlier that morning. The protests at Dumont Drilling had dribbled to a small group of students still milling around out in front. Most of the protestors had gone home.

Ian had asked him to keep a close eye on his granddaughter, and Jake had assured him he was doing exactly that. Considering he had spent the night in Sage's bed, the eye he was keeping on her was a lot closer than Ian might guess.

The ding of the elevator alerted Jake to the sheik's arrival. He was surprised when the man walked out with only his two personal bodyguards, Kiron and Kamal. Even his lawyers were absent. The men disappeared inside the conference room, and a few minutes later, Jake was even more surprised when Sage stepped out and asked him to join them.

"This is getting complicated," she said. "It's more than just business now. I'd like you to be there."

Smart lady, he thought, as he had a number of times before. There was more than money at stake. A young woman was missing. Roshan was likely into something illegal, and there was a bomber in the mix.

They went through the formalities, one of the office staff bringing in coffee, pouring for the sheik and Sage and anyone else who was interested. It usually took the Saudis a while to warm up and start talking about anything more than pleasantries, but today the sheik cut right to the chase.

"I have come to admire you, Ms. Dumont. And in some way, also to trust you." He flicked a glance at Jake. "I trust now that whatever is said in this room will go no further."

Sage met his dark gaze squarely. "You have my word, Your Highness." Her eyes went to Jake. "I speak for Mr. Cantrell, as well."

The sheik nodded, seeming satisfied. "As you know, my daughter is missing. I have had no word of her, aside from the note she left in Zahra's pocket."

"Did the note say why A'lia went off on her own?" Sage asked.

"My daughter wishes to go to school in your country. She has friends in America, people she met while she attended university in Riyadh. She believes they will help her."

"Then perhaps that's where she's gone."

"I imagine that is her plan. Unfortunately, I know little of these people, or where I might find them."

"I see."

"My daughter and I have had many discussions on this matter. I did not believe she would go so far. By her disobedience, she has dishonored not only me but our whole family." He glanced away. "And yet I find it difficult to condemn her."

Sage's voice softened. "Your daughter is a very intelligent young woman. Sometimes not everyone can fit into the same mold."

The sheik stared out the window. It was rare for a Saudi male to discuss his family with an outsider, but Jake figured these were unusual circumstances. Clearly, the man was desperate to find his child.

"A'lia is like her mother. Strong-willed and spirited. Nura was unhappy with her role as a wife and mother. She wanted something more. She also wanted more than just marriage for her daughter."

"Have you spoken to her? Have you told your wife what's happened?"

"My Nura died three years ago. A'lia took her death very hard. Perhaps that is part of the reason she left. Perhaps she felt she owed it to her mother."

"Is there anything I can do to help you find her?"

"That is why I am telling you all of this. I believe, sooner or later, my daughter will contact you. She knows only the people she has met here in Houston. And I believe she trusts you. If you hear from her, I would like you to tell her I wish to speak to her. Tell her she need not be afraid of her brother or anyone else."

Jake mulled over the words. The sheik loved his daughter and he was a fairly progressive man. But Roshan was fanatical when it came to a woman knowing and accepting her place, an attitude he had made clear. At the very least, he would believe A'lia should be severely punished for what she had done. Physical beatings of women—or worse—were commonplace in Saudi Arabia. It was just the way it was.

"If I speak to A'lia," Sage said, "I promise I'll do my best to convince her to call you. If I hear anything at all, I'll let you know."

The sheik gave a slight bow of his head, his white headdress falling forward around his shoulders. "That is all I can ask." He turned to Jake. "Is there news of the man responsible for the car bomb?"

"Not yet. We're hoping to learn more today."

"I hope you will keep me informed."

"Certainly."

Khalid returned his attention to Sage. "If you will excuse me, it is time I got back to my family."

"Of course."

He relaxed a little. "Tomorrow we will continue our discussions. My daughter has caused more than enough trouble. There is work yet for me to do here."

Jake caught a flash of relief in Sage's face.

She summoned an appropriate smile. "Then I shall see you in the morning."

With a final nod, the sheik stood up and, with his bodyguards, walked out the door.

Sage sank down in one of the leather conference room chairs. "He wants to continue the negotiations."

Jake stood beside her. "To be honest, I didn't think he would. But maybe Khalid sees it as unseemly to allow a woman's behavior to disrupt his agenda."

Sage rubbed her left temple, where an ache had begun to throb. "What he said about Roshan... A'lia's in danger, isn't she? She's risked more than her father's anger. By disobeying his wishes, she's disgraced her family. Roshan isn't going to let that pass."

"Roshan is also subject to his father's dictates. The trick is to keep the matter secret. If the sheik can manage that and bring her back into the fold, he can protect her."

"I hope she's somewhere safe."

"She's a smart girl. She had to have had a plan. If it went smoothly, she should be safe."

Sage released a slow breath. "I hope she calls. Maybe I can talk her into going home with him."

"You sure you want to?"

The question rolled through her. If the situation were different, would she help the girl escape the life she'd be forced to live under her family's iron control?

Sage refused to think of it. The deal was all that mattered. She had enough trouble already without taking on someone else's.

"I've got mountains of work on my desk at the office," she said, avoiding Jake's question. "I need to get down there."

"All right." As he walked her toward the door, his hand rode at her waist, and a tremor of awareness ran through her. She remembered those big hands moving over her body, the power of them, the skill. Jake knew women—that much was clear. He knew exactly how to please a woman, and exactly how to please her.

Sage ignored the warm tingling in her limbs and thought instead of all she had left to do. She had forgotten the USB recording they had played at her apartment last night, until Jake used his cell to phone Alex.

"I'm going to need that translation," he said. "Can you set it up?"

She couldn't hear Alex's reply, but Jake was nodding. "Great," he said. "I'm in Midtown. Meetings here are over for the day, so I'm driving Sage to the office. If you can take over for me for a couple of hours, I'll deliver a copy of the disk to the professor."

"I'll be at work," Sage interrupted. "I'll be fine."

Jake ignored her. "I should be downtown in twenty minutes."

Alex must have agreed because Jake hung up the phone.

"I'll be in my office, for heaven's sake," Sage said peevishly. "I'll be safe enough there."

"Yeah, and if that bomb had gone off twenty minutes later, you would have been safe inside Linc's car."

Her stomach rolled.

Jake turned her to face him. "I'm not going to let anyone hurt you, Sage. But I need you to let me do my job."

She swallowed. He was right. She'd begun to realize he usually was. "Okay."

He bent his head and dropped a quick kiss on her mouth. "Good girl."

They headed downstairs. Leaving her with the security guard in the lobby, Jake went to find his Jeep. Before they'd left that morning, he'd used a mirror with a telescoping handle to examine the undercarriage, assuring himself it was safe. He must have done the same now, for a few minutes later the Jeep pulled up in front of the building and Jake came inside to collect her.

"Ready?" he asked.

Sage just nodded. It was going to be another long day.

The police were waiting, seated in the reception area, when Jake walked Sage out of the elevator onto the executive floor of Marine Drilling. Detectives Brady and Vasquez rose from their chairs and started toward them.

Brady reached them first. "Sorry ta bother you, Ms. Dumont. Your assistant told us you were on your way into the office. We got some new information we need ta talk to you about."

She flicked a hopeful glance at Jake. He was damn well hoping they'd found something, too.

"Let's go into my office." Sage led the group inside and Jake closed the door. They all sat down at the round, granite-topped table in the corner. Through the windows, Jake could see people on the street below still milling about with signs, but the number of demonstrators was clearly dwindling.

Brady opened his notepad and took out a pen. "The report from the explosives unit came in last night." He glanced up. "Looks like the bomb was remotely detonated."

Sage's eyes widened. "What?"

"So the guy was there watching the car," Jake said. "He set off the bomb before we had a chance to get inside."

"Looks like it. Must have hung around after he rigged the device, otherwise he wouldna' known what time someone might get in it and drive away."

"It was a warning," Jake said. "He could have waited until we were inside the car, but he didn't. He wasn't trying to kill us. He was trying to scare us."

"But why?" Sage asked.

"Good question." Vasquez raked his fingers through his thick black hair.

"He may have intended to set the bomb off later," Brady said, "when more people were around. But it woulda' been a bigger risk. Somethin' could have gone wrong and people coulda' been killed."

"Maybe he got cold feet and changed his mind," Jake said. "Took the safer approach and set the bomb off before anyone got in the car."

"I still don't understand what he was trying to accomplish," Sage said.

"Notoriety, maybe." Vasquez leaned back in his chair. "The explosion was covered in all the papers and on TV. Speculation was the bombing had something to do with the protests. That stirred the media up again."

"It certainly seems like a lot of risk just to get media attention," Sage said.

Jake thought so, too. But so far he hadn't come up with a better motive, so he made no comment. "What can you tell us about the bomb itself? Any idea who might have made it?"

"Explosive forensics says it was combination of ammonium nitrates and fuel oil—a compound similar to Prillex."

Sage straightened in her chair. "Prillex? That's one of the explosives used in oil exploration."

"That's right," Brady drawled. "And even more interestin', they traced the electrical detonator back to a supplier who deals exclusively with the oil industry. Unfortunately, there was no way to know specifically which company purchased the device used in the car bomb."

Sage stared at the detective. "Are you saying this had nothing to do with the protests?"

Brady shook his head. "Not enough information to know for sure. Thing is, it's beginnin' to look like it had something to do with the deal you're trying to make. Any idea who might want these negotiations to fail?"

"You're not thinking it might be one of our competitors?"

"I'm not thinkin' anythin', Ms. Dumont. I'm hopin' you might have some idea where we should go from here."

Sage swallowed, shook her head. "I have no idea. What I'm working on is a business venture. The oil industry is booming. I can't imagine another company going so far as to blow up my car in order to keep us from buying used drilling equipment."

"A quarter of a billion dollars' worth of drilling equipment," Vasquez said. "That's not like buying a load of rusty nails."

"Maybe one of them wants it for themselves," Brady suggested. "Are there any other companies vying for this equipment?"

"Sheik Khalid has other potential buyers. I don't know exactly who they are, but I doubt any of our competitors want that platform badly enough to set off a bomb."

But Jake was thinking that it had nearly put an end to the negotiations. Probably would have if it hadn't been for A'lia's disappearance.

"How about on a personal level?" Brady asked. "Anyone you've done business with who might hold a grudge?"

Sage glanced at Jake and shook her head. "No."

The detectives asked a couple more questions, then rose from their chairs. Jake and Sage stood up, too.

"That's all for now," Brady said. "If you think of anythin'…"

"I'll call, believe me," Sage said.

She stared at the door as the men left the office, looking so dispirited that Jake gently grasped her shoulders.

"We'll figure this out," he said.

She gazed up at him. "Who would do this, Jake? Someone I know? Someone I've done business with? I've always tried to be completely ethical in my dealings."

He wanted to pursue the subject, ask a few questions of his own, but the phone on her desk started ringing and Sage walked over and picked it up.

She slipped into business mode, and he could see she was going to be involved in the call for some time. She nodded when he pointed toward the door and quietly left the office.

Alex was waiting outside, the slight bulge beneath the jacket of his expensive suit telling Jake he was armed.

"Cops just left," Jake told him. "Looks like the bomb was a homemade version that included a substance similar to Prillex. It's used to find oil."

"I've heard of it."

"Detonator was oil related, too, and triggered remotely. The guy was there when the car went up."

Alex's dark blond eyebrows went up. "So he was sending a message."

Jake nodded. "Police figure he was trying to get media attention or interfere with the purchase. They're looking at Marine Drilling's competitors."

"Could be, I guess."

"Maybe." Though Jake had a couple of other ideas. He glanced toward the elevator. "I've got a couple of things I need to do. Including talking to your professor friend out at the university."

Alex checked his watch. "I called him this morning. He's free after ten for a couple of hours."

"Great." Jake tipped his head toward to door to Sage's office. "Keep an eye on her, will you?"

Alex didn't smile. "Count on it."

Chapter 20

Sage thought things couldn't get any worse. But when her grandfather walked into her office, his eyes dark with concern, she discovered they could slide even further downhill.

Silver-haired and imposing, Ian stopped just inside and carefully closed the door. "So what's this I hear about a broken engagement?"

Her stomach instantly knotted. She thought he'd come to discuss the negotiations, or the bombing or what was happening with the sheik. Instead, Phillip must have called. She took a deep breath, steeled herself for the conversation ahead and came out from behind her desk.

She bent and kissed Ian's cheek. Smelling his cologne, she thought about how she loved the scent he always wore and how handsome he looked today in his dove-gray, pin-striped, three-piece suit.

"I guess you talked to Phillip?"

His expression didn't alter. "Phillip is in my office. He flew all the way back here from Scotland. He's extremely upset about this, Sage."

Then why hadn't he come to her instead of to her grandfather?

"I was going to tell you about it," she said a little defensively. "After things got back to normal. So much is going on right now. I didn't want to upset you any more than you were already."

"You could have come to me, Sage. You know that."

She glanced down at her hands, which she'd clasped in front of her. "I know. I'm sorry." She hadn't meant to hurt him. She loved him so much.

Ian just nodded. "Phillip's asked me to intercede on his behalf. He hopes I can make you understand how much you mean to him, how much he wants to marry you."

A little flare of anger sent her chin up an inch. "Then why isn't he standing here instead of you?"

Ian's lips curved slightly. "Because he knows how stubborn you can be once your mind is made up. What I'd like to know is why you felt you needed to break your engagement."

It wasn't really his business, but Sage knew how much he loved her, how important her happiness was to him. She raked her heavy hair away from her face.

"I needed some time. I wasn't sure getting married was the right thing for me to do. Phillip was due back in Houston in a couple of months. I thought we could discuss things then."

"I see."

She wondered if he did. Ian Dumont was shrewd

and intelligent. She wondered what he saw when she was with Jake. If he knew they were sleeping together and if he did, what he thought about it.

She didn't ask. As close as they were, sexual matters were off-limits to both of them.

"Phillip was hoping to take you to dinner, but naturally that is out of the question. He heard about the bomb, of course. Everyone in the office knows, and word travels fast even across the ocean. Phillip is extremely concerned. He's worried about you. He wants to talk to you, Sage. I think you owe him that much."

She did. Of course she did.

"Yes, I know. I never meant to hurt Phillip. Or be unfair to you. I just… I've got to be sure, Grandfather."

His head came up. She rarely called him that, and never at work, which was a measure of how much Phillip's arrival had upset her.

"I just want you to be happy, Sage."

Her throat tightened. "I know."

"I'll send him in."

She nodded, bit her lip. She didn't want to face Phillip. She'd been sleeping with another man. She didn't want to lie to him, but she didn't want to make things even more unpleasant.

He walked though the door as he always did—as if he were entering his own office instead of one that belonged to her. He looked good, his blond hair perfectly styled, his handsome face smooth and tanned, his Italian suit tailored perfectly to fit his lean frame.

"Sage…darling." He walked toward her, bent and kissed her cheek. "I had to come. I've thought of you every minute since you called. I didn't hear about the bomb until I was getting on the plane. I'm so glad you're all right."

"I wasn't in the car. I'm just thankful no one was injured."

"We need to talk, Sage. I don't understand what happened between us, but I'm convinced that if we discuss the whole thing openly and honestly, face-to-face, we'll be able to work things out."

He sounded sincere. But Phillip was accomplished at that. It was one of the things that made him a successful corporate executive.

"I wish that were true, Phillip, truly I do, but I haven't changed my mind. I need time to find out what sort of future I really want. I need the freedom to explore different avenues. That's the reason I ended our engagement."

A muscle ticked in his lean cheek. "By freedom you mean you want the right to see other people."

She swallowed, but refused to glance away. "Yes."

"And I suppose that includes Jake Cantrell."

Did he know? Or was he just guessing? "It means exploring my options." She released a shaky breath. "I'm not sure anymore about anything, Phillip. That's why I need more time."

He took both her hands and brought them to his lips. "We're good together, Sage. We always have been. You know that."

They *were* good together. They enjoyed the same things, had the same goals, saw the future the same way. They'd been friends as well as lovers. Her throat closed up. She felt the sting of tears. "I know that, Phillip. I wish… I…" *could love you.* "I wish things could be the way they were, but…"

"But what, Sage? I love you. I've loved you for years. Tell me you still love me."

In a way she did love him. Phillip had helped her become the woman she was today. She owed him for the strength she had gained and for the years they had shared together.

Her eyes filled with tears. "I care about you, Phillip. I always will."

He moved closer, drew her into his arms. She didn't stop him when he kissed her. Instead, she closed her eyes, praying she would feel something, some of the heat she felt with Jake, some of the passion. It wasn't there. She realized it never really had been.

Sage pulled away. "I'm sorry, Phillip. I have to do this. Have to have time to figure things out."

His expression shifted, hardened. "And in the meantime, you expect me to wait on the sidelines until you make up your mind."

"No, I…" She straightened, summoned her courage. "I don't expect you to wait. I expect you to go on with your life."

He looked into her eyes and his features softened. He reached out and touched her cheek. "If you feel that strongly, I'll respect your wishes. For now. In the future maybe something will change and you'll realize that what we had together was the right thing for both of us."

She swallowed. "Maybe I will. If I do, and you feel the same… If both of us are interested in resuming our relationship, then that's what we'll do."

But more and more, she was seeing Phillip in a different light, seeing that he wasn't the right man for her. For an instant, an image of Jake Cantrell appeared in her mind.

But Jake wasn't the right man, either. He was her lover and her protector. But they were from different worlds. Jake was a loner, a man who liked to live on the edge. She wanted stability. In time, she wanted children.

Something squeezed inside her.

Their affair couldn't last, but it wasn't over, not yet. She told herself she could protect herself against her feelings for Jake. She just had to be careful.

"Are you certain this is what you want?" Phillip asked, drawing her back to the moment. "Because as much as I love you, Sage, I won't wait forever."

She thought of all they had shared, and fresh tears burned her eyes. "It's what I want, Phillip."

At least for now. She had no idea what she would want tomorrow or at any time in the future. She drew the engagement ring off her finger and handed it back to him.

Phillip's fingers curled around it and his voice gentled. "You've always worked so hard. Perhaps I pushed too much. Perhaps giving you the time you need will make things clearer. We'll talk again, Sage. Whenever you're ready. Until then, darling, if you need me, you know where I am."

Her heart squeezed. She watched as he turned and walked out the door, closing it softly behind him. Was it truly over between them? Or would she come to her senses and beg him to take her back?

She wiped away the last of her tears and went into the bathroom to wash her face. Sage tried to imagine Phillip in her bed instead of Jake, but the image wouldn't come.

* * *

After driving out to Adam Haddad's office, Jake went in to drop off the copy of the flash drive he'd had made, which included only the portion he needed translated.

"You must be Mr. Cantrell," the professor's teaching assistant said, a pretty blonde with glasses and a perky smile.

"That's right. Jake Cantrell."

"The professor said you might be stopping by. Something came up and he had to leave. He won't be gone long. You can wait for him or come back in an hour."

"I'll be back." Jake set the flash drive on her desk. "Give him this, will you? I'm hoping he can translate it for me."

"Yes, he mentioned that. I'll see he gets it."

"Thanks."

Jake checked his watch as he left the office. With plenty of time to finish his second errand, he headed for the middle school where Felix and his young friend Desi were enrolled. He had a hunch he'd find Desi's older brother, Bo, loitering somewhere in the neighborhood.

He knew the kid. Felix had introduced the two Johnson brothers at a Little League baseball game. Felix played shortstop. He wasn't much of an athlete, but he loved the sport and was getting better all the time.

Jake turned south on Kirby toward the school, then began a methodical search of the area, driving up and down the streets, slowly expanding his search grid.

It didn't take long to find his quarry. Just as he'd figured, Bo Johnson stood on a corner with two of his friends, smoking cigarettes and watching some of the neighborhood girls walk past.

Jake pulled the Jeep over to the curb and got out of the car. "Hey, Bo. I need to talk to you a minute."

Bo looked up, saw who it was, tossed his cigarette away, and all three boys started running. But Jake had figured on that and was already in motion. Ignoring the other two, he caught up with Bo before he reached the end of the block, grabbed him by the back of his dirty red basketball jersey and pushed him up against the rough brick wall of an empty store.

"I guess you didn't hear me. I said I want to talk to you."

"Lemme go, man. I didn't do nothin'." Bo was tall, just a couple inches shorter than Jake, but he was thin to the point of scrawny.

"You did do something, Bo. You tried to push a friend of mine into using drugs. Long as I'm around that's not going to happen."

"I don't know what you're talkin' 'bout, man."

Jake slammed him back against the wall. "Felix Porter's a good kid. He's trying to stay clean, make something of himself. Far as I know, your brother's a good kid, too. You pushing him to start using?"

Bo shook his head. "No, man."

Jake shoved him against the wall yet again. "Are you?"

Some of Bo's bravado faded. He looked like the vulnerable teenager he actually was. "I wouldn't do that, man."

"Then why are you doing it to Felix?"

A slow breath whispered out. Bo wiped a trickle of sweat off his forehead. "My mom's sick, okay? She can't work like she used to. That's why I dropped outta high school. I needed to get my hands on some green so I could take care of her and my little brother."

Jake let go of Bo's ragged jersey. "What about Felix?"

"Everybody likes Felix. I figured if I could get him a little high, show him how good it felt, maybe he'd sell some stuff for me. He do that, we could both make some money and I could take care of my mom."

Jake stepped back, giving the boy a little more breathing room. "Why don't you get a job and earn some money on your own?"

Bo shook his head. "Tried that, man. Ain't no work nowhere."

That much was true. Times were tough, especially for a high school dropout. Jake looked closely at Bo's eyes. "You using?"

"No! I smoke a little dope once in a while. Not too often. Costs too much."

Jake caught the kid's arm, turned it over to look for needle marks. Saw it was clean. "You got a record?"

Bo's eyes widened. "No."

"I'll tell you what I'll do. I'll talk to a friend of mine, see if he's got any work for you."

The teen looked suspicious. "What kind of work?"

"Job's with Atlas Security." Trace was looking for a kid to help out at the office, maybe run some errands, do some filing. If Jake recommended him, Trace would give Bo a try.

"Be doing odd jobs, running errands, a little cleanup. Pay won't be a lot more than minimum wage, but it'll give you some experience, and there's potential for you to work your way up in the company." It was a stretch to imagine Bo Johnson as a security guard, but stranger things had happened.

Hope slipped into Bo's dark eyes. "This ain't some kind of joke, is it?"

"No joke, Bo. You show up at Atlas tomorrow morning at seven-thirty. Ask for Trace Rawlins." Jake handed the teen a card with the address printed on it. "I'll call him, tell him you're coming in to talk to him about the job."

Bo stared at the card as if he thought it might disappear. His chin angled up. "I don't know. I'll think about it."

"You do that. And you better think real hard."

He stuck the card into a pocket in his dirty jeans and started to walk away. Jake caught his arm.

"One more thing. You take the job, don't screw it up. You understand?"

Bo's jaw tightened.

Jake took a step closer, using his full height and weight to make his point. He clamped a hand on the boy's bony shoulder. "And if you ever try that shit on Felix again, I'll be back. The next time, we won't be talking. I'll be kicking your skinny ass." He squeezed the kid's shoulder. "You got it?"

Bo nodded and Jake let go. Turning, the boy took off running.

Jake watched until he disappeared, wondering if the kid had the guts to change his life and make something of himself.

He needed to call Trace and give him a heads-up. He'd vouch for the kid this once, and hope like hell Bo wouldn't give Trace any trouble. He wondered if the boy would actually show up in the morning.

Either way, Jake figured he had just solved Felix's problems.

* * *

Sage finished the last of her calls. She had talked to Red Williams and brought Will Bailey up to speed. In the morning, she planned to renew her campaign to convince Sheik Khalid to accept a fair price for his drilling equipment.

She leaned back in the leather chair behind her desk and closed her eyes, saw a replay of her conversation with Phillip. She couldn't stop thinking about him.

She couldn't stop thinking of Jake.

With a sigh, she got up to get a glass of water from the bathroom, then she heard Jake's familiar knock on the door.

Her insides trembled. Just knowing he was out there made her heart beat faster. She opened the door and he walked past her into the office.

"I'm heading out to the university to talk to Professor Haddad. He's finished the translation. I thought you might want to come."

"Yes...very much."

Jake's gaze moved over her and he started frowning. He reached out and caught her chin, tipped her face up and gave it a thorough inspection. "You've been crying. What's wrong?"

She thought she'd repaired her makeup well enough that he couldn't tell. But Jake was extremely perceptive.

"Phillip's back."

Jake's expression hardened; his blue eyes turned opaque. "Here? At the office?"

"He talked to Ian. He asked my grandfather to intercede on his behalf."

"You want to tell me what happened?" Jake said it

calmly. Too calmly. Sage wondered what was going through his head.

"I told him the same thing I told him before. I said I needed time. I have no idea if he knows about you. I didn't tell him. I didn't want to hurt him any more than I already have."

Jake's jaw looked hard as steel. "What else?"

"Phillip said he loved me. He said we were good together. Then he kissed me."

Jake said nothing, but a muscle ticked in his cheek. He stared at her with those fierce blue eyes, waiting for her to continue.

"I didn't... I didn't kiss him back," she finally said.

"Why not?"

Her eyes welled with tears. "Because he wasn't you."

She didn't see him move. He was just suddenly there, catching her in his arms, pulling her close, his mouth coming down over hers. It was a hard, possessive kiss meant to erase any memory of the man before him, a kiss that set her insides on fire. Sage kissed him back and tried not to think how good it felt, how right.

It was Jake who pulled away first. His arms tightened around her, and for a long moment he just held her. "We'll figure this out." He pressed his lips against her hair. "We'll find a way."

A lump rose in Sage's throat. "I wish things could be back the way they were. I wish I was still content to be with Phillip. I wish I didn't know what it was like to want someone the way I want you."

Jake kissed her again, gently this time. "You can't go back. No one can. It's just the way life is."

She dashed the tears from her cheeks. "I know."

He glanced down at her hand, saw the engagement

ring was gone, and dropped one more soft kiss on her lips. "You gonna be all right?"

She swallowed, then nodded. "Phillip deserved better treatment."

"You were honest, Sage. How many people can say that? You didn't go behind his back. You were free when we got together."

She had done the right thing. And Jake had been part of the reason. "I'm grateful for that."

He reached out and took her hand. "Come on. You need to get out of here for a while. Let's go find out what Roshan's been up to. Let's go see what's on that flash drive."

Sage relaxed at the tug of his hand. He had a way of making her feel better. For now that was all that mattered.

That and making her deal tomorrow morning. Sage let Jake lead her out the door.

Chapter 21

Jake pulled the Jeep into the University of Houston parking lot and turned off the engine. It was still hot and muggy, but the days were a little shorter, the nights cooler, and a breeze rolled in off the distant sea.

He opened Sage's door, helped her out and started walking with her across the campus. He tried not to think of what had happened in her office, how he'd felt when she'd told him Phillip had returned, and the bastard had kissed her.

But Jake couldn't forget the way his chest had tightened and his heart had squeezed like a fist. Then blind rage took over. He'd wanted to tear Phillip Stanton apart limb by limb with his bare hands.

Until that moment, he'd never known an instant of jealousy, hadn't understood what a potent force it could be. But Sage Dumont belonged to him and no other man could have her.

At least that was how he'd felt at the time.

He didn't want to consider what that might mean. He didn't want to think about his deepening feelings for her.

As they stepped off the grass onto a maze of sidewalks, a group of students wearing backpacks walked past, then a cluster of teachers carrying canvas book bags. Jake flicked a glance at Sage, tried not to think how appealing she looked with the sun on her face and her hair gleaming. It didn't matter. There wasn't a chance in hell the physical attraction they felt for each other would turn into a long-term, committed relationship.

They were nothing alike, people from different worlds, living two very different lives. Sage was a member of a rich and powerful family, while he had busted his balls working on the family farm, then held two jobs to get through city college. He'd been determined to leave the Iowa cornfields behind, and he'd done what it took to make that happen.

Special Forces had needed a different kind of determination, but he'd pushed himself to the mental and physical limits necessary to become part of that elite group of men.

He was tough to the core. Sage was a society princess.

Jake amended that. He couldn't deny that she hadn't had an easy childhood, that the life she and her mother had lived in Chicago had to have been rough. That kind of life built character—and he recognized that character in Sage.

Recognized and admired her drive, her guts and

her brains. Which was just another reason it wouldn't work.

Sage wanted to run the family business. A husband like him and, hell, maybe a couple of his kids, wouldn't have any place in her world.

At least he had plenty of money. Mercenary work paid big-time, and so did personal security at the levels he was employed. He wasn't as rich as the Dumonts, but he was a damn long way from being poor.

They arrived at the professor's office and Jake led Sage inside, grateful for the chance to get his mind off his feelings. The professor's blonde assistant spotted him as he walked toward her, and smiled up at him from behind her desk.

"Professor Haddad said to send you in as soon as you arrived." She pointed to a door leading to an inner office. "He's anxious to see you."

Jake wondered if that was good news or bad, and exactly what the professor had learned. "Thanks."

They found their way to his office, a slightly chaotic room full of books and stacks of papers. There seemed to be some kind of order to the files and notebooks sitting on the desk, but only the professor himself would understand what it was.

Haddad stood up as they entered, pulling off his black-rimmed glasses.

"Mr. Cantrell. A pleasure to meet you. Alex has told me a great deal about you."

"It's just Jake, and I hope it wasn't anything too terrible."

"No, quite the contrary." The professor, a man in his forties, had short black hair and an olive complexion beneath a neatly trimmed black beard. He turned to

Sage. "And you're Sage Dumont. I've seen your photo in the newspapers."

She smiled. "It's nice to meet you, Professor. We really appreciate your help."

"Before we begin, I must tell you, I am concerned at the implications of this recording. I'm wondering if the conversation should be reported to Homeland Security."

The hairs on the back of Jake's neck went up. He'd been thinking drugs. What else was on the damned tape that he hadn't understood?

"First let's see what you've got."

Haddad handed him the transcript of the portion of the recording Jake had given him.

Jake read the first line.

"You are certain about this? The delivery is on schedule?" Roshan was the speaker, Jake recalled.

"The last delivery will be coming in as planned. It will be picked up on Friday." Quadim had answered.

"Unless my father makes a new deal, there will be only one more load of pipe arriving after this one."

"It does not matter. The product has all been shipped. For now we are finished." Quadim.

"When will we get the money?" Roshan.

"Tariq will be there with our contact when the product is retrieved. He will receive the money in exchange and bring it back to us. You'll get your half of the profit, as usual."

Jake didn't like the sound of that. Who the hell got the other half? The contact? He had missed that part completely. The contact had to be the guy who had collected the money on the earlier shipments—assuming there were more than just this one, which it certainly sounded like.

"I will be glad when this is over." Roshan had said that. "I do not like taking risks."

Jake looked at Sage, who had been reading the transcript along with him.

"Nothing specifically about drugs," she said.

"No, but I'm fairly sure he mentioned them while we were riding that day at the ranch. I think that's the product they're discussing."

The professor's tone held a note of concern. "You believe this information concerns a shipment of drugs?"

"That's what we think. We can't take the recording to the authorities because of how we got it." And because he didn't want Sage's name or Marine Drilling spread all over the front pages of the newspapers again. "And we want to keep your name out of it."

The professor watched him closely. "Alex says you are an extremely capable man. What will you do?"

"We'll be at the docks when the men arrive to pick up whatever is in the pipe. If drugs are involved, we'll make sure they don't fall into the wrong hands."

"And if it is something more?"

Jake knew what the professor was asking. Was Roshan planning something that would threaten national security? There was no reason to suspect that. And it didn't really matter. Whatever it was, there was no way in hell Jake was letting it illegally enter the country.

"Same answer," he said. "I've got friends trained to handle this kind of thing. We'll take care of it quietly until we're sure what we've got."

The professor nodded. "All right. Alex sent you,

and I trust him." He smiled. "Did you know we were classmates at Yale?"

Sage looked up in surprise.

"He never talks much about his life before he became a pilot," Jake said.

"One day I was accosted by a group of young men in town," Haddad recalled. "Perhaps because of my heritage, I don't know. Alex happened to see me as he came out of a store, and realized I was in trouble. He was on the boxing team." The professor grinned. "I discovered that Alex Justice is a very capable man."

Jake felt the pull of a smile.

"We became friends that day. I trust Alex and so I will abide by my agreement to translate the recording and leave the rest to you."

"Thank you, Professor." Jake shook his hand and so did Sage.

"Thank you," she said.

They walked out of the office and into the sunlight. "I wonder what Rina would say if she knew Alex graduated from Yale?"

Jake smiled. "Doesn't change the fact he's not her type."

"True enough."

"*If* he's really not her type."

Sage laughed. Then her smile slipped away. "What if the professor is right and there's something more sinister in the pipe?"

"Like I said, we'll handle it. Trace is a Ranger and a communications expert, Ben's a SEAL, Alex is ex-military and he knows what he's doing."

"And so do you."

Jake glanced at her as they reached the Jeep. "That's

right, I do." He opened the passenger door, caught her waist and lifted her into the vehicle, feeling that little rush of sexual heat that always hit him when he touched her.

In this kind of work, he knew exactly what he was doing. He wished like hell he knew what he was doing when it came to Sage Dumont.

Jake started the car, but didn't pull out of the parking space.

He turned in his seat toward Sage. "There's something on your mind. You'd better spit it out before I make these calls."

She shuddered out a breath. There was definitely something on her mind and Jake had an amazing ability to ferret that out. "I was just thinking...wondering if maybe we shouldn't just bring in the police."

"It's your call. The problem is we don't have any real evidence. We can't turn over the recording or the transcript or we'll be the ones arrested. We can alert the police that something might be coming into the port illegally, but we can't back up our suspicions, and we don't even know for sure what it is."

Sage stared down at her hands, then looked up at Jake. "I'm just... I'm worried something will go wrong. I don't want anyone getting hurt."

"I won't lie to you. Something can always go wrong. But this is the kind of work I do, Sage. If things go the way we plan, we'll stop this without having an international incident. That's in your best interest, the best interest of Marine Drilling, and also the best interest of the sheik and his family."

Jake was right. So far Sheik Khalid had heard no

word from his daughter. He was worried, and rightfully so. He didn't need trouble with his son. At least not the kind that would be spread all over the newspapers.

"You're right. We need to keep this quiet. Stop it before it becomes a real problem." She looked up at him. "Do whatever it takes to make that happen."

Jake just nodded. "There's one more thing. I'm leaving you out of this. If something goes wrong, I don't want you involved."

Sage straightened. "That's not happening, Jake. I'm the one who brought the Saudis over here. I'm the one responsible for whatever it is Roshan is doing. I want to be included."

"You need to think of your career. If you let me handle this and there's trouble, you'll have deniability."

"You mean I can lie and say I didn't know what you were going to do?"

"Yeah, that's what I mean."

"I'm in or it doesn't happen."

Jake's features tightened. He wasn't happy, she could tell, but he was beginning to know her well enough to understand she wouldn't back down. Not on this. Pulling his cell phone out of his coat pocket, he pressed a number. First a call to Alex, then to Ben, explaining the situation, asking for their help, then setting up a meeting at her apartment that evening.

His last call went to Trace.

"All right, that sounds good," Jake said as the conversation progressed. "We'll lay it all out tonight, recon the area tomorrow and go in on Friday. I need you to do a preliminary search, get us some satellite pictures if you can."

Sage couldn't hear Trace's reply, but he must have agreed.

"We'll figure out what gear we need, and assemble everything tomorrow night at my apartment before we head out, use my place as our base of operations. That work for you?"

Apparently Trace said yes.

"All right, then I'll see you at Sage's tonight at nineteen hundred." Jake closed the phone and shoved it into his pocket.

"Nineteen hundred," Sage said. "You're already in military mode."

"Old habit."

He didn't say more as he put the Jeep in Reverse and backed out of the parking space. Sage didn't press him. The men were holding their initial meeting at her apartment. She was pretty sure Jake intended to keep her in the loop.

If he didn't he was in for a big surprise.

Sage was tired by the time they got to her apartment. Jake made his usual inspection of the rooms and as soon as he was sure the place was secure, she went to the kitchen and tossed her oversize leather handbag onto the table. Jake shed his suit coat and tie and popped open the first few buttons on his shirt.

It had been another long day, but through it all she had been constantly aware of him. Watching him now, she could see the strong pulse beating at the base of his suntanned throat, reminding her of the virile body beneath his clothes.

What was there about a man unbuttoning his shirt that sent erotic thoughts into a woman's head?

"I'm desperate for a Coke," she said, turning away from the temptation he presented just by standing there, and opening the fridge.

"I could use something cold to drink," Jake agreed.

She reached inside and pulled out a can of Diet Coke for herself and the real thing for Jake, handed his over, and they both cracked open the tops.

The cold sting of the liquid running down her throat settled her a little and at the same time gave her an energy boost. She had just begun to relax when the phone started ringing. Instantly, the tension she had begun to shed surged back with a vengeance.

Digging her cell out of her purse, she pressed it against her ear. "Sage Dumont."

"Ms. Dumont, it's Detective Brady." Jake bent down so that he could also hear. "We wanted you to know we've released Bert Hobson." The man who had accosted her that night in the Post Oak Grill. "We didn't have enough evidence to hold him."

Jake took the phone. "What about the people who were with him? Did Hobson give up their names?"

"He did. They all checked out. Truth is, we no longer believe Hobson or his friends had any part in the bombing."

"Hobson is no longer a suspect," Jake said to Sage.

She reached up and reclaimed the phone. "If Hobson isn't involved, who is?"

"We don't that know yet, but we will. It's just a matter of time."

She looked up at Jake and shook her head. "I'd appreciate it if you'd keep me informed." She ended the call and tossed the phone back into her purse. "The police don't think it was Hobson. What do you think?"

Jake took a swallow of his drink. "Hobson isn't our man."

"Because of the kind of bomb that was used?"

"That's right. Hobson is in the wind power business. He's got no connection to the oil industry."

She raised the Coke can, took a slow drink just to give herself time to think. "The kind of substance that was used and the detonator... Those same materials are used by the Saudis. You don't think Roshan or his friends could have had something to do with it?"

Jake shook his head. "I don't think so. Roshan wants whatever is in that load of pipe. The car bomb could very well have sent his father back to Saudi Arabia. Roshan would have been forced to go with him or find some excuse to stay. Leaving sooner than planned doesn't suit his purpose."

Jake tipped up the shiny red can and finished his drink in a single long swallow. Sage watched the muscles in his throat move up and down, watched as he crushed the empty can in one of his big hands. A tremor of heat moved through her, tugged low in her belly. So much was happening, the last thing she should be thinking about was sex. Yet just looking at Jake made her want him.

His blue eyes sharpened on her face. "Did you know your cheeks get pink when you're thinking about sex? They're pink right now."

"I—I wasn't thinking about sex."

He tossed the can into the recycle bin. "Liar." He reached for her, pulled her into his arms. She could feel his powerful erection pressing against her as his mouth came down over hers. The kiss was deep and thorough, and she gave up any pretense of resisting.

"I look at you and I want you," Jake whispered against her ear. "I like that you want me, too."

And then he was kissing her again and she was kissing him back. She didn't protest when he carried her into the bedroom and set her on her feet, unclipped his pistol from his belt and laid it on the nightstand. She stopped him when he reached for her and started to strip off her clothes.

"Not this time," she said. "This time it's my turn." Reaching toward him, she finished unbuttoning his shirt, then tugged it free of the waistband of his slacks and pulled it off his shoulders. Jake toed off his shoes and she knelt and stripped away his socks. She could feel his eyes on her as she unbuckled his belt and reached for his zipper, slid it down with a satisfying buzz.

His breathing quickened. He straightened, making him even taller, the ridge of his sex jutting forward. As she slid his slacks down his muscular legs, his eyes remained locked on her face, as hot and blue as flame.

He looked incredibly sexy in a pair of snug-fitting briefs, his arousal making them way too tight. She drew them down his long legs, freeing his erection, and he stepped out of them.

He looked even better naked.

Her heart was beating, thumping inside her chest, and her mouth felt dry. She paused to admire the thick muscles in his thighs, the ridges across his flat stomach, his deep chest and powerful biceps, the heavy bands of muscle across his shoulders.

"My turn," he said gruffly, his impatience building. Her heartbeat quickened as he made short work of removing her yellow suit and cream silk blouse. Then he lifted her out of her heels and let her slide down his body until her bare feet touched the floor.

"I always forget how small you are." Another searing kiss and her bra disappeared, along with her panties. Sage felt his hands on her breasts, cupping them, teasing the crests into peaks.

She was breathing hard, wanting him. "My turn again," she said, sounding as breathless as she felt, and went to work kissing her way down his amazing body.

Sage knelt in front of him, brushed her lips against the healing red mark on his thigh where a piece of hot metal had burned across his skin when the car bomb exploded. Reaching up, she cupped him, stroked him, then took him into her mouth.

"Jesus," he said, clenching his jaw tight. Jake hissed in a breath and slid his hand into her hair. He didn't let her work him over very long. He liked it, though. She could tell by his deep, ragged breathing, the growls of pleasure that came from his throat.

"That's enough," he said harshly. "I have to have you now."

She gasped as he hauled her up and lifted her into his arms, carried her over and settled her on the bed. Jake followed her down and began to feast on her breasts. She thought he would take her, but instead he lifted her, set her astride him, let her sink slowly down until he filled her completely.

"Your turn," he said, and her eyes closed as pleasure washed through her. For a moment she just sat there, absorbing the feel of him inside her, the way they fit so perfectly together, the thrum of her heart and the delicious sensations.

His jaw clenched when she started to move, and

she thrilled at the power she held over him, a man so big and fierce. She wondered that he could be such a thoughtful lover.

It didn't take long until she brought them both to a wild, shuddering climax, their muscles straining, their bodies damp with perspiration. With a sigh of pure pleasure she slumped against his massive chest, nestled there, and felt his hand stroking her hair.

Sage didn't remember falling asleep. She only knew a feeling of deep contentment unlike anything she had ever felt before.

Chapter 22

Jake napped for a while, not really asleep, mostly enjoying the feel of the soft woman nestled against him. Sage was exhausted from the stress of her job, plus dealing with a bomber and a missing girl.

So far they'd heard nothing from the sheik, and A'lia hadn't tried to contact Sage. Jake hoped the girl's father was making the right decision in not alerting the police.

Keeping the girl's disappearance under wraps was a helluva lot better for Sage, since it ensured her name stayed out of the papers. It was also keeping the sheik in Houston and the negotiations alive.

And it was better for A'lia, assuming she was somewhere safe. Without being hunted by the authorities, the girl would be able to make her own decisions. But sooner or later the sheik would want some assurance his daughter was safe and if that didn't happen soon, Jake figured the sheik would do whatever it took to find her.

Doing his best not to waken Sage, he eased out from under her warm, naked body and left her sleeping, her dark hair curling over the pillow. He showered, then dressed in jeans and a drab-green marines T-shirt, soft and thin from so much wear over the years.

He snagged his stainless wristwatch and checked the time, clipped his pistol back onto his belt and made his way into the kitchen. He checked the fridge to make sure Sage had Cokes and beer, and at six o'clock called Domino's Pizza to order a couple extra-large pies, fully loaded, for the meeting ahead.

Padding into Sage's office, he grabbed a yellow pad off her desk and returned to the kitchen, sat down and started making some notes.

It was nearly six-thirty when Sage emerged, freshly showered and smelling like flowers, making him remember how much he liked taking her to bed, arousing him a little before he forced his mind back to business. She was wearing a pair of khakis, a burnt-orange sleeveless top and sandals that showed the orange polish on her toes. He wanted to suck them.

"I ordered some pizza for the guys," he said, determined not to get distracted. "You have plenty of soft drinks and beer." His eyes ran over her and his mouth curved up. "Your hair's still damp and your cheeks are pink."

Her eyes widened. "I'm *not* thinking of—"

His laughter cut her off. "I know. You just look so damned luscious. It makes me want you all over again."

And damned if her cheeks didn't get even pinker. Maybe she really was thinking of sex. Or if she wasn't, he figured he'd just put the thought back in her head.

"Your friends will be here any minute," she told him a little tartly.

The reminder ended his teasing and brought his thoughts back to the work ahead. "Before they arrive, there's something I've been wanting to talk to you about."

"What's that?"

"Who benefits if your negotiations with the Saudis fall through?"

"Some other company, I guess. You were there when I told that to the police."

"That's right. Another company might benefit—or someone in your own company. Someone who doesn't want you to get the job as president."

Her head came up. She hadn't thought of that. He could see by the stubborn set of her chin that she refused to consider it now.

"That's ridiculous. The only other candidate Grandfather would consider would be one of the vice presidents, either Charlie Denton, Jonathan Hunter or Phillip. None of them would try to blow me up to get rid of me."

"The guy who planted the bomb was there watching it happen. You weren't anywhere near the car when he set it off. But the consequences of the act were the same. The threat was enough to send Khalid and his family back home. If he'd left, the deal most likely wouldn't get done. Right?"

"Yes, but—"

"You would have cost the company a boatload of money and got zip for your efforts. And you wouldn't get picked for the promotion. Think about it."

Her lips thinned. "I'm not going to think about it. I know these men. I was going to marry one of them. They wouldn't do something that awful."

Maybe they wouldn't. Then again, the possibility wasn't something Jake was willing to overlook. "I'll have to take your word for it, since I don't know them." But he'd already started checking them out. Tomorrow, he'd set Sol on it. It wouldn't take long before Trace's whiz kid knew everything there was to know about the three men, maybe even whether one of them was involved.

Sage eyed Jake sharply. She was loyal to a fault, but she was also smart. He could almost see her mind spinning, wondering if it was possible that one of the men she knew had arranged for the bombing.

She shook her head, undoubtedly thinking it couldn't be true. But the notion would stick in her head until the bomber was arrested. Sage Dumont was a lot of things, but a fool wasn't one of them.

Dusk settled in. Outside her apartment windows, the lights of the city began to blink on, strings of white and circles of bright colors that would intensify as the evening progressed. The men were due any minute. Former military men who could handle whatever Roshan was planning.

Whatever Roshan was planning. The thought sent a chill down Sage's spine.

She carried a tray of cheese and crackers into the dining room and set it in the middle of the table, along with napkins and paper plates. Sodas and beer were waiting in the refrigerator. It was going to be a testosterone-filled atmosphere the likes of which her apartment had never seen.

The intercom buzzed. *Showtime.* She walked over and pressed the button, gave permission for Alex and Ben to come up. "I'm expecting another guest," she said, and gave the guard Trace's name. "You can send him up as soon as he arrives. Thank you, Henry."

Ben and Alex walked in together, one hard-featured and dark, one smiling and fair; both handsome. Alex was no longer on the security detail unless Jake had something else he had to do. Sage's grandfather had brought in a couple of security people that Jake approved of and Ian had worked with before, which freed up Ben Slocum to help with the job tomorrow night.

Each of them carried an extra-large Domino's pizza.

"We bumped into the delivery boy in the lobby," Alex said. "Figured we'd save him the trip."

"I owe you one," Jake said. Alex set his pizza on the dining-room table and Ben carried his over to the kitchen counter.

A few minutes later, Trace walked through the door, a beautiful redhead on his arm. He pulled off his white straw cowboy hat and held it in his hand.

"Sage, this is my wife, Maggie. I hope you don't mind me bringin' her along. We figured… That is, we thought you might want some company while we're talkin' shop."

A distraction. As curious as she was about Trace's wife, it wasn't going to work. She managed to smile. "It's nice to meet you, Maggie."

"You, too," Maggie said. She was about two inches shorter than Sage, with gorgeous shoulder-length hair that curled softly around her face.

Sage felt a niggle of recognition before a memory surfaced. "I've seen your picture. You're Maggie O'Connell, the photographer." Famous in Texas as a landscape photographer, she was beginning to make a name for herself all over the country.

The woman smiled. "That's right. I'm Maggie Rawlins now."

"Yes, congratulations to you both."

"Thank you."

"Why don't we go in the kitchen while the guys get to work?" Maggie suggested. "Give us a chance for a little girl talk."

Sage's gaze swung to Jake. "Go ahead and do what you need to, but when you're finished, I want to know exactly what you're planning. I want to be in the loop, Jake. This is my problem. You're helping me solve it, but in the end, I'm the one who's going to be held responsible."

Jake looked at Trace. "I could have told you it wouldn't work."

His friend grinned. "Worth a try."

"We're just in the planning stage now," Jake said to Sage. "Once we get going, we'll need your help."

Sage relaxed. "All right. But whatever happens, don't even think of leaving me out."

The corner of Jake's mouth tipped up. "Duly noted."

Sage turned to Maggie. "How about a glass of wine?" she asked, and led the redhead into the kitchen.

Jake grabbed a Coke, followed by Trace. Ben and Alex each opened a Lone Star, and they settled themselves around Sage's sleek black lacquer dining table. The peach silk chairs were comfortable, but not practical. Be hard as hell to clean if one of them dropped a slice of pizza on the seat, God forbid.

Jake inwardly smiled. It probably wasn't too often that Sage had four ex-military sitting at her dining-room table plotting their next mission.

"Anything new on the bomber?" Alex asked, starting them in the right direction. They'd talked a few more times on the phone, come up with some preliminary plans. The rest would be laid out tonight.

"Hobson has been released," Jake said. "Police don't think he's connected."

"Sayers gave me a heads-up on that," Trace said, referring to his detective friend. "Told me Brady was going to call Sage and let her know. He says they're looking in a different direction."

Jake wondered if his theory might be right and the police were looking a little closer to home.

"You able to get those satellite photos we need?" he asked.

"Affirmative. Sol took care of it. He didn't say how he got 'em and I didn't ask." The kid could work wonders on the computer. Trace did his best to keep him reined in unless it was important.

This was important.

Trace opened the briefcase he'd brought with him, took out rolled-up satellite photos and spread them on the table. He used his laptop to weigh down one end, and Ben and Alex set their beer bottles on the other.

"This shows the pier where the *Normandy* is scheduled to dock sometime tomorrow morning. They'll start unloading cargo that day. I figure they'll be finished sometime Friday."

Jake turned toward the kitchen, heard the sound of female laughter. It seemed as if the women were getting along just fine.

He shoved back his chair and went to get Sage, hoping she could help them here. She and Maggie were chowing down on slices of pizza and sipping glasses of chilled white wine.

"If you two can quit gossiping for a minute—Sage, we could use your help."

A smug smile flitted across her face. "Of course." She grabbed the plate and her wine and walked ahead of Jake to the dining room. Maggie followed them in and both women sat down.

The guys were scarfing pizza when he joined them. Jake grabbed a slice for himself, took a bite and set the rest down on a paper plate.

He swallowed and swung his attention to Sage. "Trace says the *Normandy* will be docking tomorrow, off-loading tomorrow and Friday. That sound right to you?"

Her eyes widened. "How did he know that?"

"Only ship comin' in from the Middle East between now and Sunday," Trace answered.

She frowned. "How did you get that information?"

"Took a look at the schedule of arrivals at the Port of Houston over the next few days."

"Yes, but how did you—"

"It's what we do, Sage," Jake said, "and you don't want to know more than that."

She flicked a glance between the two of them and moistened her lips. "All right. Okay…" She took a sip of wine. "Yes, that sounds correct," she said, answering his question. "The *Normandy* is hauling one of the last two loads of five-inch pipe we purchased from the Saudis. It should be completely off-loaded by late Friday afternoon and transported to the storage area. It'll be kept there over the weekend until the trucks arrive to pick it up and disperse it to the proper locations on Monday."

"Do you know which storage area it'll be kept in?"

"It's on my computer. Let me pull up the data." Sage

hurried to her office and returned with a printout that held the shipping information.

"The *Normandy* should be docking around ten in the morning at one of the wharves in the Woodhouse Terminal—that's on the north side of the ship channel near Galena. After the pipes are off-loaded, they'll be kept in storage area C."

Trace pulled out a 24-by-36-inch map of the area. Jake didn't tell Sage she was mostly confirming info Trace had already gotten. He laid the map on top of the satellite images, located the docking site, then the storage area.

"Right here." Trace pointed to the spot, then circled it with a fluorescent marker.

"They'll wait for dark," Jake said, "then go in. They'll need time to locate the pipe or pipes that hold the merchandise and remove it."

Jake studied the map, examined the route to the area Trace had circled in yellow. "Quadim said Tariq would be there when the product was retrieved. They'll have the drugs out of the pipe. The other guys will be bringing the money. Since these kinds of folks aren't all that trusting, they probably plan to make the exchange right there in the storage area."

Ben and Alex both leaned over the table to examine the first map, then locate area C on the satellite images. Ben used the magnifying glass Jake had brought from Sage's study to get a closer look.

"Open area. Enclosed by what appears to be chain-link fence. Looks like mercury lights along the perimeter."

Alex took the glass, leaned over the table. "Lights aren't too close together. Shouldn't be hard to take a few of them out."

"I'll handle that," Trace said. "Lights'll be off long enough for you to go in. I'll turn them back on after you're under cover."

"What happens then?" Sage asked.

"The bad guys arrive to retrieve the merchandise," Ben said, "and exchange it for the money."

"And after?" she pressed.

Alex grinned, his dimples digging in. "Then we take it away from them, sweetheart."

"Like candy from a baby," Ben added.

"Not quite," Jake said. "It's trickier when you need to make it happen without any casualties."

Ben's ice-blue eyes swung to Sage. "That means we don't get to kill anyone."

Her eyebrows went up. "Oh."

He was kidding, Jake knew, but with Ben it wasn't that easy to tell.

Sage took another sip of wine. "So how will you get the stuff away from them without using weapons?"

"Oh, we'll be carrying," Alex said. "None of us has a death wish. But we'll be using tranquilizer darts and stun guns to take them out."

"Jake'll be point man," Trace added. "He'll be located somewhere on the perimeter. He'll take out as many of them as he can from his position without alerting the others, then we go in and finish the job."

"I'll be armed with a CO_2-powered air gun," Jake explained. "A Pneu-Dart X-Caliber. It's the kind of rifle they use to sedate wild animals. This model is extremely accurate."

Sage looked up at him. "I've seen you shoot. I know how good you are."

He smiled. She was right. He was one of the best.

He'd be using a night-vision scope and it was a good one. He wouldn't miss. Still, it was a single-action weapon. He'd have to reload, so he wouldn't be able to take all of them out. That would be Ben and Alex's job.

"How do you plan to get inside?" Sage asked. "The main entrance stays open, but the gate to the storage area will be locked, and a security guard patrols the grounds."

"Tomorrow we'll take an up-close look around," Trace said, "see what kind of alarm system they've got, figure a way to get by it."

"We'll time the guard's rounds," Jake said, "figure how much time we'll have to get in and take up our positions. Unfortunately, we won't be able to get too close in the daytime. There's bound to be security cameras all over the place."

Sage sat up a little straighter, her eyes lighting up. He didn't like the look on her face.

"I can get you in," she said. "I'm head of acquisitions for MDI. We have a shipment coming in—that gives me a reason to be there. If my car shows up on the cameras, no one is going to think anything about it."

Jake started shaking his head. "I told you, I don't want you involved. If something goes wrong—"

"Something is a lot more likely to go wrong if you don't have good information. I can help you get it. You need me, Jake."

Ben looked at him hard, those pale blue eyes pinning him like a laser. "She's right, you know. We need all the intel we can get. Besides, it's not like we're stealing anything. No one knows about the stuff in the pipe. Hell, we don't even know for sure it's there. We're just eliminating a possible problem before it occurs."

Alex took a swallow of his beer. "Hard to argue with that."

Jake leaned back in his chair. "I still don't like it."

For the first time Maggie spoke up. She rarely interfered in Trace's business, but when she did, her husband usually listened. So did Jake.

"If this goes wrong," she said, "the problem comes down on Sage. It ought to be her decision."

Sage smiled warmly at her, then swung her gaze back to Jake. "And my decision is to drive you and Trace to the port, help you find out what you need to know, and get out of there."

Jake scowled. He didn't like it. Not one damned bit. But his friends were putting themselves in harm's way to help him, and he didn't want them taking any more chances than they had to. "Fine, we'll do it your way."

Sage exchanged a triumphant smile with Maggie, then sat back in her chair.

"Looks like we're done for tonight," Jake said. "Tomorrow, after Trace and I finish our surveillance, we'll meet up back at the office. That work for everyone?"

"Works for me," Alex said.

"Me, too," said Ben.

"Fine. Then why don't we finish this pizza?"

"Here's to that." Alex lifted his beer and took a long swallow.

Jake started to reach for another slice, then slid his gaze to Sage. He thought about what might happen if something went wrong, and discovered he was no longer hungry.

Chapter 23

It was early Thursday, the antique gilded clock on the mantel ticking the minutes away, reminding Rina that she needed to get to her job at Smith Barney Morgan Stanley. Ryan was still out of town so she had been staying in her own apartment with A'lia, dropping by the one she shared with Ryan to water the plants—real ones instead of the silk ones she grudgingly kept in her own place, since she wasn't there that much.

She was ready to leave for work when she spotted A'lia sitting on the living-room sofa.

"Sleep all right?" she asked, walking over to talk to her, already knowing the answer. The queen-size bed in the guest room was comfortable and there was a bathroom just down the hall. But Rina had heard the TV playing softly at two o'clock in the morning.

"It is hard to get used to the change in time."

Good an excuse as any, but not the root of the problem. Rina sat down on the overstuffed sofa and gently rested a hand on A'lia's slender shoulder.

"Listen, sweetie, I know you're upset, but you can't stay holed up in here forever. We have to do something to resolve this."

The girl looked up at her from beneath thick black lashes. "You have been kind to me, Rina, and I know what you say is true. But I am afraid."

"Of your father?"

"No, but... I do not know what will happen to me if they find me. Roshan is only my half brother, and we have never gotten along. He thinks I am too outspoken for a woman."

"Your father is bound to be worried. Sooner or later you're going to have to talk to him. If you can convince him to let you stay in America, you can have the life you want."

Her eyes were big and dark, their size and color emphasized by the pink silk head scarf that covered her neck and most of her lovely face. Aside from that, she was dressed in Western clothes—jeans and a pink T-shirt with butterflies on the front.

"I wish I knew what to do," she murmured.

"Why don't you let me help you? I think I know where to begin. Let me call Sage. She knows you're missing. She called me at the office yesterday and we talked about it."

"You did not tell her—"

"No, I didn't tell her you were here. She said her meetings were still going on with your father. That means she's in touch with him every day. Let me speak to her."

Rina started to say she would phone Sage and ask her to set up a meeting between A'lia and the sheik, but as she considered the idea, she wasn't sure a phone conversation would be enough to convince Sage to help them.

The deal with Sheik Khalid was crucial to Sage's career. It was bound to influence her thinking. Better to let A'lia ask her. The young girl's pleas for help were hard to resist.

"What if she tells my father I am staying with you, and Roshan finds out?"

"I'm not going to tell her anything. I'm going to say I need to talk to her. Then we'll go see her together. You can explain everything yourself and ask her to help you."

A'lia sat quietly, her head bent, hands clasped together in her lap. "All right," she finally agreed, looking resigned. "I will do as you say, and I will pray that your friend will help me."

Rina managed to smile. "All right then. I'll call her from my office this morning, see if I can get her to let us come over tonight."

A'lia nodded, but she didn't look any happier than she had before.

They reviewed the plan as Sage prepared to leave for her meeting the following morning with the sheik.

"So we'll pick Trace up and go out to the port this afternoon."

Jake nodded. "As soon as you're finished for the day."

"Lately Khalid's been leaving a little early. If we're lucky, that will happen again today. If not, I'll come up with a reason to cut the meeting short."

"Good."

"And we'll be taking my car," Sage said, "so it won't matter if it shows up on the security cameras."

"Good so far," Jake agreed.

"When we get to the port," she continued, going over the details in her head, "I'll stop and check in, tell them I'm there to be sure the *Normandy* has arrived, and check on the progress of the off-loading. Then we'll make our way around to storage area C, and you and Trace can take a look."

Jake gazed toward the window, staring out at the sprawling city ten stories below. "I wish I could think of another way, but we don't have much time and we need to take that look."

"And we will." It wouldn't be that hard, would it? She had every right to be there and she could take whomever she wished.

Sage inwardly shivered. How had her simple plan to purchase equipment from the Saudis gone so far astray?

Nervously, she smoothed the front of her pale blue suit. "I've spent a small fortune buying clothes I wouldn't dream of wearing under different circumstances. I'll never be so glad to stop dressing in these damned long skirts."

His mouth edged up. "Be worth it if you make your deal. Maybe today will be the day."

"I think there's a chance it could happen. Now that my goal is in sight, I don't dare wind things up till after tomorrow night. I want to know what Roshan is doing and I want to make sure we stop him."

"That's the plan," Jake said.

A thought that was sobering. This afternoon she

was going on a spy mission, and tomorrow night the men would be sneaking in to retrieve whatever it was that was stashed in one or more sections of the pipe Marine Drilling had purchased from Saudi Arabia.

If there was actually something there.

Willing herself not to worry, she shifted her focus to the meeting ahead.

Will and Red were waiting in her attorney's Midtown office when she arrived, followed soon after by the Saudis. Leaving Jake outside the conference room door, they all went in and continued the negotiations, Sage doing her best to keep her mind on the job she was trying to do, and not the reconnaissance mission ahead.

As she had hoped, the meeting ended early. Khalid was clearly worried about his daughter and seemed to have trouble focusing. Tomorrow, Friday, was a day of meditation and prayer. He hoped the day would bring word of A'lia, and his family a little peace.

Afterward, having a bit of extra time, Sage made a stop downtown at her office, which was where Rina found her, sitting behind her desk, making a few last-minute calls.

"You turned off your phone," her friend chided as she opened the door and walked in with barely a knock.

Sage stood up from behind her desk, always glad to see her. "I was meeting with the sheik."

"I figured. I just… I was hoping I might be able to stop by your place tonight. There's something important I need to talk to you about."

"What is it?"

"I don't have time right now. I'm hoping later will be okay."

Sage didn't like the edginess she heard in her best friend's voice. Maybe Rina was breaking up with Ryan. They were never really suited, as far as Sage was concerned, so that might not be such bad news.

"All right, sure." She grabbed her briefcase and they walked out of her office. Jake was waiting, anxious to head for the port. On the way, they would be stopping at a coffee shop to pick up Trace.

"Will Jake be there tonight?"

Sage flicked him a glance, saw him standing near the reception desk in bodyguard mode. He was so damned big and so damned sexy that she felt a hot little twinge.

"He's my bodyguard. He'll be there."

Rina smiled. "How's that going for you?"

She couldn't stop a grin. "Amazing."

"Good call, then."

"So far." Sage had told her friend about her breakup with Phillip. She hadn't said that her relationship with Jake had everything to do with sex and nothing at all to do with building a future together. She ignored a little pang and kept the thought to herself.

"He works for you, right? So you can trust him," Rina said, an odd thought even for her.

"I trust him, yes, but what does that have to do with—"

One of the elevators across the room dinged as the door slid open, and Rina's gaze darted in that direction. "Look, I've got to run," she said. "I'll see you tonight. Seven o'clock okay?"

"Should be fine." Unless something happened

during her sojourn at the port. "I'll call if something comes up."

Rina waved over her shoulder. "See you then."

Sage looked down at her watch. Past time to leave.

Jake walked up to her. "It's almost two. You ready to go?"

To make a spy run through the Port of Houston. "I'm ready." *Sort of.*

"Good, let's head out."

Sage tightened her grip on her briefcase; Jake caught her arm and led her toward the elevator.

"You still up for this?" he asked as they crossed the lobby to the rear door, as usual.

"I haven't changed my mind, if that's what you're asking."

Jake's jaw tightened. He didn't want her to get involved. She wished she didn't have to, but as far as she was concerned, she had to see this whole thing through.

At least the demonstrations had ended. No protestors were marching around with signs, no media were lurking—at least not for the moment.

"Stay here," Jake said as they reached her Mercedes, which he had thoroughly gone over that morning in search of a bomb—an extremely unsettling thought.

A security guard had been assigned to watch the car while it sat in the lot, but he checked the undercarriage again to be sure it was safe. It reminded her how upside down her world had become. Maybe after tomorrow night, things would begin to return to normal.

Sage prayed it would be true.

Since his office was in the opposite direction, they picked Trace up at a truck stop near the juncture of the

45 and the south loop of the 610 Freeway. Sitting next to Sage in the passenger seat of her car, Jake leaned back as she drove east to the Clinton exit and made her way toward Galena.

"By the way," Trace said from the backseat, "that kid you sent, Bo Johnson, showed up to work this morning."

"That so," Jake said.

"Bo Johnson…?" Sage repeated. "Isn't that the boy who was giving Felix Porter a bad time?"

"That's right," Jake said. "Bo and I had a little chat. He won't be bothering Felix again."

Sage flicked him a sideways glance. "During this little chat, you decided to help him get a job?"

Jake shrugged. "His mother's been sick. Kid needs money. Maybe he'll find out it's better to earn it by working than by selling drugs."

"Bo didn't back away from anything I asked him to do," Trace said. "Might just work out."

"For his sake, I hope so."

Sage said nothing more, but Jake could see by the look on her face she hadn't expected him to do that. Hell, it was no big deal. Kid would probably screw up, anyway.

At the main entrance, Sage stopped the car and went to check in. Jake watched her disappear, wishing he could have kept her out of this completely. But it wasn't going to happen. Time was a factor, and they didn't have all that much.

She was gone only a few minutes. "They're still off-loading," she said as she slid back in behind the wheel. "Everything's going according to schedule, so they should be finished sometime tomorrow morning.

Then the pipe will be transported to storage area C. They lock the gate there at 5:00 p.m."

Using a small digital camera, Jake took photos along the route as she drove to the wharf where the *Normandy* was docked, then on to the fenced-in storage area where the pipe would be kept over the weekend.

Jake had been to the port on business before. Add to that the time he'd spent on the internet studying maps and information, of which there was plenty. The Woodhouse Terminal and surroundings were huge, with three wharves, several hundred thousand square feet of transit sheds, and acres of open storage. The roadways were alive with trucks, loaded and empty, as well as pickups, cars and heavy equipment. There were dozens of big round oil tanks, and containers of various sizes and shapes for other liquid storage.

Jake was happy to see that some of the tanks backed up to area C, right behind the fence. They all had ladders that wound around them to the top.

He and Trace got out of the car.

"Stay here," Jake said to Sage through the driver's window, which she had rolled down. "This won't take long."

He spotted a couple of cameras and was careful to stay out of range, his bill cap pulled low, as he reconned the grounds inside the chain-link fence. The sliding gate was open and lots of workers milled around. He took a few shots and carefully stayed out of video camera range.

Trace was off checking the alarm system, looking for the main connection. Once he had the information he needed, he'd be able to turn off the alarm and then reset it after they were inside, so the bad guys wouldn't know anyone was in there.

Jake took photos of the place where the load of pipe would be stacked, designated by a sign that read Marine Drilling International. He finished just as his friend reappeared.

"I got what we need," Trace said.

"So did I." He tipped his head toward one of the tanks. "Good vantage point up there."

Trace followed his gaze, his dark eyes shaded by the brim of a dark blue baseball cap. "Real good."

Jake took a last glance at the various items stored in the lot: metal containers and stacks of wooden boxes, pyramids of pipe in various sizes, a row of brand-new dump trucks, another of yellow bulldozers.

"Plenty of cover around," he said. "We'll figure our positions when we get to the office."

"I didn't see any security guards in the area," Sage said when the man returned.

"Probably don't start making rounds till after closing."

"Sounds right," Trace said. "We'll have to keep a sharp eye."

Jake nodded. "Let's go back to the office and lay it all out."

At least her part was over. As Sage drove back to the city, she released a sigh of relief. She still couldn't believe she had spent the afternoon spying, getting ready for a mission to stop a shipment of drugs from being smuggled into the country.

If Jake was right.

Her heart was still beating a little too fast as she

drove the Mercedes into the parking lot in front of Atlas Security, Jake sitting in the passenger seat beside her, Trace driving his own vehicle back from the coffee shop where they had picked him up.

She pulled into one of the customer parking spaces out front. The afternoon heat was beginning to take its toll and a slight headache throbbed at the base of her skull.

She had never been to Jake's office before, but the front of the single-story brick building was well-maintained, and it was nice inside, she saw as she walked in with Jake, done in tones of beige and dark green, with oak desks, and photographs of Texas landscapes on the walls.

A plump older woman with slightly frizzy blond hair and thin, penciled eyebrows sat at the reception desk, a pair of half glasses perched on her nose.

"Annie, this is Sage Dumont," Jake said. "Annie is the lady who rules the roost around here."

Sage smiled. "A pleasure to meet you."

"You, too." The woman smiled back. "You're even prettier than your pictures."

"Thank you."

"I hear you dumped that guy you were seeing. Smart move. He wasn't right for you. I had a hunch you'd figure that out."

For several moments Sage just stood there, unable to think of a single thing to say. "How did you know about Phillip?"

Annie held up the *National Enquirer* spread open on her desk. "I like to stay informed."

The sleazy tabloid wasn't exactly Sage's idea of

staying informed, but she didn't say so. She hadn't even known the article was in there.

"Don't pay any attention to Annie," Jake said. "She's always got her nose in other people's business."

"Good thing for you," the receptionist quipped, sending him a look Sage didn't understand.

"Annie knows pretty much everything that's going on in Houston," Jake finally conceded, "and I admit there are times her information comes in handy."

"And don't you forget it." Annie turned to Sage, kept her voice low. "Jake's a really nice guy. He just doesn't want anyone to know it. Got a heart of gold—" her gaze flicked over him, head to foot "—not to mention his more obvious attributes." She winked, and Sage laughed.

"I'll keep that in mind."

Jake caught her arm, flicked Annie a warning glance, and hauled Sage off toward a door at the back of the office.

In a small meeting room, Alex and Ben sat at a heavy oak table surrounded by wooden captain's chairs. Trace sat down, opened his laptop and began tapping away on the keyboard. Alex leaned back and stretched his long legs out beneath the table, while Ben stared intently at the maps spread in front of him.

Sage sat down, leaving a spot for Jake closer to the men. He began by opening the back of the small digital camera he had been using out at the port and pulling out the memory card.

Trace looked up from a screen filled with coded information. "Getting in shouldn't be tough. The system in the storage area is wireless and at least five years old. I've got the software we need to handle it."

"Great." Jake handed him the photo card. "These ought to give us a little closer look at what's on site."

Trace pushed the card into a slot in the computer. Using a wireless device in another part of the office, he printed out the pictures and went to retrieve them.

For the next half hour, the men pored over the details of the plan, each choosing a position that would provide the best possible cover.

"They'll need transportation to carry the money in and the merchandise out. Odds are they'll drive in through the gate, which means they'll have a pass code or something. Then they'll have to disable the alarm."

"I'll be running communications from just outside the fence," Trace said. "Soon as you get the parabolic set up, we'll know what's going on."

"Parabolic?" Sage asked.

"Microphone," Jake answered. "You can hear conversation clear as a bell from three hundred yards away. Trace'll be handling communications, and we'll all be wearing mics and earbuds, so we'll be in constant contact."

"I see."

"I'll be positioned near the top of a tank," Jake said. "Once they've retrieved the drugs, or whatever the hell is in there, I'll take out as many as I can. Ben and Alex will take out the others, grab the merchandise, and we're out of there."

Sage sat there, pondering the situation, while the men went over the photos and maps once more. "I wonder how Tariq will know which pipe has the drugs?" she finally asked.

"They'll have it marked some way. Judging from their conversation, this isn't the first shipment. Whoever is getting the money from the buyers—in this case, Tariq—will know exactly where to find the goods."

"What about the video cameras?" she asked. "Don't you need to worry about them?"

"We'll be dressed in black and wearing black face paint. We'll be driving one of the Atlas SUVs, but the name on the side and the license plate will be covered. Keep in mind that as long as nothing goes wrong, no one is going to check the cameras or the alarm system. No one will ever know we were there."

But what if something did go wrong? Drug dealers carried guns. They killed people every day. They would shoot Jake or anyone else who tried to take what they considered their property.

Her heart constricted. She couldn't stand to think of something happening to Jake. She couldn't imagine his powerful, dynamic presence being gone from her life. Her chest clamped down even harder as the realization struck her. When had Jake Cantrell become so important? How could she have let her emotions grow so deep where he was concerned?

She told herself she was worried about all of them. That she didn't want any of the men to get hurt, and it was true.

Sage suppressed a tremor of fear.

Chapter 24

The night was heavy, warm and dark as Rina pulled her little red SLK convertible up in front of Sage's high-rise condo building and parked in one of the guest spaces in front. Aside from her quick stop downtown to see Sage, she had spent the day in her Smith Barney Morgan Stanley office, doing her best to concentrate on the market and her customers' investments.

A'lia had stayed hidden in her apartment.

Rina shoved open the heavy glass door, and she and A'lia stepped inside the lobby, into air-conditioning so cold that goose bumps rose on her skin. A'lia fidgeted nervously beside her. She tried not to do the same.

"Are you certain she will not tell my father?" the young woman asked once again. Rina didn't have time to answer before they reached the front desk.

The security guard knew her and smiled. "Good

evening, Ms. Eckhart, it's good to see you. I'll tell Ms. Dumont you're here."

"Thank you, Henry." She turned to A'lia as they headed for the elevators. "Sage is my best friend and I trust her. More than that, we need her help. I'll do everything I can to convince her." *And Jake.*

But she wasn't completely sure what either of them would do. Sage had always been driven, always wanting to prove herself, especially to her grandfather. Rina knew how desperately she wanted to close this deal with the Saudis.

And yet her heart was kind and generous, and Rina knew she sympathized greatly with the young woman's plight.

Whatever might happen, they needed Sage's help. A'lia wouldn't be completely free or completely safe until she gained her father's approval. Sage had the best chance of helping them make that happen.

On the tenth floor, they stepped out of the elevator and walked down the hall to Sage's door. A'lia nervously adjusted the blue head scarf she wore, one of several Rina had bought her, along with two pairs of jeans and a few modest, cotton knit tops.

A shopping trip wasn't going to happen until A'lia was safe.

The door swung open when Rina knocked, and Sage greeted her with a smile. She was still wearing the business suit she'd had on at the office.

"Come on in," she said, stepping back out of the way. Her eyes widened. "Oh, my God—A'lia!" The warm smile faded, but at least she didn't slam the door in their faces.

"Surprise!" Rina said brightly, trying to lighten the mood.

Sage laid a hand over her heart as if she was having a heart attack. Maybe she was. "Yes...yes, it certainly is." She cast Rina a glare before speaking to her guest. "A'lia, I'm so glad to know you're safe. Your father has been extremely worried."

Tears filled the young woman's beautiful eyes. "I did not wish for him to worry, but I had to get away. I could not live as he wished me to."

"Why don't we go into the living room?" Sage suggested with another dark glance Rina's way.

"Where's Jake?" Rina asked.

"He's in my office working on the computer. I'm sure he'll be as...surprised to see A'lia as I am." She flashed Rina a sharp-edged smile. *Thanks for the warning,* her look said. Followed by, *Have you lost your mind?*

For the next few minutes, Rina explained how A'lia had gotten away from her cousins and bodyguard, how she had come to her for help.

"She had my business card," Rina said. "I gave it to her the weekend we were out at your ranch. She came to me because she didn't know where else to go. Now she's in trouble and you're the only person who can help her."

Heavy footsteps sounded in the hallway. "Jesus!" Jake stood there transfixed. "Christ, could things get any worse?"

A'lia started crying.

"Now see what you've done?" Rina scolded. "You big brute."

"Wait a minute! I didn't mean to..." Jake took a slow, deep breath. "Son of a bitch."

"It's all right, sweetie," Rina soothed. "Jake isn't mad at you." She drilled him with a glare. "Are you, Jake?"

"No." He strode the rest of the way into the living room. "I'm sorry, A'lia. None of this is your fault. It's just bad timing."

Rina looked up at him. "What kind of bad timing?"

"Never mind," Sage said.

Probably interfering with their plans for a hot night of sex, Rina thought. Or at least that's what she'd be planning if she was with a virile man like Jake.

She shook her head, wondering where the hell that thought had come from. Macho men were not her type, and Ryan was a really nice guy.

"The thing is," Rina said, "you both know enough about Middle East customs to understand the kind of trouble A'lia is in. She's disobeyed her father. That just isn't allowed. Her dad is undoubtedly angry, but it's Roshan she's really afraid of."

A look passed between Sage and Jake.

"You know what Roshan is like," Rina continued. "He'll want to see her punished. A'lia's afraid of him and I don't blame her."

"I don't, either," Sage said.

"Then you'll help her?"

"Help her do what?" Jake asked, from where he stood behind the sofa. "Sage has her hands full with the deal she's trying to negotiate and everything else that's been going on. She's had protests and threats. And in case you've forgotten, a couple of days ago, someone tried to blow her up."

A'lia stood up from the sofa, her eyes still glistening with tears. "I am sorry. I should not have come. You have enough trouble of your own." She started for the door, but Sage caught her arm.

"Wait, A'lia. You don't have to leave." Sage led her back to the sofa and sat down beside her. "I just wasn't expecting to see you, that's all. Why don't we talk this over?"

Rina heard Jake's muttered curse.

"Your father's really been worried," Sage said. "After the car bomb went off, I think he would have left Houston and gone back to Saudi Arabia if you hadn't run away. He told me he wouldn't leave until he'd talked you, made sure you were safe."

"I wish to talk to him, also. I must try again to explain, to make him understand. Other Muslim women are content with the lives they lead. I am different. I have this yearning, this need to see things, do things. I wish to go to school, get as much education as I can."

Sage squeezed her hand. "I'll call your father in the morning, tell him you want to see him."

"Not tomorrow," A'lia said. "Tomorrow is a day of prayer. It would not be a good time."

"All right, I'll call him Saturday morning, see if I can set something up." Sage looked at Rina. "And A'lia can stay with you until then?"

"It's not a problem. Ryan is gone for another few days and I've been talking to him on his cell. He doesn't even know I'm not staying at our apartment." Rina glanced over at Jake, whose features looked iron hard. He wasn't liking this. Not one bit.

Sage followed Rina's gaze, and so did A'lia. Just standing there with his shoulders propped against the wall and his arms crossed over his massive chest, the man was imposing.

"Jake won't say anything to your father," Sage promised. "You don't have to worry about that."

"It's not my place to interfere," he said. "I won't say a word."

Not that he didn't want to, Rina could tell.

"There is…there is one more thing. I am sorry I did not tell you, Rina." *Uh-oh.* "You see, there is a boy."

"Fuck…" Jake grumbled, so low Rina hoped A'lia didn't hear. Silently, Rina repeated the word herself.

"His name is Dan-ish Ganjani. We met in Riyadh when I was at university. No one knew except my roommate, who is also my cousin. Danny is from Pakistan, but he lives in America now. He was visiting his brother, who works in Riyadh. We met at a bookstore and he asked if he could see me. My roommate and her brother went with us. Danny and I discovered we have many things in common. We didn't plan for it to happen, but we…we fell in love. Danny has asked me to marry him."

No one said a word, not even Jake.

"Does Danny live in Houston?" Rina finally asked.

"No, in New York City. He is a computer expert. I have not called him. I must be free before I can accept his proposal of marriage."

Jake shoved away from the wall and stalked forward. "Sage, you need to consider this very carefully. There is no way in hell her father is going to approve of this. It's his duty to choose her husband. If he thinks for a moment you've gone behind his back to help his daughter, you can kiss your deal goodbye."

Sage just sat there.

"Call her father, tell him A'lia came to you for help.

Tell him she wants to see him, then let her take it from there."

"That isn't enough," Rina said. "She needs you to help her convince him. The sheik respects you, Sage. He sees you as an equal, or at least as close as a woman can get to his level. He might listen to you. It's her only chance."

Jake towered over Sage. "And your only chance to make this deal you've worked your ass off on for the last six months is for you to stay out of it."

Sage looked at A'lia, whose beautiful face was even paler than when she'd arrived.

"I want to help you, A'lia, I truly do, but I need to think about it. There are things going on right now that you don't know about. I need to see how all of that works out first. I'll give you my decision Saturday morning. No matter what happens, I'll arrange a meeting between you and your father. For now that's the best I can do."

"Sage—" Rina began.

"That's my decision, Rina. I'll phone Saturday morning. If I can help, I will. I won't know until then."

Rina didn't press her. She knew her friend well enough to realize something else was going on, something that might affect her situation with the sheik, maybe even A'lia.

"That's good enough for me," Rina said, rising to her feet.

A'lia stood up, too. "Whatever happens, I know you and Rina have done your best to help me. I will always remember."

Sage walked them to the door, then leaned over and hugged A'lia. "Rina will make sure you're okay. She's a very good friend to have."

Rina felt a sharp sting behind her eyes. "You're a very good friend to have, too," she said, and the two of them hugged.

They left the apartment, A'lia looking even more forlorn than she had before, and Rina not feeling much better. What would it be like to love someone so much you would risk your entire future, maybe your life, just to be with him?

She wondered if she would ever know.

Sage felt Jake's hands settle gently on her shoulders. She turned to look into his handsome face.

"I know I shouldn't get involved," she said. "I know you don't approve, but I just… A'lia deserves a chance to be happy."

He bent his head and very softly kissed her. "I gave you good, sound advice, and I meant every word. Staying as far away from A'lia and her troubles with her father and brother is exactly what you should do. Doesn't mean I don't admire you for wanting to help her."

"She's in trouble, Jake. If it weren't for Roshan and whatever he's planning, I might have gone ahead and agreed to talk to her father on her behalf."

"If you do, he might blow your deal right out of the water."

"I know." She released a shaky breath. "But it's the right thing to do, and in the end, I don't think I can turn away from that. After all I've learned, I understand why A'lia feels the way she does. I understand why she ran away and I don't see how I can stand by and not help her."

Jake caught her chin between his fingers. "I wondered how you'd feel if it came to something like this.

I should have known." And then he kissed her again. It was the gentlest, most tender kiss she had ever known, and it made her heart turn over. She slid her arms around his neck and for several long moments just hung on.

Her heart was beating softly and she felt close to tears. Dear God, she was falling in love with him. It couldn't be happening, but it was. She swallowed past the lump in her throat. There was no way it could work for them. Just looking at Jake and thinking of the mission he would be undertaking tomorrow night told her that.

She inhaled deeply, steeled herself and eased away. "At least I have until Saturday to make my decision."

"We'll know more by then, and you handled it just right. If Roshan and his friends are bringing drugs into the country, we'll have to tell the sheik. Resolving that problem has to come first."

"Yes."

Jake eased her back into his arms. "But nothing is going to get resolved tonight, so why don't I take you to bed?" There was hunger in those blue, blue eyes and the way he said the words made her stomach quiver.

She knew what it was like when Jake Cantrell took a woman to bed. Knew that after the hot, erotic sex, she would sleep more soundly than she had anytime before she'd met him.

She went up on her toes and kissed him, a hotter, deeper, wetter kiss than before. Jake responded as he always did, taking control, kissing her back until her toes curled inside her high heels.

As promised, he took her to bed and made love to her slowly, gently.

Sage tried not to think of the broken heart she was going to suffer when Jake was gone.

Chapter 25

Dusk had fallen. It was Friday night and time was ticking toward the mission ahead. Jake's mind was already focused in that direction.

"You ready?" he asked Sage.

"Let me get my purse."

One of his big concerns had been what to do with Sage while he was out with the men. Whatever was going down didn't change the fact that a bomber was still out there. Jake's guess was the man hadn't meant to kill Sage or anyone else, but there was no way to know for sure until the cops had him in custody.

Jake had discussed the situation with Trace and they'd decided to change their base of operations and assemble their gear at his place. Jake would leave Sage with Maggie until the mission was over.

Trace's house was a fortress, armed with every kind

of alarm system imaginable. Security was his business and he wanted the best. There was no such thing as being too careful.

On top of that, Jake had asked Rex Westcott, a guy who worked stakeouts for Trace, to position himself on the street out front. Sage would be safe till they got back.

"I've got it," she said, slinging her big leather bag over her shoulder. "I'm ready to go."

Amazingly, when he'd told her his plans, Sage hadn't argued. She was beginning to know him, to understand when to back down and accept his decisions.

"We're out of here," he said as they left the apartment and headed for the Jeep. They went over the mission on the way.

"If you find the drugs," Sage asked, "what will you do with Tariq?"

"Take him to the sheik, explain what's been going on."

"If that happens, I have to be there. I'll need to go with you."

He'd known this was coming. He wanted to say no, but he knew she deserved to go. Knew that what happened tonight would be crucial to the deal she was making, a deal that would greatly affect her future.

"Don't say no, Jake. Not this time." And the look in her eyes warned him that if he did, she would find some way to be there with or without him.

"We don't know for sure what we'll find. Until we do, there's no sense talking about it."

"I want to be there when you confront Roshan. I have to be."

Jake clenched his jaw. She was right and he knew

it. "Okay, if it goes down the way we think it will, I'll take you with me."

She didn't say more, just sat back in her seat and stared out the window. A few minutes later he pulled up in front of Trace's single-story, wood-frame house. As Jake walked Sage to the door, he felt her tremble.

"You okay?" he asked.

She caught his arm, turned him to face her. "I'm worried about you." When she looked at him with those golden-brown eyes, something squeezed inside his chest. "I don't want you getting hurt."

Jake reached out and touched her cheek. "There's a saying...you can plan the party, but you can't plan the outcome. Something can always go wrong. But if everything goes right, this'll all be over soon."

She managed a nod, gave him a halfhearted smile.

"And I like that you're worried. It's been a long time since a woman I cared about worried about me."

Sage started to say something, but the door opened and Trace stood in the entry. "Come on in. The party's about to get started."

As Jake walked inside, he saw Alex and Ben, dressed completely in black, as he and Trace were.

"Gear's loaded," Alex said.

Jake checked his pistol one last time and slid it back into the holster at his waist.

"Latest satellite photos show the pipe has been stored in the spot reserved for them in area C," Trace said. "Everything looks good to go."

Ben shoved himself to his feet, his pale blue eyes intense, his features hard with purpose, making him look like the Iceman that was his SEAL name. "Time to rock and roll."

Jake grabbed Sage, dragged her into his arms and kissed her long and deep. Trace walked over to Maggie and did the same.

"Take care of yourselves," Sage said, and Jake thought he caught the sheen of tears.

Jake ignored the tightness that had returned to his chest. He needed to focus on the mission. "Okay, kiddies, time to play."

After a last quick glance at Sage, he was gone.

"How do you stand this?" Sage asked Maggie, who gazed at the closed door the men had just disappeared through, a worried expression on her face.

"It doesn't happen that often," she replied, "and I've come to trust Trace's judgment. He was a Ranger. They're all ex-military, and they've worked together enough to form a competent team. Did you know that before we were married, Trace saved my life?"

Sage stared at her. "No, I didn't."

"Why don't we have a glass of wine and I'll tell you about it."

"I better not. I need to stay alert. If they find drugs, Jake'll be taking Tariq to the sheik. I'll need to go with them."

"As wired as you are, one glass of wine isn't going to do any more than calm your nerves. Besides, it's liable to be hours before they return."

Hours of worry. Sage's nerves were already strung so tight she was shaking. "You're right. I think I could use a drink."

She followed Maggie toward the kitchen. Dressed in jeans and a yellow cotton top, with her wavy red hair and green eyes, she was a very pretty woman.

"Don't you worry about him?" she asked as her new friend opened a white, retro-fifties refrigerator, took out a bottle of white wine and set it on the counter. The kitchen itself was charming, done in a fifties design with red-and-white-checked curtains, a Formica-topped table and chrome chairs, and sparkling white appliances that were new but built to look vintage.

"Of course I worry," Maggie said. "I love him madly. I feel so lucky that he loves me, too. But like I said, this isn't an everyday occurrence. Mostly, Trace runs the office and investigates cases that interest him, usually nothing that requires him to wear a Kevlar vest and carry night-vision goggles, sleep darts and a Beretta."

Maybe Trace had mostly settled down, but Jake was different. Missions like these were his life. He'd worked in the Middle East and South America. He was a mercenary and a highly paid bodyguard. He specialized in this sort of thing.

This is what I do, Sage.

Maggie poured them each a glass of wine and handed one to Sage. "You're in love with him, aren't you?"

Her heart twisted. She had never felt this way about a man before. "I'm trying very hard not to be."

"Why is that? It looked to me like he's pretty crazy about you, too."

Was he? It was hard to know what Jake felt for her. "It's mostly sexual attraction for both of us," she said, trying hard to convince herself. "I thought it would pass, but so far it hasn't."

"When Trace and I first started dating, I kind of thought that, too."

Sage sipped her wine. "It's different for the two of you. Trace's life is here. So is yours. Jake isn't the kind of man to settle down."

"I think he might if he found the right woman."

Sage ran a finger around the rim of her glass. "Maybe. Even if he tried, it wouldn't matter. We aren't well suited."

"Because of your career?"

"Partly. My job requires me to socialize with a certain caliber of people. I don't mean that in a snobbish way, but my grandfather runs with the country club set. MDI sponsors benefits and community events I'm required to attend. Jake would hate that kind of thing."

"Maybe. But I've learned that marriage is a give-and-take. If he loved you, I think Jake would do just fine with those kinds of things. Not all the time, of course. He's a man's man. So is Trace. But I can tell you from experience, Trace looks amazing in a tux. Jake might just surprise you."

Oh, yeah, the man was full of surprises. Sage tried not to think of the way they'd made love that morning, but she could feel the heat rising in her face.

"Even if you were right," she said, "Jake told me himself he never stays in one place very long. He gets bored, I think. There's no way he'd be happy staying in Houston for the rest of his life."

"But you would be."

"My family's here, my business. Houston is my home. I don't think Jake cares about that kind of thing."

"You could be right, I don't know. He does move

around a lot—Trace told me that. I suppose time will tell."

"I suppose." But the thought of Jake leaving made Sage's insides squeeze into a knot. Sooner or later he would be gone. If she were smart, she'd rein in her feelings before she got seriously hurt.

She looked up at Maggie and mustered a smile. "So how did your handsome husband save your life?"

For the next half hour, Maggie told her the fascinating story of a stalker who had nearly killed her, and how she'd wound up a married woman instead.

Even as Sage listened, a tiny part of her mind was thinking of Jake and worrying about him, wondering if he was safe.

The drive through the main entrance went smoothly. Even this late at night, trucks rumbled along the roads, disappearing into one location and appearing from another. There were private as well as public facilities along the twenty-five-mile-long complex that made up the Port of Houston.

Fortunately, no work was being done in the section of storage area C that housed the recently arrived load of pipe. As the black Atlas Security SUV got closer, the men finished putting on their gear and blackening their faces. Trace pulled the vehicle behind a cluster of equipment parked outside the locked gate, and they all got out.

Jake fastened the clasp on the front of his Kevlar vest, put on his mic and earbuds, and the others did the same. Ben and Alex snapped their stun guns in place and grabbed a bag each of tranq darts. Ben picked up the parabolic mic, while Trace set up his laptop on the tailgate and Jake made a final check of his air rifle and tranquilizer darts.

"Alarm's off," Trace said, hitting a key on his computer. "Power's off to the mercury lights around the perimeter. You can go in whenever you're ready."

"Can't think of a better time than now," Ben said, parabolic in hand.

"Let's kick some drug smuggler ass," Alex said with his trademark grin, and the men took off for the gate. Ben slid it open, and he and Alex disappeared inside, heading for the positions they had decided on last night.

As Jake set off for the oil storage tank behind the stack of pipes, he tested his mic and earbuds and got replies back from Trace and the other two men. With the dart gun slung over his shoulder, he climbed the stairs that wound around the tank and took a position on a platform near the top. As soon as they were all in position, Trace reset the alarm and powered up the mercury lights.

Everything was ready. Jake didn't doubt their quarry would show up sooner or later.

All they had to do was wait.

"God, it seems like they've been gone forever," Sage said, fighting the urge to get up and pace in front of the sofa. The house, a single-story residence in the University District not far from the Atlas Security office, had been remodeled to supply all the modern conveniences, and it was extremely comfortable.

In the living room, an overstuffed burgundy sofa and chairs sat on deep beige carpets. Family photos perched on tables, and Maggie Rawlins's spectacular landscape photography hung on the walls.

Maggie walked toward her out of the kitchen. "Actually, it isn't even one o'clock yet. Trace said he figured the meet would be set for sometime between midnight and two. Less people around."

"I can't stop worrying."

Maggie sat down next to her on the sofa. Both of them had switched to drinking iced tea.

"I've been around these guys for a while now," Maggie said. "I know how good they are. I remind myself of that whenever they're involved in something like this."

"Which isn't all that often." Sage repeated Maggie's earlier words.

"That's right. Life has its risks. I love Trace enough to accept the risks he sometimes takes."

Could Sage do that? Risk loving a man who worked the dangerous jobs Jake often undertook?

She didn't think so.

"Want to watch some TV?" Maggie asked. "Might make the time pass more quickly."

"Sure." But Sage knew she could sit there with her eyes glued to the screen and not have a clue what the show was about. All she could think of was Jake and how worried she was.

Please, God, don't let anything happen to him. Don't let anything happen to any of them.

She just hoped God was listening.

"Here they come." It was a little after 1:00 a.m. From his vantage point on top of the tank, Jake spotted a black van with chrome wheels rolling toward them along the road.

"Roger that." Trace's drawl crackled through the earbud.

Ben and Alex both copied the information.

The van stopped at the gate and a few minutes later the mercury lights shut down. The alarm must have been disabled, too, because a man jumped out and rolled the gate open.

Apparently, Trace wasn't the only one with state-of-the-art equipment. Drug money could buy the best of a lot of things.

The Atlas vehicle was hidden well out of sight. Through the night-vision scope on his rifle, Jake watched the black van drive through the gate to a spot behind a corrugated metal container where it couldn't be spotted from the road, and the engine fell silent.

The first man returned to the van and climbed in. Nothing happened until another car approached a few minutes later—an unimposing Buick four-door with two men inside. Had to be Tariq and the contact man, the guy who had brokered the deal. The car pulled up in front of the stack of pipe, the engine shut off and the men stepped out of the car.

It was too dark to tell which one was Tariq, but Jake figured he was on the passenger side, since he didn't have a car. The driver had to be the contact Quadim had mentioned on the recording.

Three men poured out of the van and walked over to join the new arrivals, while a fourth, the driver, stayed with the vehicle.

"They're talking about the shipment," Trace said, picking up the voices on the parabolic mic.

"One of the guys from the Buick's got a black light," Alex noted. "Looks like he's trying to locate some kind of fluorescent mark on the pipe."

"He's zeroing in on the drugs," Jake said.

Wielding flashlights, the men searched the pipe openings at the back of the stack, then came around and shone the black light on the openings in front.

"He's found the mark and located the drugs," Trace said, listening to the conversation. "He's telling the buyers to go get the money."

Jake scanned the scene through his night scope, watched one of the men use a telescoping rod with a hook on the end to drag out the packages from inside the five-inch pipe. It took a while before all the merchandise was located and retrieved.

"They're sayin' that's the last package," Trace said.

"Get ready to roll," Jake murmured. Across the compound, he spotted the driver, standing next to the van. The sleep dart was loaded. Jake lifted the rifle and rested the stock against his shoulder, sighted down the barrel and squeezed the trigger. He felt the slight kick, but there wasn't much sound. Through the night scope, he saw the man drop down behind the van, conveniently out of sight.

"Driver's out," he said, reloading the gun with another tranq dart.

"Roger," Trace said. Ben and Alex copied.

"One more shot," Jake said.

The team prepared to make their move. The minute he fired the next dart and the buyers saw one of their own go down, the rest would arm themselves and scatter. The chaos would give Ben and Alex the chance go in, and Jake the chance for another shot.

He raised the rifle, aimed at the guy heading back to the van to retrieve the money, and squeezed again. The man reached over his shoulder to grab the dart that hit solidly in the middle of his back, then went down like a sack of wheat.

Someone shouted an alarm. As Jake reloaded, they all pulled weapons and bolted like rats for cover. Problem was, wherever they went, either Ben or Alex was there ahead of them, ready to take them down.

This was the dangerous part. It was close work and the men they were after were all carrying weapons. Jake heard Alex's voice through the earbud: "Sleepy time for number three."

Through the scope, Jake saw a tussle going on between two men, one in a headlock. The struggle ended and the target crumpled to the ground.

"Four's napping peacefully," Ben reported.

That left two more unaccounted for. Someone moved off to the right and an instant later, a gunshot echoed across the compound.

Alex cursed. "One of them took a hit."

Jake held the rifle steady on the moving target. As the shooter ran toward a stack of crates, he pulled the trigger, imbedding a dart in the side of the guy's neck. The figure hit the ground and rolled, ending up sprawled facedown in the dirt.

A few feet away, Alex knelt beside the guy who'd taken a bullet. "Heart shot," he said into his mic. "It's the contact man. No other casualties."

"I'm on my way," Jake said. Slinging his rifle over his shoulder, he headed down the winding stairs, his mind moving from plan A to plan B. He climbed the chain-link fence at the back of the storage area, thank-

ful there was no barbed wire on top, vaulted over and
landed on the balls of his feet.

He spotted Ben jogging toward him. "The name on
the dead guy's license is Gamal Ali. Except for him,
they're all sleeping like lambs."

Jake glanced around. There hadn't been any sign of
a security guard all night. Probably been paid to stay
away from the area.

He knelt beside the guy lying in a growing pool of
blood. Mixed heritage, mostly black, judging from
his skin tone. The man's facial features were blunt,
his cheeks covered by a beard. Both arms sported a
maze of one-color, primitive tattoos.

"Gamal Ali," Ben said. "Sounds Middle Eastern,
but he doesn't look it."

"With all those tats, looks like a guy who's been
in prison."

"What do we do about him?"

"Drug smuggling's a dangerous game. The guy's
luck ran out. Leave him and the others where they are."
Jake checked on each one, saw they were all breathing steadily. Three Hispanics wearing earrings and
do-rags, and a white guy with a sunburn.

"Since no one was supposed to get killed," Ben
said, "what's plan B?"

On a mission, there always was one, and usually
a plan C.

"You remember that DEA agent who debriefed us
after our little adventure in Belize?" A mission they'd
gone on a few months back with his friend Johnnie
Riggs.

"Richard Haskins?" Ben said as they loaded the
drugs into the van next to the money-filled briefcase.

"Yeah, I remember him. He's a level thirteen agent. Got plenty of pull and after what went down in Belize, he owes us. We gonna tip him to this?"

"That's plan B. We leave the money and the drugs in the van, leave our friends peacefully sleeping and the problems to the DEA. They'll match one of the guns to the bullet in the dead guy. That takes everyone else out of the equation. With the contact man out of the way, there's no one to tie the deal to Tariq or Roshan. The Feds leave MDI out of it, since all the company did was buy a load of used drill pipe, and in exchange, the DEA boys get to make one helluva bust."

Trace started nodding. "That could work," he said.

Ben flicked a glance at the expensive, tricked-out van. "The bad news is, with the kind of money these guys make, they'll be out of jail in a heartbeat and royally pissed."

"Maybe, but they won't be dead. And they won't have a clue what went down."

"That's it then," Alex said. "Let's load Tariq and our gear into the SUV and get the hell out of here."

They wiped down the Buick that belonged to the dead guy, erasing any prints Tariq might have left, loaded themselves into the SUV and hit the road.

They left the alarm turned off and the gate open. It looked like a drug deal gone bad, and that was exactly what it was.

"How much do you figure they had?" Alex asked.

"Looked like pure heroin," Trace said. "I figure a million plus, inside the briefcase. After it's cut, that's about twenty million street value."

Alex whistled.

As Trace pulled the SUV onto the freeway, Jake

pulled one of the sealed packages out of a canvas bag. "I kept this one for the sheik. Proof his little boy was playing dirty."

He stuffed the heroin back into the bag and drew out his cell phone. He had Haskins's cell number from the debriefing. He'd loaded it into his phone before they'd left the house—just in case.

Haskins answered in a groggy, sleep-thickened voice, and Jake started talking, putting plan B into action.

Chapter 26

"Did you hear that?" Sage stirred on the sofa in the living room. She must have dozed off. Now she was wide-awake.

"It's them," Maggie said, coming out of her chair. She ran to the kitchen, checked to be sure it was her husband and the others, and turned off the alarm system. Sage was standing next to her when the back door swung open and the men walked in.

Sage's heart swelled. All of them were still wearing their flak vests over the black clothes they'd set off in. Now those clothes were dusty, torn in a couple of places, and their faces streaked with black paint they hadn't completely wiped away.

They looked fearsome and dear, and as Jake tossed a canvas bag onto the kitchen counter and walked toward her, she ran to him, threw her arms around his neck and just hung on.

"You're all right," she said as he pulled her tight against him. "You're okay."

"We're all okay," he said, then bent and gave her a quick, hard kiss.

Ben wound up the parade, carrying Tariq's limp body over his shoulder.

Sage recognized Roshan's bodyguard and her stomach churned. "He isn't...he isn't dead, is he?"

"Just sleeping," Ben said. "He'll be out for a couple more hours."

Sage let out a breath. "Good. That's good."

"Unfortunately, his partner wasn't so lucky," Jake told her.

"One of the bad guys shot him," Alex explained, as Ben carted Tariq to the sofa and tossed him down on the cushions.

"It wasn't what we planned," Jake added, "but the truth is, it makes our situation easier. I cut a deal with the DEA. They're picking up the money, the drugs and the guys who were buying them. You and Marine Drilling are out of it. And with the contact man out of the way, they can't connect the deal to Roshan or Tariq."

Sage sank down in one of the chrome kitchen chairs. It was almost too much to handle. "What... what happens now?"

"You and I take it from here. We load Tariq into the Jeep and pay a little visit to the sheik. There's a kilo of heroin in that bag on the counter. I don't think Khalid's going to be happy when he finds out what his son and the kid's friends have been doing."

Sage looked up at Jake, thought how fierce he looked, how completely in control. "So you were right." She shoved her hair back from her face. She was bone tired and at the same time keyed up. "First A'lia and now Roshan. I feel sorry for Khalid."

"Roshan is spoiled and selfish, which is partly the sheik's fault for indulging him so much. On the other hand, A'lia is smart and loving. One out of two isn't bad."

"Why don't I make us some coffee?" Maggie suggested.

Alex shook his head. "Thanks, but I'm heading on home."

"I'm already gone," Ben said, and both men started through the living room toward the door.

"Tell Rex we don't need him anymore," Jake said.

"Will do," said Alex as he opened the front door and headed out to the street, where the men's cars were parked.

Sage's gaze followed them. "Rex who?"

"Guy who works for Trace. He's been keeping an eye on things here just in case. Figured we didn't need any more surprises."

Sage closed her eyes and leaned back in her chair.

"You don't have to go with me," Jake said softly.

She opened her eyes. "Yes, I do. I'm just… It's a lot to handle all at once."

"I know it is, honey." He sat down in the chair beside her, took her hand between both of his. "But you know as well as I do life isn't always easy."

No, it wasn't. Her first twelve years had taught her that. Still… "A man is dead, Jake."

"A man who smuggles illegal drugs into the country. Drugs that end up hurting kids like Felix Porter. Tonight we stopped that from happening."

She thought of the young boy Jake was helping, a kid who was doing his best to stay out of trouble. The notion that they might have helped kids like Felix in some way made her feel a little better. "Yes, I guess we did."

Her words made Jake smile. As big as he was, with his face still smudged with greasepaint and his eyes so incredibly blue, he was the most virile, most attractive man she had ever met. It was insane to want him now, when everything in her world was completely upside down, but she did.

"I wish it was tomorrow," he said, his gaze locked with hers. "I wish we were somewhere else, someplace where I could give you what both of us need."

She reached out and stroked his cheek. "I was so worried." She remembered what he had said. *It's been a long time since a woman I cared about worried about me.* Those words had touched something inside her.

His eyes remained on her face. "We're going to get through this, Sage. Everything's going to be all right."

Maybe it would be. But once it was over, what would happen to her and Jake? Her heart squeezed. The pain was already starting. It was only going to get worse.

"We've got to go," Jake said, rising to his feet. "When Tariq doesn't return to the hotel, Roshan's going to get worried. We don't want him to panic and do something stupid."

She got up out of her chair. She wasn't dressed for a meeting with the sheik—she was wearing jeans and a turquoise, short-sleeved knit sweater. It would have to do.

She turned to Maggie. "Thank you for everything."

Maggie walked over and hugged her. "If you need me, just call."

Sage managed to smile. "Thanks."

"Keep me posted," Trace said.

"You bet." Jake handed Sage the canvas bag from the counter, then walked over to Tariq, who was dressed in beige slacks and a dark blue polo shirt instead of his usual black suit.

"How are we going to get him into the hotel like that?"

Jake bent down and hoisted the man over his shoulder in a fireman's carry. "We just tell the doorman he partied a little too hard. Staff at a first-class hotel like that are used to being discreet."

Adjusting the strap of the canvas bag over her shoulder, Sage grabbed her purse and hurried ahead, opening the door while Jake carried Tariq outside.

Moments later they were in the Jeep, Tariq settled in the back, and rolling down the road toward the Four Seasons Hotel. Sage had no idea what was going to happen when they got there.

Or what she was going to tell A'lia when she called as promised in the morning.

Getting inside the hotel and up to the presidential suite on the twentieth floor wasn't a problem. Jake had been there a number of times with Sage, the sheik and his entourage. And looking at Tariq hanging over Jake's shoulder, no one doubted he was dead drunk.

Jake knocked on the door to the suite. A few seconds later, the door swung open. Kiron, one of the sheik's tall, imposing bodyguards, stood there staring at the incongruous group of people in the hall. When he recognized Tariq, his black eyes widened.

"We need to speak to the sheik," Jake said when the man made no move to invite them inside.

"It's a matter of extreme importance," Sage added.

Finally, Kiron stepped back, allowing them into the suite but barring them from going any farther.

"What you ask is impossible," the bodyguard said. "I will take care of Tariq, but you cannot disturb His Highness at this late hour. You may speak to him in the morning."

Jake walked past him and dumped Tariq on an elegant white sofa. He lay there with his eyes closed and his mouth hanging open, his shoulder-length hair a black cloud around his face.

"We need to see the sheik now," Sage insisted. "It's important or we wouldn't be here. Tell him there's a problem that involves his son."

For several long moments Kiron didn't move. Then he gave a faint nod and strode out of the room.

He returned a few minutes later. "The sheik will see you, but he must have time to dress. You may wait for him there."

He pointed to a conversation area at the opposite end of the opulent living room. Jake took the canvas bag from Sage's hand and guided her in that direction. They sat down in overstuffed chairs around a gilded, glass-topped coffee table.

They waited a full twenty minutes before Sheik Khalid walked into the living room, perfectly groomed and dressed in his usual white robe and headdress. Jake and Sage both rose from their chairs as he approached.

"Your Highness," Sage said formally, letting him know how important this was. "I hope you will pardon my dress. There was no time to change."

Khalid acknowledged the remark with a frown, his gaze going to Tariq, who sprawled ignominiously on the sofa at the opposite end of the living room.

"Please…tell me what has happened. What has brought you here at this hour?"

"Perhaps we should all sit down," Jake suggested.

They returned to their seats around the low table, and the sheik sat down, as well. Jake opened the black canvas bag and pulled out the kilo of raw heroin he had taken from the storage area.

"This is what brings us here. Twenty million dollars' worth of this, and more than a million dollars in cash that is now in the hands of the Unites States Drug Enforcement Agency. I brought this so you could see for yourself what your son and his friends are involved in."

The sheik's face went pale beneath his beard. He sat there stunned as Jake and Sage spent the next half hour explaining the conversation Jake had overheard at the ranch. Leaving out the part about the flash drive recording from the limo, they went on to say that they had been able to prevent the drug deal from being completed, but in the process one of the drug smugglers had been killed.

"So far we've been able to keep you and your family out of this," Jake said. "But you need to get Roshan and the others out of the country. I'm presuming you'll see that they're properly dealt with, and do whatever is necessary to ensure nothing like this happens again."

The sheik looked devastated. "In our country, possession of an illicit drug is punished by a flogging or a very harsh jail sentence. Drug trafficking carries the same penalty as murder or rape—a public beheading."

Jake ignored the faint sound Sage made.

"Roshan is your son," she said, obviously shaken. "I do not expect you to punish him by giving him a death sentence."

The sheik stood and began to pace, his robes fanning out around his sandaled feet. The air hung heavy with uncertainty.

Finally, he stopped pacing and returned to where they sat. "There is no doubt what must be done. Quadim and the others involved in this will be imprisoned. At the very least, my son will be forced into exile. He will receive no more money, and to his family, from this night forward, he will be dead."

"Sheik Khalid," Sage began.

He fixed his attention on her. "You must not interfere in this. Roshan has broken our laws. He is fortunate that he will continue to live." The sheik turned to Kiron, who stood at the far end of the room with his hands clasped in front of him. "Bring my son and Quadim, and also Yousef." Roshan's cousin and his other bodyguard.

"We don't know if Yousef is involved," Jake said, though Quadim clearly was, since his voice was on the recording.

"I will discover the truth."

No one spoke as Kiron left to collect the men, nor while he was gone.

He returned a few minutes later. "Quadim and Yousef are gone, Your Highness."

"Gone?"

"Their rooms are empty. Their beds have not been slept in."

So Quadim and Yousef were both in the wind. No doubt now the other bodyguard was involved.

The sheik's features hardened. "And my son?"

Kiron stepped out of the way and Roshan walked into the living room. He was fully dressed in his robe and headdress, obviously waiting for news. The moment he saw Tariq sprawled on the sofa, his handsome face went pale.

"Join us, my son."

He hesitated only a moment, then started forward, stopping in front of his father. Though he tried to mask his expression, a muscle ticked in his cheek. His features were set in defiance, but his hands were shaking.

"According to our friends, you and your cousin have been busy this night." Khalid turned, pointed at Tariq. "As you can see, all did not go as planned."

Roshan drilled Jake with a glare. "I do not know what lies these people have told you, but—"

"Do not compound your shame by trying to place blame where it does not belong. The least you can do is have the courage to admit what you have done."

"I admit nothing."

"Then we will see what Tariq has to say when he awakens from his slumber." He turned to Jake. "How much longer?"

"Shouldn't be too long now."

As if on cue, Tariq began to mumble and stir. Kiron was joined by Kamal, the sheik's other bodyguard, and both men stood over Tariq as he awakened.

"Where is your cousin Quadim?" the sheik asked Roshan mildly.

His son blinked. "I assume he is in his room."

"I am afraid Quadim and Yousef are missing. That leaves you to deal with this situation on your own. Is there anything you wish to say?"

Roshan was breathing too fast, his eyes darting around the room, his composure slipping badly. He swallowed, wet his lips. "It...it was all Quadim's idea. He told me it would be easy."

Beneath his beard, the sheik's lips thinned. "How many times have you done this?"

Roshan flicked a glance toward Tariq. "It started with the first purchase Marine Drilling made of used pipe. This was the third shipment. It...it was to be our last."

"How did you get the drugs?"

Roshan wet his lips. "They came from Afghanistan into Port Ras Tanura. That was where the pipe was being loaded before it was shipped to Houston."

"Who else was involved in this?"

"No one. There were only the four of us."

For several long moments, the sheik said nothing. "Why?" he finally asked, his eyes full of sadness. "Tell me why you have done this thing?"

Roshan looked at his father and his jaw hardened. "I was tired of begging you for money. I wanted money of my own. Enough that I could leave, be out from under your control."

Resignation and regret settled in Khalid's stern face, making him look years older. "Both of my children wish to be free of me. A'lia has run away and my son has committed a heinous crime. The shame is mine to bear as much as my children."

Sage stood and faced him. "Your daughter has not

shamed you, Sheik Khalid. She has contacted me. She wishes to see you. She seeks your understanding, your approval. She loves you. She does not wish you to lose the love you feel for her in return."

The sheik stiffened. "I cannot think of A'lia now. First I must deal with my son. Until this matter is resolved, I ask that you say nothing of this to anyone."

"Of course not," Sage said.

He turned to Jake, stuffed the drugs back into the canvas bag and handed it over. "Please give this to the authorities."

"I'll see that they get it."

Both Jake and Sage made polite farewells to the sheik. Neither of them spoke as they crossed the room, but the fear Jake saw on Tariq's dark face as his eyes followed them to the door said the situation would be dealt with as harshly as the sheik had promised.

Chapter 27

Warm sunlight filtered through the curtains into the bedroom where Jake lay next to Sage in her king-size bed. She'd fallen asleep in the Jeep on the way home last night. In her apartment, while he'd been in the shower, she had undressed, then fallen asleep on top of the covers.

He'd tucked her into bed and joined her there, drawn her into his arms and let her sleep curled against him for the short remainder of the night.

She was exhausted, he knew. Worry and uncertainty did that to a person. She was out of her element in all this, finding her way through murky, unknown territory, though she was handling the situation far better than most people would.

As he lay on his side, Sage's head tucked beneath his chin, Jake thought of last night, recalling the instant he had walked through Trace's back door and seen the worry on Sage's beautiful face, the tears in her eyes as she threw herself into his arms.

He remembered the powerful surge of emotion he had felt, the feeling of rightness, the bone-deep knowledge that this was his woman, the one he hadn't realized he had been waiting for all his life.

Sage belonged to him.

The problem was what to do about it.

He listened to her deep, even breathing, and asked himself if he was willing to give up the life he had been living for more than a decade, the excitement he always felt when he started over somewhere new, the adrenaline rush of an unknown mission.

Was he willing to make those kinds of changes for Sage?

The truth was he had been moving in that direction even before he'd met her. He'd been sending down roots here in Houston, making friends, allowing himself to feel things, experience life in a way his work wouldn't allow before. Like joining the Big Brother program. Like spending time with Felix Porter and his family.

There were people he cared about in Houston, people who cared about him. A wife and family wouldn't be the burden he'd once believed. They would be his joy.

Sage would be his joy.

He waited for the punch in the gut, the voice in his head that warned, *Time to hit the road, buddy. Get the hell out before it's too late.* But the punch never came. Maybe he was finally ready to settle down, to explore a different side of himself than the tough, go-it-alone guy he'd been since his father had died.

He thought of that day and a sharp pang centered in his chest. He'd been a senior in high school, and his father's death had hit him hard. He remembered his mother's grief and how he had worked the farm every extra minute, dawn to dark, to help her.

He thought of his stepfather, the man his mother had finally married. Jake had left the farm so she would have a chance to be happy again. He thought of how he had joined the marines hoping to make a place for himself in the world.

And it had been. He was good at his job. One of the best. His kind of talent was always needed somewhere. But that existence was lonely. He had come to a point where he wanted more.

Unconsciously, he smoothed a hand over Sage's heavy, dark hair. Trouble was he wasn't sure what Sage wanted. He knew she cared about him. She had made that clear last night. Did she love him? And even if she did, would she want a hard man like him in her life?

Because the raw truth was, no matter how much he changed, he'd still be the same man. The work he did involved a certain amount of risk. Though he could choose assignments that involved less danger, there were times he'd be needed, and he knew he would go. He was who he was. Sage would have to accept that, be willing to accept him and the kind of life he lived.

She stirred beside him, but didn't awaken. They'd had almost no sleep last night. He gently tucked a lock of hair behind her ear. *So beautiful,* he thought, and felt himself harden. He'd wanted her last night, but she was so damned tired he was worried about her. He wanted her now, but she needed to sleep and regain her strength.

There were still problems ahead for her. She'd promised to call A'lia this morning, and though the girl's father hadn't agreed to a meeting, Jake figured in time he would.

And the guy who had blown up Linc's SUV was still out there. Still a threat to her. The police were making some headway—Jake didn't know how much. So far Sol had come up with squat on Jonathan Hunter and Charles Denton, Sage's competition for the upcoming MDI president's job. Jake wanted the kid to dig deeper, take another hard look.

He needed to get up and get moving. Instead, he drew Sage a little closer, ignored his raging hard-on and let her drift deeper into sleep.

Yawning behind her hand, Sage sat up in bed. A brilliant sun shone through a crack in the bedroom curtains. The place beside her on the mattress was empty, Jake no longer there. When she looked at the clock, she saw it was almost noon.

She took a deep breath and swung her feet to the side of the bed. Dammit, she should have been up hours ago. But Jake had let her sleep, and she couldn't help being grateful. She felt more herself than she had in days.

She hurried to shower and dress, choosing a pair of khaki slacks and a pretty apricot blouse edged with lace. She had promised to phone A'lia, and though the sheik hadn't agreed to see her, Sage's decision about helping his daughter had been made.

She couldn't ignore that A'lia was trying to carve out a life under very difficult circumstances. Sage had to do all she could to help.

The rich aroma of freshly brewed coffee drew her into the kitchen. Jake poured her a cup as she walked through the door, his blue eyes running over her as she took a bracing sip.

She smiled at him, a hum of pleasure coming from her throat. "I really needed this."

"You feeling better?"

He looked refreshed this morning, clean-shaven, with his short, dark hair neatly combed. He was wearing faded blue jeans and low-topped leather work boots, and a fresh, light blue T-shirt stretched over his massive chest.

"I'm rested, thanks to you."

His mouth curved into a sexy smile. "If I'd had my way, you'd have slept a little less but felt even better."

Sage laughed. "Maybe we'll have time for a, um, nap this afternoon."

His smile widened. "Sounds good to me."

"In the meantime, I've got to call A'lia."

Jake took a sip of his coffee. "You gonna to tell her about Roshan?"

"Definitely not. That's family business. I'll leave that to her father."

Jake nodded in approval. "I'm starving. How about an omelet and bacon? Maybe a couple slices of toast? I'm not a great cook but I can put that much together."

"That'd be great. I'll be back when I'm finished."

Smiling, she left him in the kitchen, thinking what a rare man he was and how much her life had changed since she'd met him. Sitting down at her desk, she picked up the phone and punched in Rina's cell number, hoping to reach her friend in her Uptown apartment.

Rina picked up on the second ring. "Hey, girlfriend.

I'm glad you called. I told A'lia you would. I said you always keep your word."

"Late night or I would have called earlier. Is she there?"

"She's here. She's chewed off half her nails waiting for the phone to ring. I'll get her."

A few seconds later A'lia's soft voice came over the line. "Hello?"

"Good morning, A'lia."

"Good morning, Sage."

"I called to tell you I spoke to your father last night."

"You did?"

"Yes, I did. I told him I'd been in touch with you. I told him you wanted to talk to him, try to explain everything that's happened. I told him you loved him and didn't want to lose that love."

A'lia started crying. "What…what did he say?"

Sage paused a moment, trying to find the right thing to say without mentioning A'lia's half brother. "Your father has a lot on his plate right now."

"His plate? I do not understand."

Sage rolled her eyes at the bad choice of words. "What I mean is he's got some things he needs to take care of. I think…once everything gets back to normal, he'll want to see you."

"He hates me."

"He doesn't hate you. He just… I'll give him tomorrow, then call him on Monday. If he agrees, we'll go see him together. I'll do what I can to help you convince him to give you his permission to go to school in this country."

"Do you…do you think he will?"

"I don't know. We'll have to wait and see, but I'm fairly sure I can arrange a meeting."

"Thank you," A'lia said softly, and Sage could hear the tears in her voice.

Rina came back on the line. "You spoke to the sheik last night?"

"Yes, in regard to a different matter."

"What was it?"

"Something that didn't involve A'lia."

"You're being evasive," Rina said.

"That's correct," Sage said, hoping her friend would understand her tone and not say too much in front of the girl. She couldn't tell anyone about Roshan. She had given the sheik her word.

"I need your help with this, Rina. I need a few more days. I'll explain everything as soon as I can."

"Okay, no problem. Do what you have to and don't worry—I'll take care of things on this end."

Relief flowed through her. "I really appreciate what you're doing for A'lia."

"She's a good kid. Unfortunately, Ryan's coming home Sunday night. He's going to expect me to be at the apartment when he gets there. A'lia can stay here, but I hate leaving her alone."

"I'll do my best to speed things up. As soon as I have something to tell you, I'll call."

"Take care of yourself," Rina said.

Sage thought of the man cooking breakfast for her in the kitchen. "Jake's here. I'll be okay." And it was true. He always seemed to be there when she needed him. She tried not to think what it would be like once all of this was over and he was gone.

She ended the call and wandered back into the

kitchen, her stomach rumbling at the savory breakfast smells.

"I put her off a few more days," she announced, pouring herself more coffee, then refilling Jake's cup.

Rounding the breakfast bar, he set two steaming plates on the table, each holding a cheese omelet, bacon, and buttered toast. Her mouth watering, Sage seated herself in front of one, while Jake sat down across from her.

"What do we have to do next?" she asked, forking in a mouthful of eggs. She gave little moan of pleasure, the omelet was so delicious.

"I've been thinking about that. It's the weekend. I doubt we'll hear from the sheik before Monday. We need to turn that last bag of heroin over to the DEA, but aside from that there's not much else we can do before the first of the week. How about we take the rest of today and tomorrow and just wind down?"

Some of the stress she'd been feeling eased from between her shoulders. "I need to check on my grandfather sometime this weekend, but aside from that, winding down sounds great. I think we deserve it."

"After last night, I think so, too."

They smiled at each other, then dug in to their food. Jake finished first, but waited politely for her to finish her last crispy piece of bacon.

"I haven't been to the gym since all this started," Sage said. "Maybe after we run your errand, we could go downstairs and work out for an hour or two."

He rolled his powerful shoulders. "I could use a good workout." His blue eyes gleamed. "Afterward, maybe we can shower, then take that nap."

Oh, yes. She felt hot just thinking about it. Showering with Jake, then another steamy round of sex before they fell asleep. "Sounds perfect."

They finished their late breakfast and cleaned up the dishes. Jake phoned Agent Haskins, his DEA connection, and set up a meeting at the Atlas Security office to hand over the bag of heroin they had taken in last night's raid.

"You're gonna come up one bag short," Jake explained to the agent over the phone. "I needed to borrow it for a couple of hours. It's all yours now."

Haskins said something Sage couldn't hear.

"You don't want to know," Jake replied. Then he added, "All right. I'll meet you at my office in twenty minutes." He ended the call and shoved his iPhone back in his pocket. He looked over at Sage. "I figured the sooner we left, the sooner we'd get back."

Sage gave a fake yawn behind her hand. "I'm feeling sleepy already."

Jake laughed and they headed for the door.

Unfortunately, the phone rang as they stepped out into the corridor. Jake held the door for Sage, who hurried back inside, ran to the kitchen and grabbed the receiver off the wall.

"Good afternoon, Your Highness." She flicked Jake a glance as he followed her back into the kitchen. "I see." Features suddenly tense, she started nodding. "Yes, I understand. I'll speak to her. I'm sure she'll be happy to meet you whenever you wish."

The sheik said something more.

"All right, I'll check with her and call you back."

She hung up the phone and took a deep breath. "The sheik's personal jet has left the country. Roshan and

Tariq are aboard—on their way back to Saudi Arabia, thank God. The sheik, his cousin Yasar, Zahra, and the sheik's two bodyguards are still here in Houston. He says he can't go home until he speaks to his daughter."

"That's good, I guess. You can be sure Roshan and Tariq will get what they deserve. I just wish Quadim and Yousef were on that plane."

"I need to set up a meeting between the sheik and A'lia. I think a neutral place would be best. Maybe tomorrow they could both come here."

Jake's smile was wry. "There goes our chance to wind down."

"I know, but—"

"But you've got a job to do. You have to do what it takes to get it done. Believe me, I understand."

Sage seemed relieved. She made a call to A'lia, got her okay, then phoned the sheik to suggest the meeting be held at her apartment. Then she hung up the phone and heaved a long, slow sigh. "They're meeting here tomorrow at eleven."

"So everything's set."

"Looks like. I'm hoping Khalid will stay a couple more days. We're really close to making our deal."

She walked over and locked her arms around Jake's neck. "You and I may not have tomorrow, but once we get back, at least we'll have the rest of today."

He kissed her lightly, thought of the nap she'd mentioned, thought of making love to her, and his body tightened. He ignored the hunger and urged her out the front door, heading once more for his office and his rendezvous with Richard Haskins.

Chapter 28

They didn't talk much on the ride to Atlas Security. It was Saturday and the office was closed. As Jake pulled into the parking lot in front of the building, he spotted Rick Haskins behind the wheel of a nondescript brown Chevy. The agent, mid-forties, medium brown hair, features deeply tanned, wore the same all-business expression he usually did.

Haskins was a damn good agent, Jake had discovered, when they'd worked together with Johnnie Riggs after a mission to Belize.

The DEA agent got out of his car at the same time Jake and Sage exited the Jeep. Jake walked toward him and they shook hands.

"Sage, meet Special Agent Richard Haskins. Rick, this is Sage Dumont."

"Nice to meet you, Ms. Dumont," he said, though

clearly he knew who she was. The drugs had arrived in a load of pipe purchased by Marine Drilling. By now Rick knew Sage was in charge of acquisitions and distribution, a vice president in the company. He would also know everything there was to know about her personal life and her powerful, wealthy family.

"It's nice to meet you, too," she said.

"This is all yours." Jake slid the strap off his shoulder and passed the canvas bag to Rick, who unzipped the bag, took a quick look at the drugs, and pulled the zipper closed. Unlocking the trunk of his car, he tossed the bag in and slammed the lid, relieving Jake of at least one problem.

"Anything else you want to tell me about all this?"

Jake thought of Roshan and the sheik, and his responsibility to Sage and her grandfather. "Not at the moment. You've got the bad guys in custody. You've probably got them singing like birds. Anything new you want to tell *us?*"

Haskins's mouth curved faintly. "Not at the moment."

Jake just smiled.

"If nothing else comes up, our deal's still on and you're out of this," Haskins said. "But until we nail things down, don't stray too far."

"Not a problem," Jake said.

Haskins flicked Sage a glance. "That goes for you, too, Ms. Dumont."

"I've got a job here in Houston, Agent Haskins. I'm not going anywhere."

The agent nodded. Jake watched as he climbed into his car, cranked the engine and drove away.

"You didn't tell him about Quadim and Yousef."

"Not yet. Unless you want the DEA descending like a horde on the sheik and his family, we wait until Khalid and his relatives are on a plane headed for home. Besides, we don't even know the two missing men's last names. Soon as we have more information, I'll let Rick know."

"With all the trouble Khalid's been having, he may leave before our deal is closed."

"Maybe."

"You think he'll give A'lia permission to stay?"

"I don't know. She's embarrassed him, caused him to lose face with his family. But then, so has Roshan. Hard to tell what he'll do."

"She might be in danger if he denies her. Yousef and Quadim are still here. They might decide to punish her themselves."

"You're right, anything could happen. Let's hope the sheik loves her enough to forgive her."

But Jake wasn't all that sure he would. Saudi rules were strict. A'lia had broken more than one. Only time and tomorrow's meeting would bring an answer.

Still standing in the parking lot in front of the office, Jake glanced toward the door. "I need to go in for a few minutes. There's a couple of things I need to check."

Sage let him guide her to the front door, then waited while he used his key to get in. She was walking next to him, heading for his desk, when a noise in the back room caught her attention and a thin black youth came out of the room and walked toward them.

"Nobody in here but me," he said. He was in his late teens, tall and thin, his eyes as dark as his skin.

She noticed he was carrying a broom. A faint sheen of perspiration covered his forehead.

"Bo," Jake said. "Trace told me you took the job. I'm glad to hear it. How's it going?"

"Good. Trace is teaching me some stuff. Thanks for, um, helping me out."

"You're helping yourself out, Bo. That's what you need to remember."

The young man smiled. There was a hint of pride in it. "Yeah, I guess I am. Thanks, anyway." He disappeared back into the rear of the building and Sage heard the swish of a broom across the floor.

"Looks like it might work out for Bo," she said, knowing he was the teenage boy Jake had mentioned.

Jake nodded. "So far so good." Sitting down at his desk, he started sorting through the stack of messages Annie had left him. Sage settled in the chair beside him, watching him prioritize the notes, toss a couple in the trash, then make a few calls.

About five minutes had passed when the bell above the door rang and Alex Justice strolled into the office. Dressed in chinos and a yellow polo shirt, his blond hair neatly trimmed and gleaming, he looked *GQ* gorgeous as always.

Sage thought of Rina. Too bad her friend had her mind made up against him. Sage liked Alex. On top of that, he was a really good-looking guy.

"So how'd it go with the sheik last night?" he asked, tossing his briefcase on his desk, then walking over to join them.

"Roshan and Tariq are on a plane back to Saudi Arabia. The sheik is taking care of their punishment personally. They weren't happy, to say the least."

"Yeah, I can imagine."

"Unfortunately, Yousef and Quadim are in the wind."

Alex's brow creased in a frown. "Not good news."

"That's for sure. I met with Haskins, gave him the last kilo of drugs."

"Deal still in place? Everything still okay?"

"Long as nothing new comes up, we're good to go. So what brings you in today?"

"Divorce case. I started out feeling sorry for the wife of the cheating husband. Looks like the guy's a straight shooter, so now I'm feeling sorry for the husband with the crazy jealous wife."

Jake chuckled. "Just part of the job."

"I guess."

The bell rang again and Sage looked up to see a young man with brown hair and black horn-rimmed glasses walk in. He waved at Jake and Alex and disappeared inside his glass-enclosed office, seating himself behind the desk.

"It's Grand Central Station in here today," Alex said.

Jake stood up from his chair, gave Sage a look. "That's Sol Greenway, Trace's computer guy. I need to talk to him. I'll be right back." He left the desk and walked into the young man's office. Through the windows, Sage could see them talking, see the young man nodding. A few minutes later, Jake returned to his desk.

"What is it?" she asked.

"Nothing much. Just a little side project I've got him working on."

With Jake, there was no way to know what that

was unless he decided to tell her, which he seemed disinclined to do.

"I'm finished," he said. "You ready to go on home?" His gaze slid over her, the heat in those incredible blue eyes impossible to miss.

"I need to check on Ian, but I think I'll call him first, find a good time to drop by." She gave Jake a sassy smile. "Maybe we should do that workout *after* our nap."

Jake grinned. "Yeah, if we have the strength."

Sage laughed as he waved goodbye to Alex and urged her toward the door.

Jake was thinking of a lazy afternoon in bed with Sage, then a good solid workout in the downstairs gym. Afterward, they'd take a long hot shower together, then maybe another "nap." Anticipation had his arousal stirring as she walked beside him into her building.

"I might as well get my mail before we go up," she said, pausing in front of a row of brass boxes.

He nodded, allowed himself the pleasure of watching the graceful way she moved, which he found sexy as hell. He liked her hands with their long slim fingers, and pretty manicured nails done in a soft peach shade. He liked it when she raked them down his back while he was inside her. Heat flowed through him. It wouldn't be long until he had her upstairs and they were making love.

He waited as she unlocked the box and pulled out the day's mail. A couple of bills and a grocery store flyer. A stack of charities wanting money. One envelope seemed to catch her eye. She turned it over a couple times, then started tearing it open.

"What is it?"

"I don't know. There's no return address." She drew out the neatly folded piece of white paper, opened it, took one look, and her face went pale. "Oh, my God."

Jake plucked the sheet from her trembling hand. It was a note made of words cut out of newspapers and magazines, pasted onto the page.

I tried to warn you. You and your company are traitors to this country. The sheik is next and this time it won't be a warning. He'll be dead.

Sonofabitch.

"Oh, my God," Sage said again.

"We need to call the police," Jake said. "Let Brady and Vasqucz know. Maybe the guy left fingerprints or maybe he licked the envelope and left some DNA." Though he doubted it. So far whoever it was had been extremely careful.

"I hate this," Sage said.

Carefully refolding the note, touching it as little as possible, Jake slipped it back into the envelope. "Stick that in your purse and try not to handle it any more than you have to. We'll call the cops as soon as we get upstairs."

Damn, he'd been afraid the guy would try something else. Whoever it was wanted the negotiations ended, and wasn't ready to quit. As a follow-up to the bombing, the note wasn't a bad idea. Sage would have to tell the sheik, and with Roshan and A'lia both giving their father fits, this time Khalid would likely head for home.

Her deal would be dead, but at least the sheik would be alive.

"I need to call Sheik Khalid," Sage said, "tell him about the note."

Jake nodded. "As soon as we talk to the police."

As he walked into the apartment, Jake used his cell to phone HPD. Since neither Brady nor Vasquez worked on Saturday, he explained to the cop on the desk what had happened, and a few minutes later Brady called him back.

"Did y'all touch the note?" he asked in his thick Texas drawl.

"It was mailed. Sage opened it. We tried to be careful. Maybe you can get some prints or some DNA."

"My partner's off for the weekend. I'll be there in thirty minutes."

Forty minutes later, Detective Jed Brady walked into the apartment wearing loose-fitting jeans and a T-shirt that covered the slight paunch above his belt buckle—weekend clothes instead of his usual suit.

Sage explained how she'd found the note in her mailbox, and Jake handed it over.

"We'll see if the crime lab boys can find somethin'. Maybe this time we'll get lucky."

"I hope so," Sage said.

"Anything new turn up lately?" Jake asked.

Brady recapped what they had found so far, stuff Jake and Sage already knew, the usual routine bullshit meant to placate a victim. But the truth was the police were no closer to catching the bomber than they'd been before.

"I need to call Sheik Khalid," Sage said, "tell him about this new threat."

"I'll handle it," Brady told her. "I've got a couple of questions I'd like to ask him. This'll give me an excuse to see him."

"I think I should go with you."

The detective shook his head. "Sorry, ma'am, not this time." He gave her a conciliatory smile. "I'll let you know if anything comes up."

Sage didn't look pleased.

"Probably better this way," Jake said. "Keeps you out of it."

"I hope you're right."

As soon as the detective was gone, Jake pulled his cell out and phoned Sol Greenway at the office.

"You had time to find anything?"

"I may have. I took your suggestions and looked in a couple of new directions."

"What'd you come up with?"

"Jonathan Hunter's a gambler. I'd noticed he traveled a lot, but I figured it was just business. This time when I looked at his airline ticket purchases, I saw he made quarterly trips to Vegas. He's a member of Grazie. That's the Venetian players club. I didn't find any indication he was in financial trouble, but their records show he gets first-class treatment. That says he gambles big-time."

"And undoubtedly loses plenty. Expensive hobby."

"For sure."

And a man with the gambling monkey on his back could use the raise that came with the promotion to president. Was it enough to hire a bomber to make sure Sage's negotiations failed?

"Anything else?" Jake asked.

"I'm not sure. I took another look at Charles Denton. Didn't find anything new on him, so I checked out his wife. Her maiden name was Shirley Tubbs. She came from a poor family, was raised in a small town south of Houston. From the articles I found in the papers, it looks like she managed to claw her way up the social ladder and finally married Denton. He isn't really wealthy, but his family is Houston aristocracy. I looked at Shirley's credit card charges. She spends money like a sailor on leave. She does a lot of charity benefits and seems to thrive on getting space in the society column of the paper."

"Interesting. Maybe she's pressing good ol' Charlie to get that promotion. More money and definitely more prestige."

"Could be."

"Thanks, kid. I owe you."

"Just doing my job."

"Yeah, right." *Like hell.* Hacking into private information was definitely not what Trace paid him to do. Well, most of the time.

Jake clicked off the phone. The police might not have anything new, but two new leads had just turned up.

He intended to follow them wherever they led.

Chapter 29

Sage waited until Jake shoved his cell phone back in the pocket of his jeans.

"You were talking to Sol, right? The computer kid?"

"That's right."

"Did the 'good ol' Charlie' you mentioned happen to be Charles Denton?"

His features tightened. "Matter of fact it did."

"What about Jonathan Hunter? Were you digging up information on him, too?"

"Your grandfather hired me to do a job, Sage. That job is to protect you. I need to figure out who set that bomb and sent that note. Both Denton and Hunter have motives to destroy your negotiations. Denton's wife is a social climber who spends money like it's going out of style. He might want the job to satisfy her need for social status. Hunter's a gambler. The promotion to president would mean a lot more money he could use to feed his habit."

"I don't believe their personal lives have anything to do with this."

"But you aren't completely sure, are you? You can't say for certain one of these men wasn't involved. Until we can totally eliminate them from suspicion, I'm going to keep digging."

Sage shook her head. "That isn't going to happen, Jake. I'm not going to stand by and let you dig up dirt on people I've known for years—people I work with every day."

"You can't stop me, Sage."

She planted her hands on her hips. "Oh, no? I'll call my grandfather. I'll tell him what you've been doing and he'll fire you. Is that what you want?"

Jake strode toward her, towered above her. "You think I'm doing this just because it's my job?"

She gasped when he reached for her, pulled her into his arms. His mouth came down hard, in an angry, burning kiss that told her how much she meant to him, how much he cared.

"I want you safe," he whispered, kissing the side of her neck. "Let me do my job." And then he kissed her again and she was lost. Helplessly, her arms went around his neck; she went up on her toes and kissed him back. His tongue swept into her mouth, tangled with hers, and heat and need poured through her.

She had never met a man who could make her feel so womanly, so hungry. So needy. Jake kissed her until she was hot and wet and close to begging him to take her.

"Jake…" she whimpered, wondering if he could hear the plea in her voice.

Triumph gleamed in his eyes as he kissed her again, then lifted her and carried her into the bedroom. They were naked within minutes, Jake above her, kissing her breasts, Sage arching beneath him, feeling the raw power of him, desperate to feel him inside her.

"Jake…please…"

"Soon," he whispered, taking his time, nipping and tasting, making her hot all over. Another drugging kiss and he eased himself inside. He felt big and hard and he filled her completely. Digging her fingers into the knotted muscles across his shoulders, she arched up in silent entreaty. The instant he started to move, she climaxed, her body trembling, her teeth sinking into her bottom lip. A soft moan escaped. Dear God, she had never known anything so glorious, so incredibly sweet.

His strokes quickened, grew deeper, harder, and she came again. Deep, saturating pleasure rushed through her, hot and fierce and consuming. Jake came a few seconds later, his powerful body tightening, muscles going rigid, head thrown back.

For long seconds neither of them moved. She could feel his heart, beating in rhythm with her own. Jake kissed her softly one last time, then lifted himself away and lay beside her, curled her against his chest.

He pressed his lips to the top of her head. "I need you safe, Sage. If neither of those men is involved, no one will ever know anything about them. You can trust me on that."

She trusted him. More than any man she had ever known. And she loved him. Dear God, she loved him, and it was going to hurt so badly when it was over between them.

She tried not to think of it, but thoughts of a life

without him tormented her, and it took a while to fall asleep.

The buzzing of the intercom announcing the arrival of a visitor awakened her. Sage tossed back the covers and leaped out of bed, hoping some new catastrophe wouldn't be waiting for her when she walked into the living room.

Jake had just finished his shower and pulled on jeans and a fresh T-shirt when he heard the intercom buzz.

He swore a silent oath at the news from the lobby desk that Ian Dumont was on his way up. No time to worry about his bare feet and damp hair. He blew out a resigned breath. At least Ian knew he was staying there. Jake wasn't sure he knew what else was going on.

Crossing to the entry, he pulled open the door, inviting the slender, silver-haired man into the apartment. His bodyguard walked in behind him, a beefy guy named Hamilton Pierce that Jake had met and knew to be good at his job.

Ham nodded a greeting. Jake nodded back.

Ian walked toward him. "Jake." Those golden eyes so much like Sage's roamed over him, missing nothing, Jake was sure.

"It's good to see you, sir." Though the timing could surely have been better, since he'd just climbed out of bed with the man's granddaughter. "Sage has been worried about you. She was hoping to see you sometime this weekend, make sure you were okay."

"I'm fine. Where is she?"

"I'm right here, Grandfather." Sage sailed into the room, a smile pasted on her face. With no time to prepare, she'd pulled on the same khaki slacks and orange top she'd been wearing, and dragged a brush through her hair. Her cheeks were rosy from sleep and making love. She looked like a woman well tumbled.

Under different circumstances, Jake might have smiled.

"I'm glad you're here," she said, leaning over to kiss her grandfather's cheek. "A couple of things have come up."

For an instant, Ian's glance flicked to Jake and one of his silver eyebrows lifted. "Is that so?"

There was a hint of something in his voice that made Jake want to squirm. He wished he could tell what the old man was thinking, but Ian Dumont was too shrewd to be easily read.

Ian kept his attention on Jake. "I see you're still taking care of my granddaughter."

Jake felt the heat at the back of his neck. He prayed his face wouldn't flush. "Yes, sir."

"It's a good thing Jake's here," Sage said a little too brightly. "This afternoon I got a note in the mail from the bomber. He made a threat against Sheik Khalid."

"The police left just a little while ago," Jake added.

"Against Khalid and not you?" Ian asked Sage.

"It was generally threatening, but no. It was definitely against the sheik. The police are informing him."

"That doesn't bode well for your deal."

"I know."

"At least the bastard isn't focused on you."

Sage looked up at him. "I'm really sorry this happened, Grandfather."

Ian's expression didn't change. "It was hardly your

fault. Whatever happens, you've done the best you could."

Sage's face fell at his words. "I haven't given up yet. I've got a meeting with the sheik and his daughter tomorrow morning. I don't think he'll leave before he sees her."

"Then maybe there's hope."

"Yes…"

But Jake could tell she was thinking about A'lia and the promise she had made to speak to the sheik on her behalf. If the deal had any chance at all of coming together, it would be over if Sage went against Khalid's wishes.

Assuming he remained in the country after his talk with the police. Then again, he'd have to wait for his jet to get back and refuel, and it was a damned long flight to Saudi Arabia, more than fourteen hours, as he recalled.

Sage was still talking to her grandfather. "The afternoon is pretty much gone," she said. "Why don't you stay for supper? We can call for takeout from the China Palace. You know how much you like Chinese."

Ian cast Jake a sidelong glance, then turned back to Sage. "Not tonight, dear heart. Maybe another time. Let me know what happens after your meeting tomorrow."

"Of course."

They chatted amiably as Sage walked him to the door, but Jake could sense her nervousness. She didn't release an easy breath until her grandfather was gone. She was worried about the deal falling through, and Jake thought maybe she was also worried that Ian might know they were sleeping together.

The old man was no fool. Jake figured he knew damned well what was going on. It didn't change a thing, as far as Jake was concerned. He wasn't ready to give Sage up, and was fairly sure he never would be.

But that would be up to her.

Meanwhile, he would give her some space, let her come to grips with her demons.

For the next few hours, he worked at the computer in her study. Sol's information had stirred up some new ideas he wanted to explore.

Whatever happened, they still had a bomber to catch.

Early the following morning, Sage dressed in her exercise tights and a cropped T-shirt and headed for the gym. She needed to relieve some stress before her meeting with the sheik, and a good hard workout usually helped.

Jake went with her. He was still her bodyguard, which her grandfather's untimely visit had reminded her. He was also used to physical exercise, and the hours they spent in bed, delicious as they were, weren't nearly enough for a man like Jake.

The gym was in the basement, so there weren't any windows. Jake unclipped his holster and laid it on a table against the wall. With the door locked behind them, they both went to work. For the first hour, Sage used the weight machines while Jake lifted heavy barbells.

In between sets, Sage allowed herself to watch him, to appreciate the way the powerful muscles in his chest and shoulders stretched the seams of his clean white T-shirt to the point of bursting. As he lay on a padded bench, pressing nearly three hundred pounds, Jake's muscles strained, rippling the sinews in his thighs and calves.

God, he was a beautiful specimen of man.

Just not the man for her. It was a thought that nagged her morning and night, a thought that made her heart clench whenever she looked at him. No matter her feelings for Jake, she was going to have to give him up. Her grandfather's visit had reminded her of that.

Ian Dumont had rescued her, been there for her when she'd needed him most. When her mother had fallen ill, it was Ian who had paid Maryann Dumont's enormous hospital bills, Ian who had seen that she received the finest medical care.

He couldn't save her mother from the vicious cancer that finally took her life, but during those agonizing days of pain and loss, he was there to give Sage comfort and make her feel safe. Through the worst days of her life, her grandfather had loved her. That love had given her the strength to go on, to become the strong woman she was today.

She owed him for everything she was. Everything she intended to become in the future. Marrying the right man was crucial to that goal. She needed someone who fit in, someone who would understand her drive and ambition. Someone her grandfather approved of.

She thought of Jake, and felt a soft pang in her heart. Marrying for love simply wasn't part of the bargain she had struck with herself when she'd accepted Ian's support and guidance over the years.

As she finished on the rowing machine, Sage took a calming breath. Today was not a day to think of the past or the future. Instead, she needed to prepare herself for her all-important meeting with the sheik. And that meant relieving as much stress as she could before his arrival.

With that in mind, she spent the next hour walking at a fast pace on the treadmill, while Jake jogged on the machine beside her. As the hour came to a close, she felt better, tired but more able to focus.

They left the gym and returned upstairs. There was time only for a quick shower and a hurried bite to eat before the sheik and Λ'lia were due. Still, by the time Sage was finished, she was ready for whatever happened.

Or at least she hoped she was.

Chapter 30

The intercom buzzed. A'lia arrived at the apartment first, walking in with Rina, who gave Sage a brief hug.

"We're a little early, but I couldn't stand the tension any longer. I think I'm more nervous that she is." Rina tipped her head toward the slender, achingly lovely girl with coffee-and-cream complexion and big brown eyes. A'lia was wearing traditional garb today, a pale gray silk caftan and matching head scarf that covered all but her face, hands and feet, probably the clothes she'd been wearing when she ran away.

"Thank you for doing this," A'lia said, taking hold of Sage's hand. "You cannot know how much your help means to me."

"I don't know what I can actually do. I guess we just have to wait and see what your father has to say."

Jake walked in just then, freshly showered and shaved and looking gorgeous.

"Good morning, ladies," he said.

"Good to see you, Jake," Rina said.

"Good morning," A'lia said to him softly, her eyes cast down.

Jake positioned himself by the door, legs slightly splayed as he settled into bodyguard mode. He was leaving this to Sage, and she thought how good he was at knowing when to take charge and when to back away.

She and A'lia talked quietly as Rina went into the kitchen to make a pot of coffee. A few minutes later, she walked back into the room carrying the antique silver service Sage had admired in a London shop and Ian had bought for her as a birthday present. Rina set the tray down but didn't pour anyone a cup.

The minutes ticked past. The sheik was late. A power play, Sage was sure. By then, A'lia was nearly in tears.

"He has changed his mind. He isn't going to come."

"He'll be here," Sage said, praying she was right. The intercom buzzed just then, announcing his arrival, keeping her own nerves from stretching even tighter.

Rina gave A'lia's hand a final squeeze and stood up from the sofa. "I think it's better if I leave you alone. I'll be in the study watching TV."

Sage didn't argue. She had no idea how this was going to play out. By now the police had told the sheik about the note and the threat. She hoped to leave him and A'lia alone to work things out, but she would just have to wait and see.

When she opened the door, Khalid walked in dramatically, his white robe and headdress floating out around him, bearded chin thrust up. His two bodyguards walked in behind him and took up positions next to Jake.

"As-salam-alaikum," Sage said, forcing herself to smile.

"Wa alaikum as-salam," the sheik replied stiffly.

A'lia greeted him formally, bowed, took his hand and kissed the back.

The sheik turned to Sage. "If you will excuse us, there are things my daughter and I need to discuss."

"Of course." Glad to give them the privacy they needed, she crossed the living room and started down the hall. Jake fell in behind her, and Khalid's bodyguards moved into the corridor outside the apartment to wait.

For the next twenty minutes, Sage had no idea what was being said. She could hardly hear their muted voices through the closed study door, and they were speaking in Arabic. As time progressed, the sheik's voice became raised in anger.

Her heart began pounding. She looked over at Jake. "You don't think he'll hurt her?"

"By custom, it's his right as her father."

"Well, I won't have it." Sage shot up from her chair. "Not in my house." Marching across the study, she jerked open the door and stormed out into the hall, glad for Jake's comforting presence as he walked behind her. She was sure she was going to find A'lia battered and bruised, maybe even bloody. Instead she found father and daughter facing off as if set to do battle.

A'lia was crying.

The sheik's features looked icy and grim.

"This is a private conversation," he said darkly.

Sage took a position between them. "I won't let you hurt her. Whatever crime you think she has committed, I won't have it. Not in my house."

Those fierce black eyes pinned her where she stood. "You dare to speak to me in this manner? Have you forgotten how much you have to lose?"

Sage swallowed hard. She knew exactly how much she had to lose. Everything she had worked for. All the years she'd put in. This deal meant everything.

She lifted her chin. "It doesn't matter. Your daughter doesn't deserve your scorn. She loves you. In forcing her to run away, you have already caused her tremendous pain." Her voice softened. "She yearns for your approval, Your Highness, but the fact is, A'lia is different. You've admitted that yourself. She's sweet and kind, and extremely smart, but she can't grow into the woman she was meant to become if she is stifled by the customs of your country."

A'lia's eyes looked round as saucers. She sank down on the sofa, trembling all over, her face ashen.

"If you love her," Sage continued, "if you want her happiness as I believe you do, you will set her free. You will be the father she adores."

Something shifted in those hard, dark features. Something she couldn't begin to read. "We are very close to closing our transaction," he reminded her with soft menace. "Are you willing to risk losing everything you have worked for by incurring my wrath?"

Sage swallowed. Sheik Khalid wasn't a man to have as an enemy. "You know that isn't what I want. But I can't stay silent and watch a young woman's life be destroyed."

Khalid said nothing for the longest time. He continued to stare into Sage's face, looking for some sign of weakness, finding only determination. His robes billowed out as he turned to his youngest daughter.

"You may remain in this country, as you wish. I will arrange for you to stay with a relative, perhaps the cousin you spoke of in New York. I will assist you in gaining entrance to university. But I will make no decision regarding your marriage to this young man I do not know. In time, perhaps, after I discover his worth, that will change. In this, my decision is final."

A'lia slid off the sofa onto the carpet and wrapped her arms around her father's legs. She bowed her head in respect. "Thank you, Father. Thank you so much. I will not disappoint you. This I promise."

He lifted her gently to her feet, eased her into his arms. "I want your happiness, my daughter. I believe these things that have been said are true, and that here you will fulfill all the promise I have seen in you. Tonight I return to Saudi Arabia, but soon arrangements will be made for me to meet this young man."

Tears streamed down A'lia's cheeks. "Thank you, Father."

He turned to look at Sage. "I have spoken to the police. It is time I returned to my homeland. My plane has arrived and is being refueled and prepared for the journey. Zahra and Yasar will remain with my daughter until permanent living arrangements can be made."

"I'll make certain they have whatever they need."

He made a formal bow. "I bid you farewell, Sage Dumont. *Ma sa-la-ma.*" The traditional goodbye.

"Ma sa-la-ma," she replied.

Turning, he walked out the door.

Behind her, A'lia wept softly.

Chapter 31

Jake escorted Sage to the office Monday morning. After her meeting with the sheik, she had phoned her grandfather and told him Khalid was leaving.

It looked as if the deal was dead.

She'd been depressed ever since, and was quiet as Jake escorted her up the elevator to her office. She was wearing a tailored, dark green suit today, but he noticed the skirt came above her knees. Pretty legs, he thought. Nice to see them again. There were definitely some benefits to having the negotiations over.

The sheik was gone, but Jake's job wasn't finished until the bomber was caught.

In the meantime, now that the sheik was on his way back to Saudi Arabia, Jake needed to phone Rick Haskins and give him the names of the other two men in the drug smuggling ring that had involved Marine Drilling.

Quadim Ahmad and Yousef Al Zahrani. Their surnames he'd gotten from A'lia, who, fortunately, was too upset about seeing her father to wonder why he wanted to know.

Using the phone in the conference room, he dialed the agent's cell number.

"Haskins," Rick answered.

"Cantrell. You got a pencil? I've got some information I want to give you."

"Jake, I'm glad you called. I need to talk to you. Both you and Ms. Dumont."

That wasn't good news. Jake warned himself not to jump to conclusions. "All right. How about we meet at my office?"

"I'd rather you came down here."

More bad news. "You still out on the West Loop?"

"Still there."

"When?"

"Now would be good."

Jake took a deep breath. "I'll have to check with Sage. Unless I call you back, we'll be there in half an hour."

"Good enough."

Rick signed off and Jake went in to confirm the meeting with Sage.

"He wants us to come to his office?" she asked, worry creeping into her voice. "That sounds pretty official. Do you know why he wants to see us?"

"If you can get away, we'll know in about thirty minutes."

She didn't waste time, just stood up from behind her desk, walked over and grabbed her purse. "All right, let's go."

* * *

The beige, six-story office building sat next to the freeway. Sage waited as Jake pushed open one of the double glass doors, then held it so she could make her way inside. Richard Haskins met them before they'd had time to give the front desk clerk their names.

"Come on back," the agent said without the usual pleasantries. Turning, he led them down the hall into a small conference room. It was stark, just chrome chairs with black vinyl seats and a Formica-topped table. Two black-and-white posters of city scenes kept the walls from being completely bare.

Sage's heart kicked up, her nerves beginning to build. The plan to intercept a group of drug smugglers had been a desperate one to begin with. A man had been killed. Jake had counted on giving the DEA credit for the bust in exchange for their protection. But would Haskins keep his word? If not, God knew what sort of trouble they could all be in.

The agent waited until she and Jake were seated.

"You want some coffee, something cold to drink?"

"We're fine," Jake answered for both of them. "What's going on, Rick?"

The agent took a seat across from them. "We've uncovered some disturbing new information about the man killed the night of the smuggling attempt."

"That right?"

"I'm afraid so. It took a few days to piece the facts together, but we finally ID'd the guy. His name was Gamal Ali."

"You knew that Friday night."

Sage remembered Jake saying it was on the man's driver's license.

"That's right. But before he changed it, his name was Jarvis Peyton. Peyton was released from Huntsville prison in 2006, where he'd been serving twenty years for armed robbery and attempted murder. The interesting part is that while he was in there, he converted to Islam. For the last two years, Homeland Security has been tracking him as a possible member of a terrorist cell."

Sage felt the color drain from her face.

"Fuck," Jake said beneath his breath. She felt his big hand grasp hers under the table and give a reassuring squeeze.

"Go on," he said.

"Under interrogation, one of the suspects taken into custody that night confessed this was the third shipment of drugs they'd smuggled into the country. We think a portion of the money Gamal Ali collected may have gone to finance terrorist activities."

Sage's heart jerked. *Oh, dear God.* And Quadim and Yousef were still missing.

Jake muttered another curse.

"We need any information you might have that could help us locate that cell."

There was no choice now. They had to tell the authorities everything. Jake's gaze went to hers. Silently she told him she understood.

"From what we know," Jake began, "the smuggling involved a man named Roshan Al Kahzaz. He's the eldest son of Sheik Khalid Al Kahzaz. You might have read something about the sheik's visit to Houston in the newspapers."

"It was headline news for a while," Haskins said.

"Khalid came here with his family to negotiate a deal with Marine Drilling." He looked at Sage.

"We were trying to buy a used offshore drilling platform and other miscellaneous equipment," she explained.

"As far as we know," Jake continued, "neither Khalid nor his immediate family had anything to do with the smuggling, which involved shipments of used pipe purchased in a smaller deal earlier in the year. But the sheik's son Roshan, his cousin Quadim and Roshan's two personal bodyguards were involved."

"Where's Roshan now?"

"He and Tariq Mohammed, one of the bodyguards, are on their way back to Saudi Arabia. According to the sheik, their punishment will be severe."

"I don't doubt it. Drug trafficking in the Middle East is a major offense."

"Roshan has diplomatic immunity," Jake said. "There wasn't much you could do to him anyway. The problem is Quadim Ahmad and Yousef Al Zharani, the cousin and the other bodyguard, have skipped. No one knows where they've gone, including the sheik."

Haskins's features hardened. "We'll need to talk to him."

"Unfortunately, the sheik's plane left for Saudi Arabia last night."

The agent's face turned red. He stood up from his chair and leaned over the table, his hands fisted on top. "So you're telling me there is no way to find these two men, men we believe may be involved in a terrorist plot."

Jake's chair grated on the floor as he rose to his full, towering height and leaned across the table in turn. "Listen, Haskins. None of this could have been predicted. Sage did everything in her power to keep this from becoming an international incident—which I'm sure the

DEA, Homeland Security and every other agency in the country would have wanted her to do. The sheik has diplomatic immunity just like his son. Even if he was still here, he wouldn't have to talk to you."

Resignation settled over Haskins's face. His shoulders slumped as he sat back down in his chair and rubbed his forehead. "We're going to need a photo ID on these two guys."

"I can help with that," Sage said. "We had security cameras installed out at our ranch before the sheik and his family came for a visit. I can have the digital cards delivered to you right away."

He nodded. "Once we narrow it down, I'll need you both to come in and ID them."

"Glad to help," Jake said.

"We may have more questions for the two of you."

"I told you most of what we know Friday night. You've heard the rest today. We made a deal. I understand you've got a problem, and if there's anything either of us think of that will help you solve it, you can believe we'll let you know. In the meantime, I expect you to keep your word."

"The situation is different now."

"Not our part in it."

Haskins just nodded. "I'll do the best I can."

Jake helped Sage out of her chair.

"Stay close," Haskins warned as they started for the door.

Jake made no reply. Sage knew he wished there was something more he could do. She just hoped Special Agent Haskins and Homeland Security found the men—and the cell—before something terrible happened.

* * *

Tuesday arrived. Jake had talked to Alex, Ben and Trace about the conversation he'd had yesterday with Richard Haskins. There wasn't much need for them to worry; he'd never mentioned their names. Still, he wished there was something they could tell the feds that would help them find that cell.

Hell, he didn't like the idea of those bastards planning to blow up a nuclear plant or a city somewhere any more than they did. He and Sage had gone back over every conversation they'd had with the Saudis, gone over the transcripts the professor had translated, but come up with a big fat zero.

For now, Jake had to leave it alone, had to get back to doing the job he was being paid to do. And that meant protecting Sage.

Last night, when they'd gone back to her apartment, he had again used the computer in her study. While Sage did some catching up on paperwork, Jake had spent nearly two hours pursuing an idea that had been niggling at the back of his mind ever since his last conversation with Sol.

Prowling the internet, he had finally located the article in the *Houston Chronicle* that broke the story of the sheik's arrival and the deal being negotiated with Marine Drilling International. The story that had set off the protests. News that was supposed to be kept secret.

Information known to only a few people in the company.

Jake wanted to know who had leaked the story.

While Sage worked at the office under the watchful eye of Ian's bodyguard, Ham Pierce, Jake ordered a coffee to-go from the counter in the Espresso Loco a few blocks away. Carrying it outside, he seated himself at one of the wire mesh tables to wait for Susan McAllister, the reporter who had written the article.

This morning he'd phoned her and dangled a carrot she couldn't resist—fresh news about the sheik and Sage Dumont—and the journalist had agreed to meet him. Susan wanted some juicy tidbit about Sage and her meeting with the sheik, and Jake was prepared to give it to her.

In exchange for a little information.

Leaning back in the white metal chair, he spotted his quarry walking toward him. He'd found a photo on the net showing a thirtysomething blonde with short, curly hair and stylish, tortoise-shell glasses, attractive in a business sort of way. Watching her approach, he saw that she was average in height, sexier than her picture had shown, not afraid to display a little bosom at the front of her light blue pantsuit.

Maybe she had done some research on him, as well, figured, being ex-military, he had an appetite for a sexy female. Until a few weeks ago, she would have been right.

Nowadays there was only one woman he wanted.

"Mr. Cantrell?"

"That's right." He stood to greet her. "Jake will do. Have a seat, Ms. McAllister."

She ran her pretty blue eyes over him head to foot. "Call me Susan. It's nice to meet you."

He smiled, tried to look friendly. "Coffee?"

"I wouldn't mind a cup, but I'd prefer a cappuccino."

He could have guessed. He got up to fetch her one, returning shortly with a paper cup shooting steam through the hole in the lid.

She blew through the hole to cool the liquid, then took a sip as he sat across from her. "So what have you got for me?"

He kept his smile in place. He could smell her soft perfume.

"The question, Susan, is what have you got for me? I have information you should be interested in. In return, I want to know who leaked the story of the sheik's arrival in Houston and the deal he'd come to negotiate with Marine Drilling. You had the byline on the piece. I want to know who gave you the information."

"I don't reveal my sources."

"Then I guess you don't want to know how the deal is progressing."

She tried to look disinterested but failed. Popping the lid off the cup, she blew across the top a few times and took another sip. "I'd like to know—of course I would. Unfortunately, my ethics won't allow me to reveal how I got that information."

He sipped his coffee, biding his time. "All right, what if I say a couple of names, and if one of them is the man who talked to you, you take a drink of your cappuccino?"

Her gaze ran over him again. She was hungry for information, or maybe that look was a different kind of hunger. He had a hunch it was both.

She eyed him shrewdly. "And you know what's happening with the deal? You can give me the facts?"

"As I said, I have information you'll be interested in knowing."

"All right, say the names."

"Charles Denton."

She just stared down at her cup.

"How about Jonathan Hunter?"

She took a sip of her coffee, giving him a yes, and smiled. "Tell me about the deal."

It was hard to speak with his jaw clamped shut. *Hunter*. Hunter had leaked the information. The man had wanted the deal to fail. Jake remembered seeing the guy coming out of Sage's office. He wanted to take the slick-looking bastard by the throat and shake him till his teeth fell out. Every bone in his body said Hunter had to be the guy who'd arranged the car bomb.

"The sheik has left Houston and gone back to his home in Saudi Arabia. I have no comment on whether or not the deal was made before his departure." Jake stood up from his chair.

"That's it? That's all you have to tell me? I could have found that out by calling the airport. What about Sage Dumont? She was in charge of the negotiations. How does she feel about the sheik leaving? She's up for a promotion, isn't she? If the deal has fallen through, chances are she won't get it, right?"

Jake smiled thinly. "No comment." He started walking.

"Hey, wait a minute." Susan hurried to catch up with him. "Look, maybe we could have a drink sometime, talk a little more about Jonathan."

He turned, stared down at her. "So now it's Jonathan? Sounds like the two of you are pretty chummy."

"Not really. He's married. What about that drink?"

"You know Hunter. How far is he willing to go to keep that deal from being made?"

"He wants to be president of the company. He wants it very badly. That's all I'm willing to say." She smiled up at him. "At least for now." She took his arm. "So how about that drink?"

Jake just smiled. "Sorry, honey, I'm just not thirsty. Thanks for the information."

Turning, he walked away.

Chapter 32

Jake strode down the sidewalk, his long legs eating up the distance back to Marine Drilling, his features more and more grim. He knew he should wait, put together as much evidence as he could before he confronted Jonathan Hunter.

Instead, when he reached the executive floor, he headed straight for Hunter's office, walked in without knocking and closed the door.

The VP smiled up at him from behind his fancy black granite desk. "Mr. Cantrell. I want to tell you how glad I am you've been looking out for our dear Sage."

Jake didn't say a word. Just strode forward, reached across the desk, grabbed hold of Hunter's tie and hauled him forward, stretching him out across the polished surface like a landed fish. Paperweights and family photos went flying; stacks of files and notes shot into the air.

"You hired the guy who blew up Sage's limo. I want his name."

Hunter clawed at the tie around his neck. "I don't… don't know what you're talking about. I didn't…didn't hire anyone."

"Bullshit." Jake dragged him to his feet on the opposite side of the desk. "Give me his name."

Hunter's eyes flashed with guilt and fear. If Jake had had the least doubt that the man was culpable, he didn't now.

"I didn't… I—I'm not…not the one."

"No?" Fury rolled through Jake. He drew back his fist, discovered it was shaking. He was afraid if he hit the bastard, he'd kill him. "You've got ten seconds."

"Sec-ur-ity!" Hunter tried to call out, but the sound came out a strangled croak.

"Six. Five. Four. Three." Jake drew back farther. "Two—"

"It was Stanton… Stanton's idea!"

Jake held himself back, but just barely. He loosened his grip a little so Hunter could speak. "Go on."

"Phillip didn't want Sage to get the president's job. He…he was planning to marry her. He didn't want her to outshine him."

"She broke their engagement weeks ago. Why would he care?" Jake jerked on the tie. "Tell me the rest."

"It…it was Stanton's idea at first. We leak the story and…and stir things up. Enough trouble, the sheik goes back home and the deal doesn't get done."

"What about the bomb?"

"Let…let me go."

Jake shoved the knot in Hunter's tie tighter, making him choke. "Not until you tell me about the bomb."

"All right, all right, I—I'll tell you."

Might as well, Jake thought. It was all over now but the shouting. He let go of Hunter's tie, but stayed well inside the man's comfort zone, using his size to deliver a subtle threat.

Hunter loosened his tie, breathed deeply and raked a hand through his black, slicked-back hair. "After the newspaper article broke, the place was overrun with demonstrators, and we thought Khalid would leave. When he didn't, I just… I couldn't let it go. I hired a guy I knew—ex-oilman, expert in exploratory demolition."

"I want his name."

"Augie… Augie Butler."

Jake made a mental note.

"Keep going."

"Butler was retired, injured in an accident on the job. I knew he needed money. I knew he could make the bomb, but I told him to make sure no one was hurt. I was clear about that. It was only meant as a warning. I thought…thought for sure the sheik would go home after that."

"But he didn't."

"No."

"What about the note?"

"I… I sent it. I pieced it together and mailed it to Sage. After everything I'd already done, I figured I had to make one last try."

"You greedy goddamned bastard." Jake drew back his fist once more, not realizing Sage had opened the door. He heard her scream as he let fly a blow that came straight from the shoulder and slammed into Jonathan Hunter's thin, pale face. Even though Jake had pulled his punch, the man went flying ass-over-teakettle across the desk, hitting his chair on the way down, sending it spinning away, moaning as he crashed to the floor.

"Jake! For God's sake, what are you doing!" Sage's eyes were wide and fearful as she started toward Hunter. Jake caught her arm and pulled her away.

"He's your guy. Him and your ex-fiancé. Stanton leaked the story to the *Chronicle* about the sheik and your deal. Apparently, he didn't want you to be his boss, and you would be if you got the job as president. He put the idea in Hunter's head and Hunter ran with it. Hired the bomber and wrote the note."

Ian walked in as Hunter staggered to his feet, blood dripping from his broken nose onto his pristine white shirt and red-striped power tie.

"What the devil...?" Ian looked at Hunter, saw one of his top executives battered and bloody, saw Jake's bleeding knuckles and knew who was to blame. His loyalty had to lie with the man who had worked for him for years.

Ian turned a hard look on Jake. "I won't tolerate this kind of behavior—not under any circumstances. You're fired, Cantrell."

"Fine by me." Turning, Jake stalked out of the office. He didn't need the fucking job. He didn't need the headache. The only thing that mattered was that Sage made no effort to stop him.

End of story, he figured. Wiping the blood off his knuckles, he crossed the carpet toward the elevator.

* * *

Sage forced her gaze away from the man teetering on the other side of the desk. She was shaking all over, trying to forget the image of Jake's big hand smashing into Jonathan Hunter's stricken face.

She turned to her grandfather, braced herself. "Jake says Jonathan is the man behind the bombing." Her glance returned to the disheveled executive, then veered out the door to Jake's retreating back. "He says…says Phillip was involved."

Ian's hard gaze swung to Hunter. "That true?"

Jonathan hesitated, glanced wildly around, trying to decide what to say. He opened his mouth, but Ian cut him off.

"Don't lie to me, Hunter. If it's true, you had better say so. If you lie, I'll find out, and it'll go a helluva lot harder on you. That I personally guarantee."

Jonathan's battered face went a pasty gray. He spoke to Sage, hoping to summon her pity. "I only meant to warn the sheik away. I knew you wouldn't get the job if the deal fell through." He returned his attention to Ian. "I've worked for this company more than twenty years. I deserved that promotion. Even Phillip thought I should get it."

"The only thing you're going to get now," Ian said harshly, "is an orange jumpsuit and time in jail to think about what you've done."

He tipped his head toward Sage. "You had better go get Cantrell. I don't condone violence, especially in the office, but I have a feeling your bodyguard's protective instincts got in the way." He raked Hunter with a look. "Since I feel like beating you to a bloody pulp myself, I understand how that might have happened." He turned back to Sage. "Go."

Sage spun and raced out of the office, her heart still hammering. She should have stood up for Jake, gone after him the instant he stormed out of the room. She should have known he had a reason to behave the way he had. But seeing the terrible blow Jonathan had taken, seeing him beaten and bleeding, and the fury in Jake's blue eyes, had held her shocked and immobile. The destruction he'd wrought with a single blow had left her stunned and shaken.

She didn't know the man who'd stood with his fists clenched and shaking, the cold-eyed, dangerous man who could use those powerful hands to kill a man if he wanted. And considering his background, likely already had.

She spotted him across the parking lot, almost to his Jeep.

"Jake! Jake, wait!" He looked up and something shifted in his features.

A little of her uncertainty remained, but when he turned, it was her Jake whose beautiful eyes met hers, Jake who pulled her into his arms.

"I'm sorry," she said breathlessly. "What happened… I just couldn't… I couldn't handle it. I'm sorry." When she wrapped her arms around his neck, he drew her gently against him.

"I'm the one who's sorry. I lost it in there. I thought of what Hunter had done, the trouble he'd caused. I imagined what could have happened to you when that bomb went off, and I lost it."

She reached up and cupped his cheek. "Jonathan got what he deserved. Ian said he wanted to beat him to a bloody pulp himself." She managed a tentative smile, realized she had tears in her eyes. "You aren't really fired."

Jake kissed her. Softly. Sweetly. Making her heart turn over.

"That's all right, I quit." He ran a thumb beneath her eyes, wiping away the wetness. "You don't need protection anymore. You're safe now, Sage."

The words should have comforted her. She didn't understand why they didn't. Except that she was in love with Jake and now that she understood the man he truly was, now that she was completely sure he wasn't the right man for her, it was only fair to him that she end their relationship.

Her heart twisted inside her.

Not now, a little voice said. *Not yet.*

So when he started back to the building, she took his arm and walked quietly beside him, let him guide her to the elevator that swept them upstairs.

There was business to finish. By now, Ian would have called the police. There would be statements to make, information to give. She thought of their interview with Richard Haskins. Lately, it seemed as if dealing with law enforcement took up most of her day.

As they stepped out of the elevator, she felt Jake's hand at her waist, guiding her back toward her office to wait for the police.

Inside her chest, her heart thumped dully. At least until this was over, she wouldn't have to say goodbye. She would have Jake a little longer.

She would take whatever time she could get.

Chapter 33

On Thursday morning, things began to settle back into a normal routine. The day before, as soon as Sage left for work, Jake had moved out of her apartment. It didn't take much effort; he had only a shaving kit and few clothes to pack. Still, he found it harder than he'd expected. Maybe he'd hoped Sage would ask him to stay. He liked living with a woman, he'd discovered. He liked living with Sage.

In the end he'd left a toothbrush, disposable razor and a change of clothes before he'd walked out the door. Somehow it didn't seem so final that way.

After Jake's confrontation with Hunter and his conversation with the police, Augie Butler had been arrested and charged with attempted murder—plus a dozen other things. Jonathan Hunter had also been charged but had hired some fancy lawyer and posted bail. Since the only thing they had against Phillip Stanton was Hunter's allegation that he had been initially involved, Jake wasn't sure what was going to happen to him.

Aside from losing his job and being blackballed throughout the oil industry by Ian Dumont.

Jake figured the high life was probably over for the no-good rotten bastard.

Though the bomb threat was over, Sage was still worried about the disappearance of Quadim and Yousef, and the possibility they were involved with a terrorist cell. Jake knew she felt responsible for bringing the men into the country. She was also depressed that the sheik had left without agreeing to a deal.

Knowing Sage wasn't good at accepting defeat, Jake was trying to give her some space until she got her head wrapped around the fact that she wasn't going to save Marine Drilling millions of dollars. And there was a good chance Charlie Denton was going to get the promotion to president.

Ian didn't play favorites when it came to business. Not even for the granddaughter he loved.

Jake figured it was up to the authorities to find the terrorists.

Thursday afternoon slipped away. It was amazing how many calls he needed to return, how many loose ends there were to tie up after being away for the past few weeks. Five o'clock came and went and Jake was still at it, but no one else had left the office, either. The place was still humming when Annie buzzed to let him know Lincoln Jones was on the way over to his desk.

"Hey, buddy, good to see you." Jake stood to shake his friend's hand. "What's up?"

"Heard they arrested the a-hole who blew up my car—thanks to you. Congratulations."

He shrugged. "Just got lucky."

"Sure you did."

"Want a cup of coffee? Got some fresh in the back."

"Sounds good." They started in that direction. "I talked to Felix," Linc said. "He told me you got Bo Johnson a job here in the office."

"Trace hired him part-time and weekends."

"Felix said you called, told him Bo was doin' real good."

"I talked to Felix on Saturday. I hope Bo keeps up the good work."

"I think he might. I saw him the other day, told him if he kept going the way he was, I'd help him get his chauffeur's license. He said he'd decided to become a private investigator. Funny, huh?"

Jake shrugged. "Stranger things have happened."

"Kid was excited about the chance to drive for me, make some extra money. He wants to get his GED."

Jake smiled. "Sounds like he's coming right along."

"Trace is good for him. I think the kid has a case of hero worship, Trace being an ex-Ranger and all. Tell you the truth, I think he has a lot of respect for you, too, Jake."

He just nodded, glad to hear the kid was straightening himself out. It didn't happen that often.

"Felix misses seeing you."

Jake ran a hand over his face. "I need to call him again. Now that this last job's wrapped up, I'll have some time. Maybe we can take in a football game or something. The Texans lost more than they won last year, but the new season's starting, and so far they're doing great. And it's always fun to catch a game."

"Felix asked about Sage. He likes her."

Jake smiled again. "So do I. I'm gonna ask her to marry me."

Linc grinned, slapped him on the back. "Good for you." They reached the back room and Jake poured them each a cup of coffee.

"I been thinking along those lines myself," Linc said, accepting a steaming mug.

Jake's eyebrows went up. "That so?"

"Me and Tanya Porter been seeing each other. I've known her a couple of years, just never thought she'd say yes if I asked her out. Finally worked up the courage. We went to the show one night and have been together ever since. I think it might be the real thing."

Jake grinned. "That's great, Linc. It'd be good for Felix to have a real dad instead of just a guy who's around part-time."

"He loves you, man."

Jake's chest felt tight. He'd just begun to open himself up to those kinds of feelings again. "He's a great kid."

"I'd be proud to call Felix my son."

"I don't blame you. I hope it works out."

Linc grinned. "Same goes."

They talked a while longer as they finished their coffee, then walked to the door. Linc waved as he crossed the parking lot, his steps so light he seemed to skip across the asphalt.

Jake waved back and returned to his desk, his friend's happiness reminding him that if he wanted some of that for himself he needed to talk to Sage. He needed to work up the courage to ask her to marry him.

The possibility she might turn him down made the coffee he'd drunk turn sour in his stomach.

He'd just sat back down at his desk to make a few more calls when the bell above the door rang and Sage walked into the office. She looked so damned pretty he wanted to drag her out of there, caveman style, and haul her off to bed.

He might have smiled at the image if he hadn't noticed the worry lines digging into her forehead as she rushed toward him. Jake shot out of his chair and intercepted her halfway.

"What is it? What's wrong?"

"I should have thought of it. I don't know why I didn't. I should have at least considered the possibility."

He took her hands; they felt ice-cold. Leading her to his desk, he sat her down in the chair next to his. "All right, what should you have thought of?"

"The shipment, Jake. I was reviewing the invoices on that old order of pipe and suddenly it hit me—there's one more load coming in."

"Take it easy. Roshan and the smugglers all said the shipment we busted was the last load of drugs."

"That's right. Of drugs. But what if there's something else in the final shipment of pipe? Something Gamal Ali wanted. Something Quadim and Yousef want—something that's far more dangerous than drugs? What if Quadim and Yousef were planning to disappear all along and—"

"And when the deal went south it just set things in motion ahead of time."

"Exactly," Sage said.

"When's that load coming in?"

"Today, Jake. The pipe may have already been un-
loaded. It'll be stored in the lot overnight, just like
before."

"If there's something in the shipment, they'll go
after it tonight. We need to talk to Haskins." Jake
grabbed Sage's hand and started hauling her toward
the door. "He may not be Homeland Security, but he's
in this up to his DEA ears."

Jake didn't stop till they reached his Jeep, where he
lifted Sage into the passenger seat. Sliding behind the
wheel, he shoved his key into the ignition, then pulled
out his cell and phoned the DEA office.

When the receptionist answered, he asked for
Special Agent Richard Haskins. "Tell him it's Jake
Cantrell."

"I'm afraid Agent Haskins is in a meeting. At the
moment he can't be disturbed."

"Tell him I'm coming in. Tell him it's important.
Tell him not to leave."

"All right, but—"

Jake closed the phone and started the engine. A few
minutes later he was on the West Loop heading south.

"This may be a wild-goose chase," he said to Sage,
"but we can't take the chance it isn't."

She just nodded. Neither of them said another word
until they reached the DEA office.

Just as before, Richard Haskins was waiting when
they walked through the door. He was wearing a plain
tan suit, his brown hair neatly combed, his wingtip
shoes gleaming. Sage walked behind him, Jake at her

side as he led them back to the same small conference room they had been in before.

"What's so urgent you couldn't leave a message on voice mail?" Haskins asked as he seated himself across from her on the table.

"We may know how you can locate the members of that cell Homeland is looking for," Jake said. And for the next half hour, they explained about the final load of pipe being shipped from Saudi Arabia, and their theory that Quadim and Yousef might have planted something for the terrorists in the shipment.

"It could be a false lead," Jake finally said, "but my gut is telling me it isn't. It just makes too much sense."

Haskins was nodding. "Smuggling the drugs into the country in the pipe worked perfectly until that last round. If you hadn't overheard them talking, it would have gone like clockwork again. If Gamal Ali was planning to smuggle a weapon of mass destruction, say, biotoxins or nuclear material, he had the perfect setup, and he knew it worked."

"Right," Jake said.

Haskins stood up from the table. "Stay here. I'll be back shortly."

The agent returned a few minutes later with photos of the members of the sheik's party, pictures taken with the security cameras out at the ranch. One of Trace's people had removed the cards from the cameras and brought them in to the agency for examination.

Haskins spread the stack of eight-by-ten photos on the conference table.

"I've set things in motion for tonight. If the men show up to retrieve the merchandise—whatever it is—

we'll be waiting. But we need to know what these guys look like."

He slid the photos in front of Sage and Jake, and they began looking them over, searching for images of the men who had disappeared.

Sage reached out and picked one of the pictures out of the glossies spread in front of her. "This is Quadim," she said.

Jake separated another from the group. "Here's his buddy, Yousef."

Sage picked out an image of Yousef walking a few paces behind Roshan toward the ranch house. Jake found one of both missing men talking together at the shooting range.

"Those are your boys," he said, sliding all four photos across the table.

"Thanks." Haskins scooped them up. "I appreciate your help with this. Both of you. I'll let you know what happens."

"Listen, Rick, if this thing goes down, it's going to be tonight. That means you haven't got a lot of time to prepare. I can help with that. I've been out there. I know the layout, how to get in and out, where to find the best cover. Let me go in with you."

Sage grabbed his arm. "Jake, please, no…" She didn't want him involved in something so dangerous. She didn't want him getting hurt.

Haskins shook his head. "Appreciate the offer, but I can't let you do that. You're a civilian."

"I'm ex-military and I'm licensed to carry. I'll stay in the background, just give you any relevant advice when we get there. Plus I'll recognize these guys if they show up. I know their size and shape, the way they move. That's better than any photo."

Haskins's face looked strained. "I don't like it."

Jake cocked his arm and pointed to the heavy steel watch on his wrist. "Time's ticking away, my friend."

Sage looked at her own wristwatch and saw it was past seven o'clock. They were down to hours, and the agents were barely getting started.

Haskins blew out a breath. "All right, fine. You're in. The truth is we can really use your help."

Her heart sank. She should have known something like this would happen. Should have known Jake wouldn't back off until it was finally over.

"I need to grab some gear," he said. "Why don't I take Sage home and meet you back here in an hour?"

"That'll work." The men shook hands and Jake led Sage out to the Jeep.

"I don't want you to do this, Jake," she said as he drove her back to his office to retrieve her car. "You've done more than enough already. Why can't you just let the DEA and Homeland Security handle it?"

"Haskins needs my help."

"It's his job, Jake. Let him do it."

Jake turned into the parking lot in front of the office and pulled up next to her Mercedes. "I want these guys, Sage. God only knows what kind of atrocity they might be planning. How would you feel if I didn't help out, and they got away with it? Took out half the population of some city?"

Her stomach clenched in alarm. Jake was right. Of course he was. It didn't mean she had to like it.

He reached out and cupped her cheek. "I'll be all right, baby, I promise."

"I'm afraid, Jake."

"Look, I'll come over when I'm finished, all right? Then you'll know I'm okay."

She looked him straight in the eye. "Do you promise you'll come? No matter how late?"

"I give you my word."

She swallowed. Nodded.

As she drove out of the lot, she watched in her rearview mirror as his Jeep pulled away. Her heart didn't stop racing until she was finally inside her apartment.

Where the thudding turned into a slow, dull ache in her chest that matched the pounding in her head.

Chapter 34

The night was crystal clear. Only a thin layer of haze dimmed the stars above the storage facility on the other side of the chain-link fence. A sliver of moon, slightly fuller than before, made the darkness a little less impenetrable.

Inside the fence that enclosed the load of pipe that had arrived that afternoon, a swarm of DEA and Homeland Security agents surrounded six men bound hand-and-foot on the ground. Quadim Ahmad and Yousef Al Zahrani were among them, along with four others Jake had never seen before.

The feds had been impressive tonight. Well organized and focused, both agencies cooperating as if they'd worked together for years.

A lot was at stake tonight. Lives were on the line.

Not until they knew what was in the cylindrical tube

retrieved from one of the pipes, placed in a lead-lined case and loaded into a bomb transport vehicle, would they know how many lives that might have been.

From Jake's vantage point in the makeshift command center outside the fence, he watched with satisfaction as the action was mopped up and the men were loaded into vans and driven off to places unknown for interrogation.

It was over. The weeks of worrying about Sage, the drug smuggling, then the fear that men invited into this country would wind up destroying it in some way.

It was over, and now Jake was free to speak to Sage on the matter nearest and dearest to his heart. Tomorrow, if the time was right, he was going to ask her to marry him.

He smiled as he removed his black flak vest and tossed it into the trunk of an agency car, then wiped some of the greasepaint off his face.

Rick walked toward him, grinning through the black stripes on his own face. He slapped Jake on the back. "Time to go home, buddy."

Home. Jake grinned back. Tonight he was going to Sage's. He'd missed sleeping beside her since he'd moved out.

He couldn't wait to get back.

Sage paced the carpet in front of the big glass windows in her living room. The lights of Houston glittered ten stories below, but she barely noticed. All she could think of was Jake. What if something had gone wrong? What if he'd been injured? Or killed?

The knot in her stomach tightened. She paced some more, went over and refilled the glass of white wine she'd poured an hour ago, hoping it would ease her nerves. She took a bracing sip, trying to remember a time in her life when the minutes had dragged so slowly, a time she had been nearly ill with worry. When her mother was in the hospital, the waiting had been endless. But somehow that was different. Her mother had had no choice. Jake did.

Even if everything went exactly as planned, even if he was fine and the terrorists were in custody, was this the life she wanted? Was Jake the kind of man she wanted in her future?

His career path was way out of her comfort zone. She didn't get involved in fighting terrorists; she went to charity benefits. Spent evenings with her grandfather at the country club.

Sage needed a man who would fit into her world. Who played golf on the weekends. The kind who bought expensive suits, enjoyed the theater and symphony concerts. The kind of man her grandfather expected her to marry.

As the clock ticked toward two, she paced some more. Waited. Prayed. Tried not to think that something had gone wrong. That maybe something had happened to Jake.

That maybe instead of Gamal Ali, this time the dead man would be Jake.

She whimpered when she heard his familiar knock, and ran to him, jerked open the door and threw herself into his arms.

"Jake...thank God."

"It's all right, baby." His big hands moved soothingly up and down her back. "Everything's okay." He was dressed completely in black, his face streaked with greasepaint. It reminded her of the time before, the night a man had been killed. It reminded her of all the reasons she needed to separate herself from Jake.

All the reasons she needed to end their relationship.

He grinned, his teeth gleaming white in the black paint on his face. "You were right. Quadim and Yousef showed up with four other men, all members of the same cell Gamal Ali belonged to. The feds swooped down on them like locusts. Only a couple of shots were fired. Only two of the men were armed. They weren't expecting trouble. They figured after the drug bust, the cops would think it was over, and they would be safe."

She pressed herself tighter against him, trembling with relief, but a sick feeling curled in the pit of her stomach.

"I've still got a few clothes here," Jake said. "I'll go shower and change and we can talk."

She just nodded. She told herself the feeling would pass, but instead, as the minutes ticked past, the uncertainty grew and her stomach swirled with nausea. By the time Jake walked out of the shower dressed in jeans and a T-shirt, his dirty clothes stuffed into a duffel he tossed on the floor beside a chair, it was too late.

"I'm tired, baby," he said as he approached. "Let's go to bed. We can talk in the morning."

Sage stood frozen. Her mouth felt dry but her palms were sweating. Slowly, she shook her head. "I wish… wish I could pick a better time. I wish I didn't have to say this at all, but tonight…tonight forced me to face the truth."

His posture stiffened, making him even taller. "What truth, Sage?"

"I'm just not… I'm not cut out for this, Jake. The

truth is, you and I… We aren't right for each other. It's as simple as that."

"I think we're perfect for one another. I know I'm not an easy man, but you can handle me and we both know it. What happened tonight…that isn't something that goes on every day."

She swallowed, forced herself not to look away. "It doesn't matter. It was never going to work. We knew that from the start. It's time…time we got on with our lives."

Jake moved closer, caught her chin between his fingers, forcing her to look up at him. "I love you, Sage. I've never said that to a woman. Never thought I'd feel this way about a woman. I want you to marry me."

"Oh, Jake…" Her eyes filled. Her heart was aching, squeezing inside her chest. She could barely see him through the blurry wetness.

"This isn't the way I planned to ask," he continued, "but I want us to spend our lives together. I want us to have kids together. I want—"

"Stop, Jake, please." Sage pressed her trembling fingers over his lips. "Don't say anything more. Please, I'm begging you."

He straightened, looked down at her as if he had never really seen her before. Inside her chest, her heart was breaking.

"You're telling me you don't love me."

The tears in her eyes slipped over onto her cheeks. A dull roaring filled her ears. She loved him. She loved him so much. "This…this isn't about love. It's about marriage. It's about a partnership that will work. It would never work with us, Jake. There is just no way."

His blue eyes seemed to chill. "Because I don't like ballet? Because I might fall asleep at some damned boring concert? You think that's what marriage is about?"

She didn't answer. Looking at his dear, handsome face, she felt a surge of love so strong, so powerful, that for a moment she couldn't breathe. Was he right? Were those things really so important? She thought of her grandfather and the life she had built for herself—a life she owed completely to him—and knew they were.

Jake drew in a deep breath, his face set in hard, grim lines. "So that's it, then. It's over."

Fresh tears brimmed. "I wish we could just go on the way we were, but it wouldn't be fair. Not to either one of us."

"No, it wouldn't." Grabbing his duffel off the floor, he headed for the door. Sage said nothing as he jerked it open and disappeared out into the hall. The sound of the door closing behind him echoed like a gunshot in the quiet room.

She crumpled onto the sofa and began to weep.

It was over. He hadn't seen it coming, had been blindsided by the look on her face when she'd told him.

She didn't want to marry him. Hell, she didn't even love him. If she had, she wouldn't have hesitated. She would have done anything to make it work between them. Sage went after what she wanted. She was strong and determined, the kind of woman he admired and respected. The kind he had stupidly fallen in love with.

For the next three days, Jake worked to put his life back in order, wrap things up.

To say his goodbyes.

"You need to think this over," Trace said. "Taking some job down in Argentina isn't going to get her out of your system. Only time will do that. Stay, Jake. You have friends here, people who care about you. You'll find another woman. Someone who loves you the way you love her. Stay here and build the life you deserve."

But Jake just shook his head. There was nothing for him in Houston. Not anymore.

As he packed up his desk, Alex and Ben both walked over to see him.

"I can't believe I'm saying this," Alex said, "but I'm gonna miss your sorry ass around here."

Jake almost smiled. "Thanks for your help on that last job."

He didn't have to say which one. They both knew it was protecting Sage, the job that was sending him away.

"Sage Dumont is a fool," Alex said, then turned and stalked away.

"When are you leaving?" Ben asked.

"Couple of days. I've got a few loose ends to tie up."

One of them was Felix Porter. He wasn't looking forward to saying goodbye to the kid. The boy meant a lot to him. He knew Felix was going to take it hard, and the truth was, Jake was going to miss him, too. He'd let down his guard with Felix, let the boy worm his way a little too deeply into his heart. His chest tightened at the thought of not being there to see the kid grow up.

At least now the boy had Linc to look after him.

Ben held out a hand. "You get down there and you need help with something, you let me know, okay?"

Jake nodded, shook Ben's hand. "Appreciate the

offer." He started for the door with his briefcase. Annie's voice stopped him as he reached the front desk.

"You just gonna give her up?" she asked. "Never knew you to be a quitter, Jake."

His jaw tightened. "The woman doesn't love me. It's as simple as that."

Annie's voice softened. "She'd be a fool not to love you, Jake. And Sage Dumont is no fool."

Jake released a slow breath. Setting down the briefcase, he walked over, caught the receptionist's face between his hands and kissed her on the lips. "I'm gonna miss you, Annie Mayberry."

She wiped a tear from her powdered cheek. "We're all gonna miss *you,* Jake."

Grabbing the briefcase, his chest squeezing painfully, Jake walked out the door.

Sage sat at her desk, staring out through the plate-glass windows across the room. The office was closed. Most of the staff had gone home for the night. She couldn't force herself to leave.

Four days had passed, but it seemed like a lifetime. She couldn't stand to think of facing her empty apartment again tonight. Couldn't stand to think of climbing into her cold, lonely bed.

Jake was so vital. So much man. She hadn't realized how empty her life would be without him.

Dear God, she missed him.

Sage wiped a tear from her cheek. She couldn't keep crying for Jake. She couldn't keep thinking about him, missing him. She was the one who had sent him away.

She looked up at the sound of her office door opening. Saw her grandfather walk in, close it firmly behind him. He strode up to her desk, his silver hair perfectly combed, his gray suit impeccable. She was thinking how dear he was to her when the sharp note in his voice jarred her back to the moment.

"All right, I've had enough of this. What the devil is going on?"

What was going on? She felt as if her life was over.

Sage summoned her courage and came up out of her chair. For her grandfather's sake, she managed to wipe the sadness out of her voice and paste on a smile. "I don't know what you mean."

"You've been crying again, haven't you? You think I can't tell? You think I don't know you well enough to see that something is terribly wrong?"

"It's…it's nothing. Just the pressure lately, and losing the deal with the sheik."

"Bullshit. I'm not an idiot, Sage. It's Cantrell, isn't it? What did that big bastard do?"

She swallowed, fought not to cry. "He asked me to marry him."

Ian's smile was one of relief. "About damned time. I figured he'd get around to it sooner or later." He frowned down at her. "So why are you crying? You're not pregnant, are you?" For an instant his smile returned. "I'd like nothing better than to have a great-grandson by that tough son of a bitch."

Sage sank down in her chair. She could hardly make her grandfather's words register in her head. She looked up at him and started crying again.

"For God's sake, stop that. I thought you loved him."

She swallowed, lifted her chin. "I do love him. How could I not love him? But loving someone… It isn't always enough."

Ian walked around to her side of the desk, drew her to her feet and into his arms. "So what's the problem, dear heart? You love him, and it's clear he's head over heels for you. Tell me why you're crying."

Sage looked up at him, her heart aching. "Because I told him no."

Ian frowned again. "Why?" His features darkened. "He didn't hit you, did he?"

"Of course not. Jake would never hurt me."

"He cheat on you?"

"No. He's too honorable a man to do that."

"Then what did he do?"

She pulled a tissue out of her top desk drawer and wiped her cheeks. "It wouldn't work, Grandfather. Surely you can see that. We just... Jake and I come from two different worlds. Can you imagine him at the country club? I'm a Dumont. I have responsibilities. You taught me that."

His voice softened. "If I did, I didn't get the lesson quite right. Your first responsibility, Sage, is to yourself. Your own happiness has to come first. Listen to me, dearest. You're a very strong woman. I always knew it would take a strong man to make you happy. When you announced your engagement to Phillip, I was more than a little surprised. I approved because I thought Phillip was what you wanted."

When she tried to turn away, Ian stopped her, forced her to look him in the face. "I'm beginning to think you were marrying Phillip because you thought it would make *me* happy. I didn't realize it at the time, but it's true, isn't it?"

Sage drew away. Walking over to the window, she looked down at the traffic far below. Cars and buses whizzed past, people hurried to unknown places. "It seemed like the right thing to do."

Ian joined her. "Has Cantrell ever embarrassed you?"

"No."

"If you're worried about his finances, I did a bit of digging on him. The man could quit work tomorrow if he wanted."

"It isn't the money. Even if he were poor, I have more than enough for both of us."

"Is your place in society really that important?"

Was it? She almost laughed. The only reason it mattered was because of Ian. "I've always just wanted you to be proud of me."

He smiled at her softly. "I've been proud of you since you were twelve years old and I drove you to your first day of school here in Houston. I thought how brave you were after all you and your mother had suffered. I always knew you'd do what it took to succeed in life, and you have. You could never disappoint me, Sage."

Her heart squeezed. Deep down she'd always known how he felt, but hearing the words opened something inside her.

She leaned close and kissed his cheek. "Thank you." She managed a smile, thought of Jake, and her sorrow returned, making her throat feel tight.

"What now?" Ian pressed.

"What about his job? What if something happened to him? I don't want to live with a man who takes those kinds of risks."

Ian sighed. "Every day of living is a risk, Sage. People step off a curb and get hit by a car. Planes crash, ships sink. You have to grab at happiness and hold on for as long as it lasts."

She hadn't thought of it that way. Her father had died. Her mother. But nearing eighty, Ian was still alive. His words settled over her like a balm, made her begin to see things in a different way. Ian was right. Marrying Jake and losing him would be devastating. Losing him now hurt just as badly.

"The truth is," her grandfather went on, "you overestimated Stanton. I think you're underestimating Cantrell." Ian reached out and touched her cheek. "And I don't think Jake would have a bit of trouble fitting in at the country club."

She looked up. "You don't?"

His smile returned. "Not as long as he had you on his arm. That man would walk through fire for you, honey. A night at the theater isn't gonna bother him at all." He took her hand, gave it a squeeze. "You sure you love him?"

The lump in her throat swelled. Inside her chest her heart was beating with hope. "Desperately," she said.

"Then I suggest you go after him. A man like Cantrell won't wait long for a woman. You want him, you'd better go get him."

Love for her grandfather made her eyes fill with tears. "Oh, Granddad, thank you."

He patted her cheek. "Go on now. Before it's too late."

He didn't have to prod her again. Sage grabbed her handbag and hurried to the door. In minutes she was behind the wheel of her car, flying down the freeway toward the off ramp that led to Jake's apartment. It was well after time for his office to close. She hoped he would be home.

She passed a police car as she roared up Buffalo Speedway, and forced herself to slow to the legal limit. By the time she pulled into the guest parking space at Jake's apartment, her nerves were strung as tight and sharp as barbed wire.

Turning off the engine, she sat back for a moment to collect herself, raked a shaky hand through her hair and wished she'd taken time to fix herself up. She didn't want to risk it.

She just wanted to be with Jake.

Chapter 35

Jake tossed a navy blue T-shirt into the suitcase he was taking to Argentina. An oil company had offered him a job protecting one of its corporate execs, and he had grabbed the position like a drowning man being tossed a rope. He couldn't get out of Houston fast enough.

Yesterday had been bad, saying his farewells at the office. Today he had gone to see Felix Porter. The kid had just been coming home from school when he'd spotted Jake's Jeep and started running toward him. Felix screeched to a halt in front of him and stuck out a hand, the way Jake had taught him.

Jake shook it, forced himself to let go. "Hey, kid."

"Jake! Man, I'm glad to see you! The Texans are playing this weekend. I was thinking…hoping me and you could go."

"Yeah, well, I was kind of thinking that myself, but…"

"But what?"

"But something's come up. There's no easy way to say this so I'm just gonna come right out with it. I'm leaving, son. I took a job down in Argentina."

The kid's face fell. "Argentina? I hardly even know where that is. Why you going down there? I thought you had a job right here."

"I did, but this is something I need to do."

Felix scuffed the toe of his worn black-and-white sneaker against the sidewalk. "So when you coming back?"

Jake swallowed. His throat felt tight. "I don't know. Not for a while." Probably never, but he didn't say that to Felix.

"What about Sage? Linc said you was gonna marry her."

"Well, that's part of the problem. Sage said no. She just didn't think it would work out."

"Why not?"

"I'm not sure, Felix. The point is, I'm leaving. I wish I didn't have to go but I do."

"I thought we was friends. Friends don't just up and leave each other."

"We'll always be friends, kid. Nothing's going to change that. I'll give you my address down there as soon as I'm settled. There's email just like here. We'll stay in touch. If you need anything, all you have to do is let me know."

Felix started shaking his head. "Ain't the same, Jake."

It wasn't the same. Not at all. Jake hauled the kid

into a hug. "I'm gonna miss you, son. I'll keep in touch. I promise." But Felix was right. Once he was gone, the distance between them would destroy the bond of friendship they had been building.

A knock sounded at the door, interrupting the memory he would just as soon forget. Jake ignored it, tossed a few pairs of socks into his suitcase and began to pack his underwear. There was no one he wanted to talk to. He just wanted to get the hell away.

The knock came again, more urgently this time, then the doorbell started chiming. Whoever was out there was damned determined to see him.

Leaving the suitcase on the bed, he strode to the door and yanked it open, and was stunned to see Sage standing in the doorway.

"Hello, Jake."

His stomach instantly knotted. That she smiled just made him mad.

"What do you want?"

Her smile slipped away. "I was hoping we could talk. There are…there are things I need to say."

He ignored the tightening in his chest. Why did she have to look so damned pretty? "We've already talked. You said what you had to say, and I got the message loud and clear."

Her chin firmed. "It's important, Jake, or I wouldn't be here." Ignoring him, she walked past him into the apartment. "It'll only take a few minutes. Then if you want me to leave, I will."

Reluctantly, he closed the door. "Look, Sage, we've been through all this already." And seeing her was only making him feel worse. "I'm trying to pack. I've got a plane to catch."

Her face fell. "You're leaving?"

"That's right. What did you expect?"

"Where…where are you going?"

"Argentina. I've taken a job down there."

She swallowed. The determined look in her golden eyes changed to uncertainty. She rested a hand on his chest and he could feel it trembling. "I don't…don't want you to go."

He frowned, noting her sudden pallor. "What is it? Has something happened? I can get Justice back on the job if—"

She shook her head, released a shaky breath. Her eyes searched his face. "It's nothing like that. What's happened is I made a terrible mistake."

"Yeah? How's that?"

"I made a mistake the night you asked me to marry you. I let you walk out the door."

The knot in his stomach pulled tighter. He couldn't handle more of this. It hurt too damned much. "What you said that night… You were right. It would never work. We just don't fit."

"That's not true. We fit perfectly. You said so yourself."

"Sage…"

Her eyes welled. Dammit, he couldn't stand to see her cry.

Her lips trembled an instant before she drew herself up. "I love you, Jake. I was just… I'm not usually that stupid. I love you and I should have said yes the minute you asked me. Because I wanted to marry you. I wanted to say yes more than anything in the world."

His chest was squeezing, his heart drumming. He'd spent every minute of the last few days trying to convince himself that Sage was right and it would never have worked between them.

"Tell me you still love me, Jake. Because I love you so much. I'm dying a little every day I spend without you."

He might be a strong man, but where this woman was concerned, he was weak. "I love you," he said, pulling her into his arms. "I'm crazy in love with you, Sage."

"Marry me?" she asked.

A deep laugh rumbled from his chest. "I'll marry you, honey. Damn straight, I'll marry you." And then he was kissing her, a long, thorough kiss that branded her as his.

He was in love with Sage Dumont and he wasn't a fool. Apparently, as Annie had said, Sage wasn't, either.

Epilogue

The wedding reception at the River Oaks Country Club was held on a perfect November day. Sage sat at the head table wearing a strapless, floor-length Vera Wang gown, her white lace veil pulled back from her face now that the ceremony was over.

In a crisp white pleated shirt and gleaming black tuxedo that perfectly fitted his tall, muscular frame, Jake laughed at something his best man, Trace Rawlins, said.

Around them, friends and family sat at linen-draped tables decorated with floral centerpieces done in silver and deep rose. Guests dined on medium rare filet mignon or fresh Alaska salmon with all the trimmings, accompanied by a fine Napa Valley chardonnay or a rich Bordeaux, part of the extravagant wedding her grandfather had insisted on providing. Dom Perignon flowed from a silver fountain, keeping fluted crystal goblets filled to the brim.

Half of Houston society had been invited, along with an interesting variety of Jake's and Sage's friends. Trace and Maggie; Annie Mayberry, Lincoln Jones and his date, Tanya Porter, sat together, along with Felix, who kept grinning ear-to-ear over the fact that Jake would be staying in Houston. Jake's mother and his stepfather also sat at the table.

Letty Cantrell Richmond was a sweet woman, older than Sage would have guessed, and fiercely proud of her son. She had cried when she'd met Sage, obviously happy that Jake had found a woman to love who clearly loved him in return. His stepfather was reserved, but he and Jake seemed to be getting along passably well.

Miscellaneous friends from the office and their spouses were there, among them Charles Denton, Michael Curtis, Red Williams, Will Bailey and Marie Castelo. Ryan Gosford, Rina's live-in boyfriend, sat at a table next to Will and his date, probably boring them with high-tech computer jargon. It was a mixed bag of people, some brought a little closer by events of the past few weeks.

Jake had introduced Sage to a tough-looking character named John Riggs, and his petite wife, Amy. She met Jake's friend Devlin Raines, and his beautiful wife, Lark, whom Sage knew from her famous designer handbags. Several expensive LARK bags sat on a shelf in Sage's closest. And their daughter, Chrissy, was the sweetest little girl.

All the guests seemed to be enjoying themselves. And though it was a Houston society affair, even Jake seemed to be having a good time.

As usual, her grandfather had been right. Jake fit into the crowd as if he had been born to it. He was a man secure in himself who didn't have to put on airs, and people respected him for that. It bothered Sage only a little that half the females in the room were drooling over him. She had pretty much expected that to happen.

Jake had no trouble being accepted—not that she really cared anymore. It was Ian's approval she had wanted all along. But until he had forced her to face the truth, she hadn't realized how important it truly was.

I'm beginning to think you were marrying Phillip to try to make me happy. Her own happiness had to come second, she had believed. Today, in marrying Jake, and by the grace of God, she was with the man she loved, a man accepted completely as part of the Dumont family.

As she sipped her champagne, she heard Jake's deep laughter, caught a glimpse of his profile. Hard jaw, sexy smile, eyes the color of a blue Texas sky... A little shiver ran through her as those eyes locked with hers and she read the desire in them, knew he saw an answering desire in hers.

They were spending the first few nights of their honeymoon at the ranch, which Jake seemed to love as much as she did. The following week they would be flying to a private island in the Grenadines, where her grandfather had arranged for them to stay in a lovely villa—a surprise wedding present.

Beneath the table Jake squeezed her hand, laughed at something Alex said. Alex and Ben were Jake's groomsmen, while Rina was Sage's maid of honor. Two of her cousins from Dallas were bridesmaids, one of them flirting outrageously with Ben, who was only flirting politely in return. Alex seemed to be doing a good job of baiting Rina, who was doing her best to ignore him.

Since the day Sage had gone to Jake and laid her heart at his feet, her world seemed to have righted itself.

A'lia was now living with a cousin in New York, getting ready to attend Columbia University next semester. Zahra and Yasar had returned to Saudi Arabia. Sage had had no word on Roshan or Tariq. Better, she thought, if she didn't know.

Quadim and Yousef had also disappeared, this time lost in the depths of the Homeland Security justice system.

And yesterday…in a phone call from the sheik, she had received an unexpected wedding gift.

"Ms. Dumont?"

Sage had instantly recognized the voice. "Sheik Khalid."

"I am told you are about to be married."

"Why, yes."

"In protecting me and my family, you have done me a great favor, one for which I am in your debt. In return, I have decided to accept the last offer your company made before I left your country. Marine Drilling is now the owner of an offshore drilling platform and the miscellaneous equipment that was included in the deal."

Her pulse shot up. "Your Highness, that is very good news."

"Consider it a wedding gift."

"Thank you. I know my grandfather will also be happy to hear of this." But mostly she couldn't wait to tell Jake. Amazing, in such a short time, how important he had become in her life.

Of course, there was no complete guarantee that because she'd made the deal she would get the job as president, even though she was a Dumont. But she had saved Marine Drilling millions and the odds were in her favor. On top of that, she had helped a young woman get a chance to live the life she chose.

Sage glanced over at Jake, found him watching her with a faint smile on his lips. She smiled in return, her heart overflowing with love for him.

More toasts were made to the bride and groom. Alex Justice rose to his feet, grinning a little too broadly, full of fun and a little too much champagne, like everyone else.

He lifted his glass in a toast. "As Shakespeare said, 'Look down, you gods, and on this couple drop a blessed crown.'" His grin broadened, dimples digging into his cheeks. "To the bride and groom."

Everyone cheered and raised their glasses. Jake turned to her and smiled. "'Doubt that the stars are fire,'" he said softly. "'Doubt the sun doth move. Doubt truth be a liar. But never doubt I love.'"

Sage's throat tightened. Dear God, Jake Cantrell quoting Shakespeare? Her eyes filled and her heart turned over.

"I love you," she said softly.

Ian's eyes twinkled. Seated next to her, he lifted his glass in a silent toast to Jake, grinned at Sage and winked.

In sheer joy, she laughed.

Jake leaned back against the headboard of the big four-poster bed watching Sage asleep beside him. The afternoon was lazy, with warm tropical breezes blowing in through the open windows, ruffling the gauzy white curtains. A slowly rotating ceiling fan pushed cool air over the light comforter Sage snuggled beneath.

Earlier, they had taken a swim in the warm Caribbean Sea, which stretched blue and beckoning beyond the terrace as far as Jake could see.

He wasn't usually one for spending downtime just loafing, lying in the sun or wandering along the beach. But he'd never had a wife before. Never been on a honeymoon.

Never known just how good life could be.

He thought of the woman beside him and how close he had been to losing her. If she hadn't come to him... If he had left the country without fighting for her...

As usual, Annie had been right.

Sage snuggled against him in slumber, and he brushed a strand of hair from her face, then bent and lightly kissed her cheek. Damn, he loved this woman.

He thought of Annie again and their last conversation. Sooner or later, she predicted, Alex Justice was going to get his comeuppance from Rina Eckhart.

"That man's had it too easy for far too long. Thinks he's irresistible to women. That little gal will show him—you just wait and see."

Sage had just laughed, but Jake had known Annie too long to dismiss her opinions out of hand. Then again, maybe this time she would be wrong.

Whatever lay ahead, for the next two weeks Jake wasn't going to think about Alex or Ben or work or anything that didn't include his wife and relaxation. There'd be time enough when he got back home to decide which assignment he was going to take. One in Houston, for sure. He was going to make a home there, just as he'd hoped to do before.

Jake watched his wife sleeping, liked the way the sun made her hair glint with gold and how her skin glowed in the soft light streaming in through the open terrace doors.

Before they'd left Houston, he and Sage had talked about where they were going to live. He couldn't handle her high-rise condo. He needed green grass and open spaces. And his apartment was way too small.

They thought maybe one of the big stately homes in the University District. The yards were large and there were lots of tall, leafy trees. It would suit them both, he figured.

Beside him Sage stirred, slowly awakened. She glanced around, smiling when she remembered where she was and that they were on their honeymoon.

She scooted backward until she was propped against the headboard beside him. "I guess we'd better get up and do something."

Jake kissed her lightly. "We'll 'do something' when we get back home. Your grandfather said to relax and enjoy ourselves. We've got an entire island to explore—whenever we get around to it." And a lovely sprawling villa, fully staffed, of course. Nothing but the best for Ian Dumont's granddaughter and her husband.

Sage grinned. "He did, didn't he?"

"Yeah, he did."

"And we deserve it."

Jake thought of all they had been through, the bomb threats and the smuggling, trying to stop a terrorist plot. "Yeah, we do."

They'd found nuclear material in the package hidden in the last pipe shipment. The plan was to assemble a dirty bomb and set it off in downtown L.A. Fortunately, the plot had failed. Though Homeland Security was still running down other possible members of the cell.

Sage smiled up at Jake. The love he saw in her eyes made his chest feel tight.

She reached up and ran her hands through his hair. "All right, then, husband of mine, I think I know exactly what we should do for the rest of the day."

One of his eyebrows went up. "Oh, yeah?"

"Yeah."

He knew this woman, knew her appetites matched his own. He didn't have to ask what she wanted to do.

Sage laughed as Jake tugged her down in the deep feather mattress and kissed her. There were hours left in the warm, sunny, tropical afternoon.

* * * * *

VEILED INTENTIONS

Delores Fossen

For Don and Orloene

Chapter 1

Detective Katelyn O'Malley stood in the entrance hall and studied each of the wedding guests as they trickled into Sacred Heart church.

If she got lucky, very lucky, maybe no one would be murdered today.

Too bad there was the little annoying buzz in the back of her head that said all hell might break loose before the bride and groom managed to say I do.

While she directed the guests to sign the registry—a duty she'd created for her cover—Katelyn continued her surveillance. She mentally dismissed two giggling teenage girls whose dresses were so skintight that they couldn't have been carrying concealed weapons, or much of anything else for that matter. Besides, if her profile of the killer was right, she wasn't looking for a female but a male in his late twenties or early thirties.

A male who'd already killed two people.

"See anything?" she heard her brother, Garrett, ask through her earpiece. He was posted outside the church. Watching their backs. And sides. It'd taken some effort, but she'd managed to get photos of thirty-nine of the forty-one guests. Not bad odds. If someone uninvited showed up, Garrett would know and could relay it to her.

Katelyn kept her voice at a whisper and spoke into the tiny communicator tucked in the neckline of her dress. "So far, so good. How about you?"

"Nothing. Well, nothing other than being hit on by one of the bridesmaids."

That wasn't anything new. Lots of women hit on her brother. "Was she armed?" Katelyn was only partly sarcastic.

"No. Unfortunately, I have firsthand knowledge that she wasn't, since she tripped over her lavender taffeta gown and fell right in my arms." He paused. "I guess this is a good time to remind you that your lieutenant will have our butts if he finds out about this little un-authorized stakeout you arranged?"

"He won't find out," Katelyn said with certainty she didn't feel. The lieutenant in question was her oldest brother and head of Homicide. And he would find out. No doubt about it. Still, if she could stop someone from being killed today, she'd gladly take the flak over her yet-to-be-an-official-part of this investigation.

"Okay, can I add then that this is probably a waste of a really great Saturday afternoon?" Garrett continued. "You're assuming the other two murders weren't just random acts of violence—"

"They weren't."

He grumbled something that Katelyn didn't want to distinguish. "All right, but even if last week's shooting was the start of some grand serial career, it's the first frickin' weekend in June. There are dozens of weddings going on in San Antonio today. Hear that, sis? *Dozens.* If our gunman's really a wacko targeting brides and grooms, he could be at any one of them."

It was true, and they'd already rehashed this subject too many times. Yes, this was a long shot. Yes, this wasn't exactly standard operating procedure. And yes, they could get reprimanded for this. But after studying all the angles, Katelyn knew in her gut that this particular ceremony was their best bet for saving lives. In her mind, this was one of those times where the means would justify the ends.

An odd sound caught her attention. A scrape of metal. Katelyn whipped her gaze to the other side of the narthex where the lanky, twenty-something photographer was adjusting his equipment. He was definitely on her list of people to be concerned about, and she made a mental note to get a look in his bag. Perhaps she'd try the bridesmaid's flirting/falling in his arms approach. She was certainly dressed for the part in the short, snug emerald silk outfit that she'd dragged from the back of her closet.

The way back.

Katelyn had added some too-high heels, heavy concealing makeup and a blond wig to go along with it. All in all, it was a very uncomfortable but hopefully convincing disguise that could work for her if needed.

"Hold on. We might have something," Garrett informed her. "*If* there's something to have in all this. A male. Brown hair, part Latino or maybe Italian. He doesn't match any of the photos. You'll have visual in under a minute because he's headed right for the church."

"Okay. I'll handle it. You stay put in case this one's a decoy."

"Be careful," he warned.

Oh, she definitely would.

More guests strolled in, bringing with them the June heat and humidity from the nearby San Antonio River. A pregnant woman with a toddler. A middle-aged couple holding hands. All innocent, she was sure of that.

And then Katelyn saw him.

That buzz in her head turned to a full roar.

He stepped into the entry. Well, he didn't step, exactly. He stalked in, smooth and slow, like a jungle cat sizing up his hunting area.

Now here was the male who fit her profile to a proverbial tee. Mahogany brown hair, not too long, not too short. Olive skin. Six-one. About a hundred and seventy-five pounds. No distinguishing marks and definitely no pretty boy. He had badass written all over him.

He wore a midnight-blue suit. Nondescript. Ditto for the crisp white dress shirt and his precisely knotted silver-gray tie. But that's where the nondescript and ditto parts ended. Katelyn had been a cop for nearly eight years and had learned to recognize something lethal when she saw it.

This guy was lethal.

His gaze swept around the room, and like his entrance, it was smooth. He made eye contact with her. Just a split second. Then, he looked away to continue his surveillance. And there was no doubt in her mind that this was surveillance for him. He dismissed the teenagers as quickly as Katelyn had, but his attention lingered a bit on the photographer, before it came back to her.

Was he suspicious?

You bet he was.

His instincts weren't lacking in any area. That meant she had to strike first.

Pulling in a hard breath to steady herself, she eased from behind the narrow table when he walked closer. She wanted a better look, among other things, and she got a dose of those *other things* right away. She caught the scent of his aftershave. Something manly and musky. It was better suited for a long night of sex than a wedding.

Or maybe that was just her imagination working overtime.

Whoa.

An imagination with seriously bad timing.

She brushed her arm against his, purposely, and the soft contact garnered her another glance. Not a dismissive one either. There was interest in the depths of those icy blue eyes. Too bad she couldn't quite make out exactly what kind of interest it was, but it was obviously time for that flirting ruse to see if she had to reel in a killer.

Katelyn smiled, making sure she let her nerves show a little. She didn't have to fake that part. She was well past being nervous. But then, this was a situation where lack of nerves would mean she was a complete idiot. Someone, maybe this man, had already killed two people. Nerves were part of the job description.

"I'm Kate." She offered her hand in greeting, and he shook it. Eventually. "Would you like to sign the guest registry?"

"No, thanks."

"Oh, okay." A roadblock. Not too surprising. Katelyn tried a different angle. "It's a keepsake for the bride and groom so they'll know who attended. Maybe I could sign it for you if you'll give me your name?"

He looked at the book, then her again. "Joe."

She almost pushed for a last name but decided it could wait. "This'll sound like a really bad line, but don't I know you from somewhere?" Katelyn asked, letting her voice purr. "You look familiar."

He spared her another glance. "No. I think I'd remember you."

There was a touch of Texas in his voice. An effortless, sliding drawl that matched his attitude.

And his aftershave.

Maybe the accent meant he was local. If so, it fit another piece of her unofficial profile.

Katelyn looked around to make sure they hadn't garnered anyone's attention. They hadn't. The guests were still ambling into the sanctuary, which was exactly where she needed them to amble. She didn't want an audience, or any bystanders, when she confronted him.

"Say, I'm a little light-headed," she lied. "I have this blood sugar thing. Nothing serious. Just makes me a little woozy. I wondered if I could just catch on to your arm before I fall flat on my face?"

He studied her. A long, snail-crawling moment. And

then, as if preparing for a root canal, he offered her his arm. She took hold of it before he changed his mind, and she got a peek inside his jacket.

He was packing a .357 Magnum in a shoulder holster.

Katelyn had anticipated a weapon, of course. However, reality caused her heart to slam against her chest. She pushed that slamming aside and got to work. It was time to move on to the next step of her plan. She needed to get him away from the guests so she could rid him of that weapon and ask a few questions.

She stumbled, just enough to make him grip her arm. That stumble was a real leap of faith on her part, since she wasn't overly confident that he would even catch her. Thankfully, there was at least one gentlemanly bone in his body, because he cooperated. After he had a good hold on her, she led him a few steps away into the narrow hallway just off the narthex.

"I can't believe this is happening," she mumbled, leaning against him so he wouldn't easily be able to reach for his gun. "Not the best time to get one of my dizzy spells. The ceremony's about to start, and I doubt you want to miss that."

She shoved him into the small vacant room that she'd already checked out. Katelyn didn't waste any time, figuring she would rather be embarrassed from a case of mistaken identity than to have a dead bride and groom.

Blocking the doorway so he couldn't leave, she drew her weapon from her holster, hidden beneath her silky jacket. "Here's how we're going to do this," she instructed. "Keep your hands where I can see them and explain to me why you brought a .357 Magnum to a wedding."

He lifted his shoulder in a casual shrug. "I carry my gun everywhere. I guess you do the same?"

If he was scared, or even remotely concerned, he certainly wasn't showing it. Too bad Katelyn couldn't say the same. Her throat was suddenly dry as dust, and she kept a firm grip on her gun to keep her hand from shaking.

"Yes, but for me, it's part of the job. I'm Detective Katelyn O'Malley, S.A.P.D., and this is what we call a stop and frisk."

He paused. Said one word of profanity under his breath. One rather crude four-letter word. He tipped his eyes to the ceiling as if seeking divine intervention.

Or something.

"Know what I think?" he asked.

"Not particularly. But I want you to remove your weapon slowly and carefully from its holster and place it on the floor. Notice those operative words. *Slowly. Carefully. Floor.* Those are major conditions here, and you're going to do that while using only two fingers. Make any sudden moves, and I'll take you down the hard way."

He looked her straight in the eye. "That wasn't what I was thinking." He disarmed himself, just as she'd instructed. Slowly, carefully, and he placed his gun on the floor directly between them.

"Oh, yeah?" Katelyn caught his shoulder and turned him around. She positioned his hands, palms flat, against the wall, and kneed his legs apart. "What exactly were you thinking?" she asked, patting him down.

The man was certainly solid. And built. Her fingers skimmed over lots of hard, sinewy muscles. Odd. She'd never noticed anything like that before when frisking a suspect. Maybe it had something to do with his memorable aftershave.

"I'm thinking you'll regret doing this," he let her know.

"I doubt it, especially since it might just save a few people from dying."

She located his wallet in his jacket pocket. Except when she got a good look at it, she realized it wasn't a wallet. And that caused her stomach to tighten into a hard knot. It also caused Katelyn to use a little profanity of her own. She flipped open the too-familiar leather case and read the name aloud.

"Joseph Rico."

"Sergeant Joe Rico," he clarified. And with that announcement, he turned back around to face her. "Homicide. S.A.P.D."

Her breath landed somewhere around that knot in her stomach.

Katelyn shook her head. The badge had to be a fake. Except it wasn't. She scratched it with her thumbnail, or rather tried to. It was as real as the one in her purse. Still, there was something off here. "Impossible. I work Homicide, and I've never seen you before in my life."

"Because I was just assigned there." He enunciated each word as if she were mentally deficient. "By the chief of police."

Judas Priest. That bit of information cleared the buzz in her head. Katelyn wasn't sure exactly where this was leading, but she knew for a fact that she wouldn't like its final destination.

Joe Rico calmly picked up his gun from the floor

and reholstered it. Somehow, he managed to look cocky even while doing that little chore. No hurried moves. No overt display of emotion.

"Well, Detective Katelyn O'Malley, I'd say we have a problem. A problem with you being here because this isn't your case. Why am I so certain of that?" He aimed his thumb at his chest. "Because it's mine."

Katelyn hadn't thought this moment could possibly get more frustrating—or embarrassing—but she was obviously wrong.

"Yours?" she demanded.

"Mine." Sergeant Rico muscled her out of the doorway and turned to leave, delivering the rest of his news from over his shoulder. "Oh, and by the way, I'm your new boss."

Chapter 2

Well, it wasn't exactly the smooth start Joe wanted for this particular investigation. While undercover, he'd been made quite easily—by his subordinate, no less. And then that subordinate had frisked him.

He was sorry to say the frisking had been more enjoyable than it should have been.

Far more.

"The chief assigned you this case?" Katelyn O'Malley asked, following him.

Since he'd already made that perfectly clear, and since he detected some resentment in her voice, he surmised that she'd heard him correctly but wasn't in agreement with the chief's decision.

Joe stopped at the edge of the narthex and pressed the transmitter of the communication device hidden in his jacket. "Did anyone come in the church in the past three minutes?" he asked the backup officer who was positioned in an office building directly across the street.

"No."

So they'd been lucky. Katelyn O'Malley's stunt hadn't allowed the sniper to walk in unchallenged. Of course, if the killer followed the method of operation of the last shooting, he or she wouldn't burst into the church until the I do's had been said. There'd be a frenzied battery of gunfire from a ski-mask-wearing shooter who wouldn't actually enter the sanctuary but would stay in the narthex and then make an easy getaway. Just the way it'd happened to the victims, Gail Prescott and Raul Hernandez.

Joe clicked off the transmitter and glanced back at Detective O'Malley.

She was staring at him as if he were a member of the fungus family.

Too bad he couldn't say the same for her.

She was attractive. Damn attractive. Not like a beauty queen either, but in a strong, athletic, kick-butt sort of way. The girl-next-door meets Buffy type.

The type he found attractive.

And no amount of denial would make his body think otherwise. Fortunately, the parts of his body that noticed her attractive looks didn't have any say in the decisions he made.

"There's been some kind of mistake." She jammed her gun back into her holster. "After the initial investigator dropped out because of family illness, I requested this case, and I was told my request was under consideration."

"It was," Joe calmly assured her. "But the considering part is finished now, and I'm the lead investigator. End of discussion."

There was nothing calm about her response. He saw some fire dance through ultraclear, cool green eyes. He'd obviously stepped on her toes, toes encased very nicely in a pair of sex-against-the-wall stilettos.

Something else about her that he truly wished he hadn't noticed.

Joe quickly pushed that, her physical attributes and the remnants of the frisking aside. What the devil was wrong with him anyway? Even if he'd been looking to spice up his love life, he darn sure wouldn't have been looking in Katelyn O'Malley's direction.

"I knew the woman who was killed last week," she added.

As if that would help her cause.

"Gail Prescott," Joe supplied. "You went to high school with her and you've maintained occasional contact with her and her family. You probably would have attended her wedding even if you hadn't been on a stakeout. Your relationship with the victim, however, doesn't give you priority in this investigation. In fact, it does just the opposite. I don't care to work with an officer who comes into a case with a personal chip on his or her shoulder."

She unclenched her teeth before she could speak. "There's no personal chip, *Sergeant.* Just my desire to bring a killer to justice."

"Good. Then, we're in agreement. I have that same desire, but that doesn't mean I'll allow you to be part of this case." But the moment the words left his mouth, Joe remembered a vital point that had come to mind. "By the way, why'd you stake out this particular church?"

The fire in those baby greens dwindled a fraction. She pulled back her shoulders as if preparing to defend herself and met him eye-to-eye. In those heels, she could almost manage it, even though he was just over six feet tall.

"Because the bride and groom met through the Perfect Match Agency, the same matchmaking service that Gail and her fiancé used," she explained. "They both also had the same florist. I thought there might be a connection so I contacted the minister here at the church—"

"You told him about this possible connection?"

"No. Of course not. There's only been one shooting, and I have no proof that there'll be another one. I didn't want the couple to bring a possible lawsuit against the department for disrupting their wedding, so I simply reminded the minister of some recent robberies in the area and offered my services as a temporary security guard. He agreed, and we came up with the idea of using the guest registry as my cover."

So she'd done her homework. He liked that. But this wasn't a time when Brownie points counted. "The florist and Perfect Match could be a coincidence. There are other possible angles."

"Yes. Gail's fiancé was Hispanic, so the shooting could have been racially motivated. Or maybe their deaths are linked to some other aspect of their personal lives." She paused. "But I don't believe that, and apparently neither do you, or you wouldn't have come here today."

Touché.

Joe fought back an urge to smile. Under different circumstances, he might have enjoyed this verbal sparring, but these weren't different circumstances. Katelyn O'Malley would be in his way, because despite her denial, this case was personal for her. In his experience, when it got personal, people made mistakes.

That wasn't going to happen on his watch.

"I came here to follow up on one particular theory. *One* theory of several," he assured her.

Joe checked the entryway. No new guests, and the others had already moved into the church. He could hear the organ start to play, an indication that the bride and groom were about to make their entrance.

Hopefully, it wouldn't be their last.

Katelyn huffed. "I know those theories as well as you—"

"Caucasian male is approaching the church," the backup officer said through Joe's communicator.

That, and the sound of hurried footsteps, interrupted whatever else she was about to say. Frantic footsteps that sent them both reaching for their guns. In the same motion, she stepped into the hallway beside him. However, the threat for which they'd braced themselves didn't materialize.

Judging from the strong family resemblance, the man who came into sight was Sergeant Garrett O'Malley. His gun was already drawn, but he held it discreetly by his side so it wouldn't easily be seen.

"Katelyn, what's going on?" her brother demanded.

Because Joe was standing arm-to-arm with her, he felt her muscles relax.

"False alarm," she let him know. Once again, she reholstered her gun. "This is Sergeant Joe Rico. Homicide. This is my brother, Sergeant Garrett O'Malley, Special Investigations."

Unlike Katelyn, Garrett didn't appear to relax. Just the opposite. It was obvious he had issues, and Joe didn't have to guess who or what those issues were.

"Rico," Garrett repeated in the same tone that he no doubt reserved for profanity. "According to the rumor mill, the chief sent you in to investigate our brother, Brayden. And possibly Katelyn and me, too."

"The chief did what?" Katelyn asked. Mouth gaping, she stepped in front of Joe and pinned her gaze to his.

This obviously wasn't the way to win friends and influence people. But that didn't matter. He had a job to do, and he'd do it, with or without the O'Malleys' approval.

"Since it appears you can answer your sister's questions," Joe said to Garrett, "I'll leave you to it and see what's happening in the church. I'd prefer that people didn't die while we're standing around chitchatting."

It was a good exit line. The only thing missing was, well, the good exit. Katelyn didn't get out of his way so he could leave, and the hallway was too narrow to go around her. He really didn't want to play bump and grind just so he could get past her.

Really.

Even if there were various parts of him that thought it might be fun.

Her hands went to her hips. "I don't know what your agenda is—"

"To do my job," Joe insisted.

That earned him a scowl. "My brothers are good cops. Don't judge either of them by the fact that I came here today. This undercover investigation was my idea and mine alone."

Since it was clear this argument wouldn't be resolved in the next couple of minutes, Joe put his gun back into his holster, firmly caught her shoulders and moved her out of his path. "I'll see you both back at headquarters when I'm finished here."

Joe turned to leave. But he still didn't manage that exit. A few steps was as far as he got. The sound stopped him in his tracks. Because it was the last thing he wanted to hear. A sound he'd anticipated, and dreaded.

A shot blasted through the church.

The emotion of her argument with Sergeant Rico evaporated instantly, and in its place, Katelyn felt the barrage of instinct and adrenaline.

Sweet heaven. The gunman had attacked after all, and she hadn't been able to stop it. She prayed the bullet had missed its target and that everyone was safe.

"The shot came from outside," Rico offered, taking the words right out of her mouth. "The west side of the building, maybe. Maybe the rear. Garrett, secure the front doors, and just in case someone else hasn't already done it, call for backup. Katelyn, you're coming with me."

Rico didn't hesitate. Neither did Garrett nor she. Her brother hurried to the front door, kicking it shut and locking it. He kept his weapon ready, secured a spot near one of the sidelight windows and then pulled out his cell phone. Rico went in the direction of the sanctuary, and Katelyn followed.

"Get down!" Rico yelled to the guests.

Most had already done just that, squeezing themselves underneath the pews. There were raw screams. Chaos. The smell of fear. And in the middle of that, Katelyn saw the bride, groom and the minister cowering between the altar and an archway of pale peach roses.

No visible evidence of blood. Thank God. They seemed unharmed.

For now.

"There's an auxiliary building out there. Two story, brown brick," she relayed to Rico. "Our gunman could be using it as a catbird seat."

He nodded and without taking his attention off the partially shot-out stained glass window, he whispered to her over his shoulder. "You don't happen to have another brother stashed in the parking lot, huh?"

"I wish. But no. We're on our own until backup arrives." Which wouldn't be for minutes. Long, critical minutes.

Where just about anything could happen.

"Good," Rico responded. "Because I have an officer out there. One who's *officially* on this case, and I didn't want any of your relatives accidentally shooting him while he's trying to do his job."

Katelyn didn't appreciate the sarcasm but welcomed all the help they could get. Maybe the officer would be able to stop the gunman before any more damage was done.

But at the moment that seemed a lot to hope for.

There'd been damage already. Even if they stopped the shooting here and now, every one of the guests would remember this horrifying ordeal for the rest of their lives. Katelyn blamed herself for that. She'd been in a position to stop this and had failed.

A second shot rang out, quickly followed by another. And another. Two of the three went through a window on the right front side of the church and tore chunks of glass from the frame. No doubt that's what the shooter had intended to do. Now he or she had a direct line of sight into the church.

Yelling and crying out, the bride, groom and minister scurried to the other side of the altar, but it wouldn't give them shelter for long. Bullets could easily eat through that wood.

"I'll make my way over there." Rico tipped his head to a set of ornate double doors, which were only a couple of yards away from the shattered window. "If necessary I'll return fire to draw the shooter's attention. I might be able to get a visual and take him out."

Yes. Or maybe the gunman would get him first. Of course, that was a chance they had to take.

"I can help." Katelyn kicked off her shoes and peeled off the silky jacket so they wouldn't get in her way. "There aren't any guests near that other window next to the doors. I'll knock out the glass and return fire, as well. Don't worry—I'll keep watch for your officer and make sure I don't send any friendly fire his way."

Rico might have disagreed with that impromptu plan, but he didn't get a chance to say anything. More shots came crashing through the building.

Heavy, thick blasts.

Nonstop, this time.

The sounds were deafening. And they drowned out the shouts, screams and prayers that increased with each new round of fire. Just as Katelyn had figured, those shots were aimed right at the wooden altar. It was the same as the first shooting, the one that had killed Gail and her fiancé. Shots and plenty of them. But that knowledge gave Katelyn no comfort whatsoever. She'd already guessed that Gail's murder wasn't some random act of violence.

For all the good it'd done her.

Her guess was right, and yet it'd still been repeated right under her nose.

The bride screamed. Maybe in pain. Maybe just from fear. Katelyn prayed it was fear.

Rico moved. Fast and low. He was almost graceful, surprising for a man his size. With Katelyn following closely behind him, they went toward the door. Along the way, he identified himself and doled out assurances to the terrified guests.

He kept close to the perimeter wall until he got to the row of the stained glass windows, and then he lowered himself to the floor and proceeded to the doors.

The shots stopped for only a couple of seconds. Not for reloading, Katelyn soon learned. And they didn't stop because the gunman was finished for the day. The break was so the person could change out rifles. The sound of the new shots told her that much since it was a different calibration. Whoever was doing this had certainly come prepared to kill but wasn't necessarily an expert marksman. The stray bullets were landing everywhere—which, of course, made the situation all the more dangerous.

Katelyn made her way right along behind Joe Rico. Trying to time it perfectly to coordinate with his efforts, she sheltered her eyes and used the grip of her gun to knock out the glass that formed the image of the archangel, Michael. The glass was solid and held in place by not just strips of lead solder but also a sturdy frame. It took several hard jabs before she managed to dislodge enough of it so she could see into the parking lot.

Pressing her back against the narrow section of wall next to the doors, she rotated her body and did a quick check outside. She had a fairly good view of the building—and the dozen or so windows facing the church. Too many windows, and the reflection of the early afternoon sun didn't make things easier. She quickly scanned them all as best she could.

No shooter in sight.

Yet, he had to be there.

Somewhere.

Because he was still firing.

While still low on the floor, Rico reached up and turned the old-fashioned brass handle on the door. He opened it a fraction and looked out. Katelyn waited for a signal so she could return fire.

And just like that, the shots stopped.

She felt another surge of adrenaline slam through her. A bad-feeling kind of surge. If the gunman wasn't shooting, then he was likely making his getaway.

That couldn't happen.

Because she knew in her heart that he would continue this until someone stopped him.

It was a risk, but Katelyn moved closer to the window so she could check the parking lot and the grounds. Rico did the same to the door. He stood, took position and aimed.

"Think," she whispered to herself. If she were a

killer, what would be her escape plan? Not the parking lot. Too visible. Not the side either since it bumped right against a fairly busy street.

No.

He'd go out the rear of the building and slip into the myriad of old shops and businesses that were crammed into this particular part of the downtown area.

Katelyn heard the sound of sirens the moment that Rico opened the door wider. Mumbling something, he peered out. He'd perhaps come to the same conclusion as she had. The gunman was getting away.

"Stay put," Rico ordered.

It was a logical order.

Katelyn needed to stay there to protect the guests. Still, part of her wanted to go after the gunman.

"Hold your positions," Garrett called out from the arched entryway that led into the church. Katelyn glanced at him and saw that he had his phone pressed to his ear. "Backup is in pursuit of a white car that just sped away."

Katelyn released the breath that she didn't even know she'd been holding. She glanced at Rico, but he didn't seem any more eager than she was to let down his guard. So they did the only thing they could do. They waited with their backs literally against the wall and their guns ready.

"Is anyone hurt?" Rico called out to the guests.

The response varied, most still layered with panic, but from what she gathered, no one had actually been shot. Nothing short of a miracle. Katelyn said a quick prayer of thanks for that and then turned to the man who'd given her so much grief about being here.

"Still think I'm the wrong person for this case?" she asked Rico.

"Yes." No hesitation whatsoever.

The analogy of butting her head against a brick wall came to mind. "But I guessed right about the gunman picking this particular wedding. Even in your book that has to count for something."

He made another check of the parking lot. "It doesn't count for much."

Crouching there among shattered glass and the smell of gunfire, it seemed petty to dislike this man because he was arrogant and hardheaded, but that didn't prevent her scowl. The scowl didn't lessen either when Garrett called out something else.

"It's over already. Backup lost the guy in pursuit," her brother announced.

"It's over," some of the guests repeated. Slowly, they began to come out of hiding. Hugging each other. Crying. Praying. Most still in shock.

Katelyn groaned and scrubbed her hand over her face. Judas. This wasn't over. In fact, that buzz in the back of her head told her it wasn't over by a long shot.

The killer had just gotten started.

Chapter 3

Joe reread the overview of the proposed mission that Lieutenant Brayden O'Malley had handed him just minutes earlier. The overview didn't read any better the second time around, and he didn't hold out hope that a third read would make it any more palatable.

There were quite a few points of contention so Joe chose the first one. "You really think the shooting day before yesterday was a result of a botched burglary of the building next to Sacred Heart church?"

"No," O'Malley readily answered. "But I'd rather have the press report that than link it with the shooting that happened a week earlier."

Joe nodded, but the two shootings wouldn't stay unlinked for long. All it would take was another incident, and unfortunately another incident was probably in the planning stages. That is, if the gunman hadn't already finalized his next hit. But the real question was—was the killer linked to the matchmaking agency or the florist?

Or neither?

The *or neither* was the most troublesome scenario of them all. If the shootings weren't connected through the businesses, then maybe they had a thrill killer or just a plain psycho on their hands.

Not that they didn't have that anyway.

But Joe preferred his psychos to keep to a discernable pattern, because with hard work and some luck, patterns could be identified.

"The shell casings taken from the two crime scenes didn't match," Katelyn said, reading from a copy of the overview. She gave a weary sigh. "So that complicates things."

"It just means our shooter likes to trade off weapons," Joe advised her. "It doesn't mean the crimes aren't related."

Another sigh from her. This one wasn't weary. It had a you-think? tinge to it.

"Arguments? Comments? Objections?" Lieutenant O'Malley asked. "If so, direct them to me and not at each other."

The man was definitely a multitasker. While he tossed out those leading questions and semireprimands, he looked through a report, scrawled his signature on it and tossed it into his out-box before he went onto the next one. But then, no one had ever accused this particular O'Malley of being inefficient. Just the opposite. The only accusation had been in the area of his preferential treatment.

"Concerns," Joe volunteered.

Time to move on to point two. He had a lot of concerns, but the major one was the woman with the short, flame-red hair who was sitting next to him. Now the question was how to voice that concern without thoroughly riling Katelyn's oldest brother, a man he had no desire to rile. Even under a cloud of suspicion, Brayden was formidable. Joe's investigation into departmental favoritism would no doubt irritate the man enough without adding more to the mix.

"Sergeant Rico thinks this case is too personal for me," Katelyn countered. "He believes I should step aside because I knew Gail."

And with that totally accurate observation, she looked across the desk that separated them and met her brother's gaze. In the next few seconds, at least a hundred or more words passed between them, even though neither spoke.

It was an interesting encounter to watch.

The lieutenant stared at her and lifted his eyebrow, just a fraction. That was it. No other change in his otherwise calm, authoritative expression. Yet the simple gesture caused Katelyn's mouth to tighten, and her grip on the chair arm whitened her knuckles. Joe could have sworn the temperature in the room dropped by a full ten degrees. It was the most efficient warning he'd ever witnessed.

"Your sister has renegade tendencies," Joe added, feeling that after what'd just happened, he was probably preaching to the choir. Still, a little choir preaching might go a long way to some changes in this mission proposal. "I'd prefer to work with another detective on this case."

And Joe already had one in mind. Detective Dawn

Davidson, a veteran officer who'd worked a serial killer case just the year before. She had the experience and from all accounts was levelheaded.

"Bringing in another detective might be a problem." The lieutenant extracted a manila folder from a stack and slid it Joe's way. "This'll be an undercover assignment, and Katelyn already has her foot in the door."

"What door?" Joe asked.

"At the matchmaking agency that might be connected to the two shootings."

Judging from the soft groan that Katelyn made and the way she sank slightly lower in her chair, this would not please him. From the lieutenant's elevated eyebrow, it didn't please him much, either.

"I must have missed that foot-in-the-door part when reading the overview," Joe commented.

Brayden pointed to the folder. "It's all in there."

Katelyn turned slightly away when he opened it and kept her attention focused on her brother. The top page in the folder was a rather lengthy questionnaire from the Perfect Match Agency, and it was dated a week earlier. It'd been filled out just two days after the first shooting.

And the name at the top?

Kate Kennedy.

Joe felt a groan coming on, as well.

"Is this your handiwork?" he asked her.

"Yes. But no one at Perfect Match has any idea that I'm a cop. *No one.* Kennedy is obviously an alias." Katelyn directed the rest of her explanation to her brother. "I wanted to get a look at the people who worked there. I figured this was the fastest way to do it."

"But not the smartest way," Joe quickly let her know. "You could have jeopardized everything by going in there on your own."

"But I didn't." Moving to the edge of her seat, she repeated it to her brother. "I can do whatever you need me to do to make this undercover assignment work."

"I'm not the one you need to convince, Katelyn. The chief assigned Sergeant Rico as the lead for this case." And the lieutenant sat back and left it at that.

The proverbial ball had just been tossed into Joe's proverbial court.

Unfortunately, he also knew how these next few minutes were about to play out.

Hell.

Katelyn O'Malley had certainly put him in a hard place with her coloring-outside-the-lines attitude. Still, it'd only compound the problem if he let his personal feelings influence the most logical way to approach this. Well, it was the most logical approach considering she'd already tossed a monkey wrench or two into the scenario.

"It wouldn't be smart for me to use another detective at this point," Joe concluded, speaking more to himself than the O'Malleys. He glanced at the questionnaire while he finished up his explanation. It figured. Katelyn had listed chili as her favorite food. "If the killer's part of the Perfect Match Agency, then he or she might be suspicious of anyone registering so soon after the second shooting."

"Guess that leaves you out then, huh?" Katelyn all but smirked at him.

Even though it was borderline petty, Joe liked it when people did that, especially when he could smirk right back. He calmly shuffled through the papers in the folder, extracted his own questionnaire and passed it to her.

Her eyes widened and skimmed over the first page. "You filled this out the same day I did?"

Let the smirking begin. "Yes."

She hissed out a breath. "Need I remind you that you just accused me of jumping the gun by going to the agency?"

"The difference is—I was on this case, and you weren't." Joe held out his hands to emphasize the space. "Big difference. I'm talking huge."

The temperature went down another notch, and her eyes narrowed to slits.

"Which brings us up-to-date, I believe," Brayden interjected. Good timing, Joe thought, since Katelyn looked ready to implode. "We have to act fast. There are only five days until Saturday. Five days until a whole host of weddings are scheduled to take place all over the city. Five days to stop a killer from striking again."

Joe was well aware of that. Those five days were already breathing down his neck. "I've learned the florist in question is doing the flower arrangements for two weddings this weekend, one Saturday, another Sunday night. But neither couple met through the Perfect Match Agency. If fact, I haven't been able to connect any of the upcoming marriages to a matchmaking agency."

"Neither have I." Katelyn pulled out her own set of notes from a leather briefcase that was leaning against her chair. "And therein lies our problem. Perfect Match doesn't release all the names of their former customers who've made wedding plans. So it becomes a needle-in-a-haystack approach."

"It's the only approach we have right now," Joe fired back. "We could stake out all the weddings in San Antonio, but it'll eat up a ton of manpower and cause people to ask too many questions and maybe even panic. Plus, there are the other ceremonies, the ones that aren't listed in the paper. We wouldn't be able to cover those. So our best bet is to go back to the source of the connection—the Perfect Match Agency. They require matched couples to meet there first for an ice-breaker, and there's one every Tuesday night, including tomorrow night."

"It starts at seven-thirty," Katelyn provided. "We don't need an invitation. We just need to be computer matched...somehow."

It didn't surprise Joe that she knew those details. She'd probably already picked out the clothes she was going to wear. And she'd done all of that before even being officially assigned to the team.

His team.

He hoped like the devil that she didn't wear those sexy stilettos and the little green outfit. He'd have enough distractions as it was.

"Detective O'Malley and I'll do this intro thing tomorrow night at Perfect Match," Joe continued, making sure he sounded like the boss. Because after the minifantasy involving her choice of fashion, he needed the reminder in the worst sort of way. "We'll pretend we were high school sweethearts and that we're surprised but happy to be reunited."

She nodded. "Good idea. And that'll explain a hasty engagement and equally hasty marriage."

"Well, hopefully." It might also make the wrong person suspicious, but he'd deal with that when and if it happened. "While we're there, we'll have a good look around the place. Without breaking the law, of course."

Another *you-think?* huff from Katelyn.

Joe ignored her and continued. "In the meantime, I'll keep going through the background checks I've been doing on the employees and the owners of Perfect Match and the florist."

"I've done background checks, as well," Katelyn informed him.

Joe bobbed his head. "Of course you have."

The woman had an incredibly effective scalpel-sharp glare. "I'm not an idiot. I did them discretely."

Joe might have questioned her on what she considered discrete, but the lieutenant spoke first. "Sounds as if you have everything under control."

Not even close.

Joe kept that sentiment to himself.

"Good." Brayden stood and reached for the jacket draped over the back of his chair. "Now, if you'll excuse me, I have an appointment with the chief. Feel free to use my office to hash out the rest of the details. Oh, and it goes without saying—keep me informed."

"Wait," Katelyn called out when her brother headed for the door. "You're both missing a key point. Yes, Sergeant Rico and I filled out these questionnaires, but that in itself doesn't give us a computer match. I hate to state the obvious here, but the *computer* does that. In fact, it generates a list of matches so the candidates can meet the people at the icebreaker. What if neither of us has any matches? What then? We can't just show up."

"I'd planned to have one of the techs go into the system and arrange for the questionnaires to be matched," Joe explained.

Katelyn shook her head. "That sounds risky. Someone at the agency might figure out—"

"A match isn't a problem," Brayden assured them. "It's all in the folder."

There was something about the lieutenant's strange, almost self-satisfied expression that sent Joe thumbing through the rest of the papers in the file. Katelyn must have had the same feeling, because she leaned closer so she could see the documents, as well.

It didn't take Joe long to find it. There it was. The dozen or so men listed as "dream date" matches for client 6341B, Kate Kennedy. His own alias, Joe Farrell, was the first name on the list.

He felt as if someone had slugged him in the solar plexus.

"You already had the tech rig the system?" Joe asked. But he didn't think that's what had generated the look on the lieutenant's face.

"No. The two of you matched without any tech interference." Brayden's eyebrows flexed. "For once, Murphy's Law worked in our favor. Let's hope that luck continues."

And with that little scud missile attack, the lieutenant left them sitting there in somewhat stunned silence.

"It had to be the chili," Joe mumbled under his breath.

Or maybe Katelyn just jotted down a whole bunch of lies while filling out the questionnaire. He hadn't, that was for sure. Unnecessary lies were just too hard to keep track of, so with the exception of his name, address and occupation, everything else was true.

Yet, they'd matched.

Even if she'd lied, that was an unsettling coincidence because it meant her lies matched his truths.

Joe quietly pushed that coincidence aside and moved on to the mission at hand.

"I'll see you at the Perfect Match tomorrow night." He stood and tucked the folder beneath his arm. "Until then, we keep doing these background checks and hope we find a smoking gun. Oh, and by the way, I insist the officers on my team follow the rules. *My* rules," he emphasized. "If you jeopardize this assignment again—"

"I won't."

"If you do, I'll have your butt and your badge."

She nodded, after a contemplative moment.

Joe almost decided to leave it at that, but there was something he couldn't leave unsaid. "I hope it's occurred to you that this plan is designed to send a killer after us."

No hesitation this time. "It has."

Good. At least underneath all that wisecracking talk, Katelyn O'Malley was smart enough to know what they were up against.

And what they were up against was a killer.

Even more, the moment they stepped inside Perfect Match, they would become the ultimate bait.

Chapter 4

Katelyn fanned herself with the Perfect Match folder.

Even though the sun was on the verge of setting, the summer heat was still escaping in filmy waves off the asphalt. It was muggy. A Texas-June kind of muggy that even the locals complained about. The air was heavy with exhaust fumes and the steamy smoke from the mesquite grills of a nearby patio restaurant. Not exactly an enticing combination, but the aroma of spicy fajitas was somehow pushing its way through the rest of the less appetizing scents.

She willed herself not to sweat as she hurried across the parking lot toward the sprawling building that housed the Perfect Match Agency. Willing didn't work. A slick bead of perspiration slithered down the center of her back, and for a couple of seconds, she entertained a pipe dream of stopping by the restaurant for a virgin frozen margarita.

This wasn't, however, the time for pipe dreams or sweat-cooling margaritas, even virgin ones. It was time to look for a killer.

Katelyn stepped through the front door of the agency, mumbled a *thank-you!* for the Arctic blast of the A/C and made her way to the reception area.

An empty area, she soon learned.

Empty, no doubt, because she was early. But then, she usually was. Brayden joked that she'd inherited some bizarre fear-of-being-late gene, but her early arrival in this case would allow her time to double-check the few things she could actually double check. Exits. Bullet-accessible windows. Security cameras, like the one mounted on the light fixture in the center of the room. It also gave her some time to take a deep breath and steady her nerves.

Someone had decorated the spacious rectangle-shaped room. Unlike her earlier visit, tonight there were bunches of gold Mylar balloons in the corners, huge bouquets of cream-colored flowers in crystal vases and bottles of champagne angled into gleaming silver ice buckets. Soft, romantic music filled the background. The stage was set for love.

But hopefully not murder.

She was armed with a Glock in her purse. It was her preferred poison when she needed to carry light. And thanks to the flexible, pencil-size device beneath her collar, she had two-way communication with headquarters. However, neither of those two security measures would give her much protection if someone opened fire through the trio of floor-to-ceiling windows. For all practical purposes, she was on her own.

An obvious drawback to being early.

The sudden clicking sound sent her reaching for her gun, but Katelyn forced herself not to draw. She needed to stay in character. It was a good thing, too. Because the click was a door opening, and the blond-haired man who came in through the side entrance wasn't carrying a weapon but another bottle of champagne.

He immediately made eye contact and smiled, a slightly too-friendly smile, before he proceeded to the table with the champagne. "Kate Kennedy, right?"

"Yes."

Katelyn didn't have to ask his name. He was Bruce Donovan. Age, twenty-nine. A local, but that sun-bleached hair, tropical tan and muscled torso seemed more suited to a California beach than the Alamo City. His official job title was office manager of the Perfect Match Agency.

He was also a prime murder suspect.

Of course, anyone associated with the agency was a suspect, but Donovan was near the top of that list. According to his background check, he'd been hit with not one but two restraining orders for stalking former girlfriends. The last incident had escalated into an assault. Combined with the fact that he was from San Antonio and a white male, it meant he fit their profile to a proverbial tee.

"I'm Bruce Donovan," he greeted. "I run things around here. In fact, I'm the one who processed your application." His face got a contemplative look for several seconds, then he snapped his fingers. "You're a P.E. teacher on break for the summer. You like old Indiana Jones movies, basketball and chili."

He grinned as if pleased with himself for recalling

that information. Katelyn didn't return the grin. If he actually memorized details about every client, it was a little unnerving. If he'd only memorized *her* details, then it went well past the unnerving stage.

"I remember because I kept thinking what a great match we'd be," he continued. "But unfortunately since I work here, I'm not allowed to pair up with any of the clients. Well, not officially anyway."

Good grief. As if he hadn't gotten his message across, he aimed another flirtatious grin in her direction.

"So do a lot of people actually find their *perfect match* at these icebreakers?" she asked.

"Depends on your definition of perfect."

"A lifelong partner," Katelyn quickly offered.

"Ah, marriage." He shrugged. "Sure, it happens." But that was as far as he took the thread of conversation.

She pointed to the wall above the table. "You should put photos of the happy couples there. It'd be great publicity."

"I'll pass on your suggestion to my boss." He placed the bottle of champagne on the table, searched through the two dozen or so plastic-encased name tags and picked up one.

Hers, apparently.

He crossed the room and reached out as if to pin it on her jacket, just over her left breast, but Katelyn intervened and took it from him instead. So he was perhaps a groping pervert in addition to being a stalker and a killer.

What a pleasant guy.

His all-American surfer-dude smile faded. He probably wasn't happy with her insistence that she pin on her own name tag.

Katelyn nodded her greeting in lieu of a handshake, and she tried to pick up on any other vibes. There was definitely that little buzz in the back of her head, but it'd been there since she'd first stepped foot in the place. And speaking of stepping, she backtracked a little toward the door so she could take cover in case Donovan was aiming for a third restraining order.

Donovan tipped his head to the glossy gold-and-white Perfect Match folder she'd tucked beneath her arm. "So did you see any immediate prospects on your list?"

"One. But it could be a coincidence." Since it was time to do a little more stage setting, she pinned on her name tag and opened the folder. She pointed to Joe's alias. "I dated a guy by that name in high school."

Something darted through his coffee-brown eyes. Concern, maybe? "Is that good or bad?"

"Definitely good. He's the one who got away, if you know what I mean."

He made a sound of superficial agreement and then quickly excused himself to leave when a man and a woman came in. Not Joe. But from the already friendly chatter and come-and-get-me smiles, these two had already decided they were a good match.

Once the two newcomers had on their name tags, Katelyn whispered their identities so the tech back at headquarters could begin background checks. In case something serious developed between them, she didn't want this couple to become the sniper's next targets.

"Kate Kennedy?" she heard the now-familiar voice say. "Is that really you?"

It was show time. She took a long breath, braced herself and turned toward him to start the charade.

Oh, mercy.

She obviously hadn't braced herself nearly enough.

At the wedding, she'd seen Joe Rico's *GQ* look, and over the past couple of days, his urban cop look of khakis and button-down dress shirts. But this was obviously his cool hot-guy look.

It worked.

Black pants, perfectly tailored. A deep crimson red crewneck pullover that hugged his chest the way men's chests should be hugged. Well, men with great chests, anyway.

Which he had.

The breeze coming in from the still-open door stirred his lightweight jacket. Also black. He'd likely worn it to conceal his .357 Magnum, but it made him look a little mysterious, confident. And dangerous.

Katelyn bet he'd never had to take a deep breath to steady himself. On the other hand, she required several more.

"Joe?" she managed to say, when she remembered how to form words. Sheez, her throat actually clamped up. She added a staged giggle of excitement to unclamp it. "It *is* you. I can't believe this."

As they'd discussed, Joe and she went to each other immediately, and he pulled her into his arms. Yep. He was definitely carrying concealed, and there was a backup in the slide holster on the rear waist of his pants.

"You're early," he whispered.

"You're not," she countered, also in a whisper.

"I was busy. We might have a little problem."

Okay. *Little* didn't sound so bad. Little problems always arose during undercover missions. "What—"

That's as far as Katelyn got.

Joe brushed his mouth over hers. A friendly sort of gesture—which they'd also discussed should happen. In theory, such a gesture was supposed to announce to the people at the agency that they were staking their personal claims on each other. Like his clothes, it worked. Katelyn heard the other couple and Bruce Donovan mention something about an apparent perfect match.

Katelyn also heard her heart pounding in her ears and felt her body turning soft and warm.

And she cursed herself.

Talk about being a hormonal wimp. Somehow, she had to make herself immune to any carnal-related reactions to Joe Rico, and she did that with a simple reminder that he was not only her boss but also the man investigating her brother.

That immediately cooled off her body.

She pulled back, both literally and figuratively.

"Incoming, six o'clock," Joe whispered.

In other words, someone was approaching from directly behind her. While Joe kept her firmly against him, she turned her head, already smiling, and came face-to-face with Addison Merrick, the owner of Perfect Match. He was also one of their suspects.

He seemed younger than Katelyn had expected, and she'd expected young. Merrick was barely twenty-six but could have passed for a teenager. Well, except for the gunmetal-gray eyes. There was something not so youthful about them.

Merrick wasn't alone. A broad-shouldered man

came into the reception area with him and took up position near the door. It was Katelyn's guess that he wasn't a client looking for love but was rather a bodyguard. Maybe this was the little problem Joe had mentioned.

"I smell success," Merrick greeted.

No all-American, surfer-dude smile from him. It was on the mechanical side. Probably no perverted, name-tag-pinning intentions, either. He looked more like the Ivy League type. And was. Old money. And from all accounts Perfect Match was a gift from his megasuccessful father. A way of keeping Addison a productive member of society. So far, it'd worked. Despite a fairly recent dip in business, it was the most successful agency of its type in the city.

"Kate Kennedy, Joe Farrell," Merrick continued. "It's a pleasure to meet you. Welcome."

She felt Joe stiffen slightly but couldn't ask him why. It probably had something to do with the guard who was studying them a little too carefully.

Joe extended his hand to Merrick. "Thanks. It looks like joining Perfect Match was the wise thing to do." He smiled lovingly at Katelyn before he slid his attention back to Merrick. "By the way, a friend of mine said he might be here tonight. Chad Benton. Have you seen him?"

Chad Benton? Katelyn had no idea what this was about. There was no one by that name associated with this case.

Merrick shook his head. "We're expecting a big crowd so you might want to check to see if your friend's name tag is on the table."

Merrick's suggestion was just the beginning, however, and not a prelude to a departure. He wasted no time latching on to her hand, and like a good host, he introduced Joe and her to the other couple. By the time he'd finished, more clients had started to trickle in.

Bruce Donovan did his hosting duties, as well. He began pouring the champagne—lots of it. Nothing like alcohol to kick up the libido and lower the defenses. The piped-in music switched to a slow, sultry beat.

"What about that little problem?" she asked Joe the moment Merrick walked away. She looped her arm through his and leaned against him, snuggling, so she could speak as softly as possible.

"Someone's watching the place."

Okay. Maybe it wasn't so little after all. "Any idea who?"

"Yeah."

Again, no explanation since groping-boy, Bruce Donovan, walked up to them with a tray of filled champagne glasses. Even when they both declined, the man didn't move far enough away for them to have a private conversation.

Joe remedied that. Smiling and whispering sweet nothings about how glad he was to see her again, he led Katelyn to the far end of the room and then just inside the hallway that led to the agency's offices. He angled them so they wouldn't be facing the camera in the reception room.

"Fiona Shipley," Joe informed her. When the static crackled in their respective communicators, he turned his off, because the now close proximity was interfering with reception. "She's parked outside watching the building."

Katelyn didn't have to ask who that was. Fiona was

a regular client at Perfect Match and a former acquaintance of Raul Hernandez, the murdered groom, and that was *former acquaintance* in a really bad way. After Fiona and Raul had met, dated and then broken up, she had apparently threatened him. The police had been looking for her but hadn't been able to locate her—not since she'd quit her job and moved out of her apartment. Apparently though, she'd come to them.

"No sign of her carrying an assault rifle, huh?" Katelyn asked, only partly joking.

"Not that I could see, but I've got two officers in a surveillance van watching her just in case." Joe glanced over his shoulder and mumbled some profanity. "Play along."

That was it. No other warning. No hint that he was about to launch into a full-contact charade.

Joe pushed her against the wall and kissed her. He pressed his body against her. Snugly against her. Until they were aligned like human puzzle parts.

Katelyn caught a glimpse of Addison Merrick watching them from the reception room. So this was Joe's version of a get-lost tactic.

Joe kept the mouth-to-mouth clinical. Well, as clinical as something like that could be, considering he had a rather hot kissing technique. No tongue involved. Just pressure. The right amount of pressure, glide and moisture to make her wish, at least temporarily, that he'd use his tongue.

He didn't stop there. His kisses traveled from her mouth. To her cheek. To her ear.

Not good.

She bit off a moan of pleasure. It seemed trivial, considering everything else that was going on, but if these forced kissing sessions continued, she would need to set some ground rules so he could go easy on her erogenous zones.

"Any suspicious activity around the perimeter of the building?" Joe murmured.

Not exactly the sensual question her body had expected to hear from the man kissing her, and it took her a moment to realize Joe was speaking to the officer monitoring the communicator under her collar.

"Fiona Shipley's still watching the place," was the response they got.

Obviously unaware of the effect he was having on her, Joe continued his inquiries while pretending to nibble on her earlobe. "Tail her if she leaves."

Normally, whispered official orders wouldn't have been a turn-on for her, but Joe's warm, moist breath hit against her neck and ear. Mercy. Not good. She didn't want to add any more hormones to this volatile mix.

Another glance at the reception area. No Addison Merrick in sight. At least their kissing session had sent him on his way.

"Merrick knew our names," Joe informed her. "I wasn't wearing a name tag, and he never looked at yours. Yet, he knew who we were."

Katelyn went back through the events of that particular introduction and realized it was true. She reprimanded herself for not noticing it, as well. "So that's what *Chad* was all about?"

Not a real person but a test. Since Merrick suggested that Joe look through the name tags, it meant he didn't know the names of all the guests. And unlike a few of the others, Joe and she weren't repeat customers. Nor had they met him when they filled out their applications.

So how had he known their names?

"This might not be such a little problem," Katelyn mumbled.

Joe quickly agreed.

In fact, it could mean the killer was already on to them.

Chapter 5

Joe should have been thinking about Addison Merrick. Specifically, about the fact the man was obviously suspicious of them.

With reason.

Both Katelyn and he had registered at Perfect Match just days after the murders. That said, only the shooter himself would have likely made the connection at this point. And that meant that Merrick was possibly their wedding sniper.

So why wasn't his attention on Merrick or the "security guard" he'd brought with him?

Because Joe was involuntarily sharing that attention with the woman he had plastered against him, that's why.

He was a fool to notice how nicely Katelyn fit in his arms. A fool to notice that she tasted almost as good as she looked. And basically, he was just a fool to have thought he could kiss her and not lust after her. That meant he had to do something about it.

Joe slid his fingers beneath her collar and temporarily turned off the audio feed on her communicator. The surveillance officers would be able to talk to them, to warn them if necessary, but they wouldn't be able to hear what he was about to admit to Detective O'Malley.

"We'd better try to keep the kissing to a minimum from now on," he whispered.

"Sure," she readily agreed.

Too readily.

Which meant all the supposedly for-show making out probably had an effect on her, as well. Joe didn't care much for the fact that it pleased him a little. This wasn't a competition, but sometimes it felt like one.

"Hey, contrary to public opinion, I'm human," Katelyn said, frowning. And probably so she wouldn't have to add more to an already uncomfortable conversation, she reconnected her communicator.

"Any indication that Addison Merrick has been investigating us?" she whispered to the person on the other end of that communicator.

Joe wished he'd thought of the question first, which was only more proof that he needed a serious mental adjustment. This case was critical. People's lives were at stake, including theirs. Heck, even his promotion to lieutenant was probably riding on this. It was no time for lust.

He repeated all of that to himself several times and hoped those reminders stayed reminders for the rest of this assignment.

"He didn't trigger any info markers to indicate an investigation," the other officer answered through the communicator. "But then, with his resources, that's not surprising."

In other words, Merrick could have done a full-scale check on them—or rather on their false identities—and they wouldn't have known.

"Hypothetically, what would Merrick have learned?" Joe asked.

He glanced at the person who stopped at the end of the hallway. Bruce Donovan. Joe didn't think it was his imagination that the man cast a suspicious glance their way. It made sense. If there'd been a computer search, Donovan would have likely been the one to do it. But the real question was—had Donovan instigated that search on his own, or had Merrick ordered it?

"The only thing Merrick could have gotten was what was in the fake files we created for you and Detective O'Malley," the officer explained. "Fake employment and financial records. Phony e-mail accounts. The addresses of the apartments that were rented to support your covers. That sort of thing. If they went after your real backgrounds, we'd know."

Katelyn opened her mouth, probably to respond to that, but she'd obviously not seen Donovan and his spying eyes. Just in case the man was eavesdropping, Joe did a quick maneuver and put his mouth right against her ear.

"Save your questions," he mumbled. "We have company."

She groaned softly.

So with this latest round of surveillance, things weren't going exactly as planned. Joe had hoped to establish the pretense of the reunited couple, leave Katelyn in the reception area and have a look around while she covered for him. He'd only managed the first of those and would likely have to save that search for another day. They would have to return anyway in two days, on Thursday, to announce their engagement. By then, he'd figure out a way to do the search.

"Fiona Shipley's about to drive away," Joe heard the backup officer announce into the communicator.

"Go after her." And that meant with the heavy scrutinization from Merrick and Donovan, it was a good time for him to get Katelyn out of there, as well. He caught her arm. "Let's say our goodbyes. We'll come back later for your car."

"Wait." She held her ground. "We still haven't looked around the place."

"And it won't happen tonight." Joe had to pull her closer to him so he could whisper. "You heard—things aren't exactly routine around here, and now we're without backup because they have to go after Fiona Shipley."

She wanted to argue. He could see it in the depth of those slightly narrowed eyes. Heck, he wanted to argue, too. And he really wanted to stay and see what he could find. But he wouldn't do that at the expense of further risking her life. There were already enough risks without him bending the rules.

Since there was no way to make this sound better, Joe just came out with it. "It's time to act as if we're ready to drag each other off to bed."

Which wouldn't be much of a stretch for him.

A few mumbled words of profanity from her, but she cooperated by sliding her arm inside his coat and around his waist. She even added a sultry chuckle and nudged him playfully with her hip.

Nope.

The pretense of dragging her off to bed wouldn't be much of a stretch at all.

Bruce Donovan stepped in front of them when they started across the reception area. "Hey, you're not leaving already, huh?" he asked, seemingly shocked.

"Kate and I have some, uh, catching up to do." Joe made sure there were enough undertones in that remark.

Too bad Donovan didn't pick up on those undertones. He placed his hand on Katelyn's arm and gave her an almost intimate rub with his fingers. His fingers even strayed a bit in the direction of Katelyn's breast.

"But you haven't even checked out the other matches on your list," Donovan reminded her. "And here I selected them just for you."

She chuckled again, a low sexy purr, and lifted her equally sexy gaze to Joe. "I've already found all the matches I need. Now it's time to play with a little fire."

With that naughty double entendre, she pushed Donovan's hand aside, tightened her grip on Joe's waist and got them moving toward the door.

"Man, I hope he's the killer," she grumbled under her breath. "Because I would *so* enjoy kicking his ass."

Joe forced himself not to smile, which was easy, since they'd hardly made it a step before Addison Merrick stopped them.

"Bruce tells me you're thinking of leaving?" Merrick asked.

Katelyn did her part with yet another sultry smile and a sensual snuggle against him.

"Yes. Thanks for arranging this," Joe added, hoping that would be the end of it.

It wasn't.

"But you can't go. Not yet. I need the two of you to sign release forms."

Since this was the first he'd heard mention of release forms, and since Merrick was a murder suspect, Joe was automatically suspicious. "We're in a bit of a hurry. Can't this wait?"

"Afraid not. It's a legal requirement. Normally, I put out the forms a little later in the evening, but if you'll come with me, I'll have you sign them in my office."

There wasn't a lot of time for Joe to debate the issue, but what a heck of an issue it was. If he declined, it could very well blow the undercover operation when it'd barely gotten started. If he said yes, it would be a meeting away from witnesses, away from the safety of being in a public place. Besides, standard procedure required—

"Let's make this quick," Katelyn insisted.

And then there was that angle. His partner making a decision without even consulting him.

Joe hoped Merrick didn't notice how much his jaw tightened.

Merrick smiled, that too-artificial smile that Joe didn't even try to interpret, and the man motioned for the guard before he turned toward the hall. It didn't surprise Joe when the guard followed. Basically, Merrick was leading them to a location where they'd be out of sight from the others, and he was taking his hired gun along with him.

And they had no backup.

Maybe he wouldn't regret Katelyn's *let's make this quick* in the next couple of minutes.

"Is this guy a friend of yours?" he asked Merrick. Joe tipped his head to the guard stalking along behind them.

"An employee," Merrick answered without even looking back. "I need someone to witness your signatures."

Of course he did.

Well, at least there was one consolation in all of this. If by some long shot Merrick wanted to do them some harm, then it'd almost certainly mean he was their sniper. Katelyn and he could perhaps end this right here, right now. Of course, that would mean a gun battle in a confined space with innocent people nearby. Not his first choice of ways to bring this to a close.

Obviously Katelyn had figured that out, as well. She kept her arm around him as they followed Merrick, but using Joe's coat as cover, she eased her hand into his slide holster located just inside the back waist of his pants. To a casual observer or the guard behind them, it probably appeared that she was copping a feel. But what she was doing was removing his reserve weapon with her left hand. It made sense because she could easily have been spotted if she'd gone after the gun in her purse.

She didn't stop there. While still keeping her left hand beneath his coat, Katelyn inched just enough away from him that things still looked intimate, but it wouldn't hinder him if he had to draw his primary.

"You're still in hot water," Joe mumbled. Good preparation *after the fact* didn't void the brash decision she'd made on her own.

"Promise?" she tossed back in that same mock purr.

He simply kept his attention on Merrick. Not easy to do, either. Why did it always feel as if he'd been smacked with a two-by-four whenever he was around Katelyn O'Malley?

Just as Joe suspected, Merrick's office was practically at the end of the hall. And also as he'd expected, the guard posted himself in the doorway behind them after they'd entered.

Other than the guard, the rest of the office looked normal. A slick thin-screen computer. Assorted files and papers. Tasteful watercolor paintings on the walls. There was also a rather large Rolodex on the corner of the glossy executive-size desk. Merrick had obviously made a lot of contacts in his line of work.

"This is a formality," Merrick explained. He rifled through his desk, presumably looking for that *formality*. Joe angled Katelyn so if necessary they could return fire in either direction, at Merrick or the guard.

But it wasn't a gun that Merrick pulled out from the drawer but two very official-looking forms.

That didn't cause Joe, however, to relax.

Keeping a grip on his weapon, Katelyn picked up a pen off Merrick's desk and scrawled her alias signature. She passed the pen to Joe, but he waited until he was certain she had good visual and position before he risked occupying his shooting hand with the pen.

"All done," she announced.

Joe agreed, and he didn't give Merrick time to say otherwise. He turned and met the guard's gaze head-on. Joe made sure that the guy understood that one way or another, they would get past him.

The guard stepped aside.

Joe didn't have to tell Katelyn to watch their backs. She did it on her own. So that she could look over his shoulder, she automatically slid herself against him under the pretense of whispering in his ear. The pretense continued to a nip of his earlobe.

"Are you purposely trying to rile me by not following regulations?" he mumbled as they went out the front door.

"Not really. It just comes natural after being a kid sister to two brothers."

Her gaze darted around the area, as well. Joe had gotten lucky with the parking space. He was almost directly in front of the building, and he got her to the car. Fast. He didn't want anyone taking shots at them, and the bullet-resistant windows gave them at least some safety.

"Sorry about that impromptu decision I made back there," she continued. "But I didn't want to tip Merrick—"

"I know what you were doing." Joe couldn't help it, he huffed. God knows why. Huffing only made him sound like an idiot, and it obviously wouldn't change his partner's approach to this case. Still, he tried. "Should I go back over the rules of chain of command?"

Now it was her time to huff. "Don't give me that. You were about to decide the same thing. There's no way you would have blown this because of the slight additional risk of going into that office."

"Maybe. But we'll never know, will we?" And so that Katelyn wouldn't continue to argue, he leaned slightly closer to her neck. "Situation report?" Joe snarled into the communicator.

"We're still following Fiona Shipley. She appears

to be just driving around but in the opposite direction of her last known residence."

Bloody hell. He hated unpredictable people and their unpredictable patterns. "Don't lose her."

The moment Joe got his assurance that they wouldn't, Katelyn turned off the audio feed function of the communicator.

"You know what you said back there about keeping the kissing to a minimum?" She didn't wait for him to answer. "Well, I know we can't avoid it, but when we're doing these phony make-out sessions, steer clear of that little place just below my ear. It's a big-time erogenous zone for me."

Joe eyed the spot and was in such an ornery mood, he considered kissing it just so he could prove that he was the one in charge here. Unfortunately, kissing any of her erogenous zones at this point would be just plain unprofessional and would likely end up giving him an erection.

Hardly a bargaining tool in this game of jockeying for control.

"Any place in particular I should avoid kissing you?" she asked.

And she was serious.

"Let's just say I'd be attentive to just about anything and leave it at that." He glanced back at the doorway of Perfect Match. Not an empty doorway, either. Addison Merrick was there, and he was staring at them.

Cursing, Joe latched on to a handful of that flame-red hair and hauled her to him. He kissed her all right, but he kept an eye on their voyeuristic host. When he was satisfied that he'd done all he could to preserve their cover, Joe started the car and drove away.

The next step was to go to Katelyn's fake apartment so they could begin the next phase of the pretense. That meant spending the next four days, and nights, together.

Alone.

"I thought you said unnecessary kissing wasn't a good idea?" she complained.

"Trust me, it was necessary."

Besides, it was too late to undo it. And it sure as heck was too late to stop what they'd put into motion. They'd either succeed together.

Or maybe die trying.

Either was possible.

Chapter 6

"I think I might have found something," she heard Joe announce from the other room.

Katelyn leaned back a little so she could glance at him through the bedroom door. For security reasons they had turned off most of the lights, but it wasn't difficult to see Joe working on his laptop at the tiny kitchen table in the equally tiny kitchen. There were no windows in that particular area so he was using the dim light over the stove to read through the latest background info on their suspects.

"Addison Merrick's longtime fiancée broke up with him last month. A bad break, too. Very messy," Joe went on. He positioned one of the other kitchen chairs in front of him and propped up his feet. "And according to his very chatty personal trainer, he's been under psychiatric care since he was a teenager. He suffers from manic-depression coupled with something called radical impulsive tendencies."

"What the heck is that last part?" She opened the suitcase that Garrett had packed for her and plundered through it for something she could wear to bed. Hopefully, it'd be something that covered a lot of skin because the apartment only had one small bedroom. The sleeping bag in the corner let her know that she'd be sharing that limited space with Joe.

Katelyn took a deep, steadying breath.

"Beats me. Maybe it means Merrick's just an irrational ticked-off killer, as opposed to all those other nonticked-off rational killers we deal with every day."

"Yeah, that'd be a nice change, huh?" she joked.

Katelyn studied the garments and realized she'd gotten her *something to cover a lot of skin* wish. There was an enormous pair of cartoon superhero pj's, no makeup whatsoever, only a toothbrush for toiletries, jeans and a T-shirt. Her underwear choices were limited to cotton and were the worst ones possible Garrett could have found in her lingerie drawer. If that's where he indeed got them. They looked like Salvation Army rejects.

She frowned.

Garrett was either trying to establish a new fashion look for her or else he wanted to make sure there was nothing alluring about her appearance. Perhaps the contents of the suitcase were her brother's version of a modern-day chastity belt.

With her limited choices, she opted for the pj's that were dotted with caped and winged crusaders. Katelyn stepped deeper into the dark bedroom, keeping the door open a crack between them so she could still hear Joe's ongoing summary of the new reports.

"I think some of the dots are starting to connect," he continued. "Get this—Merrick's shrink is a guy by the name of Dr. Allen Kent. Ring any bells?"

The moment the name registered, Katelyn hurriedly put on the pj's and walked back to the doorway. "He's Gail's ex-husband. Their divorce became final just a couple of weeks before her wedding to Raul."

Now that was an interesting connection. Their prime suspect, Addison Merrick, was in therapy with the ex-husband of their first murder victim.

"Coincidence?" she suggested.

"Maybe." Joe tossed her a glance. And did a double take before he shook his head. "But because he's an ex, he's a suspect. I'll have someone question Dr. Kent tomorrow. Too bad I can't do it myself, but I can't risk blowing our cover."

"It might be a risk no matter who does the questioning, especially since he'll just roadblock us with doctor-patient confidentiality. He might even lawyer up. Wouldn't it be a better idea just to have him followed?"

"Then I wouldn't be able to get his reaction when he's asked about his connection to Merrick."

True. And maybe it was worth the risk just to shake things up a little. It might make the sniper think twice about launching another attack over the weekend.

"What exactly are you wearing?" Joe asked.

She glanced down at the pajamas and shrugged. "I think it belongs in the sleepwear category of garments. Garrett packed for me."

That seemed to be the only explanation Joe required. He mumbled something under his breath about brotherly love, minimized Merrick's file on the computer screen and clicked on to the next one.

While she waited for it to load, she glanced at Joe's attire. He still wore the clothes he'd had on for the ice-breaker. Well, minus the jacket. His hair was no longer perfect, however. Probably because he had a habit of scratching his head and running his hand through it while in deep thought.

And then there was the stubble.

No ordinary five o'clock shadow for this guy. Nope. It fell into the category of the desperado look. Very fashionable. Equally sexy. But what made it even more so was that he wore it as naturally as that contemplative cop's look, which sadly for her was the greatest turn-on of all.

"Fiona Shipley," Joe read aloud.

Good. Back to business. It was exactly where her mind needed to be. "Anything new on her?"

"You mean other than the fact that she managed to shake the backup officers who were following her, and now no one knows where she is?"

"Yes, other than that," Katelyn grumbled.

She made her way around him to get to the fridge. Ah, she had much better luck there than her suitcase. It was stocked with fruit and other snacks, but what immediately caught her eye was the six-pack of her favorite Irish beer. It must have been Garrett's peace offering for the botched fashion choices.

"Other than a knack for disappearing," Joe said glancing over the report, "we don't really have much. We already knew she was a frequent customer at Perfect Match and that the dead groom had been one of her fairly recent dream matches."

Katelyn opened a bottle of beer and took a long sip. "Which means nothing, of course. I had over a dozen dream matches so heaven knows how many she's had over the past year."

There. She'd been trying to figure out a way to dismiss the fact that Joe had been her number one match. Not that it was important, but it'd been one of those little nagging thoughts in the back of her mind.

When he didn't respond, Katelyn glanced at him. No double take this time. Joe was staring at her. Well, he was staring at her beer, anyway.

"Want one?" she asked, lifting the bottle. "It's the good stuff. My favorite. I'll have to thank Garrett for buying it."

"Actually, I asked him to pick it up when he wanted to know what to bring over."

Katelyn had already reached for the fridge, but that brought her hand to a stop. She forced herself not to stop for too long so it wouldn't appear she was shocked by that revelation.

"Well, then. I owe you the thanks instead." She took out a beer from the fridge, handed it to him and left it at that.

Joe closed down the files and started in on his beer. It was obviously his favorite, as well.

"Agreeing to go into that back office with Merrick wasn't a safe idea," he let her know.

Oh, that.

She hadn't thought for a minute that he'd forget it. "No. But it was a smart one. Come on, you were on the verge of following him, but I just got around to saying it first."

He didn't agree, or disagree. Joe sat there, staring into space while slowly sliding his fingers through the moisture on the longneck bottle.

Judas.

Even that made her body think of erotic things that it shouldn't be thinking about.

"Talk to me about Brayden," she said to give her body something else to contemplate. "About this so-called investigation that the chief ordered regarding preferential treatment."

That got Joe's attention off blank space. He looked at her again. "Is this the part where you tell me to back off and leave your brother alone?"

"Something like that. He's had a rough time recently."

He nodded. "Yeah, I heard. I'm sorry about his wife's death."

"His wife's *murder*," Katelyn quickly corrected. "She was murdered last year, and the case is practically cold. There are no arrests and no leads. Brayden has to live with that every single moment of his life. Any idea what that does to a good cop, to know he can't solve his own wife's murder?"

Another nod.

"By nodding, I guess you mean to imply that you understand, but there's no way you could," Katelyn went on. There was a lot more emotion in her voice than she wanted. But then, she'd never thought to discuss this objectively. "Brayden loved her, and it rips his heart to shreds to know that her killer is still out there somewhere."

"I'm sorry." It probably would have been easier for him to turn his attention back to the condensation on his beer bottle, or anywhere else for that matter, but he didn't. Joe kept his gaze firmly on her. "Do you honestly think that I'd believe there's preferential treatment just because it's an allegation?"

She opened her mouth. Closed it. Frowned. And silently cursed him. It was a dirty-pool kind of question, one that diffused the indignation she'd planned to hang on to a little longer. It was a good barrier against the effects of that desperado stubble.

"Brayden is lucky to have Garrett and you," Joe said, getting up from his chair. "And you're lucky to have them." He spared her pj's another glance. "I guess."

She couldn't help it. She smiled. But she suppressed it as quickly as possible. "Does that mean Garrett had this same chat with you?"

"Twice."

Katelyn had to suppress a smile again. "I'll bet those were interesting conversations, especially considering you two are the same rank."

Joe appeared to suppress a smile of his own. "And am I supposed to believe you held something back because I outrank you?"

"Busted." She finished off her beer, tossed the bottle into a recycling bin and unstrapped the slide holster from around her waist. "Present levity and warm fuzzy feelings aside, if you hurt Brayden, I'll make you pay."

"Like I said, he's lucky to have you." He tipped his head toward the windows in the living room. "Don't stand in here too long."

Because someone might already be watching them.

If the killer hadn't already scoped them out, then he or she would be doing it very soon. It was best not to be in his direct line of fire when that happened.

He glanced at his watch. "It's almost midnight. We've got an early morning ahead of us."

"Should we turn off all the lights?" she asked, going into the bedroom ahead of him. She placed her slide holster on the nightstand next to her badge, primary weapon and the communicator that she'd already turned off. Then Katelyn stepped into the bathroom to brush her teeth.

"No. We should look...active," Joe responded. "That way, it'll convince a killer that we're on our way to becoming a bride and groom."

"Too bad I don't have a pair of those blow-up dolls we could parade past the window every now and then." She paused, and was thankful she wasn't in the same room with him so he could see the blush rise on her cheeks. "I'm *so* sorry I said that."

He chuckled softly. An incredibly sexy male sound that made her want to pound her head against the wall.

This was going to be such a long week.

From the mirror, she watched Joe add his two guns and his badge to the nightstand, making the rather small piece of furniture look even smaller under the arsenal. He had his shirt halfway stripped off before he stopped and snagged her gaze. "I don't have pajamas. If you're the blushing sort, you might want to look away."

Yeah, right. She was about a hundred percent certain her eyes had no intention of cooperating with that suggestion. She didn't even fight it. Katelyn watched his reflection. A not-so-cheap thrill. And had the privilege of seeing him toss that shirt aside. At least a dozen muscles flexed in his arms and chest as they responded to the simple gesture.

A simple gesture that caused her mouth to go dry. Mercy.

She forced herself to finish brushing her teeth and even looked away when his pants came off. Well, briefly looked away. She thanked her lucky stars that he kept on a pair of dark blue boxers.

"Will this temporary housekeeping arrangement cause any personal problems for you?" he asked.

"If that's a subtle way of asking me if I'm involved with anyone, the answer's no." It made her sound like a social leper. Which wasn't really that far off the mark. Rather than remind him that most men weren't turned on by a woman packing a badge and a couple of Glocks, Katelyn went for levity. "My last boyfriend was a sex therapist who broke up with me because he said I was too aggressive in bed."

She paused a heartbeat before she let their gazes connect again. Yep. The startled look on his face had been worth it. "It's a joke," she let him know.

Other than a slight sound of amusement, that was his only other reaction. So much for levity. When she went into the bedroom, he strolled into the bathroom to brush his teeth.

"Actually, my last boyfriend was an accountant who broke up with me because he said I was too wrapped up in my job," she confessed and climbed into bed. "Hard to make someone feel even remotely important when you're never around. He got fed up and left me for a kindergarten teacher."

Still no response.

"How about you?" she asked.

"No one current." He came out of the bathroom, and she made a point of looking away. She'd already overdosed on his great bod. No need for more. "The last woman in my life was a kindergarten teacher who left me for an accountant."

Okay. So that broke the ice that had already been thawing between them. She laughed. Then bit her lip so she wouldn't laugh again.

She aimed her finger at him. "Let's get something straight. I don't want to like you, Rico."

He leaned over as if to kiss her good-night, letting his mouth come very close to hers. Breath met breath. And then he turned off the light. "I agree completely."

She lay there silently cursing him. But not for long. His head had hardly hit the pillow on the floor before the phone rang. Since it was supposed to be her apartment, Katelyn rolled to the side of the bed and answered it.

"It's me," she heard her brother say.

"Garrett, just the man I wanted to talk to."

Joe must have felt the same because he pressed the speaker function on the phone. Probably because he wanted to hear anything official. But the official part would have to wait.

"Thanks for the expert packing job," she tossed out at Garrett. "You do know this'll cost you in slow painful ways you can't even imagine?"

"I'm trembling in my Doc Martens." But the sarcasm wasn't nearly strong enough, and it didn't come close to masking his concern. "I'll drop by in the morning, pretending to deliver breakfast. Anything I can bring you?"

"You mean other than Starbucks and some real clothes?" Katelyn inquired cautiously, feeling him out.

"Yeah. Other than that."

Heck. He was placating her.

Never a good sign.

"What about you, Rico? You need anything?" Garrett asked.

Mercy. He'd moved from placating to being nice.

"No, thanks," Joe let him know. "I've got some things in the trunk of my car."

Garrett paused. Never a good sign, either. "So the plan is for you two to pick up Katelyn's car in the morning and then not come up for air again until it's time to announce your engagement at Perfect Match on Thursday?"

"Great summary." But Katelyn had reached her threshold for beating around the bush. "Spill it, Garrett. What's wrong?"

"I'm not sure, exactly." Yet another hesitation. "Someone's digging through the fake files we created for your covers."

"We expected that," Joe pointed out. He sat up in his sleeping bag, leaning back against the side of the mattress.

"Yeah, but I didn't expect them to go at it this way. It's sloppy. Damn sloppy. And that slop leads right to Merrick. It makes me uncomfortable."

Katelyn knew exactly how he felt. Merrick might be a killer, but from all accounts he was smart. If the cyber trail led to him, then it was probably because someone wanted them to think Merrick had done it.

Bruce Donovan, maybe?

Of course, there was also the angle that by being

sloppy, Merrick was giving himself a very convincing out.

"If he's that smart," Katelyn mumbled. "We're in serious trouble."

"Yeah," Garrett agreed.

Joe glanced at her. He had that did-I-miss-something? look. At least she thought that's what that glance was about until he shrugged. "I don't care how smart Merrick is. If he's making these sloppy searches to cover the fact he's the sniper, we'll still stop him."

Well, they were all on the same page. Interesting. Most outsiders, including fellow cops, had trouble following Garrett's and her thought processes.

"There's more," Garrett continued. "It sucks, so brace yourself. I got a call from an editor friend at the *Express News*. There'll be a story about the two shootings in the morning paper. They're linking them."

"We knew this was coming," Katelyn offered.

"An article, yeah. But there'll be photos. Some apparently taken at the icebreaker tonight. There'll be one with Rico and you kissing."

Okay. So they hadn't known about this.

Judas.

A photo.

"Supposedly, it's a grainy shot, and you're in a lip lock, but still…" Garrett's explanation trailed off, leaving them with the general idea that this was not a good thing.

"How'd they get the photo?" Joe asked.

"Addison Merrick. He takes stills from the security feed. For some reason, he gave the press a couple of them when they came around sniffing for a story about two hours ago."

And because she and Joe had signed those consent forms, it was all perfectly legal.

"He's suspicious," Katelyn mumbled.

"It could be a ploy to get you to back off," Garrett suggested. "Because something like this darn sure wouldn't be good for business."

"Or maybe he's going for another sloppy tactic so he can cover his butt," Joe contributed. "The real killer probably wouldn't give up photos of potential victims, but a ruthless businessman trying to get some free publicity might." He cursed. "Or a killer who wanted to appear to be an honest businessman might."

Neither Garrett nor she disagreed with him.

"This changes nothing," Joe insisted a moment later. "We'll stick with the plan and lay low here until Thursday afternoon when we'll make a return visit to Perfect Match. If the photo's clearer than expected, or if it causes any unwanted press, then I'll deal with it."

"You do that," Garrett fired back.

Katelyn huffed because she understood that tone. It was his brotherly warning for her to be careful.

"I'm not stupid," she responded. Katelyn reached over and hung up.

Joe gave her another of those looks, except this time she was fairly sure he was puzzled. "He's worried about us," she interpreted.

And apparently, with reason.

The game had just escalated from dangerous to deadly. But then, Katelyn had known from day one that it was an inevitable escalation. Playing the killer's deadly game was the only way to stop him.

* * *

A loud ringing sound jarred Joe from the dream to beat all dreams. He snapped to a sitting position and groped for the phone, the alarm or whatever the hell was making the noise so he could stop it.

Katelyn cursed, a couple of phrases worthy of the awful racket. However, her profanity clipped off unexpectedly about a split second after she latched on to her gun and fell off the bed.

She landed right on him.

His hands were suddenly filled with her. A warm, firm, armed woman who smelled like a strange mixture of sex and gunmetal. Her eyes were still ripe with sleep, and she blinked several times, staring at him as if trying to figure out how she'd gotten in his lap.

Katelyn obviously wasn't a morning person, either.

Thankfully, the noise stopped so Joe could get his bearings. It didn't take long, especially when he realized her fall had aligned their bodies in the best, and worst, possible ways. She was straddling him, her long athletic legs resting against the sides of his hips.

And he had an erection.

It was a product of the dream he'd been having. About her. She noticed it. But then, it would have been impossible not to notice.

"One of the advantages of being a woman," she mumbled, her gaze drifting in the direction of where he was certainly testing the limits of his boxers. "We don't wear our…hearts on our sleeves."

"Smart-ass," he tossed back, because frankly he couldn't think of anything else to say.

Laughing lazily, she climbed off him. Staggered. And would have probably landed in his lap again if he hadn't caught her. Specifically, her left butt cheek. Not the particular part of her anatomy he'd wanted to grab, but it was either that or risk having accidental sex with her.

Joe was certain he didn't want that to happen.

Well, almost certain, anyway.

"I think it was the doorbell." Katelyn glanced at the clock. "Seven forty-five. It has to be Garrett. If he doesn't have coffee with him, he's a dead man."

Joe got to his feet, somehow, and fought through the haze still in his head. When the buzzing sound started again, he realized she was right. It was the doorbell. And yep, it was probably Garrett. Still, Joe wasn't about to take any chances. He pulled on his pants, grabbed his gun and headed into the living room.

"Be careful," she whispered unnecessarily.

He would. No amount of fatigue or dream remnants would cause him to do away with standard procedures. Joe eased against the wall, moving slowly. Quietly. Keeping away from the door, he lifted the blinds a fraction and peeked out.

Not Garrett.

"It's Bruce Donovan," Joe let her know.

She already had her gun, but that caused her to assume a defensive position. No more ripe sleepy blinks or lazy laughter. She morphed into the cop.

Joe took another look outside. Donovan appeared to be holding some papers and wasn't visibly armed.

Which didn't mean anything.

Donovan was the type to carry concealed.

"Back me up," Joe reminded her.

Using the door to hide his gun, Joe opened it. Not

a fraction, either. He might need the extra space if he had to fire.

"Yeah?" he greeted Donovan. Not nicely, either.

Surprise went through Donovan's eyes, and when he tried to speak, he fumbled his words. Definitely not the slick player he'd portrayed the night before at the icebreaker.

"I wanted to drop these off for Kate," Donovan said, offering the papers to Joe. "It's a copy of the release form she signed and the questionnaire she originally filled out. I thought she'd like them for her personal records. Oh, and here's the newspaper. It was on this side of the stairs so I figured it was hers."

Joe took the items with his left hand so he could still hold on to his gun. "This couldn't wait until later?"

Donovan shrugged. "I was headed to work to get an early start and decided to drop it off on my way."

"Right." The apartment wasn't on the way to Perfect Match. Donovan was checking on them. Now, the real question was why. Was it because he was the killer, or because he'd planned to hit on Katelyn again?

If it was the latter, the man had a death wish.

One more attempt by Donovan to grope her breasts, and Katelyn would almost certainly go after him. And Joe would stand back and let her.

"So are you off from work today or what?" Donovan asked.

"I decided to take a little vacation time."

"From your freelance journalism job?" Donovan paused as if waiting for Joe to confirm that. Joe didn't. "I'm the one who ran your computer matches. Personally, I figured you'd go for the blond speech therapist, but then I didn't know about your past history with Kate."

It seemed like a good idea just to nod. For a man on a delivery mission, Donovan was asking a lot of questions and providing a lot of unnecessary information.

Joe heard Katelyn move around behind him, but he had no idea what she was up to until she ducked under his arm and snuggled against him. She'd stripped off her pajama bottoms, tousled her hair around her face, and with the top that hit her at midthigh, she looked as if she'd just finished up a thoroughly satisfying round of sex. And was ready for round two.

"Kate." Donovan attempted a smile and failed.

"Morning, Mr. Donovan. It's early." She slid her left arm around Joe's waist, and with her right hand, she pressed her gun directly against the back side of the door. She aimed it at Donovan. With that Glock, she'd easily be able to shoot through the thick wood if necessary.

Donovan tipped his head to the forms he'd just given to Joe. "I decided to drop off those."

"I heard."

Her tone conveyed no interest whatsoever, and she eased her left hand slightly lower. From Joe's waist and just into his pants—which he hadn't gotten around to zipping fully. She rubbed her fingers gently over the muscles that led directly to his groin. It wasn't just an intimate gesture. It was a sexually charged one.

"Thanks," she added to Donovan.

There was a definite "get lost" at the end of it. For extra measure, she put her mouth against Joe's ear, mumbled a seriously raunchy suggestion that involved them naked on the kitchen table. She issued a good-bye, shut the door in their visitor's face and locked it.

"If Donovan had any doubts about us being lovers," Katelyn whispered as she took her hand from his pants, "he doesn't now."

No. The charade was about good as it could get. Maybe even a little too good.

Man.

Joe stood there for a moment and tried to get his lungs to work.

How the devil was he supposed to handle three and a half more days of this?

While he was staving off another erection, she took the newspaper from him, tore off the plastic wrapper and sank onto the sofa.

"Good news. We didn't make the front page." A moment later, she groaned. "But we made the second."

Katelyn held it up for him. There were three small black and white photos accompanying the article entitled Dying For Love? Theirs was in the center, and even though they were practically wrapped around each other, Katelyn's face was visible.

And clear.

Too clear.

"No," she snarled, looking directly at him. She tossed the paper aside and practically charged at him. "You're not taking me off this case."

"Your cover might have been compromised," Joe pointed out.

"*Might* is the operative word there. But if you pull me now, it'll take weeks to create another cover—if that's even possible at this point. I won't let innocent people die because there's a possibility that someone could identify me from that photo."

In addition to her hand, the woman certainly knew where to aim her arguments. Joe didn't want anyone else dying, either—including her.

"Please," she added.

That cost her. No doubt about it. It was as close to begging as Katelyn O'Malley probably ever got, and it had to have stung her pride for him to be the recipient of that request.

Joe groaned, knowing how this would play out. "I would attach a condition or two—something along the lines of insisting you follow orders and don't improvise—but I won't bother."

"Does that mean you won't cut me from the case?"

He nodded, after making her wait a couple of seconds. "Not unless I have definite proof that your cover's been blown. And don't you dare smile, O'Malley, because you know I just handed you a gift."

No smile. Not even close. But he did see a lot of relief on her face. "Thank you. You won't regret it."

Wrong.

He already did. A lot. But for better or worse, Katelyn was his best shot at stopping another murder.

God help them.

Chapter 7

"Dr. Kent's interview is about to start," Joe called out. "You were right. He lawyered up."

Katelyn hurriedly applied a slathering of some pale raspberry lipstick that her mother had packed and gave her skirt-suit a quick adjustment. The short mocha outfit wouldn't have been her first choice for a return visit to Perfect Match to announce her "engagement," but it was either that or a cherry-red slip dress she hadn't worn since college.

Heaven knows what Garrett had told their mother about this particular assignment, but it was obvious the woman believed Katelyn needed to show some leg. Maybe she'd seen the photo of Joe in the paper. That meant at their regular family Sunday brunch, Katelyn would have to do some damage control before her folks started planning a real wedding.

When she joined him in the kitchen, Joe already had the laptop opened on the table, and even though he had his attention fixed on the screen, he was also putting on his shoes. Unlike her semi-sex-kitten attire, he'd gone for the brooding businessman look. Dark blue pants and a matching button-down shirt. Since his coat was draped over the chair, that likely meant he'd be using it again to camouflage his shoulder holster.

"Did you ever meet Dr. Kent?" he asked.

"No. Never had the honor. Gail and he weren't married that long."

While she poured them both cups of coffee, she studied the video feed of the man who'd once been her friend's husband. Kent's expensive Italian suit was perfect. Ditto for his bronze-colored hair. But those eyes were all barracuda.

"Gail's mom and I use the same hairdresser," Katelyn continued. The coffee was hours old, bitter and way too strong, but she gulped it down anyway so she could have her caffeine fix. "According to her, Kent liked to play mind games, and he was always ragging on Gail, always taking shots at her self-esteem. He fought the divorce for months before finally giving in."

"Maybe he didn't give in after all," Joe commented with a shrug.

Yes. And because of that bitter divorce they'd added Dr. Allen Kent to the top of their list of murder suspects and had spent much of the previous day going through his background check.

Well, doing that and trying to avoid each other.

The close quarters weren't exactly conducive to avoidance, especially since they had to share the same computer, same reports, same bedroom and same bathroom. But they'd both done their best to keep the other at arm's length. In between that arm's length, however, the air kept crackling between them.

Katelyn sipped her coffee and tried to push that uncomfortable realization aside.

"Did Kent say why he wasn't available for an interview yesterday?" she asked.

"He claimed he couldn't rearrange his schedule."

Claimed was right. He likely wanted to discuss strategy with his lawyer before *voluntarily* coming to police headquarters for questioning. In fact, it was her guess that the lawyer by Kent's side had used a good portion of that extra twenty-four hours to coach his client as to exactly what to say.

And what not to say.

After all, Kent wasn't just linked to Merrick. He was linked to the murdered bride. That would have caused a tense moment or two for an attorney.

Detective Dawn Davidson was the officer doing the interview. Under different circumstances, Katelyn would have asked that Garrett do it, but since he'd been at the apartment twice in the past twenty-four hours, Joe decided it was an unnecessary risk to take. Even though her brother had worn a delivery man's disguise, if someone had been carefully watching the place—like Dr. Kent, for example—he might have been able to make the connection.

Davidson started with the basics and just as Joe suggested, she mentioned the *remote possibility* that the shootings were somehow *loosely associated* with clients from the Perfect Match Agency. For good measure, she even hinted at the article that had appeared in the newspaper the day before. Then, Dawn went in for the bull's-eye and asked Kent about his relationship with Addison Merrick.

"I'm afraid I can't discuss anything regarding a patient," he crisply assured her. "If that's why I'm here, then you're wasting my time."

"As slick as slime," Katelyn mumbled. "No wonder Gail divorced him."

"So Mr. Merrick is your patient?" Dawn commented. But she didn't wait for him to verify it. "He was vague about that yesterday when we questioned him."

Ah, now there was a reaction. Kent's aristocratic mouth tightened for a fraction of a second. Now the trick was to decide if that gesture meant he was riled about the detective's *got-ya* comment or Merrick's vagueness during questioning. A vagueness that would obviously make the police wonder why Merrick felt a reason to hold back information.

"It's good to see him squirm," Joe said, glancing at her. The glance turned into a double take, just as he'd done with her pj's that first night. Katelyn resisted the urge to adjust her skirt again. No matter how much she tugged and pulled, the fabric wasn't going to stretch.

Thankfully, Dawn got his attention off the skirt when she continued the interrogation. The detective went through the other questions, but they were window dressing, since it wasn't Kent's actual responses they were interested in but the way he reacted. Dawn played her part to a tee. And she made just enough eye contact and kept the right inflection in her voice to let Kent know that he was indeed a suspect. When she finished, Kent didn't waste any time getting out of there.

Joe didn't waste any time, either. He grabbed his phone and pressed a few buttons. A moment later, Katelyn heard Dawn's own phone ring on the audio feed of the computer. "Have him followed," Joe ordered when Dawn answered. "Not closely though. And I don't want him approached so he can claim harassment."

He ended the call, clipped the tiny cell phone to his belt and got up. "After I shave, we'll leave for the Perfect Match."

Katelyn almost told him that she'd prefer if he skipped that particular grooming step, but then she'd have to explain why. There was already enough male-female stuff going on between them without her letting him know that she'd liked his stubbled look.

While she put on her slide holster and checked the communicator she'd threaded under her collar, her gaze landed on the papers Joe had left on the table. Specifically, her questionnaire, which Donovan had dropped off the previous morning. It was opened to page three, the section that dealt with her preferences for leisure activities.

Had Joe been reading it?

If so, did he have any idea that the answers were true?

Katelyn didn't allow her ridiculous, hormone-induced speculations to go beyond that. After all, there were probably dozens of legitimate reasons why Joe would be reading her file.

Too bad none of those dozens of legitimate reasons readily came to mind.

Curious now, she sat at the computer and did a search to find his file. Within a couple of seconds, she'd pulled up the bogus information the department had created for him. She went one step beyond that, and with her password, she located his official record.

She glanced over her shoulder in the direction of

the bedroom, to make sure he wasn't watching. He wasn't. From the sound of his electric razor, he was in the bathroom still ridding himself of his sexy stubble.

His official photo loaded, as did the rest of the info. Joseph Luis Rico. He was thirty-two. A military brat. Two brothers, a sister. He'd lived all over the world until his eighteenth birthday, when he'd left for college and then the police academy.

"Wow," Katelyn mumbled when she glanced through the list of his awards and recognitions. He had a slew of them, including one from the governor. Those accolades accounted for not just one early promotion but two. He was a supercop by anyone's standards.

But she hadn't needed a file to tell her that.

A notation near the bottom caught her eye. Just a month before his transfer to S.A.P.D., he'd taken leave, and the code beside it was one she recognized. Whatever had generated that time off required a clean psych evaluation before he could return to the job. Interesting. He'd either killed someone in the line of duty or else the leave was of a particularly stressful, personal nature.

"Find anything?" she heard him ask.

Busted.

Katelyn didn't even try to hide it. Not that she could have anyway since his picture was right there on the screen. Instead, she pushed her questionnaire, still opened to page three, to the side so he'd know this was a tit for tat kind of invasion of privacy.

As opposed to just a plain ordinary invasion.

"You lived in England for three years," she commented. "When your father was stationed there."

"You run a six-minute mile," he countered. "While listening to Axl Rose."

Not to be outdone, she continued with, "Your brothers are both Air Force Combat Rescue Officers."

"Your mother and father were both cops."

Frowning, she swiveled around in the chair. "That wasn't on the questionnaire."

"No, but it was in your personnel file." His gaze drifted to her clothes, and her legs. "Nice skirt."

Katelyn was sure her frown deepened. "Is that a ploy to get me to forget you were in my file?"

"No. It's a ploy to let you off the hook for snooping in mine." He set a small black velvet box in her lap, right on her skirt. "If you want to know something about me, Katelyn, just ask."

She would have questioned him about that personal leave, but the box suddenly captured her complete attention. It was the right size and the right shape. Well, depending on one's perspective, it was right. It was not so right from her perspective. "Is that what I think it is?"

"It is if you think it's an engagement ring." He proceeded to fix his communicator under his collar. "We need it for the announcement."

Okay. So those two simple words, engagement ring, shouldn't have sent her stomach into a tailspin, but they did. Jeez, it was such a *girl* reaction. And for nothing, since it was all show anyway.

Katelyn opened the box as if it were live explosives and came face-to-face not with some gaudy lifestyle statement but rather a tastefully delicate diamond set in beautifully etched gold. Definitely a *wow*.

"It looks real," she mumbled.

"It is. It belonged to my grandmother."

"Oh, sheez." His grandmother's? Could this possibly get any more uncomfortable? "I can't wear something like that."

"Sure you can. Well, provided it fits." He took it from the box and slipped it onto her finger. No fanfare. No awkward pause to ponder the moment. Certainly no romantic words or gazes.

It fit.

"Okay, let's go," he ordered.

He would have probably been out the door if his phone hadn't rung. Katelyn grabbed her purse while he answered it. As she moved the meager sunlight slanting through the windows caught the facets of the diamond and sent a rainbow dancing around the room. She turned the ring around so it wouldn't happen again.

She needed rainbows about as much as she needed a real engagement to Joe Rico.

"Did he?" Joe asked.

But it wasn't a casual inquiry. Like the ring box, it snared Katelyn's attention and caused her to tune in to his conversation.

"No. No change in plans," he continued. He hung up and looked at her. "Guess where Dr. Kent's headed?"

"Perfect Match?" Katelyn repeated the words and took out the questioning inflection. Of course, that's where Kent would go. He wanted answers as to why Merrick had brought him into this investigation. And that meant if they hurried, they had the opportunity to hear what Merrick was saying to his shrink. A way to kill two birds with one stone.

Joe paused and combed his gaze over her. "You're sure Kent won't recognize you?"

"Positive."

Well, not positive, exactly. She had no idea if Gail

had ever shown Kent her photo, but she couldn't let a mere possibility hold her back now. If Donovan was at work, it would be the first time they'd have their three primary suspects under the same roof. It was perhaps the break they'd been looking for.

Or maybe it would be the very confrontation to make a killer snap.

Katelyn checked her primary and backup weapons to make sure she was ready.

As they'd planned on the trip over, Katelyn lured the receptionist from her desk with a bogus emergency request for her to show her the location of the ladies' room. Joe used the ploy to walk past the other clients who were filling out questionnaires so he could slip unannounced into the hall that led to Merrick's office. Since Dr. Kent wasn't around, that meant he was probably already in there with Merrick.

Along the way, Joe looked for the security guard and cameras to make sure he hadn't missed one. No guard today, and the only camera he spotted was the one in the reception area. It had obviously supplied the photo for the newspaper article and could still possibly be monitoring the hall. So he plastered a silly grin on his face while he was trying to eavesdrop. Best to keep up the facade of the happily engaged man.

Unlike Kent. Who didn't sound happy at all. The man was practically shouting. Joe heard him when he was still several yards from Merrick's office door. Not very shrinklike behavior. Rather, Kent seemed to be in the middle of a Prozac-required moment.

"But why even mention my name?" Kent snarled.

Thankfully they'd left the door slightly ajar. Joe saw Merrick shake his head. "I'm not sure I did."

"But you must have. Jesus H. Christ, Addison, these people think you might know something about those two shootings. Why would you purposely let them believe you're unstable by telling them you were in therapy?"

Another head shake. This one more frantic than the first. "I swear, I don't think your name even came up in conversation. And they don't suspect me. They can't. They said their visit was just routine."

Katelyn emerged from the other end of the hall, which meant she'd found a way to the office without going back past the receptionist. She puckered her lips in a *shh* gesture and quietly walked to him. One glance at the camera in the reception room, and she stepped into Joe's arms. But she didn't just step. She immediately launched into her lover's pose. She pressed her body against Joe's and brushed a kiss on his jaw.

"Routine?" Kent repeated. "There's nothing routine about a police interrogation. Please tell me your lawyer was here when you spoke to them."

"No." Merrick paled a little. "I didn't think it was necessary."

"Well, from now on, it is. I can't afford to have my name dragged through the mud again."

Again? Since Joe had spent hours pouring through Kent's file, he thought that reference might be for his messy divorce from Gail. It appeared to have cost Kent a client or two. And a small fortune.

After delivering a terse goodbye, Kent turned and stormed out. He paused when he spotted Joe and gave him only a dismissive glance. Kent might have done the same to Katelyn if she hadn't buried her face against Joe's neck.

Definitely not good.

"I thought you said he wouldn't recognize you?" Joe whispered when Kent was out of earshot.

She shook her head. "He didn't."

Which, of course, didn't answer his question at all.

"Why are you here?" Merrick asked. He was staring at them through the now fully opened door.

"We'd like to talk to you." Joe made sure he grinned. Katelyn did her part by sliding her body against his. Well, it was a little more than just a slide. She hooked her fingers onto his belt—and into the waist of his pants. "We have great news."

Merrick mumbled something indistinguishable, sighed and shoved both his hands through his hair. "Give me a couple of minutes." And to make sure he had that time to himself, he shut the door.

Joe clicked off his communicator, checked to make sure hers was off as well and looked down at her. "Put your hands in my pants this time, and I'll take you where you stand."

Katelyn didn't look quite as shocked as he'd hoped. In fact, she didn't look shocked at all. She looked, well, interested. And disgusted with herself for showing that interest.

Joe knew exactly how she felt.

"We're in trouble here, Rico." She added a shake of her head to his disgusted expression. "Because I swear that sounded more like foreplay than a threat."

He fought, hard, to hold on to what little composure he had left. "I really didn't need to hear that, okay?"

"You're right." Another headshake. She huffed and

glanced at Merrick's closed door. Like Joe, she was probably hoping the man would open it. Soon. It might save Katelyn and him both from doing something he'd almost certainly regret.

"Besides, it's just all this forced intimacy that's making us think like this," she mumbled. She even repeated a slightly different variation of it as if trying to convince herself.

Again, Joe knew exactly how she felt.

"We just have to remember that the kissing and touching are fake," she concluded.

But Joe wasn't ready to conclude things just yet. He had one point of contention left. "Including the part where you put your hand in my pants?"

"Would I do something like that just for amusement?" But she waved him off. "Don't answer that. For our own sanity, let's just say everything, and I mean *everything*, we've done for the past couple of days has been an act."

It was the right thing to say. The right thing, period. She'd given them both a much-needed out. That's why Joe couldn't understand why he didn't take that out.

Instead, he slid his hand around the back of her neck and dragged her to him. Not that he had to drag her far.

She was already so close he could almost taste her.

So that's exactly what he decided to do. He lowered his head and took her mouth as if it were his for the taking.

The jolt was instant.

No cool, gentle touch of lips. Not this. This was all fire. All pleasure. All silk and heat. Not that Katelyn expected anything less from Joe, and that made it all the more dangerous.

Did it stop her?

No.

One jolt from his mouth and she was beyond a place where reason and stopping made sense. Instead, she took. She let him claim. Ravage. And just when she thought it couldn't possibly get any better, or worse, he upped the ante with the mating of their tongues. The intimate joining of their mouths. The warmth of their bodies sliding against each other, practically fighting to get closer, to touch more.

To feel more.

It was as close to sex as they could get without clothing removal.

He made a sound. A groan of breath that was male through and through. And possibly the most erotic sound she'd ever heard.

Katelyn felt the world tilt on its axis.

This was wrong. So wrong. But everything about it seemed right.

She forced herself to back off. And she almost lost that battle. Somehow though, she got her mouth to move from his. It took another moment before she got it to speak.

"That wasn't for show," she informed him. A really dumb thing to say, but what the heck? It was hard to beat the mother of all dumb things—that kiss.

"I figured that out by myself." He ran his tongue over his bottom lip. "We can't do it again though because it…felt better than it should have."

You bet it did. And not only that. It felt better than it should have while they were standing only yards away from a murder suspect.

A suspect who opened the door.

Chapter 8

Katelyn put on the best fake smile she could manage, and while easing her right hand to her slide holster, she flashed her engagement ring at Merrick.

"Joe and I are getting married." She added some excitement to her tone, as well, and she didn't totally have to fake that part. There was excitement racing through her all right, and it wasn't all related to that kiss Joe had just laid on her. There was something downright spooky about the way Merrick was acting.

Was the man about to go psycho on them?

Joe must have considered that as well because he too adjusted his position so it would be easier for him to get to his weapon.

"Congratulations are in order," Merrick finally said after a silence that was too long and much too uncomfortable. "Come this way. We'll celebrate."

Katelyn didn't relax yet. Hopefully, celebrating was all he had in mind. She stayed side by side with Joe as they started down the hall toward the reception area.

"Say, wasn't that Dr. Allen Kent who just left your office?" Joe asked, sounding remarkably casual.

There was nothing casual, however, about Merrick's response. From over his shoulder, he gave Joe a chilly, "Yes."

Katelyn ignored the frosty tone since they needed more info from him than that solo affirmative. "Wow. He's practically a local celebrity. I'm in therapy, you know. In fact, my therapist thinks I've gone off the deep end by getting engaged to Joe. But I know it's the right thing to do. That's why we don't want to wait." She paused only long enough to draw breath. "Wonder what Dr. Kent would have to say about that?"

It was a weak attempt to get Merrick to open up. And an unsuccessful one. He didn't say a word about therapy or Dr. Kent. But his silence told her loads. That shouting session with Kent had upset him, no doubt about it, but he was keeping it inside for the most part. No fists through walls. No profanity. A still-waters-run-deep kind of person.

So how would a man like that kill?

Would he gun down happy brides and grooms because his own fiancée had crushed his hopes of having an equally happy life? If so, how could Joe and she stop him from trying to kill again?

As those questions ran through her head, Merrick paused at one of the doors. Knocked once. And opened it. Bruce Donovan was seated at a desk littered with computers and other equipment.

"We need champagne," Merrick advised him. "Meet us in reception."

Katelyn's gaze connected with Donovan's. His *disapproving* gaze. Definitely not a still-waters kind of guy. She made a mental note not to sample the champagne in case he decided to poison it.

"Something tells me they've done this before," Joe muttered to her as they watched Merrick assemble an impromptu celebration.

Their host motioned for the four other clients and the receptionist to join them. They did. The clients put their questionnaires aside. Donovan appeared with the champagne and a stack of plastic fluted glasses. Merrick popped the cork and began to pour.

"So a lot of your matched couples get engaged?" Joe asked Merrick.

He lifted a shoulder. "Some."

Katelyn pressed for more. "I'll bet you keep press releases and such of your success stories."

"Not really." And with that, Merrick stepped away to pour more champagne.

"Okay, what's wrong with this picture?" Joe whispered to her. He slipped his arm around her and launched into a mock cuddling session so they could continue their discussion without being overheard.

"The clients," Katelyn immediately offered. "I was alone in here the day I did my questionnaire. How about you?"

"Me and one very old guy."

These people weren't old or even socially desperate-looking. They were young and practically buzzing with energy.

Katelyn bit off a groan. "They don't appear to be

drunk or high so that probably means they read the article in the newspaper."

"Adrenaline junkies," Joe added.

A moment later, one of the female clients confirmed that. Katelyn heard her talking almost breathlessly about the possible link to the sniper. *Isn't it soooo scary?*

Great. Sickos. Just what they didn't need to blend with the rifle-firing sicko they already had. However, it did give Katelyn something else to consider. The shootings had perhaps boosted business. A business that had recently been sagging. Merrick couldn't have been unhappy about that particular side effect, but was he smart enough, calculating enough, to have known it would happen?

Because Katelyn had her attention on the group, she didn't miss the nudge Donovan gave his boss. Merrick turned, aiming his gaze in the direction of the reception doorway.

The still waters became a little turbulent.

Katelyn followed his narrowed gaze to a tall, attractive brunette. A woman she recognized because she'd studied her file and accompanying photos.

Fiona Shipley.

"I see her," Joe whispered.

"Just the person we've been looking for."

From the look on Merrick's face, he didn't feel the same. He handed off the champagne bottle to Donovan, whispered something terse and then stormed straight for the woman. Fortunately, one of the other clients stopped him, but that diversion wouldn't last long. Katelyn could tell from the look in Merrick's eyes that one way or another, he intended to get Fiona out of here.

"We'll intervene and talk to her," Joe insisted.

"Something tells me she won't go for the let's-be-gal-pals ploy. You need to put some moves on her before Merrick whisks her away."

Joe's eyebrow lifted. "Moves?"

She nodded. "Trust me, you've got some good ones." Great ones, in fact. The kiss had proven that.

He didn't seem flattered. "I don't guess Fiona will consider those *moves* bottom-feeding gestures since I just announced my engagement to you?"

"Let's hope not. You occupy Fiona, and I'll take care of Merrick. Maybe I can put him in a more talkative mood and learn the names of any recently engaged Perfect Match couples."

Joe caught her arm when she tried to step away. "Please tell me you're not going to try to rile him enough so he'll come after you."

Katelyn tried to look offended. "You think I'd do that?"

"Yeah, I do," he said without hesitation.

If it wouldn't have blown the lovebird facade, she would have scowled at him. "Are you saying divide and conquer's not a good idea?"

Several muscles stirred in his jaw, a definite sign he agreed with her plan but probably wouldn't approve of her methods. "You've got ten minutes max," he finally said. "Get everything you can from him. I'll do the same to Fiona. Just don't shake things up too much, okay?"

This time, it was Katelyn who stopped. "I'll say

the same to you. Fiona's the one with a hostile history, not Merrick."

In fact, this divide and conquer investigative approach suddenly didn't seem like a good idea. Even more, Katelyn didn't want to explore why it occurred to her that it wasn't good.

Judas.

She was worried about Joe.

A man who could clearly take care of himself.

"Are you about to quote regulations about approaching a potentially violent suspect without proper backup?" Joe asked.

"You wish."

He stared at her several long seconds, and cursed. "It's about that kiss?"

She nodded. "Probably."

But when she repeated that to herself, it didn't seem so much like a probably as a definitely.

Praying she was wrong, Katelyn turned to head Merrick off at the pass.

Joe made it to Fiona before Merrick did. Thanks to Katelyn. She latched on to Merrick and somehow brought him to a stop. God knows what she was saying to him, but she seemed to have captured his attention.

Fiona offered him a tentative smile when Joe approached her. The smile vanished when she glanced in Katelyn and Merrick's direction.

"Joe Farrell." He extended his hand, and she shook it. Not a delicate grip, either. She could probably hold her own in an arm wrestling competition.

"Fiona Shipley." She slid her gaze over him and up. "I haven't seen you in here before."

It was almost certainly a lie. She'd been watching the place the night of the icebreaker.

She moved slightly to the side, probably so she could keep her eye on Merrick. He did the same, angling his body so he could watch Katelyn. Since she was the only redhead in the room, she made a great visual target. The skirt helped, too. She had the best pair of legs in the room.

Maybe the world.

And maybe he was still recovering from the effects of that kiss, because everything about her suddenly seemed damn incredible. Thankfully, she'd probably do something to rile him before the night was over. That would get his mind back where it belonged.

"So you know everyone here?" Joe asked Fiona. Not exactly chitchat, either. It was an opening to bring the subject around to Merrick, the man who was glancing in her direction as much as she was glancing in his.

"No. Just Bruce and Addison."

Joe skipped right past the Bruce part and went for the jugular. "Merrick's a friend of yours?"

She gave an unnecessary adjustment to her gold hoop earring. "Something like that."

In other words, *nothing* like that. She was either Merrick's former, present or even wannabe lover. With the way she kept eyeing Katelyn, it was highly likely that it wasn't the latter.

Interesting.

"How about you?" she asked. "Are you a new client, or are you with someone?"

"I'm with my fiancée, Kate." He pointed to Katelyn but made sure he only showed minimal interest in the woman whom he'd supposedly asked to be his wife. "Old flames reunited thanks to Perfect Match. Things happened pretty fast between us."

And he let Fiona fill in the blanks. Maybe she'd think he was having second thoughts. Or maybe she'd just think he was a bottom-feeder. Either way, she didn't seem turned off with the idea of an engaged man chatting her up. But then, maybe she was trying to make Merrick jealous. Or something. There were a lot of dynamics going on in the room, and not all of them were limited to Merrick and Fiona. Some of them were obviously happening between Katelyn and him.

Since Joe could feel his self-imposed time limit ticking away, he took a pen from the receptionist's desk and passed it to Fiona. He discreetly put out his hand, palm up. "In case things don't work out with Addison, or Kate, why don't you give me a number where I can reach you? I'd like to give you a call sometime."

That got Fiona's attention. Man, did it. She gave him several more once-overs, not exactly carnal ones, either. There was some disgust. Some loathing. Even a hot flash of anger in her eyes. That's why it surprised Joe when she scribbled some numbers on his hand.

That was it. No sultry invitations, no warm goodbyes. No explanations as to why she'd give a man her number when she obviously disliked him.

"If you'll excuse me, I need to speak with Addison." Fiona tossed the pen back on the desk and stepped away.

Merrick moved toward Fiona at the same time he left Katelyn and walked toward her. Merrick said something. Something harsh, judging from the way she reacted. She looked as if the man had slapped her.

Then, she angled her eyes in Katelyn and Joe's direction. Merrick's gaze followed.

Oh, yeah. Merrick was definitely suspicious of them, and their latest round of unofficial questioning had probably made it worse.

Fiona gave Merrick a not-so-friendly glower, turned on her heel and headed for the door. Merrick aimed a similar facial expression at them and went in the opposite direction toward his office.

"Should we follow one of them?" Katelyn asked in a whisper.

"Not with that camera looming over us. We've already peaked their interest too much for one night." Way too much. "Did you learn anything new?"

"No. He's not flirtatious or chatty like Donovan." Katelyn glanced around the room. "Speaking of the devil, where is he?"

"He left not long after you started talking to Merrick."

She made a sound to indicate she didn't care for that. Neither did Joe.

"Maybe we should follow him instead?" she suggested.

"He went in the same direction as Merrick. Besides, we have this." Making sure he was out of camera angle, Joe flashed the number that Fiona had given him.

She blinked. "You got her number that fast?"

"Maybe. It could be a fake."

"Yeah, right. It's not a fake."

Joe wasn't sure if he should be complimented by that, but unfortunately it felt like a compliment.

"So what's the deal between Merrick and her?" Katelyn asked. "Are they involved?"

"That'd be my guess. It's also my guess that one or both isn't too happy about that."

"Merrick, maybe. It might explain why he had the guard here the night of the icebreaker. Maybe he wanted to keep her away from the place."

"It's possible. Merrick certainly wasn't happy to see her. I'll call her tomorrow and see if I can arrange to meet her somewhere."

"With proper backup, correct?" Katelyn whispered.

Since it didn't sound even remotely sarcastic, he stared at her. "Why this sudden fixation with backup?"

She dismissed it with a wave of her hand. "I don't know. There's this little buzz in the back of my head. It's making me antsy."

"Then obviously it's a good time for us to get out of here. We'll come back tomorrow and invite them to the wedding."

After he called Fiona, of course. If he got lucky, that number would be real so he could continue their discussion.

They went out the door. Not alone, either. Two other clients were right behind them, and the woman was still chattering about Perfect Match's possible connection to the sniper. If the sniper had indeed been inside that reception room and heard her, it would have no doubt made him or her nervous.

Or maybe not.

Maybe that's exactly what the nutcase wanted. Publicity. Recognition. A moment in the spotlight, even if that moment meant people dying.

All four of them headed toward the parking lot. Unlike the night of the mixer, Joe hadn't managed to get a decent parking spot. They were almost a full block away. In the dark.

"So did you learn anything new when you talked to Fiona?" Katelyn whispered, presumably so that the couple behind them wouldn't hear. "Like maybe how many eyelashes she had? You probably had a chance to count them when she was fluttering them at you."

Joe geared up to give her a smart-ass comeback. The glint of movement stopped him. The glint he caught out of the corner of his eye.

But it was too late.

The shot rang out before he could get Katelyn out of the way.

Katelyn felt the searing hot pain slice across her arm.

She ignored it and drew her weapon while she yelled for the couple to get down. They did, diving for cover behind a parked car. She latched on to Joe at the same moment he latched on to her, and they dragged each other to the ground.

It wasn't a second too soon.

Another bullet smashed into the building, into the exact spot where they'd been.

Katelyn couldn't take the time to berate herself, but she would sure as heck do it later. She should have paid more attention to that buzz in her head instead of dismissing it. And she darn sure shouldn't have been playing twenty questions with Joe about his encounter with Fiona Shipley.

Now that mistake might cost both of them their lives.

She checked the other couple. They were cowering, their hands protectively over their heads. All in all, it wasn't a bad position. The car would give them some measure of protection, but it wasn't the same for Joe and her. For all practical purposes, they were still out in the open.

"Let's move," Joe ordered.

Katelyn didn't waste any time. She got to her feet, and they scrambled for the narrow alley between the two buildings. He maneuvered them to the far side of an overflowing Dumpster, but it wasn't an ideal position either since bullets could go through the metal.

"Rico here," Joe said into his communicator. "We've got a shooter. Send backup to the outside perimeter of the area and await further orders."

The outside perimeter so that it wouldn't blow their cover. Not that it wouldn't anyway. But Joe was obviously hoping to salvage this mission and keep them alive.

Katelyn pulled in a few steadying breaths and glanced down at her arm. She saw the gashed fabric, and the blood. Nothing serious, she decided, but she angled her body so that Joe wouldn't notice it. He didn't need that kind of distraction now.

Another shot.

It slammed into the exterior wall and tore off a chunk of brick, sending mortar and dust flying through the air. Two more shots quickly followed, both of them gashing into the Dumpster and the wall just above their heads.

The bullets came close.

Too close. And the thought of them coming any closer set Katelyn's heart pounding.

She leaned forward slightly, trying to see if she could pinpoint the origin of those bullets so she could get off a shot.

"Don't even think about it," Joe snarled.

Katelyn started to argue, to remind him that she could return fire as well as he could, but that probably wasn't a good option anyway. The gunman clearly had an advantage, and if she moved away from cover to get a better shot, it would also leave her vulnerable. They were already too exposed as it was.

Still, that didn't stop Joe.

He aimed. And she knew that he was about to do something she'd already dismissed.

But then the shots stopped.

The waiting began.

Katelyn counted off the seconds, the quiet seconds, until she got to sixty. Joe grabbed her shoulder when she started to move and he put her right back against the wall. "Not yet." He took the end of his communicator and put it against his mouth. "Situation report."

"Additional officers are on the way," the backup officer responded.

Which meant the sniper was getting away.

Again!

Worse, it didn't exclude any of their suspects. Fiona, Merrick or Donovan could have left Perfect Match and sneaked into any of the multistory buildings across the street. For that matter, Kent could have done the same thing. He could have been lying in wait for them.

"Pick up Bruce Donovan, Dr. Kent, Addison Merrick and Fiona Shipley," Joe snarled into his communicator. "Bring them in. I want them all interrogated. And by God, they'd better have answers."

Chapter 9

Katelyn shut the bathroom door and peeled off her top. Somehow, she'd managed to keep the streak of blood from Joe, but if she didn't get rid of the evidence, she wouldn't be able to keep it from him for long. Thankfully, he'd planted himself in the living room and was still immersed in the necessary calls and reports to headquarters.

"Judas," she mumbled looking down at the shallow but angry gash that the sniper's bullet had left on her arm.

The bleeding had already stopped, and it wasn't especially painful—okay, it did hurt—but what hurt even more was the realization that it could have been worse. Much worse. The gunman could have killed Joe, the other couple and her. It was a miracle that all she had to show for the encounter was a minor two-inch abrasion, some dried blood and a pair of shredded panty hose that she'd damaged when she dove down on the sidewalk.

She stuffed the top in the cabinet beneath the sink and while she was at it, she took off her panty hose to add them to the stash. She located a first aid kit in the medicine cabinet and got to work cleaning the wound. When she finished, Katelyn covered it with a bandage and slipped on a white cotton shirt, the only other long-sleeve garment her mother had included in the bag. Maybe the quick change in clothes wouldn't make Joe suspicious.

Or maybe it would.

He was standing right in front of her when she opened the door. He had his hands bracketed on each side of the frame, essentially blocking her path.

"Everything okay?" he asked. But it wasn't a simple question. There were some dangerous undercurrents in it.

"I'm fine."

Those now infamous jaw muscles went to work against each other. "Take off your shirt, or I'll take it off for you."

Oh.

"Does this mean you want to have sex?" Katelyn tried. But it was a lousy try. Anyone with half a brain would have known it wasn't sex on his mind. Not with that warlike expression.

He waited only a second or two before he reached out, grabbed the sides of her shirt and ripped it open. A few of the buttons merely gave way and slipped through the buttonholes. Others didn't. They landed with tiny bouncing pings on the tile floor.

His gaze raced over her body, and it obviously wasn't her lacy bra or her breasts that captured his interest. His attention quickly landed on the bandage.

Katelyn braced herself for him to rip the shirt right off her. But he didn't. His touch gentled and Joe eased it off her shoulder to expose her arm.

"It's not bad," she insisted.

He didn't take her word for it. Not surprising since he'd just caught her in a lie. With that same gentle touch, those same careful movements, he lifted the bandage.

And cursed.

The jaw muscles started again.

"How did you know I was hurt?" Katelyn asked. God, her voice actually cracked.

"There was blood on the sleeve of my jacket. It's not mine. I figured it had to be yours."

She shrugged. "And here I thought I'd contained my bodily fluids."

"This isn't funny!"

Because he looked ready to lose it, she ran her hand down the length of his arm. "It's nothing. I've gotten worse from shaving my legs."

He pressed the bandage back in place, gently, and skimmed his fingertips from it, across the top of her left breast and then to her heart. "Six inches in this direction, and the bullet wouldn't have grazed you. It would have killed you."

His gaze came to hers.

Unlike his touch, there was still no gentleness in those glacier-blue eyes, but Katelyn knew without a doubt if gentleness was what she needed, he could have easily provided it.

And he did.

Without moving his hand from her heart, Joe pulled her to him. Where she felt incredibly safe and warm.

Katelyn went with it, against her better judgment. Full-blown sex would have been far less of an intimate risk than this. But her better judgment and her resolve went south. Unable to hold back a shudder of breath, she rested her head against his shoulder and took things from him that she hadn't known she needed.

They stood there for heaven knows how long. Minutes, maybe. Perhaps longer. The rhythm of her heart seemed to fall into cadence with the pulse that throbbed in his wrist. And the world seemed to just melt away.

Until the doorbell rang.

Joe immediately stepped back, drawing his gun, and their tender moment ended.

"Wait here," he ordered.

"Right, and leave you without backup. Like I'm really going to do that."

Knowing she couldn't do much to fix the shirt, she shucked it off and put on one that Joe had left in the bedroom. Katelyn had her weapon drawn before he even made it to the door.

"It's your brother," Joe let her know.

Great. She didn't want to face Garrett now. "Don't say a word about the scratch," she warned in a whisper.

But she soon learned it wasn't Garrett when Joe opened the door and let him in.

It was Brayden.

Even worse.

He was part bloodhound and all cop, and he could sniff out problems a mile away. She made sure Joe's shirt covered the bandage before she joined the two men in the living room.

"I came by to check on you," Brayden greeted. He was dressed like a delivery man, but the disguise wasn't limited to just his clothes. He was carrying a white bag. "Dad sent some chili."

"Thanks." Katelyn took the bag, knowing she should dig in right away to prove all was right with the world, but her stomach wasn't quite ready for food. She set it on the table instead.

"You can do your initial reports on the computer," Brayden instructed. "But I'll still need you to do a face-to-face at headquarters. No way around that. We'll send a cruiser for you tomorrow so it'll look as if you're being brought in for questioning. In fact, we'll bring in all the people who were at Perfect Match tonight."

Brayden gave them both a considering glance and sat on the sofa. "Did either of you fire your weapons?"

"No," she quickly volunteered.

Joe stared at her.

Brayden paused, as if waiting to see what had caused that stare. "Any reason to think your cover's been compromised?" he asked, and Brayden directed that question at Joe.

Joe leaned against the narrow snack bar that divided the kitchen from the living room. "Hard to tell. Just about everyone in Perfect Match was talking about the shootings. And that other couple was walking right behind us. Maybe the sniper just wanted to make his or her presence known."

Brayden didn't say anything for several seconds. "Well, we're rounding up Bruce Donovan and hopefully Fiona Shipley for an interrogation, so maybe we'll know something soon. Fiona checked herself into a residential mental health clinic about an hour ago. Lots of freedom for her to go from one place to the other, but it doesn't give us a lot of access to her unless she's willing to grant us that access. Oh, and we learned that Donovan owns several hunting rifles so I went ahead and requested a search warrant."

"Good," Joe said.

Katelyn muttered an agreement as well, even though Donovan probably wasn't stupid enough to leave murder weapons lying around for the cops to find. Still, it'd prevent him from getting a good night's sleep—which would apparently be her fate, as well. Joe probably wouldn't drop that *six inches over and you could have been killed* discussion.

"You intend to continue with the present mission plan?" Brayden asked Joe.

Joe stared at her again. Katelyn stared back and tried to put the words in his mouth. Or rather the word. And that word was *yes*.

He didn't say yes.

But then he didn't say no, either.

"I'll have to get back to you on that," Joe told her brother.

Brayden nodded. Made a sound of contemplation. Then looked at Joe. "Would you mind if I spoke to Katelyn in private?"

Another glare from Joe aimed in her direction, but this one had a *tell him the truth* warning in it. It was a warning she'd definitely ignore. Joe would thank her for it later, after they'd collared the sniper.

Her brother motioned for her to sit down the moment Joe left the room. "What's wrong?" Brayden asked.

She didn't sit, but put on her best butter-wouldn't-melt-in-my-mouth expression. "Why would you think anything's wrong?"

Brayden's eyebrow lifted.

So much for the nonmelting butter routine. That eyebrow was a very effective BS monitor. Still, it didn't stop her from going on the offensive. "What— being shot at isn't reason enough to make me cranky?"

His eyebrow stayed up. "You're wearing Sergeant Rico's shirt," he pointed out.

"Oh, that." Not that she'd thought for minute Brayden would miss something like that. However, since he'd broached the subject, Katelyn went with it. It might get him off the undercover assignment. "I'm not allowed to have a lover? Garrett is the wild child of the family, and you don't lecture him about it."

"Garrett doesn't sleep with his boss."

"My *temporary* boss," Katelyn corrected.

Brayden shook his head. Nothing overt. Just a simple gesture. "You know something I don't? Joe Rico's a sergeant in Homicide. You're a detective in the same department."

"For now, yes. But I figure he'll get promoted, and then he'll be moved." If not, then it might come down to her asking for a transfer, a thought that had her feeling a little nauseous. She'd worked hard to get into Homicide, damn hard, and she wouldn't just give that up. Well, unless there was no other way. Then she'd consider it.

Heaven help her.

"And I haven't actually slept with him," she said

more to herself than her brother. "I've just been flirting with the idea. *Lightly* flirting with it. And even if something happened between us, it's not against the regs per se. It's just frowned upon because it could cause, well, morale problems." She added an indignant huff just because she'd delivered Brayden's lecture for him. "Is this why you came over? To grill me about my love life?"

He caught her wrist and sat her on the coffee table in front of him. "Quit being so defensive. I came to see if you were all right."

Katelyn leaned closer into his personal space. "I. Am."

"Yes. I can see that."

She didn't want to know if he was being sarcastic, mainly because she was certain that he was. After all, his eyebrow was still cocked and locked, ready to fire, and she'd delivered her *I. Am.* comment through clenched teeth.

"I also wanted to talk to you about Sergeant Rico," he calmly went on. "And about this mission."

Since she was already on the defensive, she just stayed there. "Oh, no. Don't even think about pulling the plug on it." Katelyn held up her thumb and index finger to indicate a miniscule space. "We're this close to getting the sniper, Brayden."

"I don't doubt it." And there wasn't anything defensive-sounding about that. He eased down her hand. "Sergeant Rico and you make a good team."

That improved her posture. But she wouldn't let a compliment, if that's indeed what it was, blindside her. "What the heck is that supposed to mean?"

"It means you each have talents that balance the

other's." He leaned back against the sofa and tucked his hands behind his head. "For Rico, procedure is rote, so deeply engrained he doesn't have to think about it. The vast majority of the time, following procedure's the right thing to do. So that practically ensures a successful mission. You, on the other hand, think outside the box, and that gives you the edge when you're in an evade and escape mode."

"Thanks. I think." Suspicious, she squinted one eye. "Is this some kind of law enforcement version of a hunters versus gatherers theory?"

He smiled. "Well, sort of." His mouth quivered as if he might smile, but then he lowered his hands and continued. "Rico's never missed a shot during firearms qualification."

Another posture improving remark. *"Never?"*

"Never."

"Sheez." She let that sink in. "Even Robocop misses every now and then."

"Rico's also never blown a case. He's batting a thousand in that department."

She frowned, realizing all the blindsiding was probably leading somewhere after all. "And your point would be?"

"No point. You're smart, and that means you know if it comes down to a tight situation, then Rico can handle it. No matter how good of a shot you are—and you're good—he's better."

"And he'll be even better if I'm backing him up," she promptly added.

"Absolutely." He stood, kissed her cheek and headed for the door. "Be careful, okay?"

Katelyn nodded, and even though she wasn't

pleased with the minilecture, she went to him and returned the kiss.

She locked the door after she let him out. "One down, one to go," she grumbled. She'd probably convinced Brayden to keep this case alive, but now she had to do the same with Joe.

"Want some chili?" she called out.

She took the two plastic containers from the bag. They were still warm so she grabbed a couple of spoons and prepared herself for a feast—which she really didn't want yet—but that was beside the point. Wolfing down some chili might go a long way toward proving to Joe that she was fit for duty.

He came out of the bedroom and started that staring thing again, so Katelyn shoved both the container of chili and a spoon into his hands. "Eat," she ordered.

She did. Katelyn sat back on the coffee table and dug in. "Practically orgasmic, huh?" she asked after he'd had his first taste.

"Close." Joe sampled another heaping spoonful. "Speaking of orgasmic, you'd rather let your brother think you have the hots for me than just tell him you're hurt?"

It was a good thing she'd just swallowed that mouthful of chili, or she might have choked on it. "You eavesdropped?"

"Thin walls," he countered. "Hard not to eavesdrop."

True. But that didn't let him off the hook completely. "I didn't want him to take me off the case, all right? Sometimes, he weirds out a little when he starts to think hard about what I do for a living. It's that you're-my-kid-sister routine. It brings out his protective instincts."

"If he'd known you were wounded in the line of duty, he would have pulled you off the case. It's not protective instincts. It's procedure."

She stabbed at the chili with her spoon. "I was *scratched* in the line of duty. Big difference."

"Why do you feel the rules don't apply to you, huh? And before you start defending yourself, just hear me out. Officers who are wounded, even when it's a scratch, take time off to recoup."

"I don't have time to recoup."

He smacked his chili onto the snack bar and stared down at her. "Am I supposed to understand that?"

No. And no explanation would probably help, either. Still, that didn't stop her. "I want to be promoted to sergeant, okay? And I wish there were a stronger word than *want,* because it'd definitely apply here. In six months, I'll be too old for that promotion."

"Too old?" he repeated. "You'll be what—the ripe old age of twenty-nine?"

"Both Brayden and Garrett made sergeant by the time they were twenty-nine."

He looked at her as if she'd sprouted wings. "This is about competing with your brothers?"

She was right. He didn't get it. He couldn't. "It'd be simple if it were a competition," she muttered, frustrated. "But it's more than that. The job is who I am. If I come up short, then I'm not the person I thought I was, and I don't think I could handle that."

Katelyn glanced at him, sorry that she'd just blurted out what was probably the only deep, dark secret she had.

"And, no, I don't really expect you to understand," she added. She poked at the chili again, glad that she had something to prod. Maybe the fake violence would rid her of the alley-cat war going on inside her body.

He dragged a chair closer and sat down right in front of her so they were eye-to-eye. And only inches apart. "I understand."

Of all the things that Katelyn thought he might say, that wasn't one of them. "Which part?"

"All of it."

She hadn't expected that, either. The skeptical look she gave him no doubt prompted him to continue.

"You know how everyone in your family are either cops or former cops? Well, in my family, they're all military officers. All successful. My dad is a retired one-star general, and he never forgave me for breaking ranks to become a police officer. As much as he was sure I'd fail, that's how determined I was to succeed. Every promotion, every citation, every award is to prove to him—and me—that I made the right decision."

"Wow." That's all she could manage for a couple of seconds. Talk about revealing deep, dark secrets.

Somehow, this conversation had taken a very unsettling turn. And more. He was so close that she took in his scent—and that mixed with the understanding look on his face was a dangerous combination.

"Okay, so maybe you do get it," she managed to say. And there was way too much breath in her voice.

"Yeah. But that doesn't mean I think it's a good idea to toss out the regs and procedures. Sometimes, you just have to step back and look at the bigger picture. Like this…" He reached for her bandaged arm.

Katelyn snagged his wrist, a variation of cutting him off at the pass. Or something like that. All she knew was it wouldn't be a good time for him to touch her. "Put your hands in my shirt again, and I'll take you where you sit."

She waited for him to laugh or give her a wiseguy comeback for using his words against him.

He didn't do either.

Joe sat there staring at her. Just staring. With those intense blue eyes that seemed to make her melt.

Mercy, where did the air suddenly go?

But it was too late for her to care about such things as air, or breathing. Katelyn let go of his wrist so she could reach for him.

Joe beat her to it.

Chapter 10

The timing sucked.

Joe forced himself to remember that. Katelyn was injured and coming down from a terrifying ordeal. However, the reminder lasted for only a couple of seconds, for just the short period of time that it took him to haul her off that coffee table and onto his lap.

Her mouth came to his. Man, did it. Her moist, sweet, hot mouth. The kiss was hard and hungry, and in that moment, Joe knew he was sunk. There wasn't enough willpower in the universe to make him back away from her.

He slid an arm around her waist, another around the back of her neck and pulled her against him. To him. Until they were pressed to each other.

She wasn't a passive participant. Not that Joe had ever thought she would be. It was a battle. Her kiss was an assault. A sweet one, but still an assault. Her fingers dug into his shoulders, fighting to bring him even closer—not really possible since he'd have to be inside her to achieve that. The way things were going though, that just might happen.

Soon.

He decided not to think about why that wouldn't be a good idea.

Joe reached for her shirt, or rather *his* shirt that she was wearing, and would have ripped it off her if he hadn't tried to be considerate of her injury. Katelyn gave it no such consideration. She stripped it off and sent it flying across the room. Joe went for her bra instead but changed his mind when she shifted her legs to straddle him.

Oh, man.

There was no chance he'd talk his body or hers into slowing down so they wouldn't kill each other. So without breaking their kiss, he went with it, embracing that dangerous energy that was already on the verge of erupting.

He gripped her thigh and just kept going. Up. Not slowly, either. And not gently.

There was a lot of bare skin thanks to her short skirt, and she'd apparently removed her panty hose. The only thing he encountered along the way was the woman going after his zipper—something he preferred not to have happen anytime soon. She'd have managed it, too, if Joe hadn't maneuvered his own seeking hand around hers.

Since there wasn't time for finesse, he went for impact instead. He succeeded. Joe shoved his hand into her panties, into the fragile swatch of lace and silk.

His fingers found her. Wet and hot. He made his way through the slick moisture.

One touch, and he heard her breath shudder.

She stopped her quest for his zipper and instead anchored her hands, one on his stomach. The other slipped into her own hair. Meeting his gaze head-on, she rocked shamelessly against his hand. One stroke. Two. Three. A long, lingering caress that brought on another shudder, another erotic hitch of her breath. And he was sure he had her close to release.

He was wrong.

Katelyn located his mouth again, kissing him as if she'd escalated the war. And maybe she had. She skipped the zipper part she'd started earlier and moved her hand from his stomach. Down.

Inside his pants.

No fumbling. She got it right the first time. Those agile fingers bypassed his boxers and slid right over his erection. One stroke. Two. A rather skillful swipe of her thumb, and she had him close to begging for mercy. Or close to begging for something else.

Joe gritted his teeth and launched them forward. Her back landed on the coffee table, and he landed on her. Between her legs. All in all, it wasn't a bad place to be. For a moment, anyway. And then there was another round of jockeying for position. She rolled. Until his back landed on the table.

Katelyn went after his shirt. He went after her skirt. It was out-and-out warfare, and for some reason speed counted. They battled the clothes and won. She even got her way with his zipper and managed to shove it down.

"Now," she demanded, already aligning the parts

of them that would have made *now* happen once he rid them of their underwear.

Maybe it was the sound of her voice, or maybe there was a thread of common sense that hadn't been smothered in all that fire, but Joe remembered something he almost wished he hadn't remembered.

"I don't have a condom," he let her know.

Katelyn stopped instantly and stared at him. "Neither do I."

Her eyes were wild, unfocused, and her breaths came out in short, hot spurts. She looked on the verge of cursing, but since she didn't, Joe cursed for both of them. What he didn't do was move away from her. It would take more than a lack of a condom for that to happen.

In one swipe with his forearm, he cleared the coffee table. Chili, magazines and papers went in every direction. He didn't stop there. Because she'd already started reaching for him, specifically for his erection, Joe latched on to her panties and pulled them off her. They tore. And neither he nor Katelyn obviously cared.

Now.

It had to be now.

With the blood raging, and his heartbeat hammering, he went straight for that hot, sweet part of her that he'd already touched. But this time, he used his mouth and tongue instead of his fingers.

The taste of her went straight through him like a double shot of whiskey. And more. It was a taste he wouldn't forget, and somewhere in the back of his mind he knew he'd never be with another woman without thinking of this.

Of her.

She mumbled something and sounded as if she were

on the verge of protesting, but a well-placed stroke of his tongue stopped her.

"Okay," was all she said.

She arched her back, moaned and began to move to the rhythm of his mouth. It didn't seem possible, but he'd actually found a way to get Katelyn O'Malley to cooperate. And he pleasured them both in the process.

For a couple more seconds, anyway.

"Maybe there's a condom in the bathroom," she decided, her tone more desperate than hopeful.

Her hands were suddenly everywhere. Touching as much of him as she could possibly touch, she slid lower and caught on to his hips, dragging him to the bathroom with her.

Still, the war didn't stop.

She did though.

But only so she could take her mouth to his bare stomach. No simple kiss. No, not her. She had him seeing double when she circled his navel with her tongue and sucked not-so-tenderly. Before he could muster enough strength to stop her, she kissed his erection as intimately as he'd kissed her. She pleasured him, and from the way she moved against him, she pleasured herself, as well.

Somehow, he stood upright so he could maneuver her and hopefully reciprocate. She caught on to his shoulders and pushed him against the wall. Normally, that wouldn't have been an enjoyable experience, but he was in the zone where anything she did would have been enjoyable in this erotic battle they were waging on each other.

Joe dragged her up with him. And turned so that

she was the one against the wall. He was careful not to hurt her arm, but he wasn't so gentle with the rest of her. He kissed her. Hard.

She tasted of him.

Smelled of him.

Yet, somehow her own unique scent and taste were there, as well. Lingering around him and making him crazy.

Turning as if in some bizarre dance, they made it into the bathroom. He couldn't have told anyone how, but it qualified as a miracle.

His shoulder slammed against the jamb when she looped her arms behind his neck and leaped up to wrap her legs around his waist. With one hand he fumbled through the medicine cabinet while he used his other hand to keep her fingers out of his boxers.

She searched for a condom as well, tossing things from the glass shelves. Throughout her quest, she kept up the kisses, the touches. Until Joe was absolutely sure he couldn't take any more.

But somehow, he took more.

She made him take more.

"Truce," Katelyn mumbled. With her breath thin, her voice had hardly any sound. "There's not a condom in here."

Fighting with his own breath, he nodded. "It was a long shot anyway."

And it no longer mattered.

He'd already prepared himself for the final battle, and he didn't need a condom for what he had in mind. Joe turned and pinned her against the sink. Without her panties in the way, he wedged his knee between her legs and eased his fingers inside her.

A long, deliberate sigh left her mouth. A moan.

And a gasp of pleasure. Once again she moved into the strokes. And she moved against him. Deeper this time, though. Against his fingers, and against his body. A slow, sensual slide that brought out every basic, every carnal instinct inside him.

"Not without you," she insisted.

"Yes, without me."

But he might as well have been talking to the air because she clamped her leg along the outside of his. Holding him in place. And she got her way by sliding her hand back into his boxers.

Since it was obvious she wouldn't give up, Joe just gave in.

"Move with me, Katelyn. Move with me."

She did. She moved with him as if her very life depended on it. And with their blood raging, that wasn't too far from the truth.

Face-to-face. Body-to-body. Wet skin whispering against wet skin. His fingers, in her. Moving. Hers, on him. Clutching. Gripping. Sliding. To a frantic, feverish pace.

"Take me where I stand," she offered.

And he accepted that offer.

He snagged her gaze, because he wanted to watch her go over. Joe fought through the clawing primal need to claim and possess so he could see exactly what this did to her. It didn't matter that he felt his own body going over, as well.

Nothing mattered.

Except this.

Except her.

They took that last climb together with strokes. Touches. Caresses. And they were right there to catch each other when the fire tore free and released them both.

* * *

Katelyn so hoped the ringing in her ears was a post-orgasmic response.

No such luck.

When she heard Joe curse, she realized it was the phone. A phone she should probably answer since this was supposedly her apartment and since they were in the middle of an undercover murder investigation.

Somehow, Joe got their bodies untangled so she could make it to the bedroom. To prevent herself from having to stand around naked, she grabbed a towel and her pajama top along the way. Naked was great during the throes of passion, but now that the passion had been sated, she was already starting to feel as if she'd done the ultimate no-no.

Which in a way she had.

She'd just had sex with her boss, and even though it wasn't full-blown sex, it qualified in every possible way that counted.

Katelyn pushed that disturbing thought aside and grabbed the phone. After a couple of tries, she even managed a meager hello.

"We have a problem," Brayden immediately informed her.

Okay. So that rid her of any lust-induced cobwebs. "What's wrong?"

She tried to brace herself, but the bracing failed when she heard her brother's response.

"The sniper struck again. There's been another shooting."

Chapter 11

"It takes thirteen average-size steps to go from one side to the other," Garrett commented from the doorway of the headquarters' conference room. "But then you probably already figured that out since all you've done is pace for the past fifteen minutes."

"I beg to differ." Katelyn held up the foam cup. "I've had coffee with my pacing."

"How very multitasked of you. Try it with gum, and you'll really impress me."

Too bad their attempts at levity failed.

Mercy. Another shooting.

She tried to choke back a sigh, failed, and dropped down into one of the burgundy leather chairs that encircled a massive oval table.

Garrett glanced at Joe, who was in the adjoining room. He'd kept the door open, and the glass panel allowed them both to see that Joe was still talking on the phone. Too bad she couldn't hear what he was saying.

"You have an update on the wounded couple yet?" Garrett asked her.

"That's what Joe's getting now." She set her empty cup aside. "Their names are Melissa and Brad Garcia. They're alive. At least, they were when they arrived at the hospital a couple of hours ago, but they're both in surgery."

"I heard the shooting happened not too far from the Municipal Auditorium?"

She nodded. "They were getting married in a late night ceremony on one of those tour boats. Just the couple, a minister and two others who were witnessing the wedding."

That in itself posed some serious questions as to how the sniper had learned about the ceremony. It wasn't exactly a well-publicized event. If she could somehow pick up the information trail, it might lead her to the person responsible. And in this case, the person responsible had shot the bride and groom within seconds after they said I do.

Just the thought of that made her stomach churn. What was supposed to be the happiest night of their life had turned into a nightmare.

Katelyn shook her head, and her fingers curled into a fist. "I should have stopped him, Garrett. This shouldn't have happened."

"You know, in some cultures that remark would be considered heresy. You're not God. Heck, you're not even in the angel category." And though it was a typical cocky Garrett response, he gave her a brotherly pat on the back. "Are you close to collaring this shooter?"

"He struck twice in the same night so at least we know we're pushing the right buttons." She glanced in Joe's direction, but he was still on the phone. "Or in light of the wounded couple, maybe it was the wrong buttons."

"It's not wrong. You'll get him." Garrett unwrapped two mints that he took from his pocket, popped one in his mouth and uncurled her fist so he could put the other one in her hand. "I heard the owner of Perfect Match might be closing down the place for a couple of days. Will that affect your follow-up plans?"

"I don't know yet." She stared at the mint because it gave her some place to focus her attention. "Joe just got the news before the hospital called."

But it would definitely have an effect. After all, they were supposed to go to Perfect Match that very afternoon and invite Merrick to the wedding. Since that was a critical step in the plan, it meant they'd have to make other arrangements to see him.

Not an ideal contingency.

If they met Merrick elsewhere, it only increased problems for securing yet another location. But then, calling the man and asking him to meet them at Perfect Match might make him even more suspicious than he already was.

Garrett took a chair, turned it backward and sat across from her so they were face-to-face. When she didn't make eye contact with him, he put his finger beneath her chin, lifted and forced the eye contact. He tipped his head toward Joe. "So how hard are you falling for that jerk?"

Katelyn frowned and tossed the mint into her mouth. She cracked it with her teeth. "He's not a jerk."

"How hard are you falling for him?" Garrett flatly repeated.

The mint crunching didn't last nearly as long as Garrett's inquisitive, in-her-face expression. "As hard as a massive crate of concrete," she admitted.

Garrett made a sound of disappointment, lifted her hand and studied the ring for her fake engagement to Joe. "I thought I taught you better than that. The badge first. Family second. Lust and laundry last."

"I'm scared it's more than just lust," Katelyn whispered.

"Hell."

"Yes." She considered some profanity of her own.

"What about all the other stuff going on?" Garrett asked. "You just plan to forget that Rico's investigation could ultimately hurt Brayden?"

"Don't give me that." Katelyn managed to keep her voice at a whisper. An angry whisper. But it was still hopefully low enough that Joe wouldn't hear her. "The chief ordered that investigation, not Joe. And it could only ultimately hurt Brayden if there were some truth to it. There isn't."

"You think Rico knows that?"

"I think I'll trust him to figure it out. Judas Priest, Garrett, he's not the bad guy in all of this. Heck, maybe the chief isn't, either. Maybe he just wants to make sure he doesn't have a potential problem in the department that could affect morale." But Katelyn groaned when she heard herself. "Good grief, I sound like Brayden. And Joe."

"Scary, huh?" He took her empty coffee cup, crushed it and launched it into the trash can. "Wanna know what else sounds scary? According to the rumor mill, Rico will probably be promoted to lieutenant. If that happens, he'll almost certainly be put in charge of Special Investigations since Brodell's retiring. That means Rico will be *my* boss."

Katelyn gave him a weary smile. "You've got nothing to worry about. Joe's a good boss."

"Yeah, but there's no lust factor in this for me, just the concern that I might have to beat him to a pulp if he doesn't do right by Brayden."

"He'll do right by Brayden." And Katelyn was surprised to realize that she believed that with all her heart.

She was *so* in trouble.

One fantastic orgasm, and she was falling head over heels for a man she certainly shouldn't be falling for.

Because she couldn't sit still and because she noted a renewed concern on Joe's face, she got up and continued her pacing. Mercy, how long did it take to get a status report on patients?

"So the rumor mill is saying he'll be promoted?" Katelyn asked just to get her mind off that phone call.

"Apparently."

"And what about my promotion?"

It was a gutsy question because she knew Garrett wouldn't lie to her. But there was a good chance he might try to sugarcoat it.

He lifted a shoulder. "It's just a rumor mill. What the heck does it matter?"

She groaned. Definitely sugarcoating. In other words, the odds were against her. However, it seemed a trivial worry with people's lives in limbo. Later, when this was over, she'd spend some time worrying about that particular aspect of her life.

Joe finally put down the phone and came out into the conference room. He nodded a greeting at Garrett before his gaze came to hers.

"The Garcias are out of the woods," he let her know. "Both required surgery, but they're stable. The doctors are hopeful they'll make a full recovery. Not only that, we should be able to get an officer in there by evening to ask them some questions."

Katelyn took a deep breath and said a prayer of thanks. Finally, a break. Now if they'd just get one with stopping this sniper before he could do any more damage.

"That's my cue to get out of here," Garrett insisted. "Remember what I just told you, Sis."

"No, thanks," she tossed back.

He smiled in that secretive way that only Garrett and Mona Lisa could have managed, lifted a hand in farewell and headed out the door.

"A problem?" Joe asked, watching Garrett leave.

"No." She glared at Garrett until he was out of sight and then turned back to Joe. "Is this one connected to Perfect Match?"

"Afraid so. According to the minister, the couple met there at an icebreaker about three months ago."

Katelyn had known he would say that. The sniper was back to the pattern. "Did anyone see the shooter?"

Joe shook his head. "No one's come forward, but it's early. We have an evidence response team checking the scene now. Brayden is still rounding up Bruce Donovan and Fiona Shipley. We might have answers soon."

"What about Dr. Kent and Addison Merrick?" she asked.

"Supposedly they were at their residences, asleep.

But three of the four suspects live alone so any of them could have sneaked out to commit the crime. Fiona could have left the mental health facility, as well."

"Wait a minute—they weren't being watched?"

"They were, but it would have been easy enough to get out without being seen."

True. So no breaks in that particular area. "This time the shots were fairly accurate?"

"Accurate enough to wound two people, but there were strays. At least a dozen. And the minister's leg was grazed with a bullet." Joe scrubbed his fingers over his chin. "You're thinking about Donovan and those two rifles he owns?"

"Yes. Maybe he's a lousy shot despite being a gun owner? Or maybe he just wants to make people believe the sniper has a bad aim so it'll take suspicion off him?"

"Or maybe he's not the sniper." Joe stopped, apparently gave that some thought, and then looked at her. "What's going on in your head?"

"I was just thinking about how the sniper broke his own rules when he fired shots at us. We weren't a newlywed couple. Now with this latest shooting maybe he, or she, wants to remind everyone that he's really only after brides and grooms who meet at the agency. And if so, then it's obviously an important message to get across."

"That brings us back to motive." He flexed his eyebrows. "All four of our suspects have that in spades."

Katelyn might have dwelled on that a little longer if she hadn't noticed the paper in Joe's hand.

"It's the details for tomorrow," he said, obviously aware of what had caught her attention.

With everything else going on, she hadn't even thought that far in advance. She did now.

A wedding.

A fake one. With Joe. Tomorrow. Maybe what'd happened in the bathroom was coloring her opinion, but that suddenly sounded as nerve-racking as facing a gunman.

"The ceremony's scheduled for noon," Joe explained, handing her the paper. "The plan is for us to have officers and the SWAT team stake out every building around the church. We're hoping to catch the sniper before either of us get near anything resembling an aisle."

"That's something worth hoping for," she mumbled, going over the mission summary.

"Of course, we'll be armed and wearing bulletproof vests just in case he manages to get through."

Of course. "Sounds like you've covered the primary bases. Well, except for maybe clothes. Do we need anything special to wear?"

A wedding dress, for example?

"Brayden's taking care of that. He knew your size," Joe clarified when she stared at him.

"Better him than Garrett, I guess. I'd end up wearing pajamas to the church if you put him in charge of wardrobe."

He reached out and touched her cheek. A quick, nonsexual tap. "Are you okay?"

"Of course." She rubbed her arm in a *see?* gesture. "It really is just a scratch."

"I wasn't talking about your arm."

"Oh. That." It seemed a good time to stare at the floor. The ceiling. Or anything other than Joe. "That's the problem with the morning after. Things seem, well, awkward."

"Which is why I should have backed away."

Heck. She hadn't meant to put this all on his shoulders. "I heard recently that in some cultures a comment like that could be considered heresy. You're not a supreme being, Joe, and don't worry—what happened between us won't affect the job."

She hoped.

But she kept that inkling of doubt to herself.

"We're both consenting adults," Katelyn continued. "Besides, we didn't even fully sleep together. It was just...lust." There, that was the word she was looking for. "And now that we've taken the edge off, so to speak, everything should be fine."

Mercy, she was babbling.

And lying.

Really lying.

That episode hadn't taken the edge off anything. It'd just made her aware of how hot Joe could get her and how masterfully he could satisfy that heat—all without fully having sex with her.

"Are you finished?" he asked.

She nodded.

And Joe stole her breath by leaning forward and kissing her.

It was nothing like the frenzied lip lock at the apartment. It was gentle. Comforting. Easy.

So easy.

It seemed as if her bones turned to liquid. But that only made it more memorable.

"Sergeant Rico?" she heard someone say. "Sorry to interrupt."

Katelyn glanced at the door, fearing who might be there. It was Detective Dawn Davidson, who'd done the initial interrogation with Dr. Kent. Thankfully, the woman looked away while Katelyn broke the kiss. Not that it would diffuse much of anything. By afternoon, the rumor mill would have something savory to nibble on.

"Here's that info you requested. And the chief wants to see you right away." Dawn handed Joe the folder and quickly excused herself.

The chief's request would have been alarming enough news without the "right away" part. It was probably about the investigation into the favoritism allegations.

Oh, to be a fly on the wall.

Despite the command from the highest ranking man in the building, Joe didn't leave. He did, however, let her fully slip out of his embrace so he could open the folder.

"I asked the techs to tap into Perfect Match's files and give me a list of all of Fiona Shipley's dream matches, plus the matches of the murdered couple." He handed her half the pages. "Look through those."

It was a good task to eliminate any residual effects of that kiss, and the events of the night before. They were Fiona's files, and they were sizable. Twelve of twenty-three pages. Of course, she was a frequent customer so the high volume wasn't that surprising.

Katelyn skimmed through the names to see if anything popped out at her. One did. "Raul Hernandez," she read aloud. "But we already knew about him."

And he was very much dead.

"Kirk Masterson," Joe announced. "The second groom. Fiona's high on his list. Third, in fact."

Pleased that the pieces might be falling into place, Katelyn turned another page, and her attention immediately landed on a name near the middle. "Bingo. She was a match with Brad Garcia, our latest victim."

Finally!

But her *finally* wasn't much of a celebration. Joe checked his watch. "There was no answer when I called that number Fiona gave me so I passed it on to the tech guys so they could check it out. If it holds, I'll try to set up a meeting with her this afternoon. Maybe we can finish this today so we won't even need the ceremony."

"Yes, maybe." And then she remembered Joe's *other* appointment. "After your meeting with the chief, of course."

"Of course."

As if it were the most natural thing in the world, he gave her hand a gentle squeeze and walked out, leaving her with a thousands questions and not many answers. Too bad a lot of those questions centered around Joe and the fact that he was setting a scenario to put himself in danger.

Which was his job, she reminded herself.

And hers.

A job she needed to focus on if she wanted them both to walk away from this alive. Suddenly, that focus seemed a lot more critical than it ever had.

Katelyn sat down, cleared her mind and began to study Fiona Shipley's file. Maybe somewhere in all those names and information, there would be clues to bring down a killer.

Chapter 12

Apparently, right away meant something different to the chief than it did to Joe. He checked his watch—he'd been waiting in the hallway for the man for nearly a half hour. Either something unexpected had come up or else this was some sort of power play to remind Joe who was in charge.

As if he could forget that.

He owed a lot to Chief Mark Ryland. After all, the man had made Joe's transfer to Homicide possible. Ryland had also put tremendous trust in him by asking him to look into allegations regarding a fellow officer.

Well, maybe it was trust.

And maybe it was just something as simple as Ryland not wanting to make the investigation official unless he knew for certain there were improprieties. Or maybe he thought Joe would be relentless in getting to the truth. In doing so, however, Ryland had pitted him against not just Brayden but the entire O'Malley clan—including Katelyn.

Yet, it hadn't kept them apart.

Of course, probably nothing short of critical injury or death could have done that. There were times, like now, when Joe felt as if he were in the path of a speeding train, and there was nothing he could do to stop it.

Nothing he *wanted* to do to stop it.

Talk about confusing. They had a killer to catch, and his every other thought was of the redhead he'd left in the conference room. She deserved better than that and so did the victims.

"Bad morning?" he heard someone ask.

Not the chief. Brayden. He was coming down the hall directly toward Joe. And he wasn't alone. He had a big white box in one arm and a little boy squirming under the other. An O'Malley clone. He looked to be two or three and was a miniature version of Brayden.

"I've had easier," Joe answered. Something told him this one wasn't going to get much better. "Is this your son?"

"Yes. My mother came by to drop off something for Katelyn so she brought him with her. Colton, this is Sergeant Rico."

The child gave a little wave, but he was obviously far more interested in the fake police badge he was playing with than meeting Joe.

"I just heard the latest victims pulled through," Brayden commented, putting the boy down. Colton didn't waste any time exploring the fake moss in an equally fake plant. "Good news."

"Definitely. Maybe we'll be able to get something from them when they're out of recovery."

"Too bad though we haven't been able to locate Fiona Shipley. She hasn't returned to her apartment or the mental health facility, and that number she gave you was a fake. It's for some shop down on Commerce Street."

Well, so much for the woman hitting on him. Katelyn had been wrong about that. Fiona had probably been trying to make Merrick jealous. Or else maybe she was suspicious and had just wanted to get Joe off her back.

"We'll keep looking for her," Brayden continued. "But if you're still able to meet with Merrick this afternoon, maybe you can talk him into giving you info about where to contact her."

Joe nodded, not really hopeful about that. "We're definitely meeting with Merrick. In fact, we'll leave just as soon as I'm done here." Merrick probably wouldn't give up the information voluntarily, but maybe they could get it some other way. His mind kept going back to that Rolodex he'd spotted on Merrick's desk. If Merrick and Fiona had had an affair, then her number was probably in there.

It seemed more than a little awkward standing outside the chief's office and having such a civil conversation with the man he was supposed to be investigating. Brayden had to know why Joe was waiting to see Chief Ryland, but he didn't show it. No dark emotion simmering just below the surface. No pondering look. Just shop talk and an occasional fatherly glance in his son's direction.

"How badly was Katelyn hurt in the shooting?" Brayden asked.

Okay. So maybe not totally shop talk. That question threw Joe off balance. "Hardly more than a scratch on her arm. She's fine. How'd you know?"

The corner of his mouth lifted. "Lucky guess."

Right. The man had probably never relied on luck or guesses in his entire life.

Brayden did a no-no motion with his index finger when his son started to remove a flyer from the bulletin board. The child promptly obeyed and moved on to a hands-on examination of the carpet.

"If you're waiting for my permission to discipline Katelyn for not following procedure about an injury," Brayden told him, "the wait's unnecessary. You're her boss."

"Believe me, I haven't forgotten that." Well, maybe he had while they were in that bathroom. Joe shook his head. "No disciplinary action will be required. Not unless you want to aim it at me. I didn't report her injury even after she…informed me of it."

"Then you must have believed it wouldn't have an impact on this assignment."

"She convinced me that it wouldn't," Joe said, rather than lie to the man.

Brayden grunted. Not an ordinary grunt. But one to indicate he was deep in thought about something. "That day in my office, you said something about Katelyn coloring outside the lines."

Joe winced, recalling the words in perfect detail. "I meant—"

"She does. So does Garrett. It drives me nuts, but I swear they can sort through things that look like a junk pile to me. Like zooming in on Perfect Match after only one shooting. You managed to do that, too, but you used department resources. Katelyn didn't, because she worked on it while off-duty. Added to that, she was also dealing with the grief from her friend's murder. Yet, I believe she got to the right place about the same time you did?"

"She did." Joe smiled, but he made sure it didn't stay on his face too long. In this case being proud of her probably wasn't a good thing to display. "Is there advice somewhere in that?"

"There is. If it comes down to a situation where someone negates the rules, trust Katelyn."

Joe met him eye-to-eye and nodded. "With my life."

And it wasn't something he had to think about.

Nor was it a question.

Brayden gave him a pat on the back and turned to leave.

"What—no veiled threats about not hurting her?" Joe asked, certain that he deserved such threats. Heck, they might even make him feel less guilty.

Joe felt Colton tugging on his pant leg, looked down, and the boy flashed the fake badge at him. "Know what a frisk is?" Except instead of frisk, it was *fisk*. Joe winked at the kid, ruffled his hair and assured him that he did.

"That's something my brother taught him," Brayden explained, obviously not too pleased about it. He passed the box to Joe so he could scoop up his son in his arms. "And as for your relationship with my sister, Katelyn can take care of herself. I'm more concerned about you than her."

"Me?"

"Katelyn feels she has to work twice as hard and twice as long to prove herself. Added to that, she's not just married to the badge, she's in love with it. And she won't give that up for you or any other man."

Not exactly a newsflash. Joe had known and admired that about her from day one. "I wouldn't even think of asking her to give it up."

Brayden stared at him a moment, and Joe felt as if the man were sizing him up. Probably was. "It'll be interesting to watch."

"Know what interrogation is?" That from Colton. Except it was *terrogation.*

"I know." In fact, Joe thought he might be in the middle of one. A subtle one, where the lieutenant was getting him to ask the questions and then provide the answers, as well.

"What'll be interesting to watch?" Joe directed at Brayden.

"How Katelyn deals with you."

Joe got the feeling Brayden left off a portion of that observation. The flip side to that coin was how the heck was he going to deal with her?

"Wait," Joe said when Brayden started to walk away. "You forgot your box."

"It's for Katelyn. Make sure she gets it."

There it was again. That almost smug look that Brayden aimed his way. Or maybe it was a look of sympathy. If so, Joe needed it.

The door to the chief's office swung open. "Come in, Rico."

Definitely not a polite suggestion, and judging from the way the man gruffly gestured for him to sit down, this wouldn't be a long meeting.

"You're closing in on this sniper case?" Ryland asked, which was probably the only semblance of a greeting Joe would get.

"I hope. Detective O'Malley and I have been undercover on it all week."

"I heard. I'm not sure why Brayden paired you with her for this."

"She was the right person for the assignment," Joe calmly insisted.

Best to leave out the part of *how* she'd become the right person. Besides, it no longer mattered. She was the right person, and that had nothing to do with all the sexual stuff going on between them.

The chief put his elbows on the desk and steepled his fingers. "So what about these allegations?"

Now this was the part where Joe wouldn't leave anything out. "I haven't seen a single incident of favoritism, and I've been in contact with all three of the O'Malleys on this sniper case."

The fingers unsteepled, and the man made a huffing sound. "Did Katelyn O'Malley have anything to do with helping you out with that conclusion?"

Joe pondered that a moment. Not because he needed time to think about it, but he wanted to put a chokehold on the anger he felt over that question. "No," he said honestly.

"No," the chief repeated. "You sure you're not thinking below the belt on this, Rico?"

Joe tightened that chokehold a little more. "If you're questioning my objectivity—"

"I am. And don't look so damn riled about it. It wouldn't be the first time."

"It would be for me." If that didn't thoroughly

tick off the chief, the next thing he had to say probably would. "I'm attracted to Katelyn O'Malley, but I wouldn't lie about allegations because of my feelings for her. And if you think I'm the kind of man who'd do that, then you need to get someone else to do this investigation."

The chief studied him. Scowled. "I don't want anyone else. You've got a fresh eye since you haven't been here that long. Keep looking. If there's something to find, I want to know about it."

Ryland gave him a dismissal wave, which Joe ignored. Joe got to his feet, but instead of leaving, he stared down at the chief. "Have there even been any legitimate complaints against Lieutenant O'Malley?"

Ryland had already reached for his brown-bag lunch, but that stopped him. "A rumor or two."

"Rumors?" Joe couldn't help it. He cursed, and he didn't keep it under his breath. "And you're willing to put his career at risk for rumors?"

With his scowl tightening, Ryland snatched his lunch bag and dumped out the contents. He rifled through, found a Snickers bar, and ripped off the wrapper. "I'm willing to do whatever it takes to make sure morale stays high."

"That's the wrong way to go about it, sir." Joe's hands went on his hips. "I'll give you my final report when I'm finished with the sniper case, but there won't be anything in it that I haven't already said to you right here, right now."

And with that, Joe walked out, no doubt leaving any chance of his promotion behind in the chief's office.

Chapter 13

Katelyn had braced herself for just about anything to happen during their meeting with Addison Merrick. But what she hadn't anticipated was that things would get *interesting* before they even reached Perfect Match.

She stared in the side mirror, her heart rate automatically kicking up a few notches.

"You see it?" she asked Joe.

"Yes." He continued to drive, but like her, he was keeping an eye on the rearview mirror. "A black BMW."

"That's the one." At the moment it was three cars back, but it'd stayed close enough behind them since they left the parking lot of the apartment. "Did you happen to notice it when we got back from head-quarters?"

"No. You?"

She shook her head. And if it'd been there, Katelyn

almost certainly would have seen it. That's exactly the sort of flag that she'd been looking for. If the sniper was truly suspicious, then in all likelihood he or she would try to follow them.

And perhaps even try to kill them again.

"I can't read the license," Katelyn informed him. "How about you."

"Not yet, but it's Texas plates." Joe took the last turn toward Perfect Match.

So did the other car.

"Maybe it's Merrick?" she suggested.

"It's possible."

After all, Joe had called the man an hour ago and had asked him to meet them at Perfect Match, so it wasn't so much of a coincidence that they'd arrive at the same time.

But this just didn't feel like a coincidence.

She squinted against the sun and tried to get a glimpse of the driver of the BMW. However, in this case, the late morning sun was a serious hindrance. It glinted off the other car's windshield, making it impossible for Katelyn to see who was following them.

"The windows are bullet resistant," Joe reminded her. "We'll park and stay put to see what our visitor does."

It was a good plan, if the sit and wait didn't take too long. They still needed to work on contacting Fiona Shipley, and that wouldn't happen if they had to play games with the driver of that BMW.

Joe pulled into a parking space directly in front of the agency. The spots normally filled with cars were practically empty. The closed sign on the door likely had a lot to do with that, and the fact that there'd been a recent shooting in the area.

The BMW passed them and parked behind one of the few vehicles at the far end of the block.

Katelyn tried to see through the sunny glare, but she could only make out a shadowy figure. She slid her hand over her weapon. And waited.

Mercy, the waiting was the hardest part.

A stir of movement to her right caused her to glance in that direction. Merrick opened the front door and motioned for them to come in.

"Well, whoever's watching us, it's not Merrick," she mumbled. That left Fiona, Donovan or even Dr. Kent. Of course, it also left any other sicko they might not have considered. Some other client or rejected lover with an attitude problem. Still, Katelyn didn't think they were off the mark with their short list of suspects. It was more than likely one of those four. She just didn't know how to go about proving which one.

Merrick motioned again. This time, it wasn't so friendly. It was definitely a hurry-up signal. But Katelyn was fairly sure that no matter how frantic the man's signals got, Joe wouldn't let either of them step out of the car with that BMW still lurking about.

With a squeal of tires, the BMW backed up just enough so it could circle around to a side street, and it sped away.

"Should we pursue?" she asked Joe.

"No. Let's stick with the plan. If it follows us when we come out, we'll try to run the plates to see who's interested in what we're doing."

She smiled at Merrick and held up her index finger in a one-minute gesture. The man ducked back inside.

That didn't mean, however, that he wouldn't be spying on them from the window.

"This'll be a quick in and out," Joe said, going over the rules. "We tell Merrick about the wedding being set for tomorrow and see if he'll give us Fiona's number under the guise of us inviting her to the ceremony. And that's it. Those two things, and we get out of there."

While he checked his weapon, Katelyn stared at the building that housed Perfect Match. But not just the building. The alley up the street where someone had tried to gun them down. Yes. She definitely understood Joe's insistence of a quick in and out. Looking at that spot made her arm ache, and it didn't do much for the rest of her, either.

"What if Merrick won't tell us how to get in touch with Fiona?" she asked.

He shrugged. "The rules still apply here."

Not exactly the answer she wanted to hear. "I swear I'm going to needlepoint that on a pillow."

"No detours, Katelyn. No shortcuts." That was as much of an order as it was a warning, and void of sarcasm or humor. "This isn't the time to try to bring down a killer. We've got a plan set in motion to do that."

"Okay, okay. It just makes me crazy to think of this piece of slime walking around free while we've got two people dead and two more seriously wounded."

"I know, and we'll get the person responsible."

That soothed her a little, but not nearly enough. Even though her brain told her the shootings weren't her fault, there was still the sickening feeling that she should have been able to stop it. People were hurt because she'd failed. No words, even those coming from Joe, could ease that.

Worse, that dread had spread to other areas.

She caught his arm when he started to open the door. Unfortunately, she hadn't really thought beyond that. Well, she had, but Katelyn hadn't quite figured out how to convey the things she was feeling. "Let me just blurt this out because I don't think I can make it sound palatable. You won't take any unnecessary risks, right?"

He angled his head to stare at her. "What's this all about?"

"I've already said it won't make sense. There's just this...fear. There, I've said it. I'm afraid. Not for me, but for you. And that's so stupid because you're a cop."

Joe did something with his mouth. Not really a gape but his version of it. "You're worried about me?"

Disgusted with herself, she nodded. She would never believe anyone who told her that sex didn't change things between a man and a woman. Except she'd had sex with other men, and it *hadn't* changed things. Not like this, anyway.

Nothing had ever changed things like this.

He slid his arm around her and pulled her to him. "I can take care of myself, Katelyn. You can take care of yourself. And when all else fails, we both make great backups."

"It's that fail part that's giving me some trouble here. It can't happen, okay?"

He nodded. "Anything else before we go in there?"

Oh, she knew what he was getting at. His meeting with the chief. It was a bit of unfinished business that would have to remain unfinished a little longer. "Nothing else." Katelyn took a deep breath. "Let's do this."

She made yet another mental check of her weapons and communicator as they stepped from the car. Joe had parked close enough so they only had a few steps before they made it to the door. Moving straight into their lovers' pose, they latched on to each other.

"Kate, Joe," Merrick greeted, opening the door and motioning for them to come in. "I was surprised to get your call. I figured all our clients had been scared off by the latest shooting."

"Oh?" And that was all Joe said. All in all, it was a good leading question.

"You haven't heard?" Merrick shook his head. "It's been all over the news. There was another couple injured last night by this so-called Veiled Sniper. Unfortunately, they were former clients."

Joe nodded. Katelyn mumbled something about how horrible it all was. She certainly didn't have to fake that part.

Merrick went to the cooler tucked away in the corner and helped himself to not one but two cups of water. While he was there, he pressed some buttons on a wall pad, and music began to play. A heavy, sensual sax that didn't exactly mesh with the adrenaline surging through her.

"If you don't mind, I'd like to make this visit quick," Merrick continued. "The security guard that I hired part-time couldn't come in today. He's sick. So I'd rather not stay around here too long."

"We won't keep you. We just wanted to invite you to the wedding." Joe produced a mock invitation from his pocket. "It's tomorrow. That's short notice, we know, but we'd love for you to be there to celebrate with us."

"And not just you," Katelyn added, making sure she sounded happy and not suspicious. "We want Bruce Donovan and all the other nice people we've met here to come, as well." She snapped her fingers. "Including Fiona Shipley. I'm not sure if you know her, but Joe and she chatted."

Merrick's smile faded, and he gripped the invitation with far more force than necessary.

"Fiona was so friendly," Joe added when Merrick didn't say anything. "But I don't know how to get in touch with her. I thought maybe you'd have her number so we could call her?"

"Sorry. I'm not allowed to give out that kind of information. Tell you what though—if I see Fiona, I'll tell her. And I'll make sure Bruce gets the word, too. This might be just what we need to lighten the mood around here." He studied the invitation. "You're not worried though? I mean, because of these other shootings."

It was on the tip of Katelyn's tongue to lie, but the door behind them flew open. Only because she saw Joe reach for his gun, she forced herself not to go for hers. Not immediately anyway. That way, if it were some legitimate visitor, it wouldn't totally blow their cover for both of them to draw. One gun they could justify. Maybe.

Instead, Katelyn kept her attention firmly on Merrick in case he planned to use this as some kind of diversion to try to kill them. Merrick's eyes widened when he caught sight of Joe's weapon.

Dr. Allen Kent stepped in.

No widening of his eyes. But he did stop. He glanced at the gun. Joe. Her. And then at Merrick.

"What's going on here?" Kent demanded. "Is this some kind of robbery?"

Joe didn't exactly relax. Nor did he lower his gun. "No robbery."

It was obviously time for damage control. "We're a little shaken." Katelyn's voice quivered slightly, which although unplanned contributed to the proof that the *shaken* part wasn't all facade. She caught Joe's wrist and lowered his hand, and his weapon, to his side. "It's the shootings."

Kent nodded. "I heard. In fact, the cops came by to see me this morning." He fired a glare at Merrick. "They asked for an alibi. Can you believe that? They wanted me to provide an alibi. I live alone for Christ's sake. Am I supposed to have friends sleep over just so I won't be accused of some crime?"

"I think they're questioning anyone associated with Perfect Match," Katelyn provided. "Joe and I had to go in this morning, as well."

Kent glanced at her again, but this time it didn't stay a glance. He combed his gaze over her from head to toe. "Don't I know you?"

Oh, mercy.

That was not what she wanted to hear right now. Beside her, she felt Joe's arm stiffen. He was no doubt thinking the same thing she was. That maybe Kent had somehow connected her to Gail after all. If so, they were in trouble.

Forcing herself to remain calm, Katelyn pretended to study his face. "Maybe we've met. I've been here a couple of times. In fact, my fiancé and I met right here at Perfect Match." For good measure she thrust out her hand so he could see the engagement ring.

"Very nice," he said without even looking at it.

"We're here to invite Addison to the wedding," Joe explained. "And Fiona Shipley."

At first, she was surprised that Joe had included the woman's name, but she soon realized it was a smart thing to do.

Kent's mouth eased into a sarcastic smile. "Trust me, you don't want to invite Fiona. She's not exactly wedding guest material."

"You know her?" Joe asked.

But the answer didn't come from Kent, but from Merrick after he had shared a glance with Kent. "We both know her. I'm afraid Fiona sometimes has trouble distinguishing reality from fantasy. She's no longer a client here. That's the main reason I had security here the night of the icebreaker. Fiona has a tendency to show up uninvited."

"She seemed nice enough when I spoke to her," Joe insisted. "And I told her I'd invite her to the wedding. I'd really like to get in touch with her."

There was a long silence, and Katelyn didn't even try to fill it in with useless chitchat. Something unspoken passed between Kent and Merrick.

"I'll get the number for you," Merrick announced.

He turned and went down the hall, presumably to his office. Katelyn didn't take any chances. She positioned herself so that Joe would be able to return fire if the man came back not with an address but with a gun.

Kent picked up a pen and a sheet of note paper from the receptionist's desk. He wrote something down and then handed the paper to Joe. "That's Fiona's cell phone number. I doubt Addison has it. And don't worry. I'm not violating any doctor-patient confidentiality since I've never seen Fiona professionally. The truth is, we met here one evening and exchanged numbers. It didn't work out between us, but she continues to call dozens of times each day."

Joe stuffed the piece of paper into his pocket. "Thanks."

"I'm not doing you any favors," Kent insisted. "The truth is I'm hoping that if the two of you offer Fiona friendship, it'll be a more positive direction for her."

"And maybe she'll stop calling you?" Joe tossed back.

A little flash of anger danced through Kent's eyes before he smiled. "That, too."

Merrick returned and handed Joe a piece of paper as well, but when Katelyn glanced at the number, she realized it wasn't the same one Kent had given them. Maybe one of them would pan out.

"Now, if you'll excuse us," Kent said, taking Merrick's arm. "Addison and I have some things to discuss in private. Good luck with your wedding plans."

Joe and Katelyn started for the door, but he stopped as soon as the two men disappeared into the hall.

"You think Kent drives a black BMW?" Katelyn whispered over the music.

"We'll know soon enough."

He glanced at the corridor on the other side of the room, and she knew what he was thinking. On the pretense of going to the ladies' room, she'd used that corridor to circle around the back of the building so she could get to Merrick's office.

"I can pretend to go to the bathroom," Katelyn suggested. "I might be able to hear what they're discussing."

Joe obviously thought about it but then shook his head. "It's too risky."

"Not if you wander over toward that hall so you could keep an eye on Merrick's office. That way, you can alert me if they come out. And if they're suspicious, you can just say you're waiting for me to get out of the ladies' room. In the meantime, you can call Fiona and check on vehicles registered to Dr. Kent."

"It's still risky."

"So is waiting for the sniper to strike again. I'm betting those two know something."

"Yeah." And he repeated it before he angled his eyes in her direction. "Tell me you can take care of yourself."

Katelyn smiled. Not from joy, exactly. But from the weirdness of the moment. She'd succeeded in winning him over to her impromptu plan, but it didn't exactly leave her feeling victorious. "I'll be careful. You do the same. I'll keep my communicator on in case you need me."

Katelyn gave him one last look, one that she hoped calmed his concerns. But there was nothing calm about what she was feeling.

She drew her weapon, shielding it against her leg and started down the corridor past offices on both sides, the restrooms and then into the back bend of the U-shaped network of hallways. Thankfully, there weren't any employees or clients lingering around.

But had someone turned up the music? The sensual sound of the sax no longer seemed so sensual. It just seemed loud. Overpowering, actually. Or maybe it was because the beat now matched the heartbeat drumming in her ears.

"Everything okay?" Katelyn whispered into her communicator.

"They haven't come out," Joe let her know.

She paused at the final section of the hall that was only about ten yards from Merrick's office and took a quick look around the corner. She caught a glimpse of Joe at the end of the hall before she ducked back.

"Great," she mumbled under her breath.

Even with the music, she should have heard shouting or even a normal conversation between Merrick and Kent. Kent had certainly done some shouting the last time he was there. It was Murphy's Law that he wouldn't cooperate in the volume department today. That meant she needed to get closer.

It wasn't an actual sound that alerted her, but something did. Something that sent her spinning to the side.

Everything happened fast.

Too fast for her to go on the offensive. The man came out from one of the rooms and rammed his body against hers, slamming her against the wall. Her injured arm hit first, and the pain was immediate and searing. Katelyn saw stars.

Another body slam. He threw the full force of his weight right into her. The impact knocked the breath out of her, and while she was fighting to pull air into her lungs, Katelyn got a good look at her attacker's face.

It was Bruce Donovan.

He clamped his hand around the front of her throat. But not to try to choke her, she soon learned. He ripped the communicator from beneath her collar.

"I knew there was something wrong about you," he snarled. "Who the hell are you?"

Katelyn knew she had to act fast. Joe was no doubt already on his way, and she didn't want him walking in on this, especially since he'd have to go past Merrick and Kent first. This was not the time for a gun battle.

Ignoring the pain in her arm and lungs, Katelyn brought up her leg, and using as much force as she could marshal, she kneed Donovan in the groin. He howled in pain and immediately released the grip he had on her.

She didn't stop there.

Katelyn grabbed his forearm and slung him forward so that he was the one against the wall. Face-first. A quick pat down, and she discovered he wasn't armed.

"Kate?" she heard Joe call out.

But that wasn't all she heard. She heard footsteps coming from the other direction, as well. They were all converging toward her.

She kept her forearm pressed against Donovan's back and snatched up her gun. That couple of moments must have given him his second wind because he tried to come at her again. He whirled around, his fist ready to bash her right in the face.

"Kate!" Joe yelled.

She was vaguely aware of Joe rounding the corner. But just vaguely. Thankfully, he didn't dive in and pull a knight-in-shining-armor maneuver. He stayed back and let her do her job.

Katelyn ducked.

Donovan's attempted jab breezed past her head, and in the same motion, she delivered a snap kick to his stomach. She didn't give him a chance to get a second wind. Recoiling, she pivoted and landed another kicking blow to the back of his legs. Donovan went down to the floor, hard, gasping for breath.

It took everything inside her not to slam him right back against that wall and read him his rights. But that wasn't a smart thing to do. There was still a chance that Joe and she could keep their cover intact. If not, then they were in trouble because they were in the same building with three of their four murder suspects.

Doing some light gasping of her own, Katelyn glanced around to get her bearings. Joe was on one side, his weapon drawn. On the other side were Dr. Kent and Merrick. They stood there in stunned silence.

"Are you okay?" Joe asked. The muscles in his jaw had turned to iron. He looked ready to rip Donovan limb from limb.

Katelyn nodded. "He tried to assault me. He wasn't successful." And after delivering that news to Joe, she made certain she added a stern look that hopefully would convince him to stay in cover. "Guess all that self-defense training finally came in handy."

"She's got a gun," Donovan managed to say. He struggled to get to his feet. Staggered. And dropped back to his knees.

Katelyn angled her body so she could deliver another snap kick if necessary. "Good thing too, huh? A woman never knows when she'll need a gun."

Merrick came closer. "What's going on here?" Maybe the adrenaline was clouding her senses, but Katelyn couldn't tell if he was concerned for her, or for Donovan.

"I think she's the sniper," Donovan snarled.

Oh, great.

It was either fast thinking on his part to save his butt, or else he genuinely believed that. If it was the latter, it would explain why he'd come after her in the first place. But Katelyn wasn't about to stake her life on anything that Donovan said. Even if he wasn't the sniper, the man was slime.

"She's wearing some kind of wire." Donovan leaned into the wall so he could stand. Not easily. However, he eventually got to his feet.

"This?" Katelyn made a point of showing both Merrick and Kent her communicator when she picked it up from the floor. "It's not a wire. It's a walkie-talkie, a way for Joe and me to stay in touch when we can't be together. Call me overly devoted, but I like being able to talk with the man I love 24/7."

Joe gave a confirming nod, and turned back his collar so they could see his communicator, as well.

There were several tense seconds, several uncomfortable glances between Kent and Merrick before Merrick finally moved and took Bruce's arm. "Let's discuss this in my office."

"Wait," Donovan said, holding his ground. He fired a nasty glare at her. "If she's not the sniper, then what the hell was she doing sneaking around back here?"

"I was looking for the bathroom," Katelyn quickly provided. No glare for her. She made sure she looked upset, which wasn't that difficult considering what had just gone down. Her heart was still racing from the fight.

More tense moments. Joe walked closer to stand right by her side. Maybe for comfort. Or maybe he just wanted to be in a better position to fire if it came down to that.

"I'm sorry this happened, Kate," Merrick finally said. "I hope you'll accept my apology." And he didn't just say it, either. He *appeared* to be sorry. Of course, that sincerity could have been for all the wrong reasons. "Now, if you'll excuse me, I need to talk with Bruce in private. I trust the two of you can see yourselves out."

Yes, they could do that, but it meant turning their backs on at least one potential killer. Still, leaving was about the only way to maintain their cover. Joe obviously felt the same. He didn't reholster his gun, nor did he take her arm—a move that would have hampered her ability to return fire. However, he did gesture with his head for them to get moving.

Katelyn complied. But she glanced over her shoulder. And neither of them stopped glancing until they were out of the building and in the car.

Joe started the engine and drove away. He made it a full block before he slid his arm around her and pulled her to him. The muscles in his body were still rock-hard, and that jaw told her that he was far from winning the battle with adrenaline.

"Thanks for not jumping in fists first back there when you saw me with Donovan."

It seemed as if several times he changed his mind about what to say. "You didn't appear to need me to jump in."

Oh, that cost him. The words were right. So was the sentiment. However, he'd not said it easily. "I didn't, but Garrett forgets that sometimes."

"I can see why." That was all he said for the next couple of seconds. "Just don't expect me to forget it again if Donovan comes near you."

Chapter 14

Katelyn O'Malley slept the same way she did everything else in life—thoroughly.

At first, she'd balked at his idea of resting while they waited for Fiona to return his call, but once Joe had coaxed her into lying down on the sofa, she'd fallen asleep within minutes. He even managed to take a nap in the adjacent chair. Since they'd gotten virtually no sleep the night before, it was a necessity. He wanted to be as alert as possible for the meeting with Fiona.

And for anything else they might face today.

A lot of things had gone wrong at Perfect Match, and that was an understatement. It could have been much worse. When Donovan came after Katelyn, she'd fought him off, subdued him—all without blowing her cover.

That pissed Joe off.

Katelyn can take care of herself, Brayden had told him. It was true. She could. That didn't mean, however, that she couldn't be hurt. It sure as heck didn't mean she was invincible.

Rather than identify herself to Donovan as a police officer, read the scum his rights and/or take him down the hard way, she'd risked everything. Part of him, the cop part, greatly admired her devotion to duty. But the rest of him just wanted to grab her by the shoulders, give her a hard shake and yell at her for taking chances like that with her life.

Not that yelling would do any good, but at least then she'd know…

…what?

Joe stopped and brooded over that for a moment.

And he decided it wouldn't be a good idea to finish that thought.

He stood, brushed a loose strand of hair from her face and forced his attention away from her mouth— which somehow managed to look both innocent and sensual at the same time. He went into the bathroom so he could call headquarters.

He reached Detective Davidson who in turn transferred his call to Garrett, who'd apparently been doing the trace on the vehicle that'd followed them. Not exactly a duty in Garrett's job description. Well, not unless the case had strayed over into Special Investigations.

"Please tell me you volunteered for this extra work, Sergeant O'Malley," Joe commented.

"What can I say? I'm a glutton for cyber searches," he said sarcastically, but the sarcastic tone quickly faded. "Davidson's working on the wedding details so I figured I'd pitch in and do my part."

In this case, his part was over and above. "Thanks."

"Let's just say you owe me and leave it at that." He didn't give Joe a chance to ask him to elaborate. "Okay, here goes. There are hundreds of black BMWs registered to owners who live in the area. Guess that's not a surprise. So I did some cross-referencing with your suspects and got lucky. One of them has a late model black BMW."

"Bruce Donovan," Joe provided.

"You got it. I guess that's not a surprise either?"

"Not really. He came after Katelyn while we were visiting Merrick."

There was a short pause. "Define *came after Katelyn*."

Joe hoped this sounded better aloud, but he wasn't counting on it. "Donovan claimed he thought she was the sniper so he tried to *apprehend* her."

Another pause, a long one, and Joe didn't need to see the man's expression to know that Garrett was not happy with this latest development. "She wasn't hurt?"

"No." But the images of her pulverizing Donovan didn't do much to ease that tight fist around his heart. If she hadn't ducked, if she'd been just an inch or two out of position to deliver those snap kicks, if the man had been a fraction faster, then…

There it was again.

Those running commentaries in his head that he really didn't want to finish. But these wouldn't back off. The truth was, even if all those other things had happened, she would have no doubt found a way to kick Donovan's butt. Katelyn wouldn't have given up.

That last part didn't exactly make him feel better, either.

"She handled Donovan on her own?" Garrett asked.

"Yeah." Joe braced himself for Garrett's lecture that would no doubt contain a lot of profanity and a thorough dressing down for not protecting his sister.

A lecture that didn't come.

"She wouldn't have *appreciated* the help anyway," Garrett grumbled.

"That was my guess, too."

Now there was some profanity, but it wasn't aimed at Joe. "It doesn't make it any easier to watch."

Joe settled for a "No."

The conversation might have lacked quantity, but at the end of the next pause, Joe felt as if he'd reached some sort of truce with Katelyn's brother. It was a truce he hadn't even realized he wanted until it happened.

"So the next step is to speak to Fiona Shipley?" Garrett asked, getting them back into a comfort zone they both understood—the job.

"I'm waiting for her to return my call now." He checked his watch. That wait was now on its third hour. "I got her cell number from Dr. Kent and left her a message."

"Kent, huh? That's an interesting source for that particular bit of info."

Yes, Joe thought so, as well. "Sometimes, Garrett, I wonder if all four of them aren't in on it. Like some conspiracy to cover up something that got botched either at Perfect Match or Kent's office. They just keep coiling and winding around each other like a nest of vipers."

If he thought for one minute it would stop the sniper, Joe would haul all of them in and lock them up for as long as possible. Without physical evidence to connect them to the crimes, however, that lockup wouldn't last long. They'd lawyer up and be out before the ink dried on the paperwork.

There was a tap at the door, and he opened it to find Katelyn standing there. "Hello, Garrett," she said, leaning closer to the phone. "Thin walls," she added when Joe just looked at her.

"Thanks for the BMW info," he told Garrett. "I'll let you know how it goes with Fiona."

"*If* it goes," Katelyn corrected when he hung up.

"It'll go." But Joe was beginning to doubt it himself. If she didn't call soon, they'd have to look for her. Fiona was the one player in all of this that they hadn't had a real chance to question. Joe had absolutely no proof, but the feeling in his gut told him that she had information that could help them get a handle on this case.

Or else she was the killer.

But either way, he needed to talk to her. With the wedding only a day away, that talk had to come soon.

Joe watched as Katelyn peeled off her jacket, and in the process he felt his body rev up for all sorts of carnal possibilities. A glimpse of her lacy bra egged those possibilities on even more. But they came to a quick crash and burn when she reached for the first aid kit.

"Another *scratch?*" he asked. Joe tried to keep emotion out of his voice, but the battle was lost before he opened his mouth.

Katelyn shook her head. "Same one."

She quickly tossed the old bandage in the trash. It wasn't so fast that Joe didn't see the fresh blood.

"That fight with Donovan," he mumbled.

Hell.

"It's no big deal." She wiped the wound with antiseptic, hissed out a breath at the inevitable sting and put on a fresh bandage. "I just didn't want to get any blood on the wedding dress when I try it on to make sure it fits."

He was glad Garrett wasn't around to hear that one. Heck, he didn't even want to hear it, so he focused on the second part of her oh-so-casual comment that wasn't anywhere in the realm of being casual. "What wedding dress?"

She turned and went into the bedroom. "It was in that box Brayden gave you."

And now it was on the bed. The corner of the large rectangular box was lifted slightly, and Joe caught a glimpse of ivory silk.

"Look the other way," she instructed. "I'm about to strip down to my underwear."

His body revved up again. "Modest?" Hard to believe, especially since they had a go at each other in the bathroom the night before.

"No. Considering you've already seen me naked, modesty would be pointless. I just don't want you looking for any bruises that Donovan might have left on me."

Another immediate halt on the revving. With lots of effort, he could ignore the blood comment but not that one. "Damn it, Katelyn, did he hurt you?"

"No, but he likely bruised me when he slammed me against the wall." She discarded her top on the bed and unzipped her skirt. "Don't worry, I'm positive his bumps and bruises outnumber mine, and I seriously doubt he'll be able to sit for a while."

That didn't help one bit. "This isn't a contest. Or a joking matter."

Huffing, she sat down on the edge of the bed and pulled the dress from the box. But her attention wasn't on the heap of silk, lace and seed pearls. Her eyes lifted to connect with his. "Don't you think I know that? Care to guess what was going through my mind while I was ramming my knee into Donovan's reproductive organs? I was thinking, no, *worrying* about you. I was afraid if you came in with guns blazing and fists flying, you'd get hurt."

"Guns blazing and fists flying?" Joe was on the verge of telling her that those things would have never happened. *Never*. But it was too uncomfortably close to a lie. The truth was he'd considered blazing guns, flying fists and any other extreme force when he saw Donovan swing that punch at Katelyn.

"Great," she mumbled. "Brayden didn't pick this out. This is my mother's dress."

It took Joe a moment to pound down the anger he was still feeling over those possible bruises, but from the groan that Katelyn made, it was obvious they had another problem to deal with first.

"It's a message," she went on. "Like the one in that scene from *The Godfather* when they sent the fish wrapped up in the newspaper."

Joe shook his head, sure he'd missed something. "I don't make the connection."

"It's my mother's way of saying 'I know you won't do anything that'll result in bullet holes or bloodstains

n this wedding dress since it's practically a family
eirloom." Katelyn gave a heavy sigh. "She's wor-
ied about me."

"Well, that makes two of us."

Except he knew it wasn't limited to such a small
umber. There was Brayden, Garrett and probably a
whole multitude of other O'Malleys. Joe would have
oved to say that their concern wasn't warranted. But
t was. In less than twenty-four hours, the undercover
assignment would take them in the direction of the
church—and the sniper.

He was still in knots about that when he felt her
fingertip skim over his stomach. His bare stomach.
'Your button's undone," she said, remedying that for
him. Well, she remedied it after another brush of her
fingertip.

"You're trying to distract me from those possible
bruises," he let her know.

"Yes, I am." She smiled, undid the button again and
planted a kiss on his stomach. "Is it working?"

He fought to hang on to the anger a little longer,
but it slipped away. "Like a charm." And because
the distraction felt so damn good, he slid his finger
over the lacy edge of her bra. White lace. Against
her cream-colored skin. Talk about erotic. Of course,
it was highly possible it was erotic simply because
it was Katelyn's bra, Katelyn's breast. "What can I
say—I'm easy."

"You're a lot of things, Sergeant Joseph Luis Rico,
but easy isn't one of them. In fact, I'd say you're the
hardest thing in my life right now. And no, there are
no raunchy hidden meanings in that."

Joe smiled anyway and pushed the thoughts of

bruises and snipers aside when she grabbed a hand
ful of his shirt and hauled him onto the bed with her
He landed on top of her, but like the previous night, she
quickly did something about that. Katelyn shifted, roll
ing them both over the soft mattress, and when she'e
finished the rolling she was on top, straddling him.

"Control issues?" he asked.

But her mouth was already swooping down on his
Fast. A hungry kiss that left no doubt that she wasn't
after conversation. It was next to impossible to argue
with that, even though he should be arguing. Instead
he was just thankful he'd picked up some condoms
when he'd filled up the car with gas at the nearby convenience store.

Joe reached up, opened the front closure on her bra
and had the satisfaction of her breasts spilling out into
his hands. She was small. Firm.

Perfect.

He cupped one, then the other and ran his thumbs
over her nipples. It was obvious she enjoyed it from
the way her mouth opened, and the soft sound of pleasure she made.

Katelyn didn't take the time to savor that pleasure,
however. She pulled off her skirt, dragging it up and
over her head and flinging it aside. No pause. No hesitation. She went after his belt and zipper. And Joe surprised her, and himself, by catching on to her wrist
to stop her.

"Control issues?" he repeated. "Claustrophobia? Is
that why you like to be on top?"

She gave him an *all right, here goes* huff. "The mis-
sionary stuff is just a little scary for me, okay? It's that
whole being passive part."

"Passive?" Sex with Katelyn was anything but passive.

Another flustered huff. And a hesitation. "It just doesn't feel right. Or fair. It's almost no work being on the bottom, but yet I'd still get all the...benefits."

Interesting. She carried her belief in the bedroom that she had to work twice as hard and twice as long to get what she wanted.

As her cue that the conversation was over, she leaned down and went after his neck with a kiss. She didn't stop there. Katelyn slid her hand over the front of his pants, a move that had Joe going from seriously aroused to rock-hard. "But if it's something you want—"

Joe ended that with a kiss of his own. "The only thing I want is you, Katelyn."

That slowed her down. She lifted her head, and her gaze met his. In the depth of those green eyes, there was concern that he was sure was mirrored in his. Concern they might have actually discussed.

If his cell phone hadn't rung.

Cursing, she rolled off him so he could snatch the ringing annoyance that was still clipped to his belt. "Hello," he barked. And this had better be important. Critical, even.

"Joe?" the woman said.

Even with the untimely interruption and his reaction to it, it only took him a split second to realize it was Fiona Shipley. He said the woman's name aloud so that Katelyn would know, as well. She moved closer to him so she could hear the conversation.

There wasn't much to hear.

"I'll meet you at the coffee shop at the intersection

of Highway 1604 and San Pedro," Fiona instructed. "You know the place?"

"I'll find it."

"Good. I'll see you in one hour. And Joe? My advice is to watch your back. Someone's been following me. I think it might be this sniper."

And with that, Fiona hung up.

"I guess it won't do any good to remind you this could be a trap?" Katelyn asked.

Joe shook his head, his attention not on her but on driving through the massive parking lot that serviced not just the coffee shop but at least a half dozen other businesses. "What would you do if Merrick, Kent or even, heaven forbid, Donovan called and asked you to meet them?"

It was a cheap—and incredibly effective—way to win an argument.

She'd go, of course. With backup. Which Joe had, since there was no way she'd let him do this alone. That's why Katelyn had worn jeans and a T-shirt and stuffed her hair beneath a Rangers baseball cap. It was as close to a disguise as she could get on such short notice. The plan they'd put together on the drive over was for her to do surveillance from the car and alert him via the communicator if anyone suspicious approached the place.

"What about Fiona's *someone's been following me. I think it might be this sniper* comment?" Katelyn reminded him. "Think it's true?"

"Could be."

And that was all the more reason to stay alert. She

didn't want the sniper or anyone else sneaking up on them.

Joe drove slowly past Java Dan's. It wasn't exactly quaint and cozy with the massive floor-to-ceiling windows that fronted the place. Even though there were only about a half dozen customers, with those windows and jammed parking lot, it'd be next to impossible to make sure someone didn't pull out a rifle and start firing right through that glass.

"I'll sit in a booth near the back," Joe commented, obviously addressing her concern before Katelyn could even voice it. Something he did often. It was almost as if they could read each other's minds.

Almost.

The big exception to that was all the personal stuff going on between them. Other than his *the only thing I want is you, Katelyn* comment on the bed, they hadn't talked a lot about, well, their feelings.

She took the blame for that though.

She'd done the majority of the stonewalling, but she wouldn't be able to keep it up. Eventually, they'd be alone. Eventually, the phone wouldn't ring, and they'd get around to having that mind-blowing sex that she'd been fantasizing about. In addition to a thoroughly enjoyable experience, which it would certainly be, it'd create a bond between them that even her surly attitude and devotion to the badge might not be able to break.

Still, that wouldn't stop her.

Whatever was brewing between them wouldn't be put off by her doubts. Or her fears.

Frustrated at her inability to keep her mind on the mission, Katelyn checked the time. Since they'd left not long after Fiona's call, they still had a good fifteen minutes to spare. Well, unless the woman was the always-arrive-early type like Katelyn was. If so, then Ms. Shipley might come walking up at any moment.

She glanced in the vanity mirror to make sure her too-visible hair hadn't escaped the cap, and while she was tucking and hiding, something occurred to her. "How about this? I'll take one of the booths on the right, facing the window. That way, I can make sure no one comes in unannounced. You take Fiona to a booth on the other side of the shop."

"And what if she recognizes you?" Joe asked.

"That's what outstretched newspapers are for. I'll buy one on my way in. Look," Katelyn added when she saw the hesitancy in his eyes. "This might be the only chance we get to talk to Fiona. She might know something that can help us stop the sniper."

Joe glanced at the coffee shop. At her. And then at those windows. He shook his head. "Don't make me regret this."

Too bad she couldn't promise him that.

Katelyn wished him good luck and got out before he could change his mind. Keeping a vigilant watch and trying to stay inconspicuous, she hurried across the parking lot and into the shop. As planned, she bought a paper and ducked into one of the booths.

And waited.

Joe came in several minutes later, and he took the only booth that was available on the far side of the room. He was visible, but barely. Katelyn had to scrunch herself in the corner to keep him and the windows in sight.

"Equipment check," she whispered into her communicator.

"I hear you," Joe responded.

So the equipment cooperated. Hopefully, everything else would. She hated stakeouts in public places. There were just too many factors she couldn't control.

The door finally swung open, and Fiona walked in. Obviously this was not one of her better appearance days. Dressed all in dark colors, she had her hair pulled back and was wearing a pair of large-lens sunglasses.

"Joe," Fiona greeted.

Katelyn had a nervous moment when the waiter blocked her line of sight, but thankfully Joe and Fiona ordered quickly, and the man moved.

"I guess you know about the other couple who were shot last night?" Katelyn heard Joe ask the woman right away.

Fiona nodded and pulled off her sunglasses. Katelyn carefully examined her expression now that she could see Fiona's eyes. Her attention wasn't on Joe but the windows. Yes. She was definitely watching her back.

"Both survived," Joe continued. "A lot better outcome than the first couple, that's for sure. What were their names? Something like Ralph and Gail?"

"Raul," Fiona corrected. "We dated, briefly."

Joe didn't respond to that right away. He waited until after they had their coffee, and he took a long sip. It was a good strategy. Fiona was obviously uncomfortable with the silence and began to fidget with her sunglasses.

"The police questioned me about the deaths," Joe finally said. "I guess they did the same to you?"

"I've been, uh, unavailable." Fiona glanced out the window again. Katelyn did the same.

A longer pause this time for Joe. "You said something on the phone about being followed?"

"I think it might be the sniper." But then she immediately shook her head. "Or else it's Addison Merrick. That's one of the reasons I agreed to see you. I noticed you've been visiting him a lot—"

"How did you know that?"

A spark of surprise. Followed by more fidgeting. Another glance out the window. A glance that turned into a full stare. Katelyn followed the woman's gaze to see what had captured her attention and saw the black BMW cruise by.

Judas Priest.

"The BMW's back," Katelyn whispered into the communicator. She moved out to the edge of the seat in case she had to use her weapon.

"You were saying something about Addison," Joe prompted Fiona.

She nodded and moistened her lips. "I wondered if he'd said anything to you about me?"

The car turned, circled and came back toward the coffee shop. If it was Donovan, he was either stupid or desperate. But the real question was, what had made him want to follow Fiona?

Or had he actually followed Joe and her?

Of course, there was also the stomach-churning possibility that it wasn't Donovan at all. Maybe Donovan wasn't the only person with access to a black BMW. Maybe it was Merrick. And maybe Fiona had been right, and it was the sniper following her.

If so, this visit could turn deadly in a hurry.

"Addison's mentioned you a couple of times," Joe told her. Practically a lie, but it seemed to get Fiona's concentration back on him. It also helped her temporary attention deficit when the car darted out of sight again.

"Addison and I started dating after his fiancée broke off their engagement." She moistened her lips again and ran her index finger over her eyebrow. "He was devastated, said he needed me. He even told me that he was in love with me."

"And then what happened?" Joe asked.

She shrugged. "I don't know. I really don't. He changed, said it wasn't right for him to see me since I was a client. He said he didn't want something like that getting back to his father."

Yes. Merrick definitely wouldn't want that. From all accounts, his father wouldn't have approved of anything that might be detrimental to the business.

"Sometimes, I wonder if Addison's the Veiled Sniper," Fiona said softly. "I mean, all three of those grooms were men I once dated."

"Push that button," Katelyn whispered to Joe, knowing he would have probably jumped on it anyway.

But the pushing wasn't even necessary. Fiona continued on her own. "I think Addison needs help."

"Yeah. I've heard he's in therapy with Dr. Kent," Joe answered.

Fiona made a sound. A soft burst of sarcasm that didn't contain any humor. "Now, there's a pair. The sick trying to heal the sick." Her gaze flew to the window again. "I believe Addison's mentally unstable."

The BMW was back, slowly weaving its way through the parking lot like some demon on the prowl. Those tinted windows only made it seem more menacing.

"What makes you say that?" Joe asked, drawing Fiona's attention back to him.

"He threatened to kill me. Just two weeks ago, I went to the icebreaker at Perfect Match, and he ordered me out. He said he was going to hire a security guard and if I came back, he'd have the guard take care of me. Is that unstable enough for you?" Fiona snatched up her purse but left her sunglasses lying on the table. "Excuse me. I need to go to the ladies' room."

Unfortunately, the ladies' room was close to the booth where Katelyn was sitting. While she tried to keep an eye on the car and Fiona, she lifted the newspaper high enough so the woman couldn't see her face. It worked. Maybe because Fiona was in a serious hurry.

"Where's the BMW?" she heard Joe whisper through the communicator.

"Still circling the place. Should I call a cruiser to pull him over?"

"No. There's no law against driving around a parking lot. Plus, I don't want him to think we have any connection to the police."

Both good points, but it didn't make it any easier to sit there and watch him. "You think Fiona's opinion of Merrick is an act?"

"Could be. She's wired, and it's not from the coffee. She's either scared of Merrick or of her own shadow."

"Or maybe she's just jittery about sitting in a booth with the man she's thinks will be her next victim?"

"That, too," Joe said calmly. Too calmly for Katelyn's liking. After all, they were talking about a potential plan to murder him. "We'll tail her when she leaves and see what she's up to."

The moment Joe said the words, he fired another glance at Katelyn. She understood it without further explanation. "Keep an eye on the BMW, and I'll check on Fiona."

"Be careful," he warned.

Katelyn kept her head low and her hand on her concealed weapon when she went down the short hallway and eased open the swinging door. The bathroom was small. Just one stall. A sink. And an open window.

The room was empty.

Their murder suspect wasn't anywhere in sight.

Chapter 15

"Anything?" Katelyn called out when she heard Joe end his phone conversation with headquarters.

"Nope. No sign of Fiona."

She groaned, but it was exactly the news she'd expected. After all, Fiona had managed to elude the police most of the week, so it wasn't surprising that she'd been able to slip out of a bathroom window at the coffee shop and go on the run again.

Of course, it would have been nice if Joe and she had anticipated that little maneuver so she could have posted herself outside the window and stopped the woman. Instead, they had to accept the fact that Fiona had provided them with a lot more questions than answers and then lulled them into allowing her to escape.

Since hindsight wasn't doing much to improve her mood, Katelyn moved on to the second point of contention.

The wedding dress.

Or more specifically, her mother's wedding dress.

The metaphorical dead fish wrapped in newspaper.

In the adjoining room she heard Joe open the fridge. Maybe an early dinner would keep him occupied while she tried on the dress. It wasn't really modesty that made her want him to stay on the other side of that wall. She just didn't want him to get the idea that she had stars in her eyes and marriage—a genuine marriage—on her mind.

She didn't.

Really.

But she still found herself mumbling profanity under her breath when she held the dress in front of her and glanced at herself in the mirror.

Katelyn frowned.

What was it about lace and silk that managed to make a woman look great, even when that woman didn't want such cosmetic changes? She was practically glowing, and she wasn't the glowing sort.

Was she?

After dwelling on it for a couple of miserable seconds, she realized the idea was growing on her. Well, growing on her if the glowing part included Joe.

She was definitely in trouble.

Since it was making her depressed and since there was no chance she'd be able to do the dozen silk-covered back buttons by herself, Katelyn put the dress aside and moved on to an important logistics problem.

Her weapons.

Hiking up the satiny floor-length slip to her waist, she planted her bare foot on the bed and strapped on a leg holster. Then a second one on her other leg. They'd make great backups, but she still needed a primary position with better accessibility. It'd take her too long to work her way through the yards of silk to get to two semiautomatics. Those excess yards could get them killed—a thought she quickly pushed aside.

That thought didn't stay pushed aside, however.

It came back with a vengeance, and every worst-case scenario started racing through her head. The sniper opening fire. Joe in the path of the bullets. Or Joe protecting her by throwing himself in the path. No matter which way it played out, he'd be right there.

Directly in the path.

Of course, she'd almost certainly do the same, which meant they'd be so busy protecting each other that it would increase the risk a hundred times over.

With each image came the inevitable slam of adrenaline. An increase in her heart rate. A tightening of her muscles. Her imagination was a little too good, because her body was reacting as if the danger was right there in the room with her.

Which in a way, it was, she soon realized.

"Lara Croft has nothing on you," Joe commented.

He was standing in the doorway, one hand bracketed on the frame. A beer in his other hand. With his shirt unbuttoned, his hair mussed and that desperado stubble shadowing his sexy chin, he looked like the main player in her darkest fears. Her hottest fantasies.

And like the source of her only sanctuary.

She wasn't sure which one worried her most.

"Maybe you can put your primary in your bouquet?" he suggested.

She heard herself mumble *it's not big enough,* but the truth was his comment barely penetrated her consciousness. Katelyn turned and went to him. Not for sex. It would have been so much easier if it'd been just for that. But she needed to melt into his arms. She needed to feel that all would be right with the world. At the moment, she just wanted those frightening images of snipers and death to go away. Joe could do that for her. He could become her sanctuary.

And he cooperated.

Joe put his beer on the dresser. As if he had all the time in the world, he circled his arm around her. He drew her to him and touched his mouth to hers. Slow and lingering. Tender. A touch that gave her a little too much time to consider exactly what was happening.

Her slip was cut low in the back, and Joe skimmed a finger down her bare skin, tracing her spine all the way down.

The heat rolled through her.

"I won't have to think about this if it's fast," she whispered against his mouth.

"I know."

With that assurance, he didn't speed up. In fact, that single stroking, sliding finger on her back slowed to a trickle. Hardly a touch at all. He handled her like fragile, paper-thin crystal and fueled a lot of flames in the process.

Did he know what this was doing to her?

No doubt.

Katelyn tried to speed things up on her own. She French kissed him. Deep and hungry. And then took those kisses to his ear, and then his neck. A major attention getter, she'd already learned, and his slight rattle of breath let her know she'd gotten his attention in exactly the way she wanted to get it.

She pushed down the slip, stepped out of it, and with his cooperation, she maneuvered them across the room.

The cooperation didn't continue.

Joe stopped them just short of the bed. He leaned down. No hurried motion, either. He brushed a kiss on the top of her right breast. Then on the left. He kept going down. Kissing. Her stomach. Her hip. The lower front of her panties. Until he reached for her ankle.

Finally, she thought. Finally!

This would lead to something wild, hot and fast. A bout of mind-boggling sex that would occupy her mind so she wouldn't worry. But he slid his clever hand up, over her leg. Over her knee. And slowly, leisurely made his way to her thigh.

He was getting closer, but it definitely wasn't where she wanted his hand.

"Joe?" Katelyn whispered, trying to convey the urgency. She got off his shirt, somehow, and had the pleasure of feeling his chest muscles jump beneath her fingers.

"Shh," he answered, his warm breath brushing against her skin. He unstrapped her holsters, one by one, and laid them on the nightstand. "It's all right."

But was it? Was it really?

The room seemed to be turning. Not quickly, either. Slowly, like his touch. Like some gentle spiral pulling her down into it. She couldn't catch her breath. And why was her heart pounding so hard? It wasn't the only thing pounding, either. Every inch of her ached. Pulsed.

Burned.

This wasn't sex. It couldn't be. This was something

leaps and bounds beyond that. Something so intimate, it frightened her almost as much as those other deadly images in her head.

Shaken, Katelyn tried again, pulling Joe onto the bed next to her. She succeeded and even managed to shove down his pants and anchor her leg over his so he wouldn't move away. It didn't stop his slow, methodical hands or mouth. He kissed her. Touched her. *Really* touched her.

Those fingers moved over her. Exploring. Discovering. Pleasuring her.

He slipped his hand into her panties. He was definitely getting closer, but what she had in mind was having him inside her. Now.

"I have a condom," she said in between breaths. Just in case that was the issue here. She'd picked up some when Joe had filled up the car at the convenience store and had gotten a strange look from the clerk.

"I have some, too," he informed her right back.

Okay. So if safe sex wasn't the issue, then what the heck was?

With those same slow strokes that matched his incredibly slow kiss, he eased his fingers inside her. Not especially deep. But then, deep wasn't necessary. He got the right spot.

Definitely.

The right pace. That, too.

And he even had the perfect pressure to make her forget all about the speed that she'd thought she wanted.

No.

She wanted this instead.

And Katelyn suddenly didn't care if it took all night for him to get her there.

It occurred to her that she should be pleasuring him as well, but even that thought faded when he turned them until they were face-to-face, and he slid down her body. His hair, his face, his mouth brushed against her skin. Joe kissed her along the way, not missing any available spot, before he rid her of her panties.

In a move that had her wondering what she'd done to deserve this special treatment, or Joe, he replaced those clever fingers with his mouth.

The room didn't just turn. It whirled around. Her breath vanished. Her heart slammed against her chest. And she was lost. Willingly lost.

Katelyn moaned, arched into him and ran her own hand into his hair. Her body sought out everything he was giving her. His mouth and tongue took her higher. Higher. Higher. Until letting go was her only option.

So she did. Katelyn let go. And Joe sent her world spinning out of control.

It didn't take long before Katelyn came back down to Earth. Mere seconds. Not that Joe had expected her to languish in the aftermath, especially when she realized he'd pulled a fast one on her.

Or rather, a slow one.

That climax obviously had its intended effect—to take off the edge. To lessen some of that raw energy inside her so they could spend a little time—all right, a lot of time—just enjoying each other.

It worked.

She moved almost lazily and smiled the smile of

a sated woman—who planned to do some sating of her own.

Katelyn tugged off his boxers while she reached over and took a condom from her purse on the nightstand. She did all the work of putting it on him and made his eyes cross in the process.

When she finished, he caught the back of her neck and pulled her to him. He kissed her. Hot and deep. And did a necessary repositioning of their bodies so that she was on top of him and so that he didn't hurt her arm. He took a moment to savor the sight of her.

All that strength.

All that beauty.

Leaning forward, she slid her hands slowly over his chest, her palms gliding through the sweat that already dampened his skin. "Ready for the ride of your life?" she whispered like a challenge.

"Are you?" he fired back.

She laughed. And he savored that as well, for a moment or two, before he moved just slightly beneath her. The tip of his erection grazed her. And judging from the way her eyelids fluttered and the shudder that went through her body, he'd grazed her in just the right place.

That sent her in search of him. Not that she had to search far, but she shifted. Restlessly. Seeking. Joe did some seeking of his own.

One thrust, and he was inside her.

Oh, man.

It was better than he'd anticipated. A hell of a lot better. And his anticipation had been pretty darn high.

She reared up, her fiery hair like a halo around her face. Bracketing her hands on his chest, she began to move. Joe caught her hips, to guide her, to take them both where they needed to go.

Picking up the pace, she rocked and slid against him. Their bodies creating the friction. The deep, intimate contact. The rhythm. Until she had him close. This wasn't simply to take off the edge, either. She was obviously aiming for something he'd never forget—as if he ever could.

Then, she stopped.

Just stopped.

Joe fought through the haze and stared at her to see why she'd done that.

"What's wrong?" he managed to say.

She hovered above him, staring, and then she reached down and laced her fingers with his. "Are you okay with me being on top?"

It wasn't exactly a question he'd been expecting, and even though just about every inch of him was throbbing for release, he took the time to grasp what she was saying.

And what she was saying was a lot.

He nodded. It was the best he could manage. For some reason, his throat had clamped shut.

Katelyn returned the nod, and there was no apprehension, no hesitancy in her clear green eyes when she lowered her body and lay against him. Her bare breasts against his chest. Her face touching his.

Without fully breaking the intimate contact of their joined bodies, she slowly rolled over. Until their positions were reversed. Until he was looking down at her.

Joe held his breath.

"It's good," she said, sounding not surprised but rather pleased with her decision.

He held his breath a little longer, until she moved. Not a move to get away from him, either. But up. With some not-so-gentle pressure, she dug her heels into the mattress, lifted her hips, then wrapped her legs around him.

And sent him sliding deep inside her.

Now he breathed. Long and rough. He fought to keep a restraint on everything that she'd unleashed inside him, but it was a fight he knew he'd soon lose.

"Am I too heavy for you?" Joe asked. Not easily, but he asked it anyway because it was important.

"No." She repeated it and kissed him. "It's a lot better than I ever thought it would be."

"I know the feeling," he mumbled.

And he was absolutely sure she knew he wasn't just talking about their present position.

He tested the waters and moved inside her. A short, quick, easy stroke. The test was a success.

Man, was it ever.

After a few more of those testing strokes, his body was already pleading with him to take this, and her, to the next level. But then, Katelyn's body was doing the same. Despite her climax only minutes earlier, he felt the aftershocks gain new life before they'd even fully subsided.

Still careful not to make her feel trapped beneath him, Joe gathered her into his arms. He took everything she offered. Everything. And he made sure he gave it right back to her. He moved high against her, hard inside her. Deep. Sliding through the slick, hot moisture of her body.

When she begged him for more, he gave it to her.

He went higher still and found a responsive, sensitive spot that made her shudder.

She insisted on more.

He gave it to her.

No longer wary of her response, he pinned her hands to the bed and was pleased when she jerked and twisted beneath him. Not to get away. No, the throaty moan, the half smile, the scorching look in her eyes was the best *welcome home, Joe* he could have ever gotten.

Her legs tightened around him. They matched each other. Move for move. Frantic stroke for frantic stroke. Until the pressure built to an unbearable level. And yet they continued. Somehow. Trying to hang on to every second, every sensation.

They climbed, together.

Drawing on each other.

Feeding each other.

Pleasuring each other.

To get to the only place they wanted to go.

She came in a flash, whispering his name in rhythm to the shudders that ravaged through her. He heard her murmurs over his own heartbeat, over his heavy breath. Over hers. It was her surrender. A sweet, sensual, complete surrender.

Joe buried his face against her neck and surrendered right along with her.

Chapter 16

Naked, Joe eased out of the bed. The room was dark. Pitch black, actually. He'd been so wrapped up in Katelyn that he hadn't even noticed that the sun had set.

She stirred, reaching for him, but he kissed her hand and placed it gently on the pillow. She went back to sleep almost immediately.

He pulled on his pants. Grabbed his cell phone, and went into the living room, shutting the door between Katelyn and him. The A/C was on full-blast and he hoped the hum of the cool air seeping through the vents would create enough white noise that his conversation wouldn't wake her.

This wasn't something he especially wanted her to hear.

After he turned on the lamp, Joe took out his wallet and located the private number for Chief Ryland. It was on a business card tucked behind the only photo he carried. A posed family shot with his parents, his brothers and him. One taken years ago, when his father and he had still been on speaking terms.

He pushed that particular reminder aside, laid his wallet on the end table and pressed in the numbers. Ryland answered the phone.

"Two things," Joe started after they got past the hellos. He sat down even though he figured this might not be an especially long conversation. "There's not even a hint of impropriety or favoritism on Brayden O'Malley's part. He runs a clean department, and I don't want to be part of any witch hunt designed to bring him down."

The chief paused, made a sound to indicate he was thinking about that. "Mind sharing with me how you arrived at this conclusion?"

"I asked questions. A lot of them. In fact, I spent most of Monday and Tuesday doing just that. And I've watched how the man operates. Brayden doesn't need to rely on favoritism and impropriety. He gets the job done the old-fashioned way, through hard work and dedication. You're lucky to have him on your team."

"Pretty frank talk," Ryland grumbled.

"You mean frank talk for a man who's on the brink of a potential promotion?" Joe didn't wait for Ryland to confirm it. "And that brings me to the second thing I want to discuss. After this case, I'll need to be moved from Homicide."

"Say what? I don't think I heard you right, Rico. You want to be moved from a department you fought for months to get into?" Another of those sounds of contemplation. "Does this have anything to do with Katelyn O'Malley?"

"It does," Joe admitted. "I'm personally involved with her, and that means we shouldn't be working together."

"Well, yeah, it happens. Personal involvement, I mean. Work hard, play hard, and all that other crap we do to get us through the night. But that doesn't mean you have to leave Homicide. I can have her moved instead."

"No," Joe quickly answered. "She stays in Homicide. I'm the one requesting the transfer."

"No?" Ryland repeated. "I swear I didn't see anything in your records to indicate you'd let yourself be ruled by *playing hard.* You've been like a bulldozer, Rico, pushing and shoving your way to the top."

"Well, things change." For the first time in his career, there was something more important than the bulldozing, the pushing and the shoving. More important even than his badge.

Katelyn.

Now he had to do everything in his power to prevent her from being killed.

Ryland made Joe wait several seconds before he delivered his verdict. But the verdict wasn't exactly conclusive. "I'll get back to you on these *two things* you just dumped in my lap," Ryland finally snarled. "In the meantime, you and Katelyn O'Malley need to collar this scumhead Veiled Sniper and get the press and the whiny watchdog groups off my back."

"We're doing our best."

"Yeah, well, do better." And with the gruff farewell, the chief hung up.

Joe punched the end call button with his thumb and put the phone on the end table next to him.

"Thin walls," he heard Katelyn say. He also heard the mattress springs groan when she got off the bed. She appeared in the doorway wearing only her panties, slipping on a shirt. His shirt. "Are you sorry you just made that call?"

"No." Joe didn't even have to think about it.

The call was a necessity. But he gave some thought to her. Her hair was all messed up, in a very sexy sort of way with loose, damp strands framing her face.

And then there was her mouth.

Man, her mouth always sucker punched him. Her lips were still swollen from the torrid war they'd waged with his mouth.

"Any idea what you look like standing there?" he asked.

She glanced down at her seminaked torso and smiled. "Are you trying to distract me?"

"Maybe. But if so, your distraction's a heck of a lot better than mine."

"Is that right?" Still smiling, she crossed the room. Instead of climbing onto his lap—something he was fantasizing about—Katelyn pulled the sides of the shirt over her naked breasts and dropped down on the sofa next to him. She linked her fingers with his, brought his hand to her lips and kissed it.

"This morning I asked Brayden to transfer me to another department," she said with her mouth still against his skin. "With the latest round of retirements, I could move to Special Investigations or Vice—"

"No. That's not fair to you. I'm the newcomer. You earned your spot in Homicide."

She climbed onto his lap. Maybe it was to distract him so he couldn't win this argument. He tried not to let her succeed. His resolve faltered a little when her silky leg brushed against his arm as she straddled him. However, instead of doing anything sexual, she kissed his cheek. It was almost chaste.

Almost.

"We are so pathetic." She chuckled. "Brayden and Garrett would have so much fun if they could see this. You and me arguing with each because we're both putting the other first. It's one for the record, Joe."

Because it was peeking out at him, he gave her right nipple a gentle pinch. "Frankly, I'm glad they aren't here to see this. Having an audience would spoil the moment. And they'd probably try to beat me senseless."

She shook her head, and the swish of movement exposed her other breast. No pinch this time. But he leaned forward and nipped the tight bud with his teeth.

Katelyn sucked in her breath, gave his already hardening erection a little nudge, but she stopped him from closing his mouth around her nipple.

"Seriously," she said, pressing her fingers over his lips. "My brothers respect you. And they like you, despite all that posturing and bravado." She reached over and picked up the photo that he'd left on the end table.

"What about them?" she asked.

"I don't think they like me." Normally, this would have been the point in the conversation where Joe clammed up, but there was nothing normal about anything anymore. "My mother died six weeks ago. A drunk driver broadsided her on the way to mass one Sunday morning."

"Oh. I'm so sorry, Joe." It wasn't just lip service, either. Katelyn gathered him in her arms, held him and brushed another kiss on his cheek. When she pulled back, he saw that her eyes were misty with tears.

He almost shrugged, but decided the tough-guy facade wasn't necessary. "I didn't get to make my peace with her before she died."

She nodded. "That explains the personal leave you took right before your transfer. I read your file," Katelyn admitted.

Yes. He remembered.

She probably could have offered a sincere condolence or insisted that his dream of being a cop wasn't something for which he should have to make peace. But she didn't. Katelyn sat there and held him.

They stayed that way, wrapped around each other for heaven knows how long. Long enough for Joe to realize that walking away from Katelyn O'Malley wouldn't be just hard.

It would be impossible.

As incredible as Joe's arms were, one glance at the clock, and Katelyn knew it was time to get to work. She lifted her head from his shoulder, kissed him—for slightly longer than she'd planned—and eased off his lap.

"I need to try on the dress," she let him know. "I have to figure out where I can put my weapon."

Groaning as he got to his feet, he followed her into the bedroom and stood in the doorway, watching her. "You said the bouquet was too small to use for cover?"

"Yes." She pointed to the small silk floral arrangement that had been stuffed into the box with the dress.

"Baby's breath and miniature pink rosebuds just aren't very effective for hiding Glocks. Go figure."

She put on her bra and long slip first, and then, as if bracing herself for a flu shot, Katelyn grabbed the dress. She eased it on over her head.

The silk whispered over her skin.

A seriously nice sensation she tried to ignore.

"I'll need you to do the buttons," she said, ignoring the mirror, as well. She hitched her thumb to the back of the dress and stepped into the satiny pair of off-white shoes. Heels. Uncomfortable ones that pinched her toes. But they put the finishing touches on the costume.

Joe moved behind her. And then he moved her. He positioned her directly in front of the mirror affixed to the outside of the bathroom door. A wide, full-length mirror.

The very one she'd been trying to avoid.

"We're going to look like those plastic figures that go on top of wedding cakes," she complained as he fastened the buttons.

Not exactly true. The dress was real. Joe was real. And what she felt for him was as real as it got. Still, she'd keep that to herself. With the mission all but closing in around them, this wasn't the time to pour out her heart.

He reached in the closet, extracted his tux shirt and jacket and put them on. Since he was already wearing black pants, the only thing missing was the tie. In true badass form, he threaded it around his collar and left it loose so it dangled against the front of his shirt.

Oh, mercy.

Talk about a surefire way to lose her breath. He simply took it away.

He brushed a kiss on her neck, met her gaze in the mirror, and smiled.

To give her hands something to do, she snatched up the bouquet and the Glock. Somehow, even the sinister-looking gun couldn't kill the moment.

But the doorbell did.

Katelyn groaned when she heard the incredibly annoying sound. Joe went one step better and cursed.

"Just a minute," she called out to the visitor.

She tossed the bouquet on the bed and checked the time again. It was nearly 10:00 p.m. Not good. It was probably Garrett or Brayden, which meant something had gone wrong.

And that put her on immediate alert.

It obviously did the same for Joe. He hurriedly put on his shoes and grabbed his weapon.

The bell rang again. Not a quick jab of sound this time, but a long wail of noise, as if somebody was leaning on the darn thing. When the noise finally stopped, Katelyn heard a barely audible groan.

"Who is it?" she asked.

The person answered, something weak and muffled. It was a man, and the image of her brothers, wounded, flew through her head. She turned to run toward the door, but Joe grabbed her arm.

The feeling of panic and dread was so strong, so overwhelming, that Katelyn nearly pushed him away so she could make sure neither Garrett nor Brayden were hurt.

"Don't do it. It could be a trap," Joe reminded her.

He was right, of course. After all, they were deep

n an undercover murder investigation, and someone
ad already tried to kill them. It was procedure to stay
ack, to make sure they wouldn't be facing a gun when
hey opened that door. Still, she had to battle every-
hing inside her to keep from throwing open the door.

And more—she had to trust that Joe was doing the
ight thing.

"Stay behind me," Joe instructed. He aimed his gun
nd while staying low, he went into the living room.
He reached over and turned off the lamp.

"Please help me," the voice said from outside the
door.

She listened for anything recognizable about it, but
again it was hardly more than a murmur of pain. If it
were a trap, if the person was faking, he was doing
an incredibly convincing job. Her heart was racing.
Her breath was in her throat. And that buzz was there.
That awful buzz in her head that told her all was far
from being well.

Her eyes adjusted to the darkness, and soon the il-
lumination from the stove panel allowed her to see
the two windows that flanked the door. Not clearly,
but at least she could maneuver around and not bump
into anything.

Moving slowly, Joe inched away from the lamp toward the window that was closest to him. Katelyn
followed. Not easily though. The dress wasn't exactly meant for skulking about, but there was no way
she could take the time to undo all those buttons and
change into something more maneuverable.

Joe didn't step in front of the window but instead
crouched even lower and lifted the blinds just a fraction.

"The security lights in the parking lot are out," h
whispered.

Okay. That didn't help. Since they'd been workin;
fine the night before, she had to assume that someon
had tampered with them.

"Who's out there?" Joe yelled. He immediatel
shifted his position so that if it was indeed a trap, th
person wouldn't be able to pinpoint his position.

The only response they got was another of thos
painful groans.

Mercy. She prayed it wasn't one of her brothers.

"Call for backup," Joe said. "But tell them not tc
approach the building, to stay back and await orders.'
He tossed her his cell phone.

Katelyn snatched it from the air, flipped it open anc
would have pressed in the numbers for headquarter:
if something hadn't distracted her.

Something seeping from beneath the door onto the
tiny patch of cream-colored tile.

It was blood.

And lots of it.

Chapter 17

"Joe?" Katelyn whispered.

He glanced at her, and she tipped her head toward the floor. Joe had no trouble whatsoever spotting the dark pool of blood.

Hell.

Whoever was out there was either putting on a very convincing show with fake blood, or else the man was genuinely dying.

"Call for backup," Joe reminded her, and he shouted to the person on the other side of the door. "Who's out there?"

"Bruce," the man finally answered.

Even though Katelyn didn't waiver from calling headquarters, Joe saw the relief flash through her eyes. It wasn't her brothers out there but Bruce Donovan. That realization would help her regain her focus.

Thank God.

Because Joe was a hundred percent sure they'd both need all the focus they could get.

"Someone…shot me," Donovan added. He sounded as if he was getting weaker by the moment.

But the key words were *as if* because there were a lot of as if's about this situation that could get them killed.

"Backup's on the way," Katelyn let him know.

Joe nodded and returned his attention to the pseudo interrogation with his possibly wounded suspect. "Who shot you, Donovan?"

"Uh… I don't know. I didn't see who it was, but the bullet was fired from a gun with a silencer. I didn't hear it until it was too late. Please let me in."

Oh, yeah. Like they were going to do that any time soon. Donovan was their number one murder suspect, and this was exactly the kind of trap a guy like him would try to pull.

"I think it might have been Fiona who shot me," Donovan tried again. "I've been following her." He paused for another of those gasps. "She might be the sniper."

"It's funny you mentioned that. I was thinking the same thing about you."

"Not me." And Donovan repeated it like a mantra. A mantra that got weaker with each word.

Joe glanced at the pool of blood. It was spreading. If by some miracle Donovan was telling the truth, he was bleeding out fast.

"Should I call an ambulance?" Katelyn asked.

He nodded. "But tell them the same thing you told backup. I don't want them to approach the suspect. I want them to wait until they have clearance from either me, you or the backup officers."

"Fiona's crazy enough to do this," Donovan went on, the pitch of his voice wavering wildly. "She has this problem... She, uh, flies off the handle when a man rejects her. She's been stalking Addison."

Joe hadn't needed Donovan to tell him that. "What were you doing here anyway?"

"Watching you and Kate," he readily admitted. "I figured if Fiona wasn't the sniper, then maybe it was... the two of you. I wanted to stop anyone else from dying."

"Playing detective can be dangerous," Joe growled.

He hurried past the door to the other window and peered through the corner of the blinds. There was just enough light from the nearby apartment complex for him to see the shadowy figure lying on the small concrete entry just outside the door. The person was curled up in a fetal position—maybe out of fear. Or maybe Donovan was trying to conceal a weapon.

"Is he armed?" Katelyn whispered. She put the phone on the snack bar and aimed both her guns at the door.

Joe shook his head. "I can't tell."

And that left him with a serious dilemma. If by some miracle what Donovan said was the truth, if Fiona had indeed shot him, then the man needed help. Render assistance, was what Joe had been taught to do. That was training.

Procedure.

But if this was a trap, then the sniper was the one calling the shots. Literally. Because when backup or the ambulance arrived in the next couple of minutes, that would put them in the line of fire, as well.

If it comes down to a situation where someone negates the rules, trust Katelyn, Brayden had said.

All in all, it was damn good advice.

"What does your gut instinct say about this?" Joe asked her in a whisper.

Katelyn blinked, probably surprised that he'd put this on her shoulders, but he was positive her shoulders could handle it.

She glanced at the blood again. "I don't think Donovan's the sniper. He wouldn't have gotten this close because he doesn't trust me not to kill him on the spot. My guess is he's the bait. And I think if we open that door, then someone will open fire on us."

Joe nodded. Everything she said made sense. So he had his answer, and he took it one step further.

Moving back to the window and without touching the blinds, he looked out into the parking lot for any sign of the person who'd likely shot Donovan and was trying to use the man to draw them out.

"See anything?" Katelyn asked.

"No."

Well, nothing other than at least three dozen cars, all jammed into the space that separated the two multistory apartment buildings. But a car probably wouldn't have given the sniper a good view, since their apartment was on the second floor. No. He or she would want to be higher.

Joe's gaze combed over the masonry fence located at the back of the parking lot. It was a possibility and would provide an escape since there was an alley by it and then a street just on the other side.

But the angle was all wrong.

It was the same for the street on the left. A bad angle, and it was way too visible. This guy liked to stand back, aim and fire. He liked hiding.

That left the three-story apartment building directly across from them.

It was a good deduction, he soon realized. Because Joe caught a glint of something. Just a glimmer of movement.

"Get down," he yelled to Katelyn. And he dove for the floor.

Right before the shot came crashing through the window where he'd been standing.

Katelyn hit the floor, sheltering her face and eyes from the flying glass. Joe did the same, but in their scramble to get away from the gunfire, they ended on opposite sides of the room.

And worse, the gunfire wasn't a single shot.

Another quickly followed and tore its way through what was left of the glass. And another. Just like the night in the alley and that day at the church, it was a barrage.

"Those shots are too high to have come from Donovan," Joe shouted over the blasts.

Katelyn agreed. That meant she'd been right about him not being the sniper.

For all the good it'd done her.

They were still pinned down. Still in danger. But at least the sniper didn't seem to be shooting at Donovan. Now that she knew he might be an innocent player in this, she didn't want another bullet hitting him.

"The bedroom," Joe yelled.

Katelyn kept her weapon in her hands, but she threw open the door so that Donovan could perhaps get inside. He did. Crawling and groaning. And she saw the still-spreading stain of blood on his shoulder and the front of his shirt. No weapon, but even if he'd had one, he was likely too weak to use it.

"The ambulance is on the way," she told Donovan. "Stay down."

With Joe yelling for her to hurry, she crawled toward him. Not easily. The bulky dress got in her way. And even after she got into the bedroom, Katelyn discovered it wasn't much safer than the area they'd just left.

The single window near the head of the bed was taking a pounding as well, and there was glass strewn all over the bedding. She reached over the debris and grabbed their communicators from the nightstand. If they got separated during an escape, they'd need them.

Joe circled an arm around her waist and pushed her into the bathroom. He didn't stop there. He got them into the tiled shower. A temporary safe haven. But only temporary. Only long enough for them to come up with a plan.

The shots continued through the bedroom window and were already gashing holes in the wall. If the sniper kept the firepower pinpointed, then those bullets would eventually come through the tile.

"How about the balcony?" she asked. "It's on the opposite side of the building from those shots."

Joe's gaze met hers, and she knew it was something he had already considered. And he'd also already dismissed it because of the danger.

"Whoever that sniper is, he or she will kill anyone who tries to help us," Katelyn pointed out. "The stray shots—"

"There aren't enough stray shots," Joe insisted.

Somehow, she heard him over the racket and over the pounding of her heartbeat.

He was right.

There weren't many strays. The shots were going through the window with much better than average precision, far more accurate than the gunfire they'd encountered at the church or in the alley. This pattern was more like the first shooting.

The one that had killed Gail and her groom.

Katelyn might have taken longer to consider that inconsistency if a bullet hadn't come through the wall and the tile.

Joe shoved her down with the bits of ceramic and plaster. The deafening noise continued to crash around them.

"We'll go out the balcony," Joe instructed. "We'll climb down the fire escape and circle back around to the edge of the building. I might be able to get a good enough look to pick off the sniper."

"You think the sniper's on the roof of that apartment building?" she asked.

"I know he is. I got a glimpse of something before he fired. I'm almost positive he's on the right side of a huge ventilation shaft where no one can see him from the street."

And it would also allow the gunman refuge since it'd take a while for the cops to block off that street. Then, he could probably escape over that fence into the alley. From there he'd simply fade into the city.

Unless they stopped him first.

"What do you want me to do?" Katelyn asked.

He ducked his head when a shot rammed through another section of the tile. "After we're on the ground, one of us will need to go to the left of the building."

For a distraction. A necessary one. If she had the layout of the roof correct in her mind, the left was the sniper's blindside since he was on the right of the ventilation shaft. That meant one of them had to be the diversion while the other delivered the shot that would hopefully take him out.

"You'll be the diversion," Joe insisted.

Because it was the safer of two positions. The sniper would have to leave cover to return fire at the person creating the diversion. But if the shooter didn't do that, if the ploy didn't work, then that would leave the person on the right—Joe—in the killer's direct line of fire.

Oh, God.

It wasn't a scenario she even wanted to consider. Katelyn would have much preferred to take the more dangerous route herself. In fact, her heart screamed for her to do just that, to protect him at all cost.

But she couldn't.

She couldn't.

Because it wasn't just their lives at stake. Donovan needed medical attention, fast. The medics couldn't get to him until Joe and she stopped the sniper. If they didn't stop him, now, he'd continue to fire, he'd continue to kill.

And simply put, Joe was the best shot.

She choked back the sob that threatened to make its way past her throat. But she couldn't stop the fear. Nothing could do that. Her hand was trembling when she draped the communicator around his neck and did the same to hers.

Katelyn pressed her mouth to his. Something brief but hopefully it said a lot more than words, because they didn't have time for long explanations.

"Don't you dare fail," she insisted.

His jaw muscles went to war with each other. "You, either."

That was it as for goodbyes.

But it was enough.

"When we get outside, hurry," Joe insisted, swallowing hard. "Use every bit of speed that I know you have because I don't want you out in the open any longer than necessary. Maintain cover and fire a shot or two to get his attention. That's it. Only a shot or two, and only if it's safe."

She nodded. Took a deep breath. And the moment he said, "Let's go," Katelyn did.

They stayed on the floor, crawling their way to the balcony. There was a pause in the shots. As he'd done at the church, the gunman was probably reloading or trading weapons. Joe and she used that lapse to their advantage. They went out onto the balcony and climbed over the railing to the fire escape.

"Equipment check," she said into her communicator.

"I hear you," Joe responded.

The shots started up again. Another barrage. Another attempt to kill whoever got in the way.

Adrenaline was like a knife cutting through her lungs. The thick humid air didn't help, either. But she ran, even in the heels and the dress, Katelyn ran as if her very life depended on it. Because it did. And not just her life, but Joe's. If she blew this diversion, then the sniper would go after him.

That couldn't happen.

She slowed down as she neared the corner and checked her surroundings to make sure the angle of the shots hadn't changed. They hadn't. The sniper was still on the roof, even though she couldn't see him. Not even a glimpse.

And that was what she had to remedy. She needed him or her out in the open for at least a second or two.

"I'm in position," she relayed to Joe.

"So am I. You go on three. I'll go on four."

"One," they counted in unison.

"Two."

"Three."

Katelyn pulled her breath, darted out from behind the cover of the building. And fired.

So did the sniper.

Right at her.

Chapter 18

It'd happened too fast.

On the count of three Joe had expected to hear Katelyn's shot, and by the four count, he figured the sniper would come out from cover to take aim at her. By five, Joe was supposed to have already fired a deadly shot that would keep Katelyn out of harm's way.

He was wrong.

Things didn't happen as planned.

Katelyn fired. He'd heard that all right. But then, the sniper fired, too. Immediately. Not a second later as he should have done.

A thousand thoughts went through Joe's head. None good. This was what he feared most. Not losing a promotion. Not blowing a case. But losing Katelyn.

He couldn't lose her.

"Say something!" Joe demanded into his communicator. And he held his breath.

"I'm okay."

Those two words were the most welcome two words he'd ever heard. Joe leaned his shoulder against the building and let it support him.

"He missed," Katelyn added. "I'll try again—"

"No! He'll be looking for you. He aimed right at you, Katelyn, and that means he's not hiding *behind* the ventilation shaft but he's crouched down in front of it."

"Okay," and she repeated it. "So how about this? I strip off the dress and toss it into the parking lot. It's big enough and light-colored enough to make a great distraction. When he fires at it, I'll shoot to draw him out, and then you can do your Robocop thing."

He didn't have enough breath left to ask about that Robocop reference, and from the ragged pauses in her own breathing and the sound of tearing fabric, he could tell she was already getting out of that dress.

Joe moved into position.

"On three," Katelyn said. And she didn't hesitate long enough for him to change his mind.

"One. Two. Three."

Nothing.

Then, something.

A blast of sound. From Katelyn's gun. And once again, the sniper fired right at her without so much as lifting his head. But this time, Joe did see the barrel of the rifle.

"Talk to me, Katelyn," Joe barked.

She didn't.

Not one word.

"Talk to me!" he repeated.

"She dove into some shrubs," Joe heard someone say through his communicator. Not Katelyn. But Garrett.

"Is she all right?" Joe immediately asked.

"Hard to say."

Not the reassurance Joe needed, especially since she wasn't giving him that reassurance herself. He consoled himself with the possibility her communicator had been damaged in the fall.

"How about you?" Garrett again. "You have a visual on this sniper?"

"If I did, he'd already be dead."

But what Joe did have was the next best thing. He knew the sniper's position. If he aimed just below where he'd seen that rifle, then he could perhaps kill him before he did any more damage.

First though, he had to make sure Katelyn was all right.

"Katelyn?" Joe barked. "If you're there, talk to me."

The next few seconds dragged into an eternity.

"We'll keep monitoring this line, and I'll do some adjusting to see if we can increase reception so we can contact her," Garrett explained. "We're assembling a team to go on the roof, but we're still a good ten, maybe fifteen minutes out."

At the moment, ten or fifteen was a couple of lifetimes. They didn't have lifetimes.

"Make sure that masonry fence is covered," Joe insisted.

"It is. Don't worry. If this guy tries to get down, he won't get far."

Maybe. But it was a risk Joe didn't want to take. He wanted to end it here and now—after he made sure Katelyn was safe.

More seconds. Long ones. And just when Joe was ready to break into a run and check on Katelyn, her voice came through the communicator. "Joe, can you hear me?"

"Loud and clear." Thank God. He was glad he was still leaning against that wall. "I thought I'd lost you."

"No way. My communicator fell off, and I had to find it. Are you okay?"

"I am now. Stay put. I'll get this guy."

"Wait. That sounds scary. I don't want the details though," Katelyn quickly added. "Just please don't do anything… Mercy, I was about to say dangerous, but it will be. It just will be."

She was right, and there was nothing they could do about it. "Remember, stay put."

"Joe, I'm in love with you," she blurted out.

Okay. So he hadn't exactly been expecting her to say that. And she likely didn't know her brother and heaven knows who else was listening in on their conversation. Joe didn't have to inform her of that, or time to respond.

He saw the rifle again, and he automatically zoomed in on it. He took aim. Shut out everything else. His focus pinpointed to that one spot.

And he fired.

Fired.

Fired.

Silence followed.

The sounds of the city and the nearby street slowly began to penetrate his consciousness. He shut them out as well, all the sounds, all the flurries of movement on the street, and Joe concentrated just on that one spot on the roof. A sign of activity, any activity, and he'd fire again.

"I think you got him," Katelyn said into the communicator.

"So do I. Maintain your position just in case."

And if the sniper was indeed dead, then it was all over.

Well, maybe.

"Please tell me you weren't hurt," she demanded.

"I'm fine. You?"

"Just a scratch or two."

Joe cursed. "Our definitions of scratches aren't the same." He'd have a medic check her out ASAP.

She paused and Joe could hear her heavy breath. Or was that his? "It'll either be Fiona or Dr. Kent on that roof," Katelyn said. "Because I think all of this was done to cover up the first shooting, those first two murders."

So Katelyn had come to the same conclusion he had. Not surprising at all. Either Kent had wanted to get back at his ex-wife or else Fiona had wanted to eliminate the happy groom. It explained the reason the first shots had been accurate. Either Fiona or Kent had fired with intent to kill. Everything else had been sloppy, a dangerous facade designed to mask the killer's motive.

Until tonight.

Tonight had been to eliminate Katelyn and him because they'd obviously gotten too close to the truth.

Heck, the sniper had almost succeeded.

"We have a visual of a body on the roof," Garrett said through the communicator.

It was the only green light he needed. Joe turned to find Katelyn.

She found him first.

He'd hardly gotten to the back corner when he almost ran into her. They skidded to a stop. Stared at each other. There was indeed a thin scratch on her chin, but other than that, she was fine.

Katelyn launched herself into his arms. He was right there to catch her.

And kiss her.

It was probably their shortest kiss ever.

"Sergeant Rico?" someone immediately called out. Brayden. He was already on the scene, and after another glance, Joe realized he wasn't the only one. At least a half dozen other officers were there, as well.

With the wedding dress thrown over his shoulder, Brayden approached them and handed it to Katelyn as she eased out of Joe's embrace.

"The press is here," Brayden said.

Which meant there'd likely be pictures. She put on the dress—probably because it beat the alternative of being photographed in her slip.

Her brother gave her arm a gentle squeeze and whispered, "Good job." Brayden said the same to Joe before they were interrupted for an update on Donovan. The man was alive and would be taken to the hospital.

The routine chaos started. The inevitable aftermath of a violent crime. There was the wail of the ambulance coming for Donovan. Shouts. Orders. The smell of gunfire and leftover adrenaline. It wasn't surprising Joe soon found himself engulfed in it.

A medic pulled Katelyn aside, checking her scratch, while Garrett came over the communicator with an update of his own.

"The sniper's Dr. Allen Kent," he heard Garrett say. "And he's a DOA. Good shooting, Rico."

So it was really over.

Well, except for one not so minor detail. There was Katelyn's comment about being in love with him.

That required Joe to take a deep breath or two.

Now that they weren't in a life-and-death situation, he wanted to get her take on it. Maybe it'd been the adrenaline and fear talking and not...

Hell, he didn't even want to finish that.

Joe turned to find her, but she'd already disappeared into the gathering crowd of officers and medics.

Chapter 19

Katelyn raked her thumb over the volume dial of her clip-on CD player and cranked up the music as loud as she could stand it. Axl Rose did his part, his gritty voice belting out the words to "Sweet Child O' Mine" as her running shoes pounded against the sidewalk.

She ran fast. Much faster than her usual Sunday morning pace from her apartment to her parents' home. She pushed herself hard. Harder. Until her muscles protested. Until her heart pounded.

But it still wasn't fast enough.

The thoughts she'd been trying to keep at bay caught up with her, and no matter how much she kicked up the pace, no matter how high she cranked up the volume, the thoughts just kept coming.

Thoughts of a killer and his victims.

Joe and she had stopped Dr. Allen Kent. A cold-blooded killer who according to his own computer diary had refused to give up the woman he loved, or go to jail for murdering her. He'd been willing to hurt or even kill others to cover that crime, and by Kent's own admission, he'd wanted Joe and her dead after he became suspicious of them.

But in the end, Joe and she had prevented Kent from killing others—including Bruce Donovan. He was alive and recovering in the hospital. Fiona Shipley, Addison Merrick and the other Perfect Match clients were all safe, as well. Heck, even a lot of the paperwork for the case had been finished.

The only thing missing was Joe.

They'd spoken, of course. Briefly. In the halls at headquarters as they were shuffled from one interview to the other. She'd had time to give him back his grandmother's ring and little else since a great deal of the past day and a half had involved hours of separate sessions with Internal Affairs and supervisors. All routine. All part of the checks and balances to make sure deadly force had been warranted.

Not that anyone had ever thought differently. Kent had had to be stopped.

The interviews were just time-consuming square fillers. But now those interviews were done, the squares had been filled, and Joe still hadn't contacted her.

Katelyn ran harder.

The night of the shooting, she'd told him that she loved him—on an open communicator, she'd since learned. Her brothers and probably plenty of other people had heard her, so certainly Joe hadn't missed it. Or maybe he had. Maybe he'd *wanted* to miss it.

And maybe the excessive endorphins from the run were simply making her crazy.

She slowed into a cooldown, hoping it'd cool her

thoughts. It didn't. The *I love you* she'd told him kept going through her head. An *I love you* that was real, and yet it hadn't been said to her in return. No amount of running could take the sting out of that. She felt as if her heart were breaking into a million pieces.

How was it possible that she'd lived twenty-eight and a half years without Joe Rico when he now seemed more important than her next breath?

Katelyn did some extra minutes of cooldown to give herself time for a serious attitude adjustment. That didn't work, either. Since she felt on the verge of crying, she cut through the backyard, hoping to sneak into her parents' house and grab a shower before the rest of the O'Malley clan showed up for Sunday brunch. Of course, she didn't hold out much hope that mere soap and water could make her feel better, but at least that way she could cry in private.

"There you are," her father greeted before Katelyn even got through the door.

Not that a greeting in itself was unusual, but her father wasn't cooking. He wasn't even wearing his Kiss The Cook apron, and there wasn't so much as a whiff of waffles and bacon.

Katelyn turned off her music, slipped off her headphones and peered past her father into the sprawling country-style kitchen. Her family was already there. Her brothers, her mother and even Colton. With the exception of Colton, they were all staring at her as if she had the answers to questions that she didn't know had been asked.

"Aunt Kay-lin!" Colton shouted.

"Hey, short stuff." He bolted for her, and Katelyn scooped him up in her arms, giving him a full circle spin around. She planted a sloppy kiss on his cheek. A kiss that earned her a giggle.

"Any idea what's going on?" Katelyn whispered to her nephew. Not that she expected an answer from a two-and-a-half-year-old.

Colton cupped his small hand around his mouth and tried to whisper back. "It's a secret."

That didn't narrow it down much.

"Mom," Katelyn greeted, giving her a kiss on the cheek, as well. There wasn't a strand of her mother's auburn hair out of place, and she'd already applied makeup. Hardly her normal Sunday routine.

Her mom brushed her fingers over the scratch on Katelyn's chin, issued a disapproving grunt, and that's when Katelyn noticed she had no megamug of coffee in her hands. Definitely abnormal. The woman stood shoulder-to-shoulder next to Brayden and appeared to have been waiting for her. Heck, all four of them appeared to be waiting.

"What?" Katelyn asked cautiously. "Did something go wrong with the Kent case?"

"Everything's fine," Brayden said. "The last few ends were tied up when Fiona Shipley volunteered to go back into therapy for her relationship issues."

"Yeah. Therapy with a shrink who doesn't m-u-r-d-e-r people," Garrett added, obviously spelling it out since Colton was listening. "Oh, and Bruce Donovan wanted me to tell you how sorry he was about the incident in the hall at Perfect Match, and he wanted to thank you for saving his life."

Nothing wrong with any of that—which only made Katelyn more suspicious. "So if it's not the Kent case, why are all of you staring at me?" And then it hit her.

"Wait, does this have anything to do with the investigation into the favoritism allegations?"

"No," Brayden assured her. "The chief decided to terminate the inquiry for lack of evidence."

In other words, Joe had intervened, and justice had been served. "So if it's not that or the Kent case, then what is it?"

Her brothers exchanged a couple of glances, lifted eyebrows and other assorted facial gestures before Brayden extended his hand to her. "Congratulations, Sergeant O'Malley."

It took several moments for that to sink in. "I got the promotion?" she gasped.

Somehow, amazingly, Katelyn had forgotten all about it.

The hugs started. Ditto for the excited kisses and well wishes from her parents. Katelyn braced herself for the flood of joy, the rush of success. And it happened. Sort of. But it was more of a trickle than a flood.

"What about Joe?" she asked. Colton wriggled out of her grip. "Did he make lieutenant?"

Garrett and Brayden traded another of those ocular volleys, and this time they included their parents in the raised eyebrow exchanges.

"Told you," Garrett assured them.

"Told them what?" But Katelyn wasn't entirely sure she wanted to hear this.

Garrett shrugged as if the answer were obvious. "That you're in love with Joe Rico."

She huffed, a short burst of air that hopefully was a vague enough reaction so she wouldn't have to out-and-out lie. She didn't want to discuss this with anyone until she'd had time to…heck, she didn't even know what she wanted to do about it. Sulking, maybe even crying, was a distinct possibility.

"Well, are you?" her mother asked, staring at her with eyes that were a genetic copy of her own.

Katelyn went on the offensive. Not with her mother. But she aimed her offensive attention at Brayden. "Did Joe get the promotion or not?"

"He got it. He'll be put in charge of Special Investigations."

But the answer hadn't come from anyone with an O'Malley surname. Katelyn's gaze flew across the room, to the adjoining family room.

And there was Joe.

Sitting on the sofa.

He got up, slid his hands into the pockets of his great-fitting jeans and ambled toward her. "Congratulations, Sergeant."

He smiled.

Just smiled.

Now here was the rush, and the rest of the room faded away. "Congratulations, Lieutenant."

"Joe dropped by to bring back my wedding dress," her mother explained, causing the room to reenter the fringes of Katelyn's consciousness. But even that couldn't get her attention off the hot-looking man walking toward her. "You left it at headquarters the night of the shooting."

"*One* of the reasons I came was to return the dress," Joe clarified. "I'm also here to ask Katelyn something."

From that look, the question wasn't about Kent or a report. Her heart landed in the vicinity of her knees.

"Oh, yeah?" Garrett commented. He nudged Brayden with his elbow.

Joe nodded, without taking his eyes away from her. "I wanted to ask her to marry me."

Okay. Another rush.

Well, more like an avalanche.

Katelyn was sure her family was doing a lot of glance exchanges, elbow nudges and the like, but she didn't care. Joe was going to ask her to marry him.

"And what do you think she'll say?" Garrett, again.

Joe stopped right in front of her. "I'm hoping she'll say yes once she's knows I'm in love with her and that I want to spend the rest of my life with her." He hooked his finger into the waist of her running shorts and pulled her to him. He touched his mouth to Katelyn's.

She felt that simple kiss from head to toe. "I'm positive she'll say yes."

"Positive?" Joe questioned, the corner of his mouth lifting.

"It's a sure thing."

So this was what it was like to be totally in love. Sweet heaven. There was nothing like it. Not the thrill of an arrest, not the promotion. Not even the badge. Just an overwhelming sense that everything was right.

The room went silent. For a moment or two. Until her mother squealed. A second wave of congratulations, hugs and well wishes started, and she found herself in some very loving arms, including Joe's.

"You knew about this?" Katelyn whispered to Garrett, noting that he was grinning as much as the others. "And you approve?"

He shrugged. "Hey, what can I say? Joe makes you happy."

Yes, he did.

And Joe obviously wanted to continue to make her happy in private because after several more minutes of celebrating, he politely asked if he could have just a few moments alone with her. Under her father's direction, the O'Malleys scattered like proverbial flies.

Joe never once let go of her. "Are you upset I chose a public proposal?" he asked.

"Not at all."

"Well, I thought it was only fair after your public announcement on the communicator."

Katelyn winced, but that public announcement would save them some time. Everyone at headquarters probably already knew how she felt about Joe Rico.

"I'd like to invite your family to the wedding," she said while she could still speak. The kiss he gave her seriously put a damper on what was left of that particular ability. "Any objections?"

He shook his head. "None. Knowing you, you'll be able to talk them into coming."

Between her father and her, it was practically guaranteed.

"It'll be a new beginning." Joe took her hand and slipped his grandmother's ring back on her finger. "A new start. A new life. Oh, and lots of great sex."

Katelyn ran her tongue over her bottom lip and felt a nice jolt when she tasted him there. "Great sex, huh?" She smiled. "But you left something out—the happily ever after part."

"I didn't leave it out." Joe laced their fingers together. Drew her against him. "With us, happily ever after is a given."

Yes. It was.

A true perfect match.

And Joe let her know that with a long, lingering kiss.

* * * * *

We hope you enjoyed reading
Against the Sun
by *New York Times* bestselling author
KAT MARTIN
and
Veiled Intentions
by *USA TODAY* bestselling author
DELORES FOSSEN

Originally MIRA® Books and
Harlequin® series stories!

From passionate, suspenseful and dramatic
love stories to inspirational or historical,
Harlequin offers different lines to
satisfy every romance reader.

New books in each line
are available every month.

BACHALO1018R

SPECIAL EXCERPT FROM

Callen Laramie left Coldwater, Texas, and never looked
back. Now, with the only father he's ever known getting
married, Callen finds himself returning for the talk-of-
the-town Christmas wedding. But there's more to this
visit than Callen ever expected—especially once he's
reunited with the once off-limits Shelby McCall...

Read on for a sneak peek at
Lone Star Christmas,
the first book in the Coldwater Texas series
from USA TODAY bestselling author Delores Fossen.

"My brain tells me it's not a good idea to kiss you, that it could lead
to sex. And other things. Things you might not be ready for."

She groaned, pushed back from the table and finished her glass of
wine. "I'm not brokenhearted."

"I believe you, but you're only a couple of months out of a long-
term relationship."

Great. It was a one-two punch. Either she got accused of the
whole broken-heart business or else she was rebounding. There was
no getting around it.

Was there?

"Just how long does the rebound period last anyway?" she asked.
"I hope less than three weeks because after that, you'll be gone."

He stared at her, set aside his wineglass. "You could get hurt."

"I could get lucky." And since that was way more forward than
she'd intended, Shelby added a smile, leaned closer. "What if I give
you some kind of disclaimer, like a business contract? I agree not to
hold you responsible for any hurt that might happen when you drive
away again?"

She could see him working that out in his mind. Of course, that
wouldn't stop her from getting hurt. Nor would it stop him from

blaming himself. That was just Callen. And that meant he was probably going to babble off a couple reasons why they shouldn't go at each other again.

He didn't.

Callen went after her again. He reached out, took hold of her arms and pulled her onto his lap. He kissed her again. Despite the quick maneuvering, the kiss was slow and easy, as if he was giving her a chance to change her mind. *As if.* He had her exactly where she wanted him to have her.

His arms came around her, not that she had plans to go anywhere, but his grip was as gentle as the kiss. He didn't urge her closer, didn't tighten what she was sure would be clever fingers on her waist and back. He just kissed her while she sat there.

Shelby sank into the kiss, letting the feel of his mouth light little flames all over her body. Of course, they didn't stay little, but that was his fault because he slid his mouth and tongue first to the spot just beneath her right ear. Then lower, to her neck. He might as well have struck a match and set her ablaze because the need quit merely pulsing and took on an urgency.

She was pretty sure Callen was in on that urgency, too, because finally his grip tightened enough to pull her closer to him. It was a safe kind of "closer," though, since she was sideways on his lap. Not touching the suddenly very needy center of her body to the center of his.

He cursed under his breath, and she thought he was cursing both of them before he buried his face in her neck. Thankfully for her that meant his mouth was buried there, too, and with his breath gusting some, it was creating a very nice sensation. One that sped that urgency along.

"I'm going to hell for what I'm thinking about doing to you," he said, intriguing her.

"That good, huh?"

Don't miss
Lone Star Christmas *by Delores Fossen,*
available October 2018 wherever
HQN Books and ebooks are sold.

www.HQNBooks.com

Copyright © 2018 by Delores Fossen

PHEXPDF0918

INTRIGUE

EDGE-OF-YOUR-SEAT INTRIGUE, FEARLESS ROMANCE.

Save **$1.00**

on the purchase of ANY Harlequin® Intrigue book.

Available wherever books are sold, including most bookstores, supermarkets, drugstores and discount stores.

Save **$1.00**

on the purchase of any Harlequin® Intrigue book.

Coupon valid until December 31, 2018.
Redeemable at participating outlets in the U.S. and Canada only.
Limit one coupon per customer.

52616062

Canadian Retailers: Harlequin Enterprises Limited will pay the face value of this coupon plus 10.25¢ if submitted by customer for this product only. Any other use constitutes fraud. Coupon is nonassignable. Void if taxed, prohibited or restricted by law. Consumer must pay any government taxes. Void if copied. Inmar Promotional Services ("IPS") customers submit coupons and proof of sales to Harlequin Enterprises Limited, P.O. Box 31000, Scarborough, ON M1R 0E7, Canada. Non-IPS retailer—for reimbursement submit coupons and proof of sales directly to Harlequin Enterprises Limited, Retail Marketing Department, 22 Adelaide St. West, 40th Floor, Toronto, Ontario M5H 4E3, Canada.

U.S. Retailers: Harlequin Enterprises Limited will pay the face value of this coupon plus 8¢ if submitted by customer for this product only. Any other use constitutes fraud. Coupon is nonassignable. Void if taxed, prohibited or restricted by law. Consumer must pay any government taxes. Void if copied. For reimbursement submit coupons and proof of sales directly to Harlequin Enterprises, Ltd 482, NCH Marketing Services, P.O. Box 880001, El Paso, TX 88588-0001, U.S.A. Cash value 1/100 cents.

5   65373 00076   2   (8100)0 12394

® and ™ are trademarks owned and used by the trademark owner and/or its licensee.

© 2018 Harlequin Enterprises Limited

HICOUP54272R

INTRIGUE

NEW YORK TIMES BESTSELLING AUTHOR

B.J. DANIELS

TAKES READERS BACK TO HER
FAN-FAVORITE WHITEHORSE, MONTANA
MINISERIES WITH A SUSPENSE-PACKED
TRILOGY!

Suspicion and shadows are around every corner in
Whitehorse, Montana: The Clementine Sisters!

September 2018   October 2018   November 2018

www.Harlequin.com

HIBJDTCS14493